LOVER'S KNOT

Also by EMILIE RICHARDS

The Shenandoah Album Series

ENDLESS CHAIN
WEDDING RING
LOVER'S KNOT

THE PARTING GLASS
PROSPECT STREET
FOX RIVER
WHISKEY ISLAND
BEAUTIFUL LIES
RISING TIDES
IRON LACE

prescriptions." She barked again in punctuation.

His brow wrinkled. He was a large man, narrow shouldered and wide hipped. He was too large to be fast on his feet and too old to have superior reflexes. She wondered if it was time for the *Post* to do another article on rent-a-cops and whether the guards were really prepared to keep the peace.

She managed a wobbly path toward the pharmacy at the back of the store, telling herself she was almost halfway through her excursion. In just moments she could reverse the last fifteen minutes. She pictured it. She would travel home the way she had come, slip off the loafers, the sweatshirt and jeans, and slide under the soft sage-green comforter. There was a glass of water beside the bed. She could take her medicine and close her eyes. If she was lucky, Isaac would sleep in the guest bed to avoid contamination. By morning the antibiotics might kick in.

There was a short line at the counter. Under a flickering fluorescent light, she stood at the end and imagined easing back into bed and closing her eyes. The clerks were working at top speed, all too aware that they had to serve everyone in line before the doors were locked. Such efficiency was unusual here. She told herself she should always arrive just before closing.

It was five to eleven before she took her place at the counter. She told the man her name and while he went to the bins to find her order, she fished for her wallet. By the time he returned, she had her credit and insurance cards ready, and he rang up the sale in record time.

On her way out, she passed the security guard. "You feel better now," he told her as he headed for the back of the store.

Mentally she cancelled the article and nodded her thanks.

A sari-clad clerk unlocked the door to let her out. The moment Kendra was over the threshold, she heard the lock turn again. The rain was slushier and falling faster by the time she started back around the building.

The anger that had brought her this far was fading, leaving a queasy feeling in her stomach.

She was too weak to nurture anger and too sick to figure out what to do about her marriage. Isaac's preoccupation with his job was nothing new. In the past she had wondered if shared sixty-hour workweeks were the reason they were still together. If they didn't have time to talk about anything more important than the latest headline or what patch of Mother Nature ACRE had saved from development, then they could pretend that time was their only enemy. They didn't have to face the truth, that enthusiastic sex and stimulating conversation were not the only building blocks of a good marriage. That most couples shared values, hopes, dreams. That most couples had plans for their future that did not begin and end with "more of the same." That most couples in their mid-thirties had found time to discuss having children.

She had been grappling with this for months. Unfortunately, she had been grappling alone. Isaac liked things the way they were. They had challenging jobs, a healthy income, enough time each week for a couple of dinners out to catch up on what they were doing. They took trips every summer, received coveted invitations to some of the capital's best parties and maintained enough friendships that their condo was always crowded when they gave the occasional party of their own.

She had tried and failed to make Isaac see that they were nothing more than roommates who successfully slept together. But the idea of something more, of a relationship built on deeper emotion, a relationship in which they put each other first, seemed beyond him. In response, he had reminded her about friends who had recently divorced. This couple because of infidelity, that one because the husband spent more on cocaine than the mortgage payment. Their own problems were inconsequential. Maybe Kendra needed a new challenge at work. Maybe she would be happier if she found a subject to investigate that was worthy of another series.

She was afraid she might be happier if she just walked away. From D.C., from the condo with its sleek leather furniture and tinted glass tables, from the husband she had vowed to love and honor until death parted them.

She wondered how long it would take Isaac to notice.

She didn't see the stranger crouching beside her car until she was right on top of him. The man was dressed for winter, with a knitted watch cap pulled tightly over his head and ears. His coat collar was flipped to shield the sides of his face. Between the clothing, the rain and the dim light, she couldn't see enough of him to note race, age or identifying features.

Kendra had street smarts galore. She had pursued stories in some of the worst neighborhoods in the city and lived to tell them. Now she realized that not thinking clearly was the most compelling reason for not venturing out when ill. Fear thundered through her, and knees already weakened began to shake.

The man stood and raised a handgun, pointing it directly at her chest. "Gimme your keys."

The keys were in her purse. Any other night she would have taken them out in the store and had them ready. She would have approached the car cautiously and used the remote to turn on the lights. Once she was certain all was safe, she would have unlocked her door with the keyless entry system. More important, she would have parked under a light, out in the open. Or she would have waited for a spot in front.

She remembered that the security guard had been walking toward the back of the store. Were there monitors there, as well? Please Lord, was someone inside watching?

"I said gimme those keys, bitch!"

"They're—" slowly she slid the purse strap down her arm, careful not to make sudden moves "—in my purse. Here. It's yours." She gathered the strap in her fist until she could hold the purse out to him, afraid if she swung it in his direction, the motion would set off a fatal chain reaction.

He gestured with the gun. "You think I have enough hands for that?"

"No. Look . . ." She unzipped the purse slowly, making sure he could see every move. It was bright orange, with Prada's logo in silver metal on the front. Isaac had given it to her on her birthday, an extravagant, flamboyant gift with a cartoon card he had drawn himself. She had loved both as a sign that there was a more playful man residing deep inside him.

Now she wanted nothing more than to grind the purse into the gunman's face.

He waved the gun, moving closer. "I don't got all day."

She held the purse open and turned it. "See? Nothing in here to worry about. I'm going to reach in and get them for you."

"Just do it!"

She slipped her hand inside. She was so frightened that she swayed on her feet. She wondered what he would do if she simply passed out. Would he drive over her? Shoot her? Kick her body out of the way so he could steal her purse and her car, and leave her in a wet undiscovered heap in the lot?

Frantically, she searched. She could not find the keys. She felt her wallet, a small hairbrush, a package of tissues. "I . . . I . . . Oh God, I forgot, I put them in my pocket." She slipped her hand out of the purse. "I'm sorry."

"You gonna be dead if you don't get moving!"

She fumbled, dropping the purse onto the wet pavement, and reached inside her jeans for the keys. She always kept them in her purse, and now she remembered why. They didn't easily fit in a pocket. She had enough keys to unlock Fort Knox. Office, car, garage, storage locker, front-door keys . . .

Isaac teased her about them. Isaac . . . Isaac . . .

She edged the keys out of the pocket with trembling, sweaty hands, a few at a time, until only the keyless entry was still stuck between the layers of denim. She slid it out and grabbed it to hand the keys over. As she clutched the pad, her thumb skirted wildly across it.

The car lights began to flash, and the horn honked. The alarm screeched, the sound widening and escalating and torturing.

She had hit the panic button. Not on purpose. Please, God, never on purpose . . .

The evening suddenly seemed like a dream. Her illness, the rain, the unfamiliar sensations of a fever-racked body, her decision to come here. The fear that was like an electric current sizzling over her skin and melting all her connective tissue so that she could no longer move or think or breathe.

When she heard the first explosion she wasn't sure exactly what it was. Yet another in the cacophony meant to alert the world to another carjacking? The front door slamming as the security guard lumbered out to stop the crime in progress?

She didn't have time to consider that the explosion, or the one that followed, might be gunshots. Blessedly, Kendra slid to the ground and finally found the oblivion she had wished for.

CHAPTER TWO

As he made his way into the rehabilitation hospital where Kendra was a patient, Isaac Taylor flipped off his cell phone and slid it into the leather holster that was as much a part of his everyday wardrobe as clean boxers and dark socks. If he didn't, he knew it would continue to ring.

He wasn't supposed to be here. In order to come, he had cancelled two afternoon meetings, and one of those would undoubtedly come back to haunt him. ACRE was a non-profit agency, but it operated with the work ethic of a Fortune 500 company. If you intended to beat the big guys at their own game, you had to think the way they did. Nobody took a job at ACRE because he wanted more time in the great outdoors

ACRE was trying to save, one real-life acre at a time.

He was still thinking about the more important meeting as he crossed through the carpeted reception area and around the welcome desk. At noon he had been scheduled to persuade a landowner that ACRE's offer for his property was more advantageous than that of a major development company. For more than a month his staff had prepared a volume of charts and surveys, tax codes, legal opinions and long-range analyses. Isaac had planned to present the volume with a focused, persuasive sales job. Instead, in twenty minutes, the landowner, a man named Gary Forsythe, would discover that Isaac's assistant was standing in for her boss at the Bombay Club. Isaac doubted Forsythe would be pleased.

He was halfway down a corridor before he realized he had chosen the wrong one. In his thirty-seven years he had visited plenty of hospitals. From Bangkok to Boston, every one he'd set foot in had been an incomprehensible maze. He stalked back the way he had come, choosing the next in a series of corridors that radiated from the entrance like the framework of a spider's web.

Kendra would be surprised to see him. For that matter, he was surprised he was here. When he'd learned she was to be released, he'd offered to bring her home, but she had refused. Instead she had arranged for a coworker at the *Washington Post* to do the honors. Kendra was slow, still a little wobbly, yes, but she wasn't going to fall on her face getting up to their condo. She didn't need Isaac.

But she *had* needed him the night she was shot.

She hadn't said that, of course. One thing he could always depend on was Kendra's unemotional, practical approach to life. This was something they shared. They were like the twin blades of a kayak paddle, each cutting cleanly through the water with an economy of motion, dipping low on one side, then the other. No rivalry, no recriminations, no resentment.

But she *had* needed him that one night, and he had failed her. Now that fact weighed heavily on both of them, a silent burden borne by two sets of shoulders. If he had left work when he should have, he could have arrived at the drugstore in time to get Kendra's medication. If he'd left work in time, she wouldn't have dragged herself out into the cold night air to be shot by a man who stole cars the way some men sold insurance or taught high school physics.

If he had just left work.

So he had left work today. He supposed it was a form of penance. Or it was an unspoken pledge.

You mean more to me than the job, Kendra. Look, here I am. In the flesh this time, no matter what it costs me.

"Mr. Taylor?"

By the time he halted, he was already a good three feet beyond the woman who had spoken. He turned and recognized Rashi Gupta, the physician in charge of Kendra's recovery.

He held out his hand. "Dr. Gupta, I'm sorry. I didn't notice you."

She took the hand briefly. "Yes, you seem like a man with a mission."

Dr. Gupta was slender and attractive, forty, perhaps, with dark skin and almond-shaped eyes. She wore an unbuttoned white lab coat over a navy skirt and blouse, and a trio of gold necklaces twinkled in the fluorescent light. Her black hair waved over her ears and collar.

From their first conversation, he had known that medically Kendra was in good hands. He was less secure about the Indian doctor's holistic approach. Had Kendra's injury been a suicide attempt, he would have understand Dr. Gupta's desire to probe the nuances of a relationship that had always suited both its partners. But the shooting had been wholly arbitrary. And he had yet to see what the doctor's probing had accomplished.

He tried not to sound impatient. "I'm going to pick up Kendra in a few minutes. Or at least that's what I thought?"

"Oh, yes, she will be going home as promised. Do you have a few moments to talk to me first?"

His inclination was to say no. He was anxious to get his wife home and comfortably settled so he could get back to work and find out what had transpired with Gary Forsythe. He knew that this afternoon, no matter what, he had to leave the office by five to spend the evening at home.

At his hesitation, Dr. Gupta stepped closer. "I must talk with you. Now or very soon. We can do it over coffee." Without waiting for his assent, she started down the hallway in the direction he had just come from. She ducked into a small deli near the reception area, and he followed her through a short line, filling a cup with coffee that smelled as if it had been heating in the stainless-steel pot all night.

The room was only half filled, a mixture of staff and visitors. A small boy in a lime-green T-shirt screamed and tried to launch himself from a booster seat at the other end of the room. The child's mother looked too exhausted to care.

"Do you wonder at the story there?" Dr. Gupta asked. "What member of the family is here, and what this young mother discovered today to make her so tired?"

Isaac never wondered about the lives of strangers. At some point in his own, he had learned the futility of trying to figure out motivations.

"I imagine the news in this place can be pretty dismal." He pulled tops off half-and-half containers and dumped the contents into his coffee. "I know we're lucky." He looked up. "Unless there's something you haven't told us?"

Dr. Gupta paused before she spoke. "Not

everyone in your situation would describe it as lucky."

He was annoyed. "Kendra was shot. Twice. The bullet nicked the spinal cord, surgery was required to halt the bleeding, there was some paralysis, which has subsided with time and good care." He forced a smile. "We can thank you for that last part. And we do."

"Mr. Taylor, the bullet damaged more than your wife's spine and internal organs."

Now he was angry, a feeling he didn't like. He looked away from her, observing the young woman grab the child's shoulder. She gave him a hard shake, and the screaming intensified. Isaac's anger ramped up a notch.

"If she shakes that baby again, we need to intercede." His tone was casual. His feelings weren't.

Dr. Gupta turned in time to see the woman reach for the child and pull him from the chair. Then, as they both watched, she settled the boy on her lap and stroked his hair, murmuring as she did. In a moment the screams subsided.

"People handle bad news in different ways." Dr. Gupta faced him again. "Some of them take it out on their children. Our young mother seems to have enough sense to know she was wrong."

Isaac went back to the subject at hand. "I know complete recovery will take time. The shooting was traumatic. Kendra's still a little shaky. I support her decision to take a leave of absence from the *Post.*"

Isaac stopped, because even though he did support Kendra's choice not to return to work for six months, he also knew the consequences. The *Washington Post* always had a pack of candidates hungry to become the next Woodward or Bernstein. She had worked hard to move up the journalistic ladder to investigative reporting, and a long hiatus would knock her down at least a few rungs.

Dr. Gupta hadn't touched her coffee and didn't now. "I'm afraid that saying your wife is only a little shaky is like saying she was only a little injured."

"What would you like me to say?"

"Perhaps you can tell me how you feel about everything that has happened?"

"I'm not the patient."

"No, you are the most important person in the patient's life."

He sat quietly a moment trying to figure out what she wanted. "I feel a lot of things," he said at last. "Relieved she's recovering, for one."

" 'Relieved' is an interesting word. It almost implies guilt, doesn't it? As if you are relieved that after what you have done, the worst did not catch up to you."

"Isn't that a stretch?"

"Is it?"

He wished she was not quite so good at getting right to the heart of matters. "Shouldn't you just say what you need to, so we can end this? I'd like to get my wife."

"Your wife was extremely sick the night she went out to the drugstore. As it turns out, she had pneumonia, which very much complicated her recovery. She asked you to get the medication, and you were too busy. I imagine you have regrets about this?" The last sentence was clearly a question she expected him to answer.

"Of course I do." He was almost surprised the words escaped his clenched jaw.

"But there is more. . . ."

"I don't know what you mean."

Her eyes were the color of milk chocolate and as expressive as her lovely, long-fingered hands. She used both now to prompt him, the fingers turned upward as if to beckon words hiding inside him.

He shook his head. "Okay, I was upset with her. After the worst was over and I knew she was going to recover. Is that what you need to hear? That I question why she went out in the first place? One dose wasn't going to make much difference in her recovery. And as it turns out, after we spoke I left to get her prescriptions, hoping I could get there before the store closed."

"Instead you arrived as she was being loaded into the ambulance."

For just a moment, despite his attempt to remain logical and calm, he experienced the same panic he had felt that night. It fractured quickly inside him, but left him vulnerable. "Yes."

"And now you ask yourself why she did this to you?"

"No, I don't ask myself why she did this to *me.* I ask myself why she did it. And the answer is pretty clear. She wasn't thinking straight. She was upset with me for not doing what I'd promised, what I should have done, so she left to take care of herself. She didn't know I was rushing to the store, because I didn't phone her back to tell her. I didn't take the time because I had no idea she'd do something that foolish. That's it. End of story."

He pushed his chair back to get up, but the doctor put her hand on his arm.

"If the story had ended, Mr. Taylor, would you be so upset?"

He didn't stand. "I'm not upset. We just aren't getting anywhere."

"Your wife's recovery is my job. Not simply her physical recovery, her emotional recovery, too. One is going as expected, one is not. I am concerned that she seems to have given up on you as a source of support."

He leaned forward. "I don't know what you're talking about."

"I am talking about her plan to move out to your vacation cabin in the Shenandoah Valley."

For a moment he didn't believe he'd heard her right. "I'm sorry?"

"She hasn't told you?"

Her hand no longer weighted him to the chair. It didn't have to. "This is the first I've heard of it."

"Then I am sorry to bring you this news.

But perhaps it's best that we talk it over, so you are prepared."

He couldn't take this in. It was inconceivable to him. Kendra would need more physical therapy. She would need checkups. She would need *him.*

Or . . . perhaps not.

"It's not a vacation cabin." He wasn't sure why he had chosen the most trivial point for starters. "We . . . I own some property out there. In Toms Brook, near the river. The cabin's old. It's not an A-frame chalet with views all the way to West Virginia. Is that the way she's made it sound?"

"It's livable?"

Isaac really didn't know. Kendra had wanted an occasional retreat outside the city, and she had made friends in the Valley. She'd found a local handyman who had put in plumbing, renovated a small bathroom, updated decades-old wiring. The man had done the work for a quarter of what anyone in the D.C. area would have charged. She had asked Isaac to come and take a look at the project, but he had always found an excuse not to. He didn't think the cabin was finished, but he really wasn't certain. To his knowledge, Kendra had never even stayed there overnight.

"Apparently she thinks it's livable," he said. "Apparently she thinks a lot of things."

"Do you understand why she's doing this?"

"Why don't you give me a clue?"

She lifted one beautifully shaped brow at his tone. "This will be something for the two of you to discuss. Kendra tells me you work long hours, that your job is important. Would you be available to her even if she was in town?"

"You want me to say I'll drop everything and fly to her bedside the moment she needs a glass of water or a tissue?"

She sat back. "If you *need* to say it. But I doubt you do. Not to me, and probably not to your wife." She paused. "And not like that."

Isaac was rarely rude, and now he was sorry. The apology was in his voice. "You took me by surprise."

"Perhaps what you *will* need to say is that you understand she feels her life is no longer under her control. That you know much has been taken from her in the past few weeks, and you sympathize with her need to come to terms with it."

"You underestimate Kendra. She's a strong woman."

"Kendra no longer feels at peace in her own skin. She no longer feels whole. She no longer feels secure. She must find her way in this new world where a woman can nearly be killed for going out to the drugstore on a rainy night."

"She's a reporter. She understands violence."

"There is much we don't understand until it knocks at our front doors, Mr. Taylor. Do not underestimate the impact of those few terrifying moments on all the moments that will follow."

Dr. Gupta glanced at her watch and shook her head. "I will be available to you, and I have colleagues who will be happy to talk to both of you as you work through all that has happened."

He rose as she did. "I think Kendra and I can work things out together. We always have."

She searched his eyes. "Have you? I wonder. Or, like most people, have you merely ignored the fragments that don't fit into the picture you hold of your marriage?"

She left him with this, left him dissatisfied that out of respect he had allowed her the final word. Left him wondering exactly how Kendra could believe that hiding in a ramshackle log cabin several hours from Washington would put the lingering effects of the shooting to rest.

Kendra swung both legs over the side of her hospital bed, a maneuver that required both hands to nudge her left leg into place. Then slowly, carefully, she shifted her weight to her feet, gripping the rail as she did. When she was balanced, she moved slowly across the floor to the mirror on the closet door. Her left foot still dragged, but the fact she was moving on her own steam was such a miracle, she felt only pride.

She ran her fingers through pecan-colored curls that the hospital salon had cut from her shoulders to her collar yesterday. She liked the new look, although it released the curls from any semblance of order. But she would be managing her own care now, and easier was better. She would be bathing in well water, too, and there was no guarantee the old well by the river was going to tolerate anything but the most perfunctory showers.

She eyed her image and ticked off what she saw. She had lost weight and hadn't needed to. Now her face was thin, almost gaunt, and there were shadows under her hazel eyes. She was pale, which meant that the freckles that had haunted her as a child stood out in sharper relief. Years ago her sister Jamie had told her she looked like a puppy in Disney's *101 Dalmatians.* To Jamie, at four, this had been the greatest of compliments.

Sandy, who was picking her up in a few minutes, had brought Kendra the clothes she wore. Yesterday she had assessed Kendra's figure and whistled disparagingly. "Girl, we got to get you some clothes that won't slide right off that skinny ass." And she had gone right out to do it.

The clothes fit perfectly. Sandy had a stellar eye for fashion, which had landed her a job in the *Post*'s Style section. For Kendra's trip home she had chosen a gauzy peach skirt and a lightweight cream-colored sweater. Kendra's taste ran more toward

Ralph Lauren than JLo, but Sandy had found a compromise.

She heard a wolf whistle from the doorway and turned around too fast, nearly tripping on her own feet. Somehow she managed to keep her balance. “Isaac? What are you doing here?”

“I came to take you home. I didn’t expect to find a supermodel.” He moved across the room as he spoke and took her elbow to steady her.

She was aware of the strength in his fingers, the solid weight of his body against hers, the inches she had to tilt her head to gaze up at him. His golden brown eyes stared down at her steadily, unsmiling. He lowered his head and gave her a quick kiss.

“I’m okay. Just turned too fast.”

“You look terrific.”

Her hand went to her hair before she realized what she was doing. She supposed it was the most natural of responses, ingrained in her gender. “Thanks.”

He reached out and lightly ruffled her curls. “I’ve never seen it this short.”

“It’s easier to take care of. And summer is coming.”

For a moment he still didn't smile; then he managed one. "I like it. A lot."

"I was expecting Sandy."

He stepped away. He was dressed for work—gray slacks, navy sports coat, pale yellow dress shirt that teased out the blond streaks in his hair. If there had been a tie, he had stripped it off.

"I told Sandy I'd come. I didn't want to miss this. It's a big day." He held up a shopping bag. "I brought you a welcome home present."

For a moment she didn't take it. She felt like a fraud. She wouldn't be going home, at least not for long, and she had to tell her husband.

"Want to sit?" he asked.

"No. No, I'm fine." She reached for the bag. "I'm, well, just surprised, that's all."

"That was the point."

She reached into the bag and pulled out a package wrapped in siren-red paper with silver ribbon. "Maybe I'd better sit."

He didn't try to help her to the bed. Isaac had learned that lesson a week ago. An aide had chastised him for trying to make things too easy. Now she made the trip with a minimum of fuss. She slid the box free of the ribbon and tore the paper loose. Inside was a sterling silver cigarette case, an antique etched with art deco fans. She pictured it in the clutch purse of a flapper.

"You want me to take up smoking?"

His smile was more natural this time. "It's the perfect size for business cards."

"It'll hold a credit card and money, too, if I want to travel light some evening." She shined it with her palm. "I love it."

"You missed the card."

"Oh?" She saw he was right. She opened the plain white envelope and drew out a sheet of watercolor paper folded into quarters. On the front he had drawn a perfect caricature of her, brown curls flying, heels clicking midair, arms flapping like wings, a smile as wide as the Potomac. Underneath the computer had printed "I Am Woman."

She opened the card. The printed message read "Watch Me Soar." Underneath it, Isaac had written, "And you will. You're on your way. Welcome home."

Tears stung her eyes. The tears were new, the product of a life that had flipped out of control and taken her emotions with it. "Who is this crazy lady?"

"Maybe you don't feel like clicking your heels just yet, but you will soon enough."

Almost from the moment she awakened from surgery, she had told herself she would move on quickly, that she would not let the carjacker destroy her life or self-confidence. She had thought that just repeating the vow often enough was all it would take. But she had been wrong.

She looked up. "It's inspiring. Thank you."

"Are you ready to go home?"

She was surprised by how little she wanted to leave. She had not yearned for the condo with its view of city streets. She had not yearned for the crushing weight of deadlines, the crowded newsroom, the ringing of telephones. She had yearned for Isaac, but that wasn't new. She had yearned for him before the shooting, too.

For a moment she couldn't answer. Fear gripped her. Outside, spring was at its peak. D.C. did spring with minimum fuss and maximum appeal. One moment the trees were bare, the next they were suffused in blossoms. Cherries, Japanese magnolias, redbuds and dogwoods. She could walk out into the sun, leaving behind a rainy night in March when she had nearly died.

it were that easy.

...endra?"

"I'm not going home." She looked over at him. "Not for long. I'm moving out to the Valley. I want to recover there. I don't think I can do it here."

He didn't look surprised. She searched his face. "Who told you?"

"Dr. Gupta. I saw her on the way to your room."

She took that in, relieved that she had not been required to break the news. "You probably think I've lost my mind."

"It's occurred to me. Let's discuss it at home, okay?"

She was afraid to drive through the District's streets, to park underground and take an elevator to their floor. Once inside the condo, she wondered, would she have the courage to leave again?

She looked away. "This is hard to explain, and harder to believe, but I'm not feeling all that brave right now."

"You don't have to explain. But I bet they have plans for your bed." His voice softened. "Nothing's going to happen. I'm here to make sure of it."

She was spared a response. In moments

they were enveloped by a swarm of staff who had come to help with last-minute arrangements. Kendra was tucked into a wheelchair and her overnight bag unceremoniously plopped on her lap. Isaac was shooed out of the room to pick up the car. She was wheeled to the elevator. By the time the first wave of fear had peaked, she was in the car and Isaac was reaching over to help with her seat belt. She fastened it with trembling hands, hoping that this, at least, would help her feel anchored to something.

Isaac drove without speaking. The streets were crowded, not unusual at lunchtime. Some part of her marveled at the sheer number of cars. Each driver knew exactly where he or she was going, exactly what needed to be done. She had always felt the same way and had never once thought how odd it was to be that certain.

Another part of her, a larger part, was terrified they would not make it through the traffic without an accident.

"I've taken care of your plants," Isaac said, once they were away from the hospital. "I didn't want you to come home to wilted ferns and African violets."

She wet her lips. "Thank you."

"Did they feed you lunch? I forgot to ask. We could stop. Would you like that?"

"No." The response was emphatic, more so than she had intended. "They fed me."

"We'll be home in a little while. Why don't you close your eyes and relax? I'll tell you when we get there."

More often than not, when she closed her eyes she saw the man who had shot her, the fury on his face, the gun swinging in her direction. She had nothing to fear from him now. He had been caught with her car not far from the drugstore and had pleaded guilty. He was in jail and would be for some time to come. But none of that seemed to help.

She searched for something to say. "What are you missing at work today? Don't tell me nothing, because I know better."

"Right now I'm missing lunch at the Bombay Club. Nothing someone else can't take care of."

She glanced at his profile. Isaac was easy to look at, if not traditionally handsome. Wide, high cheekbones, strong jaw, dark upswept brows. He tanned easily, and his skin always had a healthy glow. Three years of braces had perfected the smile that could so easily make her forget all the things that went unsaid between them.

"You'll want to get back after you drop me off," she said.

"Only if you're feeling comfortable. I can clear my schedule."

He hadn't cleared it. She heard that. He had expected to return. Now, faced with a woman who hadn't even been sure she could leave the hospital, he was reconsidering.

"I'll be fine," she promised.

They drove the rest of the way without speaking. She flinched as he pulled into the condo garage. It was well lit, the space large enough that it was unlikely anyone would be hiding, but when he turned off the engine, she had to force herself to unsnap the seat belt and reach for the door handle.

"Wait until I come around," he said.

He helped her out, then opened the back to get her overnight bag. She had given her flowers to other patients early that morning. She had little to show for the weeks she'd spent in rehabilitation except improved muscle tone, a lopsided gait that was, nevertheless, the difference between mobility and paralysis, and the prospect of a normal life once she was fully recovered.

"There's no nurse's aide present. Am I allowed to escort you?"

She moved closer and took his arm. They walked slowly, but she managed well. Her gaze darted right and left. The garage seemed empty.

The ride up was uneventful. Their hallway was longer than she had remembered. The inside of their condo was filled with red tulips, yellow daffodils and hyacinth-purple balloons.

"It's wonderful." Kendra's voice was husky. "Are they all from you?"

"The balloons are from your colleagues. The daffodils are from Sam and Elisa. The tulips are mine."

"I feel welcomed."

"You've been missed." He wrapped her in his arms. This kiss was not perfunctory. "Welcome home," he said, when he finally pulled away.

"Either you're making me dizzy, or I'm still recovering."

"Sit. I'll get you something to drink. Pepsi? Snapple?"

"Why don't you get yourself something for lunch?"

He waited until she was seated, then headed for the tiny kitchen. She pulled the old quilt from the back of the sofa and draped it over her legs, because, suddenly, she was chilled. She wondered how long the peace would last, how long she would be allowed to bask in flowers and balloons before her convalescence became the topic of conversation again.

It didn't take long. He returned with a sandwich. She wondered when he had found the time to shop for bread and ham. Had an assistant volunteered? Had he gone online and scheduled a delivery, hurriedly checking off items he thought she might need?

"Are you really going to be all right?" he asked. "I can stay, or I can call Sandy. She said she'd come if you needed her."

"I'll be fine. We have a security alarm. I'll probably use it."

He ate in silence, as if he couldn't fill up quickly enough. He had broad shoulders and an athlete's build. He always ate as if he were training for a decathlon. When he had finished, he took his plate back to the kitchen, returning minutes later with a glass of milk.

"We might as well talk about this," she said. "There's nothing to gain from putting it off."

"It's been a big day. Maybe we should wait."

"I know you don't understand. I know you think I've lost my mind. But I need to get out of here."

"I could try to get vacation time. Not next week, but the week after doesn't look too grim. We could go away together. Someplace quiet."

She searched for the right words, but there weren't any. "I need to get away from *everything,*" she said at last.

He sipped his milk, but his eyes didn't leave hers. "I gather that means me."

"I hope you'll stay there with me when you can."

"This doesn't make sense." He got up and began to pace. "I know you've been through a tough time. I understand that. But what's the point of leaving everything familiar?"

"And why should I stay? My job's on hold. You're never home. What friends I've had time to make have high-octane professions. I don't think I'm going to enjoy strolling our neighborhood for a while. There's nothing here for me."

He stopped pacing. "Your husband is here. Your home."

She settled on the second part. "This condo isn't my home. It's a place we bought because it was a good investment and we could afford it without dipping into my trust fund. But we can't even have a cat. I'm lucky they let me raise houseplants. We look out over more buildings just like this one, filled with more people who work too hard. We bought the furniture from the previous owners so we wouldn't even have to shop."

Clearly nothing she had said made any sense to him. He was frowning when he spoke.

"Let's try a different tack. You just got out of the hospital. You still need physical therapy. The doctor has to follow your progress, and you're not that keen on being alone. So you respond by moving to the middle of nowhere? You'll be completely alone out there. If you fall, if you run a fever, if you wake up terrified, who will know? Who will take care of you?"

"I could be alone here, too. The chances are good I would be."

"It's really about me, isn't it. It's about—"

She held up a hand to stave off his words. "No, it's about me. I don't want to be here. It's that simple and that complicated. I can't breathe right now. I need a place where I can heal. I need a place to get in touch with everything."

"How long have you been thinking about this?"

"Since I woke up unsure I'd ever walk again. I told myself then that if a miracle occurred, I would leave the city."

"You would leave *me.*"

She didn't deny it. "I can't ask you to give up your job and come with me."

"Would you want me to if I could?"

She shook her head. "I have to take time to sort out my life and put it all back together. I don't expect you to understand or help. I don't understand it myself."

"The night you were shot, you told me you weren't sure my best would ever be good enough again. Have you decided it isn't?"

She was surprised he remembered her words. She hadn't thought of them. But the sentiment? The sentiment had plagued her continually. Their lives had changed, and there was no going back. She didn't think Isaac understood that. She wasn't sure *she* did, but at least she was aware of the change, even if she couldn't see all its shapes and boundaries.

"I don't know that we can ever be good for each other again." Her throat felt swollen, as if she were choking back more than hurtful words. "I'm not the person I was a couple of weeks ago. I'll never be that person again. It's going to take a while to find out who this new Kendra Taylor is."

She saw from his expression that he had delved as far as he could or would. This was not the kind of conversation in which Isaac shone. The pause was significant. She could see him switching gears, putting aside whatever emotion he felt.

"The cabin's ready to live in? You got that far in the renovations?"

"Anything but fancy, but it's habitable." She made herself look at him. "I want the land and the cabin, Isaac. I want it to be mine so I can do whatever needs to be done without always getting your permission. I'll trade you my share of this condo. They should be roughly equivalent. Or I'll pay you outright if they're not. It should be simple enough, changing names on deeds."

"It's gone that far? We're splitting assets?"

"Just this one. But I need to make a home."

She saw him sorting through responses. She imagined them all, had imagined them for the entire week since her plan had solidified. In the end, though, he gave her the one she'd known he would.

"Do whatever you want. You don't need my permission. And someday, if need be, I'll sign it over to you." He glanced at his watch. "Do you want me to call Sandy?"

"No. I'll be all right. I'll probably take a nap."

"Then I'm heading back to work. Call if you need anything. I'll be home in time for dinner."

The balloons danced when he closed the door behind him. Kendra stopped swallowing tears and let them flow.

CHAPTER THREE

A brand-new car was sitting in the clearing in front of the cabin when Isaac and Kendra drove up. Even though Kendra's sedan had been recovered, she hadn't wanted it anymore. As soon as she arrived home from the hospital, she had traded it in for a new forest-green Lexus RX with all-wheel drive. She claimed she would need a car that drove efficiently on dirt and gravel roads, but Isaac suspected the real reason was simpler. The sedan had nearly gotten her killed, and she would never forget that.

Sam and Elisa Kinkade, Kendra's minister and his wife, had picked up the new car on a trip into the city and delivered it here. Isaac had met the Kinkades after a story that Kendra had done about them almost a year ago, and liked them both. Sam was a minister with a healthy social conscience, for which he had twice suffered the rigors of prison. Elisa was a doctor from Guatemala who had suffered her own nightmares. Isaac was not a believer in happy endings, but he thought these two deserved one.

Until now, Kendra hadn't even seen her new SUV. She hadn't been willing to make the trip to the showroom, and her salesperson had driven to the condo to collect the sedan as a courtesy.

"You'll finally get to check out your new car," Isaac said.

"Looks good, doesn't it?"

The car said a lot about his wife. Luxury, yes, but not obviously. Kendra hadn't gone for the top of the line, although she easily could have afforded it. She hadn't seen the point of more car than she needed, or shown any need to flaunt inherited wealth. She would drive the SUV carefully and for as long as she sensibly could. When he'd met her, she had been driving a twelve-year-old BMW that had traveled from coast to coast half a dozen times.

She sat forward to peer out the front window. "From here you can't see most of the changes, but you *can* see the logs. Dabney removed the siding that covered them. And he re-roofed the front porch."

"I don't really remember what it looked like."

"It's been a long time since you were here, hasn't it?"

"Not long enough."

"Please come in and look around."

"What did you think? That I was going to drop you off and speed away?" He was sorry the moment he'd said it, and sorrier for the edge in his voice.

She was calmer. "I didn't think that. I just didn't know if you'd want to come inside."

He rarely apologized—he'd spent his childhood being forced to say he was sorry for everything except the air he breathed—but he did soften his tone. "I'm sure I'll feel better about your move if you can prove there's a decent bathroom."

"There was always running water and a toilet. Your grandmother lived the way a lot of people in that generation did."

He didn't like to hear anyone call the woman he'd inherited the cabin and land from his "grandmother." He had never met Leah Spurlock Jackson and felt no connection. His adoptive father had made it clear his pitiful specimen of a son had descended from poor white trash. It was no surprise to Colonel Grant Taylor when Isaac only made Bs in algebra or wasn't chosen for the best soccer teams at whatever Air Force base on which they were living.

Isaac, who had excelled at almost everything he touched, was well beyond believing anything his father had said about him. But the little he knew about his birth family reinforced this particular rant. His mother had worked in a bar and hadn't been sure who his father was. And for most of her life, his grandmother had lived in this primitive cabin with no husband in residence.

He unhooked his seat belt and grabbed the keys, although out here there was little chance anyone was going to steal the car. First they would have to navigate the rutted dirt road that led to the clearing.

"I'll unload. Why don't you open up?" He turned back to Kendra. "Unless you've changed your mind?"

She shook her head. He opened his door, and once he was out, he slammed it harder than he needed to.

When he opened the trunk, Kendra insisted on taking a shopping bag filled with miscellaneous kitchen items she'd collected from the condo. She had left more than half for him, although both of them knew he would probably be eating all his meals out.

"Do you know what they call this architectural style?" she asked as they moved slowly toward the cabin.

"Lean-to?"

"It's a dogtrot cabin. The early settlers were restricted by the length of the available logs and the weight they could lift. So they built small homes, and when it came time to add on, they just built another house across from the first and connected them with a roof and flooring. A dog could trot right between the houses, and that's where the dogs stayed on a hot day or at night. The design acts sort of like a tunnel and sucks in any cool breezes. A lot of houses started this way, then they were covered with siding, and the middle porch became a room or a hallway. There are more of them around than you'd guess."

"Uh-huh."

His lack of enthusiasm didn't stop her. "Your interest is noted. At least part of the house was built before your grandmother's time, and the front porch was added later. I don't know when."

"Would you find it so intriguing if this were your family home? Instead of the brownstone in Manhattan? Or the estate in Saratoga Springs?"

"I'd find it more intriguing. I like the history here."

"To each his own."

Again she ignored him. "When you look at all the mini-mansions going up in the D.C. suburbs, it's hard to imagine anyone raising a family in a house as small as this one, isn't it?"

"I imagine some people just added on."

"I'd like to do that here, but I don't want to destroy the integrity of the design."

"Anyone else would raze this place."

"That was my first thought. Don't forget, I wanted to build a new house on the site."

And *he* hadn't wanted to. From the day three years ago when he had discovered he'd been left this land and cabin as an inheritance, Isaac had not wanted anything to do with it. Still, he was a practical man, and he had seen the investment potential at a time when the stock market was tanking. So he held on, knowing that by the time he retired, the property would be worth a great deal. He'd only grudgingly agreed to the minor renovations because a structure might make selling the property that much easier when the time came.

"Now I wish I'd gone along with you," he said. "I'd feel better knowing you were living in a modern house."

"Don't worry. Once I found out there were logs under the siding, I never would have taken it down."

They reached the steps up to the narrow porch that ran along the front of both structures and the bisecting dogtrot. He held out a hand. "Watch your step. Why hasn't your carpenter built a railing?"

"He moved to Tennessee two weeks ago to live closer to his children." Kendra took Isaac's hand. Hers felt as light as air, and her skin was the color of eggshells. She was putting a good face on things, but she looked drained.

"You mean you don't have anybody to finish putting this place in order?"

"I'll find somebody now that I'm out here. I have resources."

He tried and couldn't imagine Kendra living in this place alone. "The railing's just for starters. The ground needs to be graded or one day you're going to take a spill. The boards on the porch look like they need to be replaced. The—"

"Have you noticed the view?"

He heard what she hadn't said. *Stop complaining and try to see what I do. I want you to understand why I'm here.*

"There's nothing wrong with the view. Move it closer to D.C. and we'd be millionaires." Of course, his wife already was, but Isaac didn't point that out. Kendra's trust fund had never been one of their problems.

The clearing around the house was flat enough, although the property sloped gently at the back, and eventually, after a drop, ended at the North Fork of the Shenandoah River. There were several newly greening trees—oaks, he guessed—planted for shade, and what he recognized as a stand of sycamores. Woods were threatening to encroach on both sides, although it looked as if the good hardwoods had been taken several decades ago. Through the thick unfettered canopy he saw blooming dogwoods and the vestiges of redbuds.

The prevailing feeling here was of civilization being swallowed alive, of vines creeping toward the house to strangle it, of seedlings that would grow overnight into beanstalks crowned with maniacal giants. He glimpsed what looked like a marsh along the edge of the woods on one side. He imagined moccasins and rattlesnakes. The woods were probably full of bears.

He, who was dedicated to saving the world's wild places.

"Come see it from inside," Kendra said.

They were in the dogtrot now. At the other end he could see the river in the distance. Despite himself, he wondered if the man who had built this cabin had planned it this way. If he had wanted to look down on the sparkling Shenandoah each morning. Or perhaps his wife had insisted she wanted to see the river as she sat on the porch and snapped beans or did her weekly mending.

"It'll look better when I've had a chance to shop."

Kendra unlocked the door on her left. At least the lock was new and looked sturdy.

"I'm going to furnish it with antiques. But I've bought enough basics to make it livable."

Isaac followed her inside. He could tell by the way her foot dragged, as well as by her pallor, that this trip had cost her a great deal. He felt a fresh twinge of anger.

"What do you think?" she asked.

The room felt dark and cramped. The ceiling was low, and although he didn't need to, he felt as if he should crouch. Kendra pulled back cream-colored curtains as she went, and although there weren't many windows, the light helped.

"I'll need to wash the windows," she said. "And apparently it's not that hard to add them to these cabins, I might just do it when I find a good contractor. I don't want a museum, I want a home."

But not with him. Isaac heard that clearly. Kendra knew this would never feel like home to him or fit with plans he had for his life. But that no longer seemed to concern her.

"Come see the kitchen," she said.

The kitchen was just the other end of the room. Dabney had done a good job of adding cabinets and a pantry. The sink, deep and rectangular, was an antique—he guessed it was one Kendra had found. A small round table sat in the corner for meals.

"Simple but efficient," she said. "Do you like it?"

"Looks easy to use."

"We got the cabinets out of an old house that was being torn down. They're hickory. I love them. And the countertop is slate from an old school building south of here."

He hadn't known she was putting so much thought or energy into this project. Apparently there was a lot he hadn't known.

"I'll show you the other part."

He stopped her before she could pass. "Don't do this."

She didn't move, and she didn't look at him. "I thought we'd worked this out."

"Look at you. You're already exhausted."

"Let me show you your grandmother's garden. Or what's left of it. I think she spent a lot of time there."

He dropped his hands. "Fine. You can show me after I move everything else inside."

He made four trips to the car. She hadn't brought much. Casual clothes, her computer, a small television set, more things for the kitchen, her plants, sheets and towels. He guessed she hadn't wanted to look as if she was moving away for good. As she felt stronger, she would probably return to the condo, perhaps while he was gone, and claim more of her things.

He looked up as he carried the next to the last load and found her standing beside the second wing.

"Elisa and Sam must have come inside. They made the bed and put fresh flowers beside it. I've got brand-new towels in the bathroom."

He was glad the Kinkades would be nearby to watch over his wife.

"Come see, Isaac. Just a glance."

Reluctantly, he followed her into the bedroom and saw a queen-size bed made up with fresh white sheets, and a sitting area with a comfortable love seat and a low round table.

"And the bathroom." She moved slowly across the room and flung open the door of what he had guessed was a closet. The bathroom was small but clearly functional. The shower stall was just large enough to turn around in.

"Looks like you've got everything you need here."

"Just about."

He wondered what she meant by that.

Everything except you? Everything except a divorce?

He went back to the car and returned with the final load. This one was filled with old quilts she had collected, including the ragged one his grandmother had left him, along with the land. He set this box just inside the bedroom door and glanced at his watch.

"I'd like to avoid rush hour in the city."

"You could stay the night."

He considered this. It would help her ease into life in the cabin. A good husband would stay. He did not feel like a good husband today.

"I have a meeting early in the morning. Do you want to show me the garden now?"

Silently she led him down the steps. He watched her carefully balance, and closed his eyes when she swayed at the bottom. He was an inch from throwing her in the car and heading back to the city.

She picked her way carefully along a path that needed mowing. "It's over here."

About thirty yards from the house, he saw an area that looked as if it might once have been neatly laid out in raised beds with paths in between. Of course, now it was so overgrown nothing remained except the barest of garden skeletons.

"There are some timbers along the edges. I'm sure there was a split-rail fence to keep out deer, or at least help. It's huge, isn't it? She must have raised all her food for the winter."

"Maybe."

She pointed west. "What's left of an orchard is that way. I'm going to see if I can find an arborist to help me restore what I can."

He put his hands on her shoulders and turned her to face him. "I don't want to leave you here. If you need to get away, won't you choose someplace else? Visit friends. Rent a house in a suburb. Spend a year in Europe?"

"I have to do this."

They stared at each other. She didn't look as brave as he knew she wanted to. There was ambivalence lurking behind her attempt at confidence.

If he could read her this clearly, he wondered, what did she see when she looked at *him?* Worry that he hadn't done enough to persuade her? Fear for her safety? Or, worst of all, some splinter of relief that she was no longer his daily problem, that he could go about his life undisturbed, work the hours he was accustomed to, stop trying to transform her into the person she had been?

He dropped his hands. "I have a little time. I can make you something for dinner. Help you unpack."

"I'll be fine. I'll take it slow. But everyday stuff is the best form of therapy."

"And you feel well enough to do that everyday stuff?"

"I'm okay."

He was emptied of protest. "Then I'll leave you to it. If you're sure."

"I am."

"Just remember, I'm only a phone call away, K.C."

Her expression changed into something sadder. "You haven't called me that in years."

Ten years ago she had been introduced to him at a party as K. C. Dunkirk, her byline at a small suburban weekly. He hadn't gotten around to calling her Kendra for a year. K.C. had slipped away some time after they were married. A lot of things had slipped away.

"Maybe it's because I don't know who you are anymore," he said.

She put her arms around his shoulders and pulled him close. “I love you, Isaac. Everything else is changing, but that never will.”

He kissed her; then he pulled her close. She felt as hollow-boned as a bird. He was afraid that the moment he released her she would take flight.

“I don’t know when I can come again,” he warned.

“I’ll be here when you do.”

When he was behind the steering wheel of his car, he looked up and saw that she was still standing where he had left her. He wondered if she would make it up the steps. He wondered when or if he would stop worrying.

She could always change her mind.

Kendra watched Isaac’s Prius disappearing into the woods and felt panic pulling her down for the third time.

“I don’t have to stay.” She closed her eyes and tried to imagine where she would go instead. Nowhere.

She took deep breaths and, minutes later, opened her eyes. The sun shone, and the air was alive with birdsong. Try as she might, she could not hear a single car. Isaac's high-efficiency engine was silent at the low speed he would use on these roads. Besides, even if he'd been driving a diesel truck, Isaac was probably too far away to hear her call.

Isaac was gone.

"Welcome home, Kendra." She started back to the porch, but once she was at the steps, she thought better of trying them. Instead she hiked herself to the edge and used her hands to move her left leg. The effort cost her every drop of strength she had left. She broke into a sweat, and for a moment she was afraid the subtle nausea she'd experienced all day was going to overwhelm her. She lay down carefully and gazed up at the porch roof.

Her physical therapist had told her that recovery was a fine balance between pushing herself and not pushing herself. Today she had landed heavily on the side of the first.

Kendra had spent very little time asking herself why the carjacking had happened to her. She didn't believe in a universe that protected one person at the expense of another. She didn't expect favoritism from

God, but she *had* asked herself how she had let anger at Isaac lead her into that dark parking lot when she had been too sick to fend for herself.

The answer hadn't pleased her. She had been angry at Isaac for a long time. Angry that he held no new aspirations for their marriage. Angry that the man who could sense every undercurrent at work had no idea she was unhappy. Or, worse, that he knew it and thought the unhappiness would simply pass without intervention.

The night she'd been shot, she had set out to prove something. By doing so, she had set in motion a chain of events that now had her staring up at a beadboard ceiling.

"Well, who'd have thought it?"

She liked the sound of her voice here. She was soft-spoken, easy to miss in a noisy newsroom, easy to ignore when the man she was speaking to had more important things on his mind. Here her voice seemed to fill the silence between the calls of cardinals and the chittering of chickadees. It sounded important, as if there was every reason to sit up and take notice. It sounded at home, as if it belonged with the rustling of treetops, the scurrying of squirrels.

"I will make myself happy here." She liked the sound of this. She could almost believe it.

The panic was subsiding. The air was growing cooler. A breeze through the dogtrot played with her hair and cooled her cheeks. The nausea diminished. She wasn't on a timetable. Sam and Elisa had made the bed. She had towels, food, water. She was okay. She could count nailheads or knots in the timber until sunset was a memory. She had nowhere to go and nothing to do. No one expected anything of her now.

She wondered how Isaac was feeling as he drove back toward D.C. Sad. She truly believed that would be part of it. He had closed his eyes to the problems between them for so long that all this had come as an unwelcome surprise. Angry. That too. Isaac wanted his world to be governed by rules and logic. Now he suspected mental foul play and didn't know how to find the culprit.

Relieved.

Relief was the one that was an ache inside her. But she knew this was not something she imagined. This new wife, with the injured spine and the damaged organs, this wife who required waiting on and hand-holding, this wife who he apparently considered too fragile to make love to . . . This wife was someone he wasn't certain how to cope with. Isaac would never refuse to try. But having taken that decision out of his hands, she was certain he was grateful.

She sighed. This, too, sounded natural here. She thought that perhaps Isaac's grandmother had indulged in many such sighs on this porch. If it was true, Kendra was sorry.

In the late afternoon she slowly unpacked the boxes, noting all the things she hadn't had room to bring. For this first trip to the cabin she had chosen only the most practical items, and others, like the quilts, that had sentimental value. She planned to ask Isaac to ship some of the small antique pieces she had defiantly collected to offset the institutional furniture that had come with their condo. The carpenter's chest, the pie safe, the yellowware bowls she'd had no room to display in the condo's galley kitchen. The moment she felt strong enough to drive, she would shop for more antiques in the Valley and fill the old cabin with them.

She wondered when that would be.

By six she knew she wasn't going to have the energy to cook dinner. There was no microwave to heat frozen food. She had a narrow four-burner stove, a dorm-size refrigerator and no small appliances. She decided to buy a slow cooker as soon as she could, so in the mornings she could fashion a dinner for later, when energy was only a memory.

She settled on an apple and took it to the front porch. There was no furniture there, but she would remedy that, as well. As soon as she was able.

She was sitting on the edge, back against a pillar, when she heard a car approaching. The sky was still light, and she suspected friends, but her hands began to perspire despite the cool air of evening. She was completely alone here, and even if she called for help, it would take a long time to arrive.

With relief she noted that the old pickup that finally chugged its way up to the clearing held two women. The relief turned to pleasure when she recognized one. She got clumsily to her feet.

"Helen . . ." She looked at the steps and realized she wasn't up to negotiating them to greet her closest neighbor.

Helen Henry swung her legs over the passenger seat of the truck and dusted off a printed sack of a dress. "I heard you were coming today. No reason to think that rascal of a preacher would get it wrong."

A pretty young woman with a cloud of red-blond hair got out on the driver's side and came around to help Helen. Kendra remembered that this was Cissy, who, along with her husband and baby daughter, lived with Helen. Kendra had met the girl briefly at the church where Sam Kinkade was the minister.

Helen, a woman in her eighties, was still vigorous, and she brushed aside Cissy's attempts to help her down. "Day comes I can't get myself out of this pickup, I'll just lie down and die. I'm not down yet, am I?"

"Ms. Henry, you'll probably die standing up giving somebody a lecture."

Helen couldn't suppress a smile, although clearly she tried. She slid down and landed with a *thud,* but it didn't seem to faze her.

She turned, then spun around and held up a cardboard box. "Brought you supper.

That's what neighbors do around here when somebody moves in."

Suddenly Kendra's apple seemed even less appealing. "That's so kind of you." She looked down at the steps. "I'd come and help, but I'm afraid these stairs just don't look too good to me right now."

"You stay right where you are. We made enough to keep you in leftovers until you get on your feet." Helen thrust the box at Cissy and started up to the cabin porch. "Where'd the railing go?"

"Rotted through. I think Dabney was planning to put up a new one and didn't get around to it."

"Man snuck out of town like a snake-oil peddler. We'll send Zeke over to put up a new one. That boy can build anything—can't he, Cissy. Maybe Caleb could help."

"Zeke's my husband," Cissy explained. She took the steps carefully, since it was hard to see around the box. "Zeke Claiborne. Caleb's my little brother, Caleb Mowrey. I don't think Caleb knows which side of a hammer is which. But Ms. Henry's right about Zeke. He'll be glad to do it, but he might not be able to get to it right away. He's going out of town in a day or two."

Helen was tall and broad, and, judging from the leathery texture of her skin, much of her past had been lived outdoors. She had thin white hair that was plumped up by a good perm and eyes that sparkled behind thick glasses. Cissy was small boned, with fragile features and Kendra's propensity to freckle. The two women made an interesting pair.

"I can't tell you how much I appreciate the offer," Kendra said, "but I'm afraid I need a lot more than a railing. I'm going to have to find somebody who has at least a couple of weeks to help me get things in better order." She tried to remember details about Cissy and her husband. "Zeke makes musical instruments, right? He has his own shop."

"If you can call a part of his daddy's barn a shop," Helen said. "But the boy is showing a lot of promise. His banjos are something to behold."

"He sold a guitar to one of the Statler Brothers," Cissy said proudly.

"Sounds like he's really on his way," Kendra said.

"We . . . I was sorry to hear about you being shot and all," Cissy said. "We were all real worried."

"We put you on the prayer list at church. Never thought that did much good," Helen said. "But it gave us all something to do when you were so far away. I mean, even if the Good Lord does what He has to when He has to, at least He knew you had a lot of friends who were worried."

Kendra felt a familiar choking sensation. Tears waiting to be swallowed. "Something worked. Here I am. Thank you for that."

"Glad you're better."

"Cissy, I didn't mean to leave you standing there," Kendra said. "The kitchen's this way."

She led them inside, and Cissy put the box on the table in the corner. "There's chicken potpie, Valley style," Cissy said. "That's one of Ms. Henry's specialties. A green bean casserole Zeke's mama made for you. A lime Jell-O salad with pears. I made that, and I made you a loaf of pumpkin bread, too. Marian, that's Zeke's mama, she also put in half a dozen chocolate cupcakes and a dozen sugar cookies."

"See that you eat every bit of it," Helen said. "You're going to be a country girl, you got to get some meat on those bones."

Kendra had not seen so much food in one

place since she'd gone to one of Community Church's potluck suppers. "This is so much. Thank you both. And you'll thank Marian for me?"

"We're your closest neighbors," Helen pointed out. "Me over that way—" she pointed "—the Clairbornes in that direction. It's been a right long time since anybody lived in this house, and I'm glad to see it in use again."

"Would you like to see the rest of it?"

Helen shook her head. "Looks good enough to live in, though it could do with some spit and polish, or maybe a bulldozer. But you've had a big day and need some rest. We'll be back."

Kendra followed them back to the porch and watched as Cissy helped Helen down the steps. This time Helen made no protest.

At the bottom, the older woman turned and looked up at Kendra. "I knew the woman who used to live here, you know. Leah Spurlock, that was her name before she married old Tom Jackson. That's how we all think of her, as a Spurlock. She raised a daughter here, but it was always a little bitty place."

Kendra had never told anyone that Isaac

had inherited this property from Leah, or why. She had wanted to know more before she made that announcement, and she had hoped to overcome Isaac's resistance first. Now she was tempted to tell Helen, to see what tales Helen could recount. But she was too tired to start that conversation.

"I'd like to add on," she said instead. "But I don't know quite how. I don't want to build a modern house onto this one. I'd want something rustic."

"There's an old barn for sale down the road, not far from where it crosses Carter's Mill. Log barn, maybe even chestnut. You might could use the timber."

Kendra liked the sound of that. "I wouldn't know how to go about it."

"I know just the man to talk to. Manning Rosslyn. Lives up not too far from the church. Got his own company. They take down old buildings people don't want anymore, number the pieces like some kind of puzzle, then put them back up in different places. He does additions, too. Preserves whatever he can. Knowing Manning, he's probably already bid on that barn." Helen smiled a little. "And this place, it would surely appeal to him. He used to be sweet on Rachel, way back in the fifties. Rachel, she was Leah's daughter."

Rachel, she was Isaac's mother.

Kendra recognized a bonus when it came her way. "I'll give him a call. Manning Rosslyn."

"Rosslyn and Rosslyn. Now that Manning's getting up in years, his son's in the business with him. Cash is his name." Helen pointed to the garden area. "That was Leah's garden. She was more or less the granny woman in these parts. You know what that means?"

"I guess not."

"Nobody could much afford a doctor. We did a lot of healing on our own. But Leah, she was the best. She knew what to use for almost any problem there was. Grew plants in that patch the likes of which nobody else around here ever tried. She'd take care of sick people, stay with them and follow whatever directions their doctors gave her. But she added her own brand of medicine right alongside theirs. I think the doctors knew and just turned their heads. There wasn't much anybody could do when my mama was dying, but when Daddy was going, nobody else could ease his pain. Leah knew how. I was always real grateful to her for that."

Kendra liked what she'd heard about Leah. She wondered if Isaac would, or if he was so prejudiced against his biological family that no good news would seep through.

She gestured to the side of the clearing. "The garden's still visible, at least the bare outline of it. I'm going to see if there's anything there that can be saved."

"Just watch out for varmints when you do. Be better just to mow it all down and start fresh." Helen hiked a worn leather purse higher on her shoulder. "You remember, we're just one phone call away. I put our phone number in that box with the food. And the Clairbornes', too. And some of the other neighbors'. You've got friends here. Don't be afraid to call them."

Kendra hoped that the tears that were such a new and disconcerting addition to her emotional repertoire would stop making appearances. "Thanks," she said in a husky voice.

"No bother at all. You take care of yourself now, and we'll expect a visit once you're all settled."

Kendra knew the offer was genuine. She planned to accept it.

CHAPTER FOUR

On Sunday morning Kendra sipped a cup of French-press coffee on the front porch. She had been at the cabin for four days, and although every night she had wrestled with the usual nightmare, last night she had slept for several hours at a stretch. She was spending so much time outdoors in the sweetly scented spring air that, finally, sleep had claimed dominance.

This morning was an especially lovely one. Softly filtered sunbeams lit the gentle green of the surrounding woods. The fine mist that had played around the tree trunks like ghostly wood nymphs was gone, and shapes had emerged. Earlier a trio of deer had nibbled at the edges of the clearing, casually observing her observing them.

Every day she visually measured the

newly emerging leaves on the closest tree shading the house, noting the subtle differences. Today she was almost certain it was an oak. Next week, when the telephone company installed a land line to the cabin and she could access the Internet, she would visit an online bookseller and order guides to help identify her environment.

On waking, she had considered attempting the drive to Community Church, but by the time she had warmed a fresh biscuit she realized she wasn't ready to brave the hour-long service. In fact, she still hadn't turned the key in the ignition of her new car. Each day she practiced sitting behind the wheel, thinking positive thoughts. Each day she stayed a little longer, felt a little calmer. Today, at some point, she was going to attempt her first drive. But small steps were in order.

Coffee on the porch had become a ritual. Now she could not imagine a time when she hadn't sat quietly for some portion of each day and observed the world around her. Without a guide, she'd made up names for the birds she couldn't identify. The cell phone bird had a song with brief, regular pauses between trilled repeats. The doorbell bird could make itself heard over the noisiest party.

She heard a rustling on the ground and casually glanced over the porch's edge, expecting chipmunks or squirrels. Instead, she saw the head of a snake. She froze, and her heart began to pound. The snake was coming from under the porch. And coming.

And coming.

By the time the snake was completely free, the part of her brain that was still working told her it was a good seven feet long.

She made mental notes so she could describe it to someone. The scales were shiny and black, although the underbelly looked white. There was good news. She neither saw nor heard rattles, and the head was not the triangular shape of a pit viper. She and Isaac had hiked in enough wild terrain for her to have a basic knowledge of poisonous snakes. This one was harmless.

Of course the bad news was that the longest snake she had ever seen, probably the longest snake in existence, was living under her porch.

"Oh, Lord." She closed her eyes, then snapped them open again. If ever there was a right moment to observe the world around her, this would be the one. The snake slithered—and there, she thought, was an appropriate verb—toward the woods east of the house and, after a while, disappeared.

"I am not alone here. More good news." She tried to think what she should do.

She wasn't particularly afraid of snakes. She had handled them with supervision, observed them behind glass, appreciated, at a distance, snakes on the trails she and Isaac hiked. Never, though, had she lived on top of one. At times she had been annoyed by the neighbors on the floor below her D.C. condo. But those young men were paragons in comparison to Slithering Godzilla, who was now having a leisurely breakfast of bird or beast before his next nap under her new home.

Maybe he didn't live there. Maybe he had just dropped in, found it not to his liking and gone to find better digs.

She pondered that. When she'd decided to renovate, one of the first things she'd asked Dabney to do was chink the logs. Elsewhere, he had plugged up every possible hole, too. She knew country houses came with field mice bonuses, and she had wanted the best possible prevention. The snake would have a tough time getting inside either portion of the cabin. Heck, this snake was so big he'd have trouble worming his way through a porthole.

So, rationally, there was little chance this guy was going to get inside. Besides, snakes were more frightened of people than people were of snakes. Not that she'd ever met anyone who had psychoanalyzed a snake and could honestly make that comparison.

She kept her eyes wide open while she finished her coffee, but there were no more surprises. Her plan for the morning—pre-snake—had included a visit to Leah's garden. Yesterday Cissy had stopped by with freshly baked biscuits and a well-thumbed paperback she had bought at a book sale in Woodstock.

"It's about herbs and such," she'd said. "I thought you might like it. Look, it has pictures." She'd paged through, pointing out the illustrations. "You might find something in that garden that looks like these. You know, something still growing from when Ms. Spurlock lived here."

Kendra had been touched by the girl's thoughtfulness. And the biscuits had been impossible to resist. She'd already eaten three.

Now it was time to decide who was master of this property. If she was really going to remain here any length of time, she had to come to terms with the wildlife.

Inside, she pulled on her oldest jeans, a long-sleeve linen shirt, a brimmed straw hat and hiking boots that laced well above her ankles. She had to do this before the sun came out in earnest. Book in hand, along with an old weed cutter she had found hanging on a nail at the back of the house, she made her way down the steps and over to the garden.

Leah had been an ambitious gardener. That much was clear. Of course, Kendra knew ambition and survival often went hand in hand. Leah had lived on poverty's doorstep. This garden had surely fed her as well as provided remedies for her neighbors and others in the community.

Although she knew too little about the woman, she did know that after marrying Tom Jackson, Leah had eventually moved into a modern house in New Market, about twenty-five miles to the south. But Kendra wondered if Leah had come back afterward to tend this garden. She had been dead for twelve years, so it was difficult to tell when the garden had been abandoned. Mother Nature could stage a takeover in just a year or two.

For a moment, teetering at the garden's edge, she reconsidered her decision. Then she made the plunge. The weed cutter—at least that was what she called it—had a rectangular blade with serrated edges. The blade was attached to the bottom of a broomstick-like handle. Under better circumstances she would have found it lightweight, but even a dinner plate felt heavy these days. She set the book on the ground and began to swing at the nearest weeds, cutting a path through the dead stalks of last year's foliage. Today, a simple path. Soon enough, a look at what was left of the garden beds.

By the time she trimmed a section three feet by about six, sweat was pouring down her cheeks. She was so exhausted that she wondered if she would make it back to the house. The beds flanking the path had been built up for drainage. After carefully checking the ground, she sank down on the bed at her right. Face in hands, she breathed deeply.

The sun was higher now, but the air was still cool. She was shaking from her efforts, and her arms felt as if she had been lifting fifty-pound weights. She'd had pneumonia. She'd barely survived two bullets. She'd had major surgery. Of course she was weak. Of course she had no stamina.

Of course she wanted to feel normal again, to be the fearless, energetic woman who had never taken no for an answer.

She sat that way until the trembling began to subside. It was time to stop for the morning. When the sun started its afternoon descent, she would try to cut another swath, only smaller this time.

She leaned back and realized that she was resting on newly emerging foliage, silkier and softer than the weeds at the edge. She turned around to examine it. The patch surprised her. It was crowded with the same plant—too crowded, of course, since no one had dealt with it in at least a decade except to mow weeds in fall. But the new leaves were a soft green oval with a pointed tip, and they emerged directly from the ground. She dug down a little and found that the root was a massive clump not far under the soil.

She felt a thrill of discovery. In her experience, weeds partied with friends, and they invited everybody they knew to join them. This plant had been set here many years ago to form a mat to repel gate-crashers.

She dug up a small clump to take back to the house with her. It took a few minutes to get it out of the ground with nothing more than fingernails and determination. Mentally she added good gardening tools to her growing shopping list.

Halfway back to the house, clutching her fuzzy-leafed prize against the linen shirt that had never been made for gardening, she realized that although she still felt weak, she no longer felt as discouraged. She hadn't done much, but she *had* done something. Surely this was the way true healing began. This was the way people moved forward.

With such beautiful weather, lunch on the porch seemed like a good idea. Kendra borrowed one of the two ladderback chairs from her kitchen table and set it against the front wall. She planned to have another of Cissy's featherweight biscuits with deli ham she'd brought from the city and cold green bean casserole. She still had to force herself to eat every day, but with less effort. Now, though, by the time she dragged the chair through the door and went back for a glass of cold tea, she was too tired to fix a meal.

Instead she rested and sipped, listening for more birds to name.

The sound that greeted her several minutes later was a car engine. She supposed she was getting used to living alone in the country. This time she was only mildly rattled.

The car was an SUV with a number of miles behind it. With pleasure she recognized Sam and Elisa, and got to her feet to greet them. She knew that after delivering her car, they had gone out of town. Elisa's brother Ramon was a freshman at James Madison University in Harrisonburg, farther south, and they had gone to visit him, returning home late last night. Elisa had called once to check on her, and she had been delighted to hear that Helen and Cissy had Kendra in their crosshairs.

Kendra held her hands high. "I repent. I'll come to church just as soon as I'm able. You can count on me."

"You'd better," Sam said. He waited for Elisa and slung his arm around her shoulders as they headed up the path. "Don't think you've disappeared from sight out here."

Elisa was carrying a grocery bag. When they got to the porch, Kendra embraced them both clumsily. "You look great. A few days off agrees with you."

"And *you* look pale." Elisa put the back of her hand against Kendra's cheek. "Are you overdoing it?"

"I've only dog-paddled from bank to bank of the river a couple of times since I arrived."

"You sit."

"There's only one chair. Let's go inside. Tell me about Ramon." Elisa's brother was a handsome, charismatic young man who, like his sister, had experienced too many hard times. Despite a formal education with substantial gaps, he had received such a high score on the SATs that he had been offered admission to several important universities. He had chosen James Madison, not only for its excellent reputation but for its proximity to Elisa and Sam. They were helping him make up the deficits in his education.

They followed her inside, and Sam made himself at home on the sofa, while Elisa carried her groceries into the kitchen. Although she had been born Alicia, she had called herself Elisa for so long that she had decided to go by it permanently. She was slender, with straight black hair that fell to her shoulders. Her English was perfect and only lightly accented. An obstetrician trained in Guatemala, she was now in the process of jumping through hoops so she could be licensed to practice in Virginia. She had to complete a two-year residency and a three-part exam, but she was under consideration at the University of Virginia and at several hospitals in the D.C. area.

She set the groceries on the counter and began to unpack. "Ramon still likes the university and sends his love. He's taking classes through the summer to catch up but will have a break in early May. We'll have a party."

"I'll look forward to that." Kendra meant it.

"There's nothing fancy in this bag. Bread, cheese, fruit, some deli salads. Enough to keep you for a few days." Elisa looked up. "You're not up to going shopping yet, are you? I don't want to nag, but it won't help if you push too hard."

"I did a little gardening today, that's all. And I stopped well before I was ready to collapse."

"Make sure you do, okay? I don't want to lose my good friend."

Kendra crossed her heart. "I promise."

They joined Sam on the sofa, and he put his arms around both of them. He was dark haired, blue eyed, and so appealing in his clerical robe that the attendance of young women in his congregation had increased. "This place is pretty basic. Are you getting along here? The parsonage has a guest room."

"Isaac thinks I've lost my mind."

"I think you're trying to find your heart, and this is the kind of place where you can listen to it beat for a while. Just don't forget we're only a few heartbeats away if you need us."

"You've been so good to me."

"We could never be good enough. Your story changed the course of our lives."

Kendra's story about Elisa and Ramon's

separate escapes from Guatemala and their long search to find each other had only been one link in the chain of events that had freed them from the nightmare of their past, but the story had also helped Kendra move from features into investigative reporting. Elisa and Ramon had fled false murder charges, the result of political oppression, but had since been cleared to find new lives in Virginia.

"I have to meet with the deacons in just a little while." Sam gave Kendra's shoulder a squeeze before he stood. "Have you driven the car yet?"

"You ought to see me slide behind the wheel."

"Ready for something more?"

She had been relaxed, and now she wasn't. "You want me to take Elisa home?"

"If you think you're up to it."

It seemed like a good way to start, even though Kendra was now breathing faster and her hands were no longer steady. "Elisa can take over if I can't do it."

"That's what I thought. So I'm taking off now. If you don't want to drive home alone, you can stay at our place until I get there, and we'll drive you back."

Elisa got up to see her husband out. When she returned, she went to the refrigerator. "Did you eat yet?"

"I was gathering strength."

"Will you let me put something together for both of us?"

"I feel so helpless." Kendra was surprised at the edge in her own voice. "I've been taking care of myself since I was nine and the nanny started passing out regularly after dinner."

"Sounds like there's a story there."

"She had a bottle of scotch hidden under the sink with the cleaning supplies. I had to put her *and* my baby sister Jamie to bed."

"That's a lot of years." Elisa took out plastic containers, opening them to peek inside. "You never told your mother?"

"Riva wasn't much of a judge of people. I knew the possibilities weren't good that the next nanny would be any better."

"The devil you know?"

"I'm not trying to be maudlin. Just to say that it bothers me a lot that I need help now."

"We are not talking about taking food out of the refrigerator, are we? I suspect we're discussing the car."

"I've driven coast to coast practically nonstop, on narrow winding roads where I might meet a car and have to back up a mile before I could pull over. And it's not like the carjacker shot me while I was inside."

"Which is not to say that if you get back inside, someone else will want your car and try to take it from you."

Kendra was silent. Having someone else speak the truth and bring it out in the open helped.

"I should have bought a clunker," she said at last.

"I'll be with you." Elisa turned on the stove and prepared to heat their lunch. "And if it doesn't go well, we will just try again later. Sam wouldn't have mentioned it today except that we're both concerned you're here alone. And since you won't ask for help, we hope you will begin to drive soon."

They ate outside on the porch, and Kendra told her friend about the snake. Elisa was properly impressed. When the conversation turned to the cabin, Kendra explained about Helen and the barn.

"Have you called Manning Rosslyn?" Elisa asked. "He sometimes attends the church with his wife. He's an older man. Tall and broad. She is younger, blond and thin."

"I haven't called yet. But I'd like to see the barn. Maybe we could drive out that way and look at it."

They finished eating and took their empty plates into the kitchen. As Kendra rinsed, Elisa prowled the living room, looking at the few personal touches Kendra had added.

She held up the corner of the Lover's Knot quilt Kendra had draped over the rocker. "This is what they call a signature quilt, isn't it? An old one."

"I seem to collect them. That one is an heirloom from Isaac's family." Kendra had begun collecting antique quilts more than a year ago. She had four that she'd bought in D.C. area shops. But the Lover's Knot was her favorite. She knew little about it—only that Leah had done her best to ensure that the quilt, along with this house and land, would make its way to the grandson she had never known.

The quilt was double-bed size and not an inch more. The binding was wearing thin. There were age spots, and about a third of the fabric blocks were noticeably faded. Although the color choices—scrap prints of greens, blues, purples and reds—were lovely, two things set the quilt apart.

The first were the signatures, all neatly embroidered in several strands of black thread but scattered over the surface as if they'd been sprinkled at random. The other was the quilting itself. Quilts of the era had often been stitched with parallel intersecting lines or half circles traced from dinner plates and saucers. Accomplished quilters had added complicated feathers and wreaths, vines or flowers. The Lover's Knot quilt had lines that meandered with no discernible pattern or plan.

This was not a quilt that had won prizes at a county fair. Yet the top itself was far too well designed and the pattern too complex to be a simple utility quilt stitched in haste to warm a cold bed.

"It looks at home here," Elisa said, smoothing it back into place.

Kendra hoped that if the quilt had been made in this cabin, Helen might know some of the people whose names were embroidered on it or where to find their descendants. But first she had to tell Helen about Isaac's relationship to Leah. She had never wanted to hide their connection; she only wanted to proceed carefully. Now she realized that if she waited too long, it would look as if she was ashamed.

"The quilt never looked at home in the condo," she told Elisa. "I doubt Isaac will notice it's missing."

"He's not taking the move well, is he."

Kendra dried her hands. "It's not logical. He can't get past that. But he'll throw himself back into work now that I'm gone."

"He will be visiting?"

Kendra wondered. Isaac had told her not to expect him for a while. She wasn't sure if that was to punish her or merely because he had taken so much time off while she was in the hospital that he now had to make it up.

"I don't know," she said. "I'm supposed to call if I need anything."

Wisely, Elisa said nothing.

Kendra brushed her hair and got her keys from the bedroom. Then she joined her friend on the porch. "Now or never, huh?"

"Now or later. The right moment is your decision."

Kendra gazed at the car. It really deserved better than a driver who was terrified to turn the key. She wiped her damp palms on the legs of her jeans. "Let's do it."

"I will be right beside you."

Kendra crossed the clearing and unlocked the door to slide behind the wheel. Elisa got in beside her and put on her seat belt. Kendra followed suit. She took a deep, shaky breath, then, before she could change her mind, put the key in the ignition. The car purred to life.

Kendra's hand was trembling on the gearshift. But she shifted into Reverse and touched the gas pedal. She backed up slowly until she could turn the wheel and position the car on the gravel drive that led out to Fitch Crossing Road.

"How am I doing so far?" she said, her voice pitched too high.

"You drive like a pro."

"That was only Reverse."

"If worse comes to worst you can turn around and back up all the way to the parsonage."

Despite herself, Kendra laughed. "I can do this."

"I have no doubts. Let's go see that barn."

The driveway was worse than she remembered, but the new car knew exactly what to do with the ruts and bumps. By the time she finished carefully navigating her way to Fitch Crossing, she felt confident enough to pull onto the larger road. She had it to herself and gently increased her speed.

"Sam drove the car to the cabin," Elisa said. "He claimed since it was new it might have some kinks that needed working out, so he told me to drive ours, and he drove this one."

"And you fell for that?"

"I let him have his fun."

Kendra drove faster until her speed approached half of what was considered normal on the country road. But her hands no longer had a death grip on the wheel, and her spine was unlocking, one vertebra at a time. In a matter of minutes they neared Carter's Mill Road, and Kendra slowed to a crawl.

"I hope the barn will have a For Sale sign."

They spotted it just before the crossroads. The two-story barn stood back on a hillside, about fifty yards from Fitch Crossing, an architectural skeleton that had been stripped of siding so that only the huge old logs were exposed. Kendra judged it had held perhaps six stalls on each side, with lots of room in between for extras. There was a hand-lettered sign tacked up on the end facing the road.

"It won't last long," Elisa said. "Somebody's going to buy it. There is such an emphasis these days on using old things in new ways. Someone will see the possibilities."

Kendra pulled into the drive leading up to the barn and stopped with the engine running. "It's a lot of barn."

"It would triple the size of your house."

Kendra had seen enough. She was definitely interested. "I'll call Manning Rosslyn and see what he has to say." She backed out to take Elisa home.

At the brick ranch parsonage, Elisa patted her arm in congratulations. "You drive like you were born to it. You will be all right going back?"

Kendra didn't want to give that too much thought. "I'm on the road again, I guess."

Driving home, she forced herself to breathe deeply when other cars passed and panic stirred. But by the time she pulled up to the clearing, she knew she could get behind the wheel again tomorrow. And to make sure she would, she promised herself a shopping trip to buy porch furniture.

Inside, she hung the keys on a nail and settled into the rocker, pulling Leah's quilt over legs that were still faintly trembling. As she rocked she fingered the panels, closing her eyes and letting her mind drift.

Despite Isaac's lack of interest, she planned to indulge her curiosity about the woman he had never known. But even after seven years of marriage, she was just as curious about the real Isaac Taylor. She wasn't sure what uncovering information about Isaac's birth family would teach her about the man, but she hoped it would teach her something.

She snuggled deeper into the Lover's Knot quilt and wondered if the woman who had pieced and quilted it had ever felt confused or lonely. Had Leah come to this cabin to escape someone, or to find herself? Had she accomplished either?

Not for the first time, Kendra felt a strong kinship with Isaac's grandmother. She closed her eyes and tried to imagine exactly what Leah would choose to say about her life.

CHAPTER FIVE

Blackburn Farm
Lock Hollow, Virginia
October 14, 1932

Dear Puss,

Since you said you was feeling puny, I am sending in this envelope some of Mama's special bitters for purifying the blood. Which is good as a tonic if you boil it in some water and drink it after a few minutes though you surely won't like the taste. I guess now that she's gone I'll be the one making this and giving it out to folks hear about from this day onward. I feel the weight of that.

If you keep feeling puny you can boil some sassafras bark and drink the tea, but better to come home and let me take care of you.

Birdie gets up every morning and does what she has to, which is about all I can say. She is a good sister to me, but I don't know if I can help her the way she needs. I am praying she will smile again soon.

Jesse Spurlock has not come round.
Always your best friend,

Leah Blackburn

Flossie and Dyer Blackburn were as healthy and strong as any residents of Lock Hollow. It was ironic that Flossie, who had doctored so many of her neighbors, succumbed to typhoid fever a week after her husband, when others with no healing skills were spared.

Birdie, Leah Blackburn's older sister, claimed she was the first to know their mother would follow their father to his grave. She had taken over Flossie's nursing care when Leah, who had been at the bedside for a full night and day, could no longer keep her eyes open.

"You go on now and sleep a spell. Let me watch over her," Birdie told her sister, and Leah, who was afraid their mother would either get better or pass without anyone to note it, had let her.

Later Birdie had recounted the events of the next hours. She had stoked the fire in the woodstove, because Mama had complained of being cold despite three layers of quilts. As she moved the logs, a spark leapt from the fire and into the room.

"It appeared to me right then," she said, "that Mama would be gone by morning. It surely was a sign."

Leah was skeptical. She had witnessed sparks showering the room before. Once a big one had set fire to a rug that Mama had plaited from strips of wool, and Mama had gone after it so furiously that Leah had been forced to remind her that both the rug and broom were suffering. No one had died that day, nor on others when the fire burned white hot.

But Birdie needed comfort. Leah thought that, in some curious way, Birdie's belief that she had predicted their mother's death helped her through the aftermath. Birdie had always believed in signs and omens.

They helped her make sense of the world into which she had been born, a world that had not been kind to her.

In 1919 poliomyelitis had come calling in the mountains and hollows of Virginia, and eight-year-old Birdie had been one of the first to feel its feverish fingers. She had nearly died from the encounter, and when the worst was over, she'd been left with a crippled leg and a body that into maturity remained as frail and weak as a child's.

Two days before Birdie was struck down, their mother had visited a neighbor and walked through the house without sitting down before leaving by a different door. This was a certain invitation to bad luck. At Birdie's bedside, the neighbor had reminded Mama of this foolish act, and Mama had ordered her never to set foot in the Blackburn house again. But Birdie, nearly delirious with fever, remembered that conversation. For years afterward she whispered the story, like a haunted bedtime tale, to Leah.

In the month since they buried their parents, Birdie had said little. It was not the way in these mountains to grieve loudly. Quietly she had turned the mirror to the wall and made certain the bodies of their parents were carried out of the house feet first, traditions that were important to her if not to Leah.

Twice, neighbors—some who had also lost loved ones—had filed silently past the coffins a neighbor had brought by wagon team to the Blackburn farm. Their parents had died within a week of each other, but there had been separate funerals, with the lumberjack preacher who lived down near Dark Hollow coming each time to assure those in attendance that the Blackburns were in a better place.

Since that time, Birdie had mourned in silence. She had been Mama's pet. Flossie Blackburn had been known for many miles as a fine seamstress, and she had carefully taught those skills to her oldest daughter. "Sewing is something it don't take strong legs to learn," she told Birdie. "And up close, you can see right smart, Birdie girl."

Birdie learned the finer points of making a home, their mother's closely guarded recipe for green tomato pickles, the proper distance to mark and stitch a quilt so the batting stayed smooth. After butchering in the fall, Birdie always received the choicest cuts of meat. After harvest, she was given the tenderest vegetables. Every night Mama brushed Birdie's hair more than the customary one hundred strokes. She embroidered the collars and cuffs of Birdie's nightdresses with daisies and roses.

Birdie lost more than a mother; she lost the person who tried hardest to shield her from the reality of her life. At her mother's graveside, Leah had silently sworn to Flossie that she would never abandon her sister.

Even without that graveside promise, Leah was certain her mother had known this. Birdie had been Mama's pet, but Leah had been her confidante and helper. Flossie had tucked Birdie under her wing, but she set Leah free to fly as far as she desired. She taught her younger daughter to read and read often, to observe the world around her, to make friends with chores she was required to do so she always had something to look forward to. She insisted that Leah get the few years of formal education available to her in their remote hollow and performed her daughter's chores herself, so that Leah could walk the necessary miles.

But best of all, Flossie passed to Leah the secrets of how to heal and give comfort.

Flossie herself had been the seventh daughter in a large West Virginia family, a position that nearly guaranteed she would have the healing touch. As if fate had wanted to make certain of it, two weeks before she was born, her father died in a logging accident. The granny midwife who presided over the birth told the neighbor women that Flossie, having never looked into her father's eyes, was destined to heal folks far and wide.

Perhaps the granny really believed this, or perhaps she simply gauged the deep exhaustion and melancholy of the baby's mother and knew that if she did not find a way to set this child apart from her many brothers and sisters, Flossie would not survive her childhood.

Whichever it was, the pronouncement that Flossie was special served her well. As soon as she was weaned, she was sent to live with a widowed neighbor known for her healing skills. And five years later, when the widow moved to Virginia's mountains to be closer to her son, Flossie went along.

In the years that followed, Flossie took

her role seriously. She served as an apprentice, learning the medicinal roles of plants, how and when to collect them, or grow them or nurture them so they increased in their forest habitats. She learned to dry and powder roots, to make tinctures, liniments and salves. Once she married Dyer Blackburn and moved to Lock Hollow, she read whatever literature she had access to, poring over the Watkins products almanacs, and *Domestic Medicine, or Poor Man's Friend, in the Hours of Affliction, Pain and Sickness* by Dr. John C. Gunn of Knoxville, Tennessee. From observation she formed her own opinions and discarded superstitions. When she finally gave birth to a daughter who could tramp the mountains with her, she taught Leah to be thoughtful and attentive, and to relish the power that came from healing the sick.

"You'll always be looked up to, where'er you go. Naught will make you dearer to friends and neighbors than to ease their pain and make their young'uns well."

It was with that in mind that Leah rose early on a Saturday, dressed, and performed her morning chores quickly and efficiently. She brought in wood for the cookstove and fanned the coals to flame. Then, while the kettle heated, she went outside and fed the chickens and the hog that would provide meat for the winter come butchering time.

The air was cool and sweet with just the tinge of smoke from their fire. Somewhere beyond the yard, an indigo bunting sang. Leah swept the path leading to the picket fence that surrounded the house and examined the remains of the hollyhocks that Mama had planted at the beginning of the summer. There had been no frost, although it was nearly time. From each plant she broke off dried blossoms in which the seeds were fully developed and slipped them in her apron pocket. She would save them to plant in the spring, in case the originals didn't reappear. Every year she would make sure some were growing right there against the fence in her mother's honor.

When she returned to the house, Birdie was pouring water over carefully measured coffee grounds. The Blackburn farm was as self-sufficient as any in the Blue Ridge, but coffee was something they could not grow themselves. In the worst of times, people in Lock Hollow roasted and ground dandelion roots or corn kernels. But the Blackburns had never resorted to this. Their father had been a careful, wily farmer who made the best use of good land and ran a steam-powered sawmill on the outskirts when times were rough. They had never wanted for any necessity.

"Did you have good dreams?" Leah asked her sister as she went to the basin beside the doorway to wash her hands.

"I've a mind to just stay up all night. My brain goes a-running, and I cain't sleep anyway."

"I can give you something for that, you know I can."

"There's nothing you can give me that will bring back Mama and Daddy."

"I can ease your misery." Although Birdie only rarely complained, Leah knew she was often in pain. The polio that had damaged her muscles had not destroyed her ability to feel. Sometimes at night Leah would hear her sister sobbing, and she would rub her legs and smooth away the cramps.

"You've enough to fret over, Leah, what with this land belonging to you now, and me nothing but a burden."

Leah had known that when her parents

died, the farm would be left to her. Two years before her death, their mother had shown them the will and explained.

"This is our last will and testament, your daddy's and mine. Now it says in here that the farm will belong to Leah alone, but, Leah, we know you'll give Birdie a place as long as she wants one. We're leaving it to you so's you can do the work that'll need doing without having to get papers signed. But you both understand what I'm saying?"

Leah hadn't needed a piece of paper to confirm what she'd always known. Birdie might be five years Leah's senior, but in the ways that mattered, Leah was the older sister. And caring for Birdie was no hardship. She adored her sister and always had.

"I sure won't listen to that kind of talk," she told Birdie now. "You couldn't be a burden if you tried. Who would keep this house and cook the meals? I aim to make sure we're both provided for, but that don't mean we got reason to fret. We got food stored up. We got a pig to slaughter comes time. We got apples on the trees, and walnuts and chinquapins in the woods."

"And you got men who come a-calling, all

the while hoping you'll look them over and make a choice."

Leah saw her sister's impish smile. Birdie was beautiful, particularly at times, like now, when she wasn't wearing the thick glasses that helped bring the distant world into focus. She had black hair that fell in thick waves to her shoulders on those rare occasions when she wore it down. Her eyes were as blue as a June sky, and her skin was clear and rosy.

Perhaps it was her poor vision, or perhaps only the way she viewed life, but Birdie always appeared to be staring into the distance. Once Flossie had told Leah that Birdie had heaven in her sights. Leah knew her mother was convinced that before too many years, Birdie would be one of God's sweetest angels.

"Men may be a-calling," she told Birdie, "but that don't mean I'm buying. I've set my sights as high as an eagle's nest."

"You mean your sights rise higher than Verle Lewis?"

"A heap." Verle was just one of the men who had been nosing around the Blackburn farm with the excuse the sisters might need help. Leah thought he would work out fine for splitting firewood or picking apples, but she was afraid that the woman who married Verle Lewis would find him asleep in the sunshine more often than she would find him farming.

"You cain't be too picky, Leah. We need a man working the land, and not a one is looking at me."

Leah tossed back her long brown braid. "And that would be the problem with the ones who've come by. Not a one can see past a wart on his own nose. If they could, it'd be you they was after, not me. Not only are you the prettiest, nobody for three counties can make biscuits like you do, or fry up an old biddy hen and make it taste like a chick just peeked out of the shell."

"I dried up on the vine before I fully bloomed." Birdie didn't look sorry. "No man's looking for a puny wife, not so's you'd know it, anyway. A man wants a wife he can kill off slowly with too many young'uns and too much to do. Me, I'd die before he could even get started."

"His loss, then. And maybe mine. 'Cause now *I* got to put up with all that."

"You're strong. You'll outlive any man."

"And maybe kill off a few while I'm at it."

Both girls laughed. Leah slung her arm over her sister's shoulders. "Let's have breakfast, then I'm off for the day. You'll be fine without me?"

"My fingers are itching to get to them new red chicken sacks. I washed and ironed 'em good, and today I'm gonna cut the pieces for our Lover's Knot quilts."

Leah made a noise low in her throat, as if she was delighted that her sister was cutting fabric for both of them. In truth, she was glad that Birdie's self-imposed mourning period seemed to be ending. For herself, quilting was as far from her mind as usual. She would rather shovel out the barn or smoke honeybees from a hollow tree than thread a needle. Quilting was something Birdie and Flossie had always done together. Now Leah was afraid that she was going to have to keep her sister company at the quilt frame, or in the evenings while she pieced blocks on the sewing machine.

Birdie fixed biscuits, stewed tomatoes and slices of salty ham, and when they sat down together, Leah ate with relish. While Birdie cleaned the kitchen, Leah made ham biscuits from the leftovers, wrapped them in a feedsack napkin perfectly hemmed by her sister and tucked it into an oak basket. She would pick apples along the way and find cool, clear spring water to quench her thirst. She added a tin cup for the latter.

"I'll be home come suppertime," she promised her sister. "The dogs'll watch out for you."

"Whatever happens'll happen. God's will be done."

Leah thought about that as she started down the road. Her sister was a contradiction. Birdie believed every superstition that had made its way to their mountain home, while also believing that all things rested in the hands of God. In contrast, Leah believed that she made her own destiny. She couldn't imagine that lives were changed by something as silly as whether a wren built his nest near her house or a floor was swept after dark. Nor could she imagine a busybody God with the time or desire to control every living being.

She left the road once she was beyond the barn and scooped a few apples off the ground at the outskirts of their orchard. One of the dogs tried to follow, but she sent him back to stay with Birdie. It was more likely that trouble would come calling than that she would stumble over it in her beloved mountains.

She didn't even feel the pull as she climbed to the top of the ridge that ran along the northern perimeter of the Blackburns' land. This was the way she often walked to visit Puss Cade when Puss wasn't staying in Stanardsville, taking care of her brother's young children now that his wife had passed away.

Leah and Puss had been friends since they were old enough to find their way across meadows and hills when chores were done. The Cades and the Blackburns had always lent each other a hand when barns were raised or apple butter was simmered and canned in the fall. Together they butchered hogs, and this year Birdie and Leah would join them rather than have a butchering day at the Blackburn place. Come winter, with only two of them, they would not need the quantity of meat they had salted and smoked in the past.

When the path diverged, she didn't turn toward the Cade place. Instead she went farther up the mountain, walking another mile before she slowed to look for the spot she remembered visiting with her mother last year. The woods, pungent with autumn's crumbling leaves, were deep here, escaping for the time being, at least, the constant cutting and plowing of new fields that kept crops abundant. A field wore out and a farmer let it go to pastureland, choosing a new area and cutting or "deadening" the trees by chopping deeply into the bark in a circle around the trunk, so that the tree would die and be easier to remove in the future. Then crops were planted and the cycle began again.

This area was still heavily wooded, although the abundant and useful chestnut trees had died off in Leah's childhood, and those that hadn't been toppled were ghostly reminders of the disease that had destroyed this valuable resource. Once upon a time timber had been cut here, but the trees had grown back thick and tall. All the plants that made their home beneath the trees were lush and well-nourished by the rich soil of the forest floor.

She stopped to get her bearings. Had she known that this job would be left to her, she would have paid even closer attention to her mother's words. Flossie had been so filled with robust good health, busy every moment, never tiring. That she and Dyer could be so quickly struck down, and neither Leah nor Birdie touched by the fever, still seemed impossible.

Clearing her mind, she stood in the quiet woods and listened. The birds had ceased their trilling and chattering as she moved farther inside. She heard rustling, and once something crashing through the brush. But bears had been gone here for as long as she remembered, hunted and killed by men who liked the taste of their meat or feared for the safety of families.

After a while she started farther into the woods, separating vines and briars with a long stick so she could pass more easily.

She was nearly where she wanted to go when she heard another crash. She stopped to listen. The bears might be gone but some residents of the hollow turned their hogs loose to forage, notching their ears so they could be rounded up and claimed when needed for butchering. There were stories about evil-tempered boars that decades ago had escaped capture and still roamed the forest, looking for revenge. She'd never believed it, but she knew better than to discount the possibility.

A shrill warble came from the direction of the crash, not the call of any bird she had ever heard. Then the warble turned into an expertly whistled rendition of "I Have No One to Love Me."

Leah slapped her hands on her hips. "Jesse Spurlock, you come out this minute!"

The crashing began again, and a young man stepped out from between trees at the side of a thicket. "Leah Blackburn. Who would have guessed it?"

She put a hand over her heart, but she wasn't sure if it was the surprise of his presence or simply his presence alone. Jesse Spurlock was a sight. Maybe they had grown up together, and maybe she was used to seeing him, but lately she couldn't remember the little black-haired boy who had built a play cabin out of firewood and charged her a piece of molasses candy for a peek. Or the older one who had hid with her in the caves up the side of Little Lock Mountain and left her, when he tired, to find her way out alone.

This grown-up version was someone else. Jesse had broad shoulders and the Spurlock cheekbones—some people said there was Cherokee blood running through the lines. His upswept eyebrows loomed over golden brown eyes, and his jaw announced he could be stubborn.

And why would anyone who'd ever met him question that?

"Just what are you doing here?" she demanded.

"Seems to me these are Spurlock woods."

"I don't see a fence. Do you see a fence?" She looked around, as if one might materialize.

"Don't need a fence. Everybody knows this land is ours. Did I scare the starch out of your backbone?"

"Nothing scares me. Are you trying to tell me I cain't be here? That you've come to chase me off?"

" 'Course not. But you'll need an escort. You're looking at him."

Even as she pretended to glare, she desperately wanted to smooth her hair. She hadn't worn a hat, and she was sure the braid that she'd tucked and pinned was now a nest of twigs and leaves. And why had she worn her oldest dress? The worn brown print was the most sensible thing for squeezing between trees and untangling briars. But she had known, hadn't she, that Jesse might come looking for her?

"Did you know I'd be here?" She fought off the instinct to fix her hair and tugged down her skirt instead. Her legs were bare and probably scratched, and she wore the heavy scuffed shoes her mother had worn for years before her. She could picture herself as clearly as if she were staring in Mama's dresser mirror.

"It's just possible somebody mentioned you'd be collecting yarbs today," he said with a grin. "But I cain't be sure."

Jesse grinning was something like the answer to a prayer. Leah's heart did a little jig even as she told herself to be careful.

"You must really want to protect the Spurlocks from intruders, you ranging all the way out into these woods a-looking for me when you didn't know for sure I was coming."

"A man cain't be too careful."

"Well, that goes double for a woman."

"You're a woman now? Seems like yesterday you were just a girl."

"Seems like yesterday you were just a boy riding your pa's old sow for a day's fun."

"You remember that? Maybe you had a reason to think about me?"

Jesse was not one of the young men who had come calling on Leah after the deaths of her parents. He had come with his family to pay a sympathy call, and he had come to both funerals, looking appropriately somber. But a month had passed since her mother's funeral, and although the Spurlock sons-in-law had come to chop wood and harvest corn, Jesse had not appeared again.

"I suppose, if I had a mind to, I could wonder why you weren't with Glenn and Wilbur when they come to harvest our corn," she said.

"Didn't need but two doing it."

She pondered that. "I got no more time to stand here and talk to you. I got work to do if you'll let me."

"Maybe I'll just come along."

She chose her direction again and started off. Asked to guess, she would have said he would follow, and he did. She could hear him right behind her as she searched for the area she'd visited with her mother for the past two autumns.

"You want to tell me what it is you're looking for?" he asked behind her.

"Bloodroot. A big patch."

"What do you need it for?"

She thought of all the uses for the plant. She knew she was showing off, but she couldn't help herself. "You got to use it right. I tell you, you cain't just go a-digging it and using it any old way. Make a tea, and it helps a sore throat, croup, a cough. Some folks say the sap'll heal a sore on the skin that nothing else will, a killing sore. But you use too much, you'll wish you hadn't. It's poison. Hurts your head and your stomach."

"You still want to get some?"

"You just got to know how to use it. Mama has a patch of it near the house, but not enough to dig the root. There's a patch up here, a big one. But you cain't dig till after the greenery goes away. I'll dig some root today and dry it."

"Some folks say your ma taught you everything she knew, that you'll be helping your neighbors just the way she did."

"She was better'n I'll ever be. But I'll do what I can."

"You and Birdie, you're making do?"

She detected a note of sympathy in his voice. She glanced behind her and wished they could walk side by side. She liked to look at him. Maybe too much.

Her head snapped to the front, and she picked up her pace. "We are."

"There's talk you need a man living there."

"I aim to be sure we don't."

"I reckon you might change your mind if the right one happened along."

Her heart did another jig. If there had been a list of eligible young men for two hundred miles around, Jesse Spurlock was the most likely candidate for first place. Not only was he handsome and intelligent, he was a natural-born leader. Men already looked up to him, asking his help in settling disputes and solving problems. His father died when Jesse was her age, seventeen, but the man inside Jesse had already formed. And his stepfather, Luther Collins, had helped shape what remained.

The Spurlocks had always been well regarded by neighbors, and like the Blackburns, they had been successful enough to lend a hand to those who had less than they did. In every way, Jesse set local hearts fluttering.

He had set hers fluttering for two years, although the only person who knew it was

Puss. Not even Birdie knew how she felt about Jesse Spurlock.

The silence stretched until she spotted the clearing where the bloodroot grew. The stalks were withered and brown. Had she not known what they looked like in the spring, she would not be certain what they were, but she had paid close attention to landmarks. She knew she was right.

“Well, you saw me all the way,” she said. “I could offer a ham biscuit and an apple in return.”

“Only fitting.” He smiled to show he was teasing.

“There’s a spring nearby. I brought a cup.”

“I know where it is. I’ll bring it to you.”

She unpacked her basket and handed him the cup. When he was out of sight, she sank to a rock and finally felt her hair to re-pin what she could.

She knew this was no chance encounter. Two possibilities occurred to her. One, that Jesse had noticed her the way she had noticed him. That she had not imagined the smiles they had exchanged, or the way he had examined her when he thought no one else was looking. The way he seemed to appear when an accidental meeting seemed unlikely.

The second possibility . . . well, even giving words to it in her head made her throat clench. Maybe Jesse was here to ask for permission to court her sister.

Jesse and Birdie, who were the same age, had always been friends. While other children had made fun of Birdie, Jesse had never once been unkind. He had lost a little sister to the polio that had partially spared Birdie. For a man who could be brash and sometimes temperamental, he could also be considerate. Birdie thought the world of him, although she never dwelled on it, but Leah didn't know what her sister would say if Jesse asked her to marry him. Birdie had little interest in men. As if she realized what childbirth might do to her frail body, she had expressed no interest in marriage or the things that came with it.

Still, Birdie was beautiful and accomplished at the things her health and eyesight allowed. Leah loved her sister, but could she put her own feelings aside and rejoice at her good fortune? If indeed Birdie even considered Jesse as a husband?

He returned before she could work out that problem in her heart.

"There's one cup but enough water for two if you're willing," he said.

"If it's a question of dying of thirst or sharing with you, I propose we share."

He laughed, a rich rumble in his chest that made her want to place her hand over it and feel the vibrations.

"I don't see a bit of digging." He perched next to her and gave her the cup for the first drink.

"I always eat first. Once I've gone and dug what I need, I'll be too dirty." She gave him the biscuit wrapped in a napkin, and she set the cup between them.

He bit into the biscuit, and his gaze warmed. "My granny made biscuits this good."

"They're Birdie's. She does all our cooking. Even when Mama was alive, Birdie did the baking. I don't bake if I don't have to."

"How do you propose to feed a husband?"

"With Birdie's cooking."

He considered that; then he cocked his head and took the cup. "And what if Birdie gets married?"

For a moment she didn't breathe. She concentrated on the sounds around her. The cooing of a mourning dove. Leaves scurrying along the ground. A squirrel crashing from one branch to another.

She lowered her lashes. "I suppose I'd have to learn to cook, unless I'm an old maid living in Birdie's house."

"From what I hear, that's not gonna happen."

"No?"

"You got every fellow for fifty miles thinking he's some kind of Romeo."

"Me and the Blackburn farm."

"I don't rightly think it's the farm." His smile was lazy and self-assured.

She brightened. "Then what could it be?"

"Might be those green eyes."

"A man would marry a woman just for the color of her eyes?"

"Not just for that."

She knew better than to continue this, but she was helpless. "What else?"

He set down the cup. "Any number of things. You and your sister are the prettiest girls in the county."

She had said she was never afraid, but of

course that had been a lie. She was afraid right now, afraid he was going to tell her he was in love with Birdie. She tried to postpone that declaration.

"How are you at digging for roots?"

"I might be persuaded."

She reached for the cup with a hand that wasn't quite steady. He reached for it at the same moment. Their hands touched, and before she could withdraw hers, he captured it, wrapping his fingers over it so that she could not pull away.

"What might *you* be persuaded to do?" he asked.

She narrowed her eyes. "You mean because my father's not here to protect me?"

"No, I mean because you might need another man to take on that job. One who might want to protect you for the rest of your life."

She felt such a rush of joy she couldn't speak. She just looked at him, but she knew the answer was in her eyes.

"It's me you want?" she asked in something close to a whisper.

"It's always been you, Leah. Never anyone else."

"Why did you stay away, then? After Mama and Daddy died."

"You needed to grieve. I didn't want to mix myself up in that. I didn't want you coming to me because you were grateful or scared."

"I told you, I don't get scared."

"I've been scared you might find someone else while I stayed away."

"Oh, Jesse . . ."

He put his arm around her and pulled her close. When he kissed her, it was better than anything she had ever imagined. Jesse, her childhood friend and tormentor. Jesse, the man who wanted her as much as she wanted him.

"What about Birdie?" she asked when he reluctantly pulled away. "I cain't leave her alone. She won't be able to manage. She has to be with me."

"If you want, we'll stay at your place with Birdie. Ma and Luther can stay on at mine. When they're gone, we'll work it out. Sell one, farm both." He shrugged. "It don't hardly matter, Leah. Birdie can live with us wherever we are. We'll be together. Where we're living won't make a difference."

He put his arms around her and pulled

her against him, closer this time, and with more insistence.

She gave in to the embrace and to the man, and as she kissed him back, she gave him her answer.

CHAPTER SIX

Isaac woke up earlier now that Kendra wasn't sleeping beside him. At first, after the shooting, he had launched himself upright every morning in a frantic, instinctive effort to find his wife. Now he woke up well before his alarm went off but fully aware that he was alone, and why.

He supposed there was an advantage to not being able to sleep. He could avoid the worst of rush hour, beating many of the State Department employees and university students who poured into Foggy Bottom. He could arrive at ACRE headquarters and partially clear his desk before the majority of the staff arrived. Some days, if he woke up particularly early, he jogged the miles to work, showering and changing into suitable clothes once he arrived. By the time he made it to his desk, the restless energy that plagued him had dissipated. He could control his impatience with bureaucracy, and channel dogged determination into positive outcomes.

This morning he was awake before six, too late to jog but with plenty of time to shower, dress and navigate traffic. By nine, when the support staff arrived, he would be well into his day.

After the shower, he considered calling Kendra, but waking her made little sense. More truthfully, their occasional phone calls left him dissatisfied, even angry, and he wasn't in the mood to risk another.

If Kendra missed him or their life together, she was giving no sign. She was polite. She asked about his job, about friends who were "their" friends, about the way he spent his evenings. But nothing *he* asked drew much response. She was making short trips into the world. She had bought a table and chairs for the front porch, and some gardening tools. The telephone company had hooked up a land line, and now she could access the Internet.

Then, as if this meant nothing, she announced she might buy a barn and use the logs to add on to the cabin. She would find out soon if that made any sense. Maybe even today.

Clearly, if Kendra planned to add to the cabin, she planned to make it a real home. He wondered how she would reconcile this with her job and marriage. Particularly her marriage.

He was still thinking about her when he pulled into his designated slot in ACRE's parking garage. Parking was at a premium in the city, and ACRE had only a dozen slots in the garage, all for executives.

He remembered the first day he'd driven to work after his promotion to managing director—feeling guilty that his staff still had to carpool or take the Metro, pleased that he had worked his way into this new position, another rung on the ladder to a political appointment where his voice might be even more effective.

The move to his position at ACRE had been smooth. With undergraduate degrees in economics and environmental technology, plus a law degree, he had started as a fund-raiser at the Sierra Club. When the Maryland chapter of ACRE offered him an administrative position, he accepted it and rose quickly through the ranks to state director. He showed a knack for raising money and organizing innovative programs, as well as making important political contacts in Annapolis and D.C., so no one was surprised when he was tapped to work in the national headquarters.

ACRE would not be Isaac's final stop. Compared to its big brothers, the Sierra Club, the Nature Conservancy or the World Wildlife Fund, ACRE was the shrimpy kid tagging along at the edge of the crowd. Unlike its counterparts, ACRE really had concentrated on preserving one acre at a time.

Personally, he didn't think small. The world's resources were too precious and vanishing too quickly to rescue in tiny parcels. He was encouraged that Dennis Lavin, the new executive director, wanted to take the organization in a different direction. But Isaac's personal plan was to continue the climb at ACRE or a similar nonprofit, then move into government when an administration that was truly committed to environmental protection took office. By then he might well have enough connections for a job where he could make a real difference.

He had managed to banish thoughts of

Kendra with thoughts of his future, but they came back as he locked the car, his eyes open for interlopers. Every time he pictured the carjacking or remembered the moment he had learned she was on the way to the hospital, he felt sick.

The gloomy garage didn't help. Rather than take the dark ramp up to the elevator, he walked down into the spring sunshine. Outside, he crossed to Gene's Beans, which all the ACRE staff frequented because the little hole-in-the-wall had stood tall against the corporate giants determined to take over the coffee world. Gene knew every employee's preferences, and he was always on the premises.

Isaac was on his way inside when he glimpsed a ragged cat scratching itself at the corner of the brick building beside the alley that provided parking slots for Gene's staff. The ginger tabby looked as if he had grown up on D.C.'s streets. He was Garfield without the paunch, but judging by the way he eyed Isaac, he had all the comic strip cat's sass and bravado, plus an ear that had been noticeably chewed up in a fight. Isaac turned for a closer look.

"Hey, fellow. Looking for a handout?"

The cat had cynical eyes. He tilted his misshapen head, as if to say, *I know your game, buster, and I ain't playin'.*

"Somebody tied a can or two to that tail, didn't they," Isaac said.

The cat struck a pose that clearly said, *What's it to you?*

Isaac went inside for his breakfast.

The cat was still beside Gene's Dumpster when he returned, but it dodged the hand he held out and abandoned him for something more promising in the alley. Isaac crossed the street to start his day.

Dennis Lavin was just getting to the office, too. He was nearly Isaac's height, twenty years his senior and bald enough to make a comb-over futile. Probably to draw attention elsewhere, he had grown a salt-and-pepper beard and mustache that were always perfectly trimmed. Isaac wondered if the beard was also a statement that Dennis was a liberal in whom ACRE could place its faith, even if his suits and approach to management were strictly Brooks Brothers standard issue.

"I like to see my staff putting in long hours," Dennis said, clapping him on the shoulder. "Good to see you making up some of those days you missed, even though we didn't begrudge a one of them. Your wife's recovering nicely?"

Isaac knew better than to say he didn't know, but it didn't matter, because Dennis immediately began a recital of all he intended to accomplish that day, ending with a curt wave as he headed for his office suite.

By nine, Isaac was glad he had arrived early. He'd managed to cull his e-mail, respond to three serious inquiries from potential donors, and write a short summary of the speech he planned to give at an upcoming conference on America's rain forests.

His staff had trickled in all morning, stopping to exchange a few pleasantries. His assistant, Heather Griswold, left a homemade chocolate chip muffin on his desk, another team member left an article from the *New York Times.* By ten they assembled in the closest conference room to compare notes on the week to come. In the afternoon, he would go over his notes and theirs with senior management.

By the time they had traded jokes and stories, coordinated calendars and discussed the most important issues of the day, the morning was nearly over. Isaac got to the final item on the agenda.

"Pallatine Mountain." He looked up. "Mr. Forsythe is still considering his options. No one's heard any different?"

Heather, who had met with Gary Forsythe on the day Kendra was discharged from the rehabilitation hospital, turned up her hands. They were wide and capable, with blunt fingernails covered in clear polish. Heather always looked as if she had stepped off the Appalachian Trail into casual business clothes. Her blond hair was short and spiky; her square face was unadorned by makeup. Even though she was only a few inches over five feet, she could carry a forty-pound pack without breaking a sweat, and men who weren't threatened found her attractive.

"He seemed open-minded the day we had lunch," she said. "He claimed the decision would take some time. But he hasn't returned my calls."

Pallatine Mountain in central Virginia was Isaac's pet project, a larger property than ACRE usually took on. To him, it represented a swing in the way things would be done in the future, preservation on a grander scale. Pallatine seemed key to ACRE's march into the future.

"This is one of the most important transactions we can make," he reminded them. "I don't want to lose an entire mountainside to some developer who plans to build a ski resort or a hunting lodge. Any ideas?"

For the next twenty minutes they batted around possibilities, and Heather took notes.

At noon the meeting broke up, and his team members went back to their desks or off to lunch. Isaac and Heather were the last out.

"Are you eating in?" she asked.

"I didn't bring anything."

"Want to grab sandwiches?"

They continued discussing the meeting as they headed for a shop on the next block and took a place in the line that was already out the door.

"I didn't want to say anything in there," Heather said, "but I was getting all kinds of vibes from Gary Forsythe."

"You should have mentioned that."

She pursed her lips, as if deciding how to phrase her concerns. "Thing is, you've had a lot on your mind. And I have nothing more than a feeling. Mr. Forsythe seems torn.

He's not a rich man. Land rich, maybe, but that's all. I think he wants to do what's right, but he has grown children, and he'd like to leave them and any future grandchildren a solid legacy."

"So far that's not really news."

"Well, he mentioned a couple of daughters and then, after some hesitation, a son. Turns out the son is an attorney."

Isaac imagined a young man with leather-bound volumes open to the inheritance laws of the State of Virginia. "I'm beginning to get a picture here."

Her expression softened. "Afraid so. But then, you're an attorney yourself."

"I never wanted to practice law, only understand it."

"I have a feeling the son's interested in money, and there's always going to be a developer who can outclass us. The son probably doesn't have any particular attachment to the mountain, the way his father does. Mr. Forsythe told me that when he was a boy, his father took him all over Pallatine hunting black bear. It's funny, isn't it? I couldn't be more opposed to hunting, but half the time it's hunters who want to keep America's wild places intact."

"I guess Gary didn't take his lawyer son hunting enough."

"He said his son was a city boy. Actually, he said, 'My son never did understand the way his old man thinks.' Maybe I'm making too much out of it. Or maybe . . ."

Isaac waited. He was not patient, but neither was he a prodder.

"Well, it bothers me," Heather said as they moved into the sandwich shop and closer to the counter.

"What bothers you, exactly?"

"I know we need to protect Pallatine. I'm convinced. But it's hard to know what to do. Do I want to be responsible for a rift in this family? I can imagine being a fly on the wall at a Forsythe reunion in, say, 2015. They'll still be talking about poor Gary, who gave away the only thing of worth the family ever owned."

"We're talking about a land deal in the millions here. He's not signing it over free and clear. He'll walk away a rich man."

"But he would walk away a lot richer if he sold to a developer. And who's to say that wouldn't be okay? People would use the land and enjoy it. They'd be close to nature when they zoomed down the slopes."

"Slopes that had been cleared by fleets of bulldozers. Slopes marred by ski lifts and condos and mountain lodges. You want another Wintergreen? Without the environmental conscience?" Wintergreen was a ski resort farther south. Some 6,000 of its 11,000 acres had been set aside for wilderness preservation, and various environmentally sensitive practices were in place. But now there were golf courses and ski slopes, as well as myriad homes and condos, on land that had once been pristine Blue Ridge, and no one could guarantee that same high level of ecological commitment for new projects, like Pallatine.

"You know, Isaac, you're always so sure of yourself. Don't you ever have doubts? You set a goal, and you don't let anything get between you and it. I'm pretty bullheaded, but I guess I see more shades of gray."

He had indeed found her bullheaded but he didn't smile. This was an important distinction, and she needed to understand it. "I see all the shades. But I also see that if you take too long weighing and dodging the important decisions, nothing will get done. It's our job to secure Pallatine for the future, however we do it. I'll be sorry if Forsythe's son punishes his dad for making a good decision. But that won't affect mine."

They reached the counter. He ordered tuna on rye, and at the last moment asked for two sandwiches, one without mayo.

"You're hungry today," she said. "Are you eating okay?"

"The second one's for a friend."

When their sandwiches arrived, they took them back to their desks and got down to work. After his afternoon meeting, Isaac came back to settle in yet again, and hours later he was surprised when Heather knocked on his door to say she was leaving.

"It's seven," she said. "And you got here early, didn't you?"

He felt a quick stab of guilt; then he remembered that Kendra was not waiting at home. He could work all night and no one would know the difference.

"You go on," he said. "I'll leave in a little while. I'm just finishing up."

She said goodbye, and he could hear her gathering things off her desk. In a few minutes the building was quiet. He doubted he was the last one left, but he wasn't entirely sure.

He put his hands over his head and stretched. For just a moment he imagined what it would feel like to go home to his wife, to take her to bed or take her to dinner. Those pleasures, which had once seemed so incidental to the larger picture of his life, now seemed central. He didn't recall ever being lonely. Perhaps he had been as a child, before he learned how futile it was to wish for things he could never have.

Now he wished, as he had so many times, that he had left work last month when Kendra needed his help. One decision, and his life had changed forever. One, careless, self-absorbed decision.

He was finished here for the night, even if no one was waiting at home for him.

He gathered papers into his briefcase and saw the white foam container with the extra sandwich. He gathered that, too, and headed for the elevator.

Outside, the sky was turning dark and the night turning cool. He walked across the street to Gene's Beans and peered into the alley beside it. The ginger tabby was scrounging behind the Dumpster, only its ragged tail visible.

"Hey, old man," Isaac said. "I brought you something."

The cat ignored him, but when Isaac opened the container and placed it on the ground, the smell of tuna told the tale. The cat quickly backed away from the Dumpster, turned and approached warily. Isaac moved slowly away from the container and watched as the cat devoured the food. As hungry as he clearly was, the cat never lost sight of Isaac as he ate.

"You know," Isaac said, "I can relate to your life, but I won't bore you with the details."

The cat finished the sandwich; then he carefully licked his front paws. He was still vigilant, though, keeping Isaac in sight at all times.

There was nothing left to say. Not to the cat, anyway. Isaac crossed the street to the garage.

Kendra was swinging the weed cutter through the second row of Leah's garden when Manning Rosslyn arrived. She was expecting him, so the sound of his car didn't worry her. She greeted him after he stepped out of a white pickup that had

Rosslyn and Rosslyn, Historic Restoration, Architectural Renewal lettered in black and gray on the doors. Twilight was just beginning to descend.

"Mrs. Taylor?" They shook hands.

"Kendra," she said, wiping perspiration from her forehead with the back of her hand. "And you're Manning. Thanks for coming."

"Glad to do it. How did you hear about me?"

She explained about Helen. "When Helen says jump, we jump, right?"

He grinned. He was a large man, maybe as old as seventy if, as Helen said, he'd been sweet on Isaac's mother. But he looked younger. If he'd played sports in high school or college, most likely he'd been a halfback for some lucky team. His hairline had receded, but what was left was gray, with some traces of brown. He had pleasant features, dark eyes that crinkled at the corners, sun-spotted skin. He wore a polo shirt with Rosslyn and Rosslyn embroidered on the pocket, dark jeans and muddy work boots.

She liked him on sight, guessing, at the same time, that this was a man who usually got his way. Most likely the good-old-boy facade covered iron determination, an excellent combination to get things done in this neck of the woods.

"I do what Ms. Henry tells me, same as everyone else hereabouts." He spoke with the accent common to central Virginia, remnants of a nineteenth-century Scottish heritage. She could identify the "about" that sounded like "aboot."

"Well, come see the house and we'll talk as we go. I told you I'm interested in the barn up the road. I see it's still for sale."

He walked beside her toward the porch. "I contacted the owner. It's yours if you want it. If you don't, I'll probably take it off his hands. I've had a good look at it. Not all the wood is worth saving. It's a mixture of chestnut, oak, poplar, some spruce. Beams in the ceiling are cedar. Too bad it was stripped of its siding, got some rot started—but I think we can salvage most of it."

"Did he give you a price?"

"We negotiated. He'll let us have it for under ten thousand, exact number depending on when we come and get it. He's not being unreasonable, but taking it down and hauling it here will add to that number. Let's see what you want to do with it first."

With a visitor standing there, Kendra felt awkward reaching the porch her usual way. She'd been in the garden a long time, though, waiting for Manning, and her left leg felt too weak to negotiate the steps.

"Feel free to take the stairs, but I get up this way," she told him. With an effort, she pulled herself up to the edge of the porch and managed to swing her legs over, helping with her hands.

Manning watched her. "No matter what we decide today, I'll send my son over tomorrow to put up a railing. Nothing fancy, just something to get you up and down a little easier."

"Zeke Claiborne was going to do it, but he's been out of town. Sam Kinkade offered to find somebody at church next week. Elisa warned me not to let Sam anywhere near the place with a saw and nails."

"Cash will make quick work of it."

Kendra dusted off her jeans. "Cash. The perfect name for a businessman."

"John Cashel Rosslyn, son from my second marriage, so he's still a youngster like you. He goes by Cash. Says he doesn't have to take credit for anything that way. As sons go, he's not the worst in town."

She smiled at the way he downplayed the pride in his voice. "If he's too busy, I'm managing this way. But I appreciate the offer."

"He'll be here. Let's see what we're up against. It's too dark for a real assessment. We'll just do a quick one tonight."

"I gather you've seen the place before."

"Sure have." He didn't elaborate.

"Dabney Higby did some work for me. He took off the old siding, re-chinked the logs." She opened the door into the living room.

"I hope he saved the wood."

"There's a pile way in the back, where the driveway ends. He hauled anything with no value to the landfill."

"I know Dabney. He's not much of a preservationist, but he's not the worst, either. You wanted the logs exposed?"

"The wood siding was covered with sheets of asphalt, patterned like bricks. It was coming loose, and it was ugly."

"He chinked the logs?"

"It seemed important."

"Did he do anything with the foundation?"

She was beginning to worry. "Not that I know of."

"See, the biggest problems these old places have are poor foundations and settling. If we have to jack it up or level it, it'll have to be re-chinked. And I would have used something authentic, or more authentic. Truth is, though, this house isn't ever going to make the historical register. There are a lot of older, better cabins in the area. First part, where we're standing, that was most likely just built as a hunting cabin. Ms. Spurlock—she's the woman used to own it—she built the second cabin and turned it into a dogtrot when she moved here in the thirties. Easiest way to give her and Rachel, her daughter, a little more room."

Kendra was glad Rachel's name had come up. "I still want to preserve it."

"I'm all for saving anything valuable, but don't save this because you think you ought to. Nobody would fault you for tearing it to the ground."

Kendra didn't want to explain why she wanted to preserve the cabin. Until she told Helen about Isaac's relationship to Leah and Rachel, she didn't want anyone else to know.

"The thing is, I also want more room, more light, more air."

"Then you need to think of this as a work in progress. History? What day in history would you go back to, anyway? Take down the second part? Dogtrot's a part of the history here, just like the two-room houses with central fireplaces the Germans from Pennsylvania built."

She was really beginning to like him. "So you're saying if we add on, use those barn logs, we're just continuing the history."

"You've got it. So let's look at it that way. What do you want here? What would give you the room you need and make you happy? That's what everybody else who ever lived here had to decide, too."

She knew what she missed. A real kitchen, with room to move around, room for friends to gather and eat. A master bathroom with a tub she could relax in. And she wanted a great room, with windows looking over the river. The view from that end of the dogtrot was spectacular.

She told him, and he nodded.

"How about this ceiling? I feel like I'm bending over," he said.

"I know. It's low here *and* in the other part, yes."

"It's false. I expect somebody put up this

cheap old beadboard sometime in the forties or so to make the place easier to heat. If you still want to go to all that trouble, I can knock out the ceilings for you. We could turn this room and the one across from it into studies or bedrooms, make the dogtrot an entry hall, use the barn to build a great room looking over the river, with a master bedroom on one side and a real bathroom off that."

"We'll need a new well if we're going to use all that water. The one here is easily exhausted."

"Cash's a dowser."

"You mean he walks around with a forked stick and finds water?"

"I'll guarantee his work. Never seen him fail. And you've got a river out there. There's bound to be good water nearby."

"You really think all that's possible here?"

"Give me about half an hour to poke around. I'll come back in when I have a better idea."

She busied herself heating a rotisserie chicken and mixing up a salad to go with it. She hadn't expected to have time to get to it, but she had finished eating by the time he returned. It was nearly dark outside.

"What you'll have, when we finish, is a house that looks like it's been standing here a good while, but one with everything you said you wanted. Won't be cheap."

"Money's not a big issue."

"This house has problems and not a lot of charm. No question. It's going to be a mess for a while. No fun living here with us on the job. You're still willing?"

"How much of a mess?"

"Somewhere along the way, we'll move you out for a week or two. Then we'll move you back in. But you'll have to live with some noise and a lot of company."

"For how long?"

"Well, you're lucky. I've got two crews. Both of them were tied up, but one finished early and doesn't have to start the next job until mid-summer. The other was due to work over in Strasburg for a few months, but the bank pulled the loan. The owners'll get their financing, but they'll have to get back to the end of the line."

"You mean you could start soon?"

"It's looking that way. Two crews for a while, and if we have to take that barn down fast to save you a couple of thousand dollars, we might as well bring it in and get to work the moment we can."

She had come to recuperate and find herself again. She had planned on solitude. Yet how could she pass up this opportunity? In the days between her call and Manning's arrival, she'd checked his work thoroughly, even driven to three sites to talk to the owners. The praise was unanimous, but she'd been warned Manning was hard to schedule and a perfectionist who worked slowly. He was the right man for this job. Logic and intuition told her so. They also told her it was now or possibly never.

"Put me on the schedule," she said.

"I'll send Cash out tomorrow to build that railing. I expect he'll want to see the place and form his own opinions. I'll have him do all the things it was too dark to do tonight. And I'll start putting together some plans for you. Your job is to think of everything you want. He'll drop off a checklist and some books to look through. You need to think about decks, porches, fireplaces, laundry rooms . . ."

She tried to listen as he ticked off the possibilities, but her mind wandered. She imagined this house, part of a living history, opened to the beauty of the setting. A place where friends would come and fill the rooms, a place where she and Isaac could absorb the serenity, the magnificence, of the Shenandoah Valley and the river below them.

She and Isaac. A commitment to this house meant a commitment to living here for at least a part of each year. And what would that do to her relationship with her husband? The husband who despised this area and everything it represented.

Yet whose life did she need to live?

"So we're agreed?" Manning asked.

She hesitated; then she nodded. "Sounds like the right way to proceed."

"You don't have to see me out, Kendra."

"I'll walk you to the porch."

Outside, stars were beginning to light the sky. A moon hung low on the horizon, nearly obscured by the woods.

Kendra decided to prod a little. "Helen told me you spent a lot of time here as a teenager."

"She did, did she?" He looked up at the sky, too. "Yeah, I was sweet on Rachel Spurlock. The way a man is sweet on a woman once in his whole life. I've been married twice, loved both of those women more than I thought a man should. But Rachel, that was something different."

She was touched. She liked Manning more and more.

"I'd like to know more about this house," she said. "I like history. I heard Rachel left town when she was still very young?"

"Rachel was a loner. I was about the only person she trusted. She never felt like she fit in here, even though she was pretty enough to turn the head of every man who saw her. But she took offense easily. Anyone looked sideways at her and she thought it meant something. She was headstrong, too. She thought her mother was trying to smother her. She wanted more from life than Toms Brook. Today she would have had a hundred good options. Back then, it was running away, or staying here and marrying me."

"I didn't mean to bring up a sore subject."

"It worked out the way it was supposed to. She never would have supported my plans to spend hunting season out in the woods and holidays with our families. To go to church on Sundays, raise children. She wanted to see the world, did Rachel. And I guess she wanted to see it alone."

Kendra wondered if some of Isaac's restless energy had come directly from his birth mother. She'd always thought his need for activity came from his upbringing, the overseas moves from base to base, the cockeyed views of an alien world he'd glimpsed from the windows of Air Force housing.

"Well, I'm glad you stayed behind," she said. "Look what you're going to do with Rachel's old house. You're going to open it to the world beyond. I wonder what she would think. Or her mother."

"Ms. Spurlock used to sit right there on an old cane-bottom stool." He pointed back toward the river and the end of the dogtrot. "She'd shuck corn or snap beans or bundle her herbs to sell to anyone who wanted them. Looking at the river was her favorite pastime, one of the few times she rested."

Kendra couldn't resist one more probe. She was, after all, a journalist. "I'm sure Leah was devastated when her daughter left."

He continued staring toward the river. "She was."

Kendra thought he had finished, but he

added, almost to himself, “She tried to find her, you know. Spent the rest of her years looking, as far as I can tell. Rachel called me once, but she wouldn’t tell me from where. At least I could tell Ms. Spurlock that much, that Rachel was still alive, even if I couldn’t tell her what Rachel said.”

Kendra couldn’t let that go. “It must have been something you were afraid to share.” It wasn’t a question, but it was a lead, if he took it.

“Rachel was furious with her mother. She said Ms. Spurlock was not the angel she seemed like to everyone else. She said she would spend her days in hell.”

The evening had turned cool, but the goose bumps rising on Kendra’s flesh had nothing to do with the temperature. “That must have been hard to hear. You must have been worried about her.”

He looked down, as if he had just remembered she was there. “I didn’t mean to go on and on. Maybe it’s standing right here. It was the first place I ever kissed Rachel.”

“I can’t help being curious. What a thing to say. Did she explain?”

He stared a moment, then he shook his head. She had seen that shake a thousand times, and she knew what it meant. She had reached a dead end. If there was anything else, she was not going to learn it. Not to-night.

"It was never a happy house," he said. "Not the way it should have been. But they loved each other, those two women. So it was a shame they never saw each other again to put things to rights." He stuck out his hand. "Glad to do business with you, Kendra. We'll talk again soon."

She shook and thanked him; then she watched him depart. And all the while she thought about Isaac's mother and grand-mother, and the sad history that had been revealed this night.

CHAPTER SEVEN

Cash Rosslyn was younger than Kendra had expected. And earlier. He appeared on her porch just after seven, with a cap in his hand and his father's grin. She took one look and knew that this charmer had probably sold one-way tickets to half the female hearts in Shenandoah County.

He was probably not much more than thirty. His hair was a little too long, a cane-syrup brown; his eyes were a flawless merger of blue and green. A deep tan made the color even more startling.

"Kendra Taylor," she said, holding out her hand. Now she was glad she'd risen and showered when the birds began their morning serenade.

"Sorry I'm so early, but this was the best

time for me. We're going to start on the barn this afternoon."

"That soon?"

"The owner has plans for that hill. We start today, the price drops a lot."

"Clearly I chose the right people to work with."

The grin flashed again. He was adept at using it, but it also seemed perfectly natural. "Yes, ma'am, you sure did. We *are* the best, no question about it. If you've got it, flaunt it."

She laughed. This was a man who enjoyed himself, and she bet if he wasn't enjoying himself, he simply moved on to something better.

"Would you like coffee? I just made a pot."

He followed her inside, running his hands over the walls as he moved toward the kitchen. He stopped halfway, pulled out a pocket knife and began tapping the handle along the length of one of the middle logs on the outside wall.

"You got some rot here. Mind if I probe a little?"

"Be my guest."

He flicked open the knife. "These long

cracks? They're called checks. Usually not a problem, just a natural part of settling, but I'm guessing some moisture got inside this one." He slipped the knife in the crack and moved it around.

"Don't tell me you're going to have to pull logs out of the middle of the house and replace them."

"Nothing so drastic. This one isn't going to be much of a problem, anyway—at least I don't think so. But I'll be checking outside, mostly." He snapped the knife shut. "Usually we can do what we call the Dutchman's repair, carve out the rotted part and piece in sound wood. I'm guessing there will be problems outside. The house needs gutters, maybe even a new roof. I'll know more after I do the whole inspection."

"Milk? Sugar?"

"Black as sin."

She poured him a mug, one of her Wal-Mart purchases. In the condo she had a set of sleek white stoneware from a home decor shop in Georgetown. Here she had settled on mugs with sunflowers and cardinals, and liked their cheery greeting every morning.

"My dad tell you the two buildings were built decades apart?"

"He thought so."

"Notching of the logs is different. Had you noticed? If you want to come outside, I can show you."

She was entranced that she had stumbled into history just by making one phone call. She poured herself another cup of coffee and followed him down the steps and around the side of the building, where it was easier to see how the house had been constructed.

Cash was in lecture mode. "Now this is a dovetail notch. You don't see this a lot. Whoever put this cabin together knew what he was doing. The other side? A half dovetail, which is a lot more common and easier to do. Not well done there, I'm afraid."

As they walked, he demonstrated the difference, which was, for the most part, a function of the angle of the notches. By the time they stood looking down at the river, Kendra was at peace with her decision. Cash hadn't made the full inspection, but without question it was going to take work to keep this structure intact. Like his father, he believed that starting from the ground up would be better. But more important, he'd also made it clear he would abide by her wishes.

No one except a New Yorker named Kendra Taylor cared what happened to this little piece of Virginia, but Cash and his father were the men to move the house solidly into the twenty-first century.

"I'm growing awfully fond of this view," she said.

"There's a lot of grading and foundation work we'll need to do here, and keeping the cabin will make it harder. Now that I've seen it for myself, I'll help my dad draw up some preliminary plans. I brought some books for you to look through, and a list of questions. When you're ready, we'll work out the details. But there'll be a lot of coming and going. You're up for this?"

"I don't see how I can say no."

"Then I'm not going to build anything too permanent in the way of a railing. We might want to enlarge that porch, or tear it down. So today I'll just stick up something temporary. Don't be judging my craftsmanship."

She wondered if he was still hoping she would change her mind and take the cabin down. "How long have you been doing this?"

"Since I gave up on mint juleps and the winner's circle."

"Kentucky?"

"Horses and racing. I still do some training, but this is what I do to make a living. For at least as long as it'll take me to finish this project."

He was as different from the men she knew as D.C. from Louisville, and a welcome change.

"I've been thinking about visiting somebody. Now might be a good time, since you'll be working here," she said.

"Might be. Though maybe you need to get used to it."

"Maybe I do. But not today."

They finished their tour, with Cash stopping twice to poke around the foundation. When they reached the front, it was in time to see Godzilla slithering toward the woods for breakfast.

"Now that's some snake," Cash said after a long, low whistle. "Never saw one quite that big."

Kendra forced herself to breathe. "I really

wish it would find another place to live. You don't know what it is, do you?"

"Black rat snake, near as I can tell. Nothing to worry you. You won't have a mouse in the house, that's for sure."

"How about a snake?"

"Well, they can climb near about anything. Seen 'em in trees raiding nests. But he's got what he needs out here, and your house is secure. I don't think you'll find him in bed with you, if that's what you're worried about. That's not a snake you'll want to go after with a hoe. You'd need a steamroller."

"Is there such a thing as snake repellant?"

"Sure is. But save yourself some money and just put up a No Vacancy sign. Works about as well. He'll probably leave when we get going here. He won't want the company, and I've got a couple of men who'd sooner shoot him than look at him."

She liked Cash, and she supposed if her life was going to be in turmoil for the next few months, she might as well enjoy the people who were causing the disturbance.

She thanked him for coming and added, "I was injured about a month ago, and the steps are hard for me without something to hang on to."

"Car accident?"

"In a manner of speaking, I guess. I was shot because a man in a D.C. parking lot wanted my car."

The whistle again. A low, mournful sound, a freight train at midnight. "Your neighbors will be watching out for you here," he promised.

She liked the sound of that. "Well, I'm off to see Helen Henry, one of those very people."

"Ms. Henry? Now there's a character. She'll get you quilting. See if she don't."

"Little chance of that."

He stuck out his hand. "We'll shake on it. And you can buy me a six-pack of some fancy microbrew when you go off to buy those needles and pins you'll need."

"And what do I get if you're wrong?"

"Heck, I'll shave ten bucks off your bill."

She extended her hand. "It's a deal."

With a smile on her face, she returned to the house for her car keys.

Kendra went out for breakfast first, which meant a trip to the Milestone Restaurant, a glorified truck stop with a buffet. She read the paper and indulged in pancakes and sausage, although she left most of her food on her plate. Between articles, she listened to the men who drove the big rigs comparing war stories. By the time she finished she thought it was late enough to visit Helen and Cissy.

She pulled up in front of their place just in time to see Cissy backing out in the old pickup. Cissy rolled down her window, and Kendra went to say hello. A blond toddler with pigtails sticking straight out from both sides of her head and eyes as big as the world around her was sitting in a car seat beside her, singing to herself.

"Meet Reese," Cissy said. "Reese, this is Miss Kendra."

Reese turned to assess her. She was absolutely adorable in a green smocked dress and tiny white tennis shoes with bells tied in the bows. Kendra's traitorous biological clock ticked a little faster.

"Hello, Reese," she said. "I'm glad to meet you."

"You got cookies?"

Kendra managed a laugh. "How old are you?"

Reese raised an eyebrow.

"Old enough not to ask for things she can't have this early. She's two and a half." Cissy turned to her daughter. "No cookies."

Reese pouted.

Cissy ignored her. "My brother's home from school today, and we're going off to buy him some new shoes. Caleb lives up the road with the Clairbornes." She lowered her voice. "If I'm any judge, Reese's grandma will have homemade doughnuts waiting when we pick him up."

Kendra had never lived in a place where family ties were such an ever present and somewhat convoluted part of daily life. "Reese is precious. And smart."

"Her nickname is Hellion."

"Is Mrs. Henry up? Will I disturb her?"

"She's up with the sun every morning. Reese helps with that—don't you, girl?"

Reese went back to her song, in no language Kendra had ever heard.

"I'll just go up and visit with her a while," Kendra said. "If you don't think she'll mind?"

"She'll mind if you don't. She fretting a lot, you being out there by yourself and all.

Do her good to see you getting around so well."

"I'll tell her about the renovation. Rosslyn and Rosslyn are going to take down the old barn and add some rooms to the house. And right now Cash is putting up a railing along the steps, so when Zeke comes back, he won't have to worry."

"Sorry he couldn't get to it first, but he had a bluegrass festival just ripe for some banjo picking. You'll make Ms. Henry's day. Ms. Henry, she's happiest when people do what she tells them."

Kendra stepped back and waved, and Cissy put the truck in Reverse again and drove off. Some would say Cissy was too young to be a mother. But she seemed to be doing a good job with her little girl. Kendra wondered at the way things fell into place.

Up on Helen's porch, she knocked cautiously on the screen door.

Helen trundled into the room to push it open. "Look who's here."

"You feel like a visitor?"

They chatted a little. Kendra turned down more coffee, and Helen gave her a quick tour of the downstairs. This was an old Virginia farmhouse with a comfortable, if not perfectly assembled, ambience. Paint and decorator touches were attractive and recent. Kendra suspected another's hand in that, perhaps Helen's daughter or granddaughter.

She knew that Elisa had lived here before marrying Sam, and that Helen's offer of lodging had been a godsend. Cissy and Zeke lived here now with Reese, supposedly to keep an eye on Helen. But Kendra wasn't really sure who was taking care of whom. Helen Henry was a kinder woman than she wanted anyone to know.

"Where do you do your quilting?" Kendra asked. "I've seen some of your work. It's spectacular."

Helen pointed to the ceiling. "Up there in my bedroom. Just something I learned as a girl. We all quilted then. We had regular quilting bees in this house when I was growing up, out in the parlor. Sometimes even Leah Spurlock joined us, though she wasn't much of a needle-woman."

The lead-in was too perfect. "You know, Helen, I'm here because I want to talk about Leah."

"You had a chance to talk to Manning Rosslyn yet?"

"I did. But I haven't really been straight with either of you. And I wanted to clear that up."

"This sounds like it might be interesting."

Helen went back into the living room and settled on the sofa. Kendra took a seat across from her.

"We didn't buy our property," Kendra said. "It was left to my husband. By Leah."

"If you don't mind me saying so, that sounds fishy. Leah died a long time ago."

"It's a long story."

"I got nothing but time. Not sure how much, as a matter of fact, so you ought to dive right in."

Kendra made herself comfortable. "Isaac, my husband, is Rachel Spurlock's son. We know Rachel ran away from Toms Brook when she was in her teens. We don't know much about what she did or where she went afterward, but we do know at one point she ended up in Kansas City. She was in her thirties by then, old enough to know better, but she gave birth to Isaac, then gave him up for adoption."

"If she gave him up, how come Leah left the boy her cabin and land?"

"That's where it gets interesting. Everything we do know, we know from Leah's stepson, Mark Jackson. He's an attorney out in California now."

"I might remember him, from when he was a boy here. Lived over at the other end of the county, so I didn't see him much, but his mother and daddy would stop by my vegetable stand in town. I remember them that way."

"You probably know this part. Leah nursed Mark's mother. The mother was sick a long time, and Mark said Leah was faithful and gentle to the end. Even though he was young, he remembers his mother telling him no one could have been kinder. Some years later, Leah and Mark's father, Tom, met again and decided to marry. She moved to New Market with him. Mark was almost grown by then, but she finished raising him. Apparently the Jacksons were happy together, and Mark has nothing but good things to say about Leah."

Helen considered this for a moment. "Not many people had anything bad to say. She was a pretty woman, and a pretty woman by herself, well, it sets other women watching, if you know what I mean. I was a widow, too. Me, I didn't have a thing to worry about like that, since I turned old before my time, but Leah, well, she caught more than one man's eye, and some of them were married. But there was never anything that went on I ever heard about. She was a good Christian woman, and she didn't encourage men, and that's a fact."

As a journalist, Kendra had learned not to be judgmental, but she was relieved. This was an improvement over what she'd thought she might hear. Manning's account of his phone call with Rachel still haunted her.

Rachel said Leah was not the angel she seemed like to everyone else. She said Leah would spend her days in hell.

"There's got to be more to it," Helen said.

"Mark was never told much about Leah's past. He knew she had a daughter, and that was about it. Then Leah passed away, and before she died, she made Tom promise he would find Rachel's child."

"How did she *know* Rachel had a child?"

"Rachel called Leah sometime after Isaac's birth and told her about the baby.

She wouldn't say whether it was a girl or a boy, or where the baby was born. After all those years, she was finally going to come back and visit. She said she would tell Leah more when she came. Then she died before she could make the trip."

"Must have broken Leah's heart."

"Rachel was working in a bar. There was a fire, and several people were killed before anyone could get to them. She was one of them."

"A terrible way to meet your Maker."

"Mark said Leah started trying to find her grandchild right afterward, but she died before she found out much. So Mark's father took up the search. He died about six years ago, but not before he asked Mark to continue. Tom left everything to Mark, but Leah left her land here and a quilt she'd made to her grandchild. Mark put the land in trust, with the provision that if Rachel's son or daughter wasn't found in his lifetime, the land would be sold and the money donated to Tom and Leah's church down in New Market."

"How did he find your husband?"

"He did what Leah and Tom never felt comfortable doing. When he hit a brick wall, he put it in the hands of a private investigator. Isaac was adopted at birth by an Air Force officer and his wife. It was a private adoption, and they looked good on paper. Maybe Rachel thought being brought up as an Air Force brat would give her son the discipline she never had, I don't know. We'll never be sure."

"He have a good life?"

Kendra gave one shake of her head. "Colonel Taylor wanted his own son, not somebody else's."

"Your husband had a lot to bear."

Kendra had already revealed more than she was comfortable with. But she had a reason. "Here's why I've told you that part. I want you to understand why Isaac is so negative about the land and anything to do with his birth family. His adopted father never let him forget his roots. He grew up being told he came from trailer trash. He's angry at everyone in the picture, even though he's not the kind of man who would ever say so."

"That explain why he's not here with you?"

"Some of it, yes."

Helen pursed her lips and nodded. "Well,

it makes some sense, that's for sure. I can see why Leah couldn't let it go, but maybe she should have let it die with her. Rachel didn't give her the baby to raise. She wanted her baby to have a fresh start."

"I hoped maybe you had some insight into that. Why she couldn't let go."

Helen took off her glasses and held them up to the light, then she wiped them on the hem of her housedress before she put them on again, taking her time. "Here's what I think, and it's not worth a lot."

"It's worth more than anything I can come up with on my own."

"Leah moved here sometime in the thirties, as near as I can remember it. She was young, and she came alone. There was no husband in sight, but she had a ring on her finger. We thought she was a widow, but I remember my mama saying she thought maybe Leah's husband had left her. And maybe she moved here to get over it."

Kendra winced. Isaac's family really did sound like characters from a Grand Old Soap Opry.

"I don't know how she came to own the cabin and the land," Helen said. "It was abandoned when she got here. I don't remember anyone ever living there, as a matter of fact. Not before she did."

"Manning thought maybe it was an old hunting cabin."

"Could have been. Anyway, she showed up pregnant, too. She had her baby here. Never took off that ring, although if my husband up and disappeared on me, I would have pawned the ring and had a good dinner out."

"So Rachel was born here?"

"You'd never know it, though. Didn't fit in. She got teased some because her mama wasn't from here. It was hard times, and strangers didn't sit too well, you see. But except for women worrying 'cause Leah was too pretty, people liked her well enough. Rachel, now, she was a different story. Just didn't seem like one of us."

Kendra was forming a picture of Rachel. "So why do you think Leah wanted so badly to find Isaac?"

"Rachel was all she had, you know. Oh, she had the cabin and the land around it, not a lot of land, but enough so she could make do. And eventually she had Tom and Mark. But they weren't blood. No, Rachel was her life and whatever joy she got from it. And with Rachel gone, maybe all she thought she had left of her daughter was that baby, wherever it was. She must have wanted to pass on some of that family feeling."

Kendra knew this was only a theory, but it made sense to her. A woman alone. A woman scorned. A child she adored who had run away. And in the end, the only thing left of that child was a grandson or granddaughter who knew nothing of its birth family and needed to—at least in Leah's mind.

She let the story sink in a little, staring at the fireplace that had been outfitted for spring with poplar logs and dried flowers.

"You said a quilt?" Helen asked after a while.

"A Lover's Knot quilt. An unusual signature quilt, actually. I'd love for you to look at it. Maybe you can tell me who some of the people are. They must be from around here. I have other signature quilts I've bought. I guess I'm becoming a collector. Will you come and see them?"

"Sounds intriguing. But like I said, Leah, she wasn't much of a quilter. A quilt, that's a surprise."

Kendra thought she had probably left

Helen with enough to think about. She got to her feet. "I hope you understand that I wasn't trying to hide Isaac's ties to Leah and Rachel. I just wanted to feel my way before I made any announcements."

Helen got up, too. "And Mark Jackson? He can't help any more?"

"Mark says his father wouldn't tell him much about Leah's past. Mark did his part by finding Isaac and passing on the property."

"So Tom Jackson didn't know. Or he was hiding something."

"That's my guess, too."

"Well, it's enough to get my brain spinning, that's for sure. And I'll want to see that quilt. I'll stop over when it's convenient."

"I'd love that. I have a phone now." Kendra gave Helen a card she'd scribbled her number on. "That's just in case you want to be sure I'm there."

Helen walked her to the door. "You're turning into a country girl. You know we drop in when we feel like it."

"I'm about to have a lot of company. The more the merrier." Kendra told her about Manning and Cash, and the work on the house.

She pushed the screen door open, but turned before she closed it again. "Do you think Leah would object? To the renovations, I mean? It's funny, but I don't want to upset a woman who isn't even alive."

"Your husband will be more likely to stay in the house if you fix it up a bit, won't he?"

Kendra didn't know.

Helen touched her shoulder. Just a light, quick touch, but a lot of touching for her. "I'd say that anything you do to make a home there will make Leah happy."

"I think I needed to hear that."

"You come back anytime. You're always welcome here."

There wasn't much time to process the conversation on the way home. It was just past ten, but Kendra was already as tired as if she had canoed the length of the North Fork. The day was shaping up to be particularly glorious. She knew better than to do any gardening until she'd had a good rest. Instead, she decided to take a notepad out to the porch and make herself comfortable in her new chair. Then she would consider what she had learned about Leah from Helen.

She half expected to hear the pounding

of a hammer as she drove up her rutted lane, but instead she heard voices and what sounded like a child's laughter. She was in the clearing before she had time to guess who might be waiting.

An unfamiliar burgundy minivan sporting Michigan plates was parked in her usual spot. The side door was open, and Kendra could see blankets and pillows and what looked like plastic cartons stacked between two captain's chairs, one of which held a child's car seat. She pulled up beside it and got out. By the time she had circled the van, a young woman was coming down the porch steps, steps that now sported a primitive railing.

Kendra stopped. The woman had dark hair that fell in waves from a scrunchie on top of her head. She was slender and graceful, with a long torso, narrow hips and perfect legs shown to their best advantage in cut-off denim shorts. A red shirt was tied just above the waist, and she wore simple suede sandals. Her oval face was fine-boned, her forehead punctuated by a deep widow's peak.

The world did not spin slower on its axis, and time didn't stop. But for a moment

Kendra felt suspended, as if this reunion, which had eluded her for so long, couldn't possibly be real.

Then she straightened her shoulders and braced herself. "Jamie."

"Hey, sis," Jamie said. "Guess it's long time no see."

CHAPTER EIGHT

"How on earth did you find me?" Kendra sailed ahead with the conversation, although she was sure the prevailing wind had abandoned her.

"Riva."

The fact that their mother remembered where Kendra was living surprised her. Before moving into the cabin, Kendra had left Riva a brief message, but she hadn't received a response. Not that she had expected one. Riva had already done her maternal duty. After the carjacking, she'd wired a huge basket of chocolates, champagne and delicate designer nightwear for Kendra to enjoy as she lay in Intensive Care, nourished entirely by tubes that snaked in and out of standard-issue hospital garb.

"She must have an assistant who can

write," Kendra said. "Someone who actually jotted down the basics."

"She's shacking up with some Frenchman in Marseilles, and she claims the household staff was well-trained by his wife."

Kendra didn't ask where the Frenchman's wife was living. Riva never squinted over fine print.

"And from this you found your way here? You didn't talk to Isaac?"

"Do you suppose he would have told me?" Jamie sounded curious, as if the possibility intrigued her.

Kendra wasn't sure. Isaac had never met her sister. Kendra herself hadn't seen Jamie in seven years.

"Mommy!"

Jamie whirled. Only then did Kendra see the reason for the crowded minivan and the car seat. A dark-haired little girl in a fairy princess costume came to the top of the steps. "Alison went potty in her diapers."

"Alison?" Kendra said.

"There's a lot you don't know, isn't there?"

"Is that Hannah?"

"I've got to see about Alison. Come meet them."

Kendra felt as if someone's fist was pressed into her belly. "Anything else I should know? Boyfriends, sons, groupies?"

Jamie didn't answer. She turned away, exposing a wide expanse of tanned flesh where her shirt and shorts didn't meet. Kendra noted the tattoo of an orchid at the base of her sister's spine.

The railing was sturdy, although it looked as if Cash needed to add a few more slats. She wondered where he had gone, but all thoughts of him disappeared when she was face-to-face with the child.

"Hannah," Jamie said, "this is your aunt Kendra."

Kendra didn't know what to say. She was staring at a perfect replica of her sister, the Jamie she had rescued from parents with more money than maturity, the Jamie she had tried, in her own childish way, to save, to buffer, to teach. Jamie, before the drugs, the men, the wanderlust. Jamie before years of anger drove her away.

Hannah held out her hand. "I am Hannah Clousell," she said. "But I am really a princess."

"This doesn't surprise me at all," Kendra

said somberly, taking her niece's slightly grubby hand.

She didn't want to let go. She wanted to pull this child behind her, to protect her the way she had not been able to protect her mother. Hannah was Jamie at six, blue eyes with no trace of sadness, dark hair brushing the top of her earlobes and the sweet hollow at her nape, Jamie's narrow aristocratic nose, so at odds with a sweet, encompassing smile.

"Hannah, where is Alison exactly?" Jamie asked.

"In the bathroom. She is not eating soap."

"You turn your head for one minute," Jamie muttered, taking off for the bedroom wing of the dogtrot.

Hannah took back her hand with a slight tug. "Alison will eat almost anything," she explained. "Except endive, which is not my favorite."

"Mine either."

"This house is unusual. It's two houses, both unlocked. In the winter you'll have to wear a coat to make breakfast."

"Maybe not. I'm adding rooms. We might close in the porch."

"Where will we sleep?"

Kendra was at a loss. Things were moving too quickly. “Where would you like to?”

“Well, not in the van. We camped coming here, but I am tired of tents.”

“There’s definitely room inside.”

“That would be better.” Hannah seemed to consider. “Yes,” she said in her precise way. “That’s what we’ll do. But not in your bed. Alison is not trustworthy.”

Kendra looked up to see Jamie backing out of her bedroom with the untrustworthy Alison slung over her shoulder. Kendra glimpsed copper-red curls and the chubby, compact body of a preschooler.

“Disaster averted,” Jamie said. “Diaper changed. I’ll dispose of it at the landfill or wherever these things go in the country. She’s almost done with diapers, but we still don’t travel in big-girl panties.” She squatted and set the little girl on her feet.

To Kendra, Alison looked as if she had just been conjured by leprechauns. She had pale Celtic skin, with cheeks stained a delicate rose. Freckles sprinkled her nose. Spiky auburn lashes lined eyes as green as Blarney’s hills.

“Alison Callahan, this is Aunt Kendra,” Jamie said, straightening Alison’s T-shirt.

The kelly green shirt was just long enough to cover her bottom. It sported the white outline of dancing shamrocks and the words *Murphy's Irish Pub.* It was her sole item of clothing.

"I poop in my pants," Alison said solemnly.

Kendra looked at her sister, then back at the little girl. "Well, that happens. I'm glad to meet you."

"I hungry."

"Don't worry," Jamie said. "We have tons of food. I don't expect you to feed us. I'll make peanut butter sandwiches."

"I turn to a peanut," Alison said. "I could."

"How old are you?" Kendra stooped to have a better look. "Three?"

"This old!" Alison held up two fingers and crooked one more. "See?"

"Two?"

"And three-quarters," Hannah said. "It's best to be accurate. She has issues."

"Oh . . ."

"Two and quarts," Alison said, nodding vehemently. "That's right."

Kendra stood and faced her sister. "I guess you thought I wouldn't be interested." She said this in a low voice, careful to keep anger from it.

"Hannah, would you mind getting the picnic basket out of the van?" Jamie said. "The little one? Can you carry it by yourself?"

Hannah rolled her eyes and started down the steps. Alison held up her arms, and Jamie swung her daughter to her hip.

"We have a lot to say to each other," Jamie said. "But not now, okay?"

"You come from nowhere with two children in tow, one I've never even heard about, and I'm not supposed to react?"

"You can react all you want once they're in bed, okay?"

"You're planning to stay, then?"

"If you'll have us."

Kendra considered. She was even more exhausted than she'd thought. She could feel herself about to say things she would normally never permit, but there was no energy left for silence.

"Do you know how much money I spent trying to find you after you disappeared? How many times I nearly did? But I was always a day behind. Then that one meeting, followed by your letter telling me about

Hannah, telling me to stay away from you both."

"I don't expect you to understand, sis."

"Sis." Kendra shook her head in disbelief.

"We're here now. Can't that be good enough to get us through dinner? I shopped for groceries. I'll cook and clean up. You can get acquainted with your nieces."

"Just tell me why you're here." Kendra could hear Hannah approaching. "That will help."

"To take care of you," Jamie said. "If you'll let me."

Jimmy Dunkirk never should have married, but more obviously, he never should have married Riva Delacroix. Jimmy was the last hope and scion of an East Coast newspaper empire that, generations before, had nearly rivaled Hearst's for papers and bravado. Instead, Jimmy, who had no interest in the written word, dismantled and sold the remains, invested the spoils in Manhattan real estate and later, on a whim, a substantial amount in a new company named Microsoft, which seemed to show promise. From that moment on, all his energy went into daredevil exploits, one of which finally killed him.

Riva Delacroix was the indulged and pampered daughter of the New Orleans Garden District Delacroixes. Raised from birth to be queen of carnival, eighteen-year-old Riva was abandoned by her parents when, after two dances at the Twelfth Night Revelers tableau ball, she eloped with Jimmy to start a new life far away from flying doubloons, boiled crawfish and the literary remains of Tennessee Williams.

Kendra always wondered when her father had realized his mistake. The day he discovered his wife indulged in impassioned conversations with the Virgin if he didn't give her everything she wanted? The night Riva showed a dismaying lack of understanding about Jimmy's affairs and stabbed him with a letter opener? The month she saw her marriage was in need of an anchor and threw away her birth control pills to provide one?

Kendra was the product of that lapse, a lapse that kept Jimmy semi-tethered to Riva's side. Jamie was the product of the *next* lapse, nine years later, timed once again to keep a straying Jimmy at heel. By then Jimmy had abandoned any thoughts of becoming a family man. He didn't like children, their demands, their insistence on being loved. More important, he didn't like his wife, whose behavior dipped from mildly neurotic to wildly insane, depending on which drugs the doctors prescribed or Riva bought on shadowed street corners.

Jimmy left before Jamie was born. Riva left soon afterward. On occasion both parents stopped by the Upper East Side brownstone, but Kendra and Jamie were left with increasingly incompetent staff hired by the same mother who might weep for an hour after she tried and failed to choose the right dress for a cocktail party.

Starved for family and affection, Kendra attached herself to the helpless baby with the trusting blue eyes. From the moment she saw her little sister, Kendra knew she was the only force that stood between Jamie and disaster.

Now Kendra lay in her bed, head pillowed on her arms, and wondered how even as a child she could have believed Jamie had a chance. With Jimmy in residence during Kendra's childhood, some decent choices had been made about who would care for her and what schools she would attend. But Jamie's care had been almost entirely at Riva's whim, and although Kendra had done what she could, she'd been a child with a child's lack of influence.

Jamie had grown up in a world where she was smothered by maternal affection, then peremptorily abandoned. She was Riva's "poor little baby," the sweet little "beignet" who had been so cruelly deserted by her heartless father. Jamie was tugged between Riva's bipolar personalities, until she frequently dissolved into a helpless puddle of misery.

In between Riva's appearances, Kendra did what she could. And when Jamie was eleven, Kendra gathered up her little sister and brought her to Chicago, where she was attending Northwestern University. Kendra set up housekeeping with a Filipino nanny who embraced Jamie as her own.

Their father died in a skydiving accident that year, and what little influence he had exerted over their mother disappeared. Riva dropped into their lives on her way to everywhere, trailing clouds of ecstasy or misery, telling glamorous stories that made the impressionable and love-hungry Jamie yearn for the life from which her sister had snatched her. Kendra, trying to provide stability, remained in Chicago after graduation, taking any newspaper job she could find in order to work her way into serious journalism.

Then, one day, when the increasingly rebellious Jamie was seventeen, she simply disappeared.

Since then, Kendra had seen her sister only once. Seven years ago she had tracked Jamie to a Brooklyn flophouse. At first Jamie hadn't even recognized her. Kendra had begged her to come home. She had promised to help her straighten out her life, but when she returned the next morning to plead with her again, Jamie had moved on.

A letter arrived months later. Jamie had given birth to a little girl named Hannah. She did not want Kendra's help, and she would not tolerate her interference. If Kendra tried to find her, Jamie and her daughter would disappear for good.

After that there had been sporadic phone calls and ground rules. Hannah, as a subject, was off-limits. And for once in her life, Riva kept any details she knew to herself.

Jamie refused to visit and said that when she was ready for a relationship, she would find her sister.

Now she had.

From the beginning, Kendra had felt an affinity for Leah Spurlock, whose missing daughter had never returned. Kendra had given up hope of seeing Jamie again, but now here she was, in the house where Leah had waited and prayed. The irony was not lost on Kendra.

Surprisingly, she had managed a nap after Jamie's announcement that she had come to Virginia to take care of her. Perhaps the notion that the sister who had swallowed so many of Kendra's waking hours wanted to give something back had pushed her over the edge of exhaustion. She no more believed Jamie's words than she believed that Isaac would have a change of heart and learn to love this property. Perhaps she'd slept because she knew she would need every bit of energy in the days ahead.

Footsteps ran past her door. Childish footsteps. Nieces. Two of them, which was new information. The girls had different last names, so apparently they also had different fathers. Kendra struggled for objectivity. The girls looked well nourished and relatively clean. Although Hannah reminded Kendra of herself at that age, too mature and too helpful, she seemed happy enough. She was obviously a bright child, and Alison, who was eternally curious, seemed happy and bright enough, as well.

But what kind of life had these little girls led?

The footsteps stopped outside Kendra's door. She pushed herself upright and called a greeting. Hannah opened the door a crack and peeked inside. "We are to bring you tea when you wake up. Are you awake?"

"You don't have to do that."

Hannah looked as if she wasn't sure what to say.

"Of course it would be very nice if you did," Kendra added quickly.

"There will be Oreos, too." The door closed.

Kendra didn't want to smile, but she was afraid if she didn't, she was going to cry.

"Damn you, Jamie." She punched her pillow, then punched it again for good measure.

She was sitting propped up with pillows

when the door opened the next time. The whole crew entered, led by Hannah who carried a tall glass of iced tea. Alison was next, with a plate showcasing three Oreos formed shamrock-style in the middle and a sandwich cut into quarters around the edges. Jamie held the door.

"Do you remember our tea parties, Ken?" Her hair was down now, spilling over her shoulders and partway down her back. At seventeen she had been gawky and coltish. Clearly this beautiful creature had emerged during the Big Absence. While Kendra resembled Jimmy, Jamie was a Delacroix through and through. Riva's parents had shown little interest in their granddaughters, but Kendra thought they had missed their best chance for a Mardi Gras queen when they ignored this one.

"I remember Kool-Aid at a wrought-iron table and graham crackers with our dolls," Kendra said.

"You were pretty well beyond the age of dolls, but you were patient. I had a hundred to choose from. Every time Riva or Jimmy showed up, they had a doll under one arm."

"They're in storage," Kendra said without thinking.

Jamie stopped at the end of the bed. "You're serious?"

"You know me, Jamie. I plan for everything. Even the possibility you might have an address to send them to one day."

Jamie's eyes met hers; then she looked down at her daughters. "Girls, one day there's going to be a lovely surprise in the mail."

The girls were too busy waiting for Kendra to take their offerings to pay much attention. Kendra noted the enthusiasm, and reached for the plate and the glass. "I have never seen anything more welcome," she told them.

"Three!" Alison jumped up and down. "Three cookies."

"If you don't open the cookies and lick off the filling, Alison will be unhappy," Hannah said. "She is a creature of habit."

Kendra set the tea on the bedside table and opened the first cookie, doing exactly as she'd been instructed. Alison vaulted onto the bed and threw her arms around her. Kendra pulled her on to her lap, careful to position her so she was not resting against her surgical scar.

"Would you like one?" she asked the little girl.

"Yours."

Jamie interceded. "She's had two already. Better not. It was the only way we could be sure the cookies would make their way to the bedside."

Hannah scooted up on the bed, as well, perching on the end. "The tea has mint and sugar. Two teaspoons. Oh, lemon, too. We weren't sure what you like in it. We decided on everything."

"I love it that way."

"Did you sleep?" Jamie asked. "Or were we too noisy?"

"I slept."

"How do you feel? I mean in general."

"I'm doing okay. I feel a little better every day."

"I wanted to come sooner. I wanted to come right away, as soon as Riva got around to telling me what had happened. But I had exams."

"Exams?"

"I'm in college. Hannah's private school is on the same schedule. That's why we were able to get away."

This was news to Kendra. "I didn't know."

"I realize that."

"It's an odd sort of secret, isn't it?"

"I'm studying architecture and interior design. I can't decide what I want to do when I graduate, so I'm hedging my bets."

Kendra was trying to process this. "You're in Michigan? I noticed your plates."

"Yes. Southfield."

"For a while?"

"I'm halfway through my third year."

Kendra realized the girls were waiting for her to taste the tea. She took a long slow sip and licked her lips. "I've never had better," she told them.

"Down now," Alison said, squirming, and Kendra helped her scoot off her lap.

"We'll leave you alone," Jamie said. "Is there anything else we can get you? I thought I'd make pasta for supper, if that's all right."

"You really don't have to wait on me."

"Okay. Do you like mushrooms?"

A plaintive tune answered before Kendra could. She recognized the Bangles' "Walk Like an Egyptian," and the source, a cell phone. Jamie pulled a small one out of her pocket and held it away to check the number.

"Tell you what," Jamie said. "I'll just stick the mushrooms on the side, and you can decide later."

The entourage left, with Jamie speaking softly into the phone. The door closed behind them. Kendra realized she was tired all over again.

By the time the afternoon had waned and garlic was sizzling in a frying pan, Kendra had learned more about her sister. Jamie was an indulgent mother. Like Riva, she stroked and cuddled, and she gave in easily. Alison ate too many snacks, and Hannah made too many decisions.

Jamie was preoccupied, too, the way their own mother had been. As the afternoon droned on, she fielded four new phone calls, and each seemed to take more out of her. Hannah automatically took charge of her sister when "Egyptian" began to play. Jamie took the phone out of the room to conduct whatever business was so important.

Jamie smoked. To her credit, she did it outside, away from her daughters. She told Kendra she quit when she was pregnant with Alison but had started again recently.

"I smoke when I'm stressed," she said. "It's bad, I know. Don't lecture."

Alison fell asleep on the sofa in the late afternoon, too tired to keep her eyes open another minute. Kendra would have put her to bed hours before, tucked in with a story. Hannah occupied herself lining up stones on the edge of the porch until Kendra gave her a notebook and a collection of colored pencils. Jamie went for a walk, cell phone pressed to her ear.

Once dinner preparations were at hand and Alison awoke, cranky and hungry, things slid further downhill. Hannah complained that her mother had forgotten to bring Alison's favorite blanket. She had reminded Jamie, and still Jamie had forgotten. Alison wanted to watch her favorite video and could not be persuaded that Aunt Kendra's television did not come equipped to show it. Hannah wanted cheese and crackers, and the only cheese she liked was gone.

Jamie was beginning to look frazzled. "We threw everything in the van and took off the day finals ended. I'm sorry, but it's hard to study and be organized. And we're all tired from the drive. We'll feel better tomorrow, and the girls and I will shop for something to entertain them."

Kendra still hadn't had a moment to talk privately with her sister, and she was beginning to doubt she would. Jamie did nothing to calm the atmosphere. When the girls whined, she tried to coax them out of it, roughhousing in the yard, or organizing a game of tag. She cuddled; she tickled; she never said no. She was the mistress of "maybe," a word that only kept them guessing.

By the time they sat down to an excellent meal of sautéed chicken and peppers in homemade marinara sauce, the girls were too overwrought to eat. After three arguments that left Kendra more exhausted than she'd felt since the shooting, Jamie put down her fork.

"Okay, here's what we're going to do," she told her daughters. "You're going to take showers in Aunt Kendra's bathroom. Then you're getting into your pajamas and bed."

"There is no bed," Hannah said.

"We have our air mattresses, and we can sleep in here. Once you're ready, you can listen to music until you fall asleep."

"I not sleepy," Alison said. "I sleeped already."

Jamie's cell phone sounded. "Sorry. I have to take this." She got up and walked outside.

Kendra was afraid it was going to be a very long evening.

After the girls were bathed and settled, the food put away and the dishes washed, Kendra found her way to the front porch and settled into one of her new chairs. Jamie had refused to let her do a thing, but she was still as tired as if she had handled the evening's chores by herself.

Darkness was creeping across the clearing when her sister finally joined her.

"Don't say it," Jamie warned.

Kendra rested her head on the back of her chair and waited for the stars to come out.

"Traveling is a disruption," Jamie said. "They'll settle in. I'm sorry they fell apart."

"I was just remembering the way you always dissolved when Riva came to visit. I'm sorry. But that's what came to mind."

"Riva had no idea in the world what a child needed."

Kendra knew when to stay silent.

"You don't think *I* do, either," Jamie said at last.

"I don't know what to think. I didn't even know about Alison until today. Suddenly you want my opinion?"

"I'm asking for it, yes."

"Well, I know better than to give it."

Jamie stood and walked to the edge of the porch. She pulled out a pack of cigarettes and a lighter, and lit up. She smoked a while before she spoke. "You've always been sure what's best. For everybody. That's why I ran away. You were so sure about my life, and I hated every decision you made for me."

Kendra closed her eyes. She didn't care about the stars anymore. "I kind of got that impression. Something about you disappearing the way you did. I got to pick up the pieces of my life while wondering if you were dead somewhere or in jail, or out on some street corner selling yourself or scoring drugs."

"I'm sorry, Ken. I was a kid. A stupid, conflicted, irresponsible, rebellious kid. And there you were, not my mother but my sister, who thought you knew everything about what was best for me."

"I had great role models. I just figured I would do everything differently from the way Jimmy and Riva did it, and I'd be fine."

"None of it was your fault."

"Oh? I'm off the hook? A moment ago it didn't sound like it."

"You're angry at me. I understand that. You have a right to be."

"You were a kid. I get that part. But you haven't been a kid in a long time, damn it. Where have you been?"

Jamie finished her cigarette. She tossed it on the ground below, then went down the steps to make sure it was out. Back on the porch, she faced her sister. "I was ashamed. I was a mess. I don't know how much lower I could have sunk without dying. It took Hannah to make me clean up my act. And it was slow work. I've had help along the way, but I didn't want to face you until I was sure I could hold up my head."

"And then there's Alison."

"I'm not sorry I had her, Ken. Don't try to make me sorry."

"Who is Alison's father? Is he someone you're with?"

"Someone I *was* with. He's out of our lives now. The pregnancy wasn't intentional. Fertility is one of my big talents. I was on the Pill. It didn't matter."

Kendra felt her insides knot in protest. "It's a funny world."

"Please believe me. I'm doing a good job with the girls. I want them. I love them. I work hard at being a mother. I didn't give them reliable fathers, and they'll pay the price for that, but I can give them the best mother in the world. Me."

"Being a mother is hard work. It's a lot more than wanting to be one." The moment the words escaped, Kendra wished they hadn't. She was angry at this sister who had stayed away, this sister who could give birth to beautiful children and treat them like playmates, this sister who had probably never, despite tonight's disclaimers, given Kendra's agony over losing her a moment's thought.

Jamie tapped another cigarette out of her pack. Kendra saw that her hands were shaking.

"You're so good at being a mother, Ken, why haven't you given it a try? You've been married a while now, right? I don't see any little ones running around the cabin. Or maybe your children wouldn't run. Maybe they'd sit in the corner and read Dostoevsky, or design computer programs to keep the rest of us in line."

Kendra thought of half a dozen replies. She'd already raised one child, thanks, and look what it had gotten her. She had a career that mattered more than two o'clock feedings. She had a husband who wanted to change the world, not diapers.

In the end, though, she told the truth. "I can't have children. Riva saw to that."

Jamie dropped the unlit cigarette on the floor and didn't bother to retrieve it. "What are you talking about?"

"Isaac and I never really got around to trying. But I wanted children, and I thought eventually he would, as well. The possibility was always there. I got a lot of mileage off that, I guess. Knowing I could. That it was a matter of choice, a matter of getting my marriage to the right place. Then I was shot."

Jamie came to sit beside her. "Were you injured so badly you won't be able to get pregnant?"

"I had emergency surgery. To stop the bleeding and repair the damage. Two bullets. One exited, one didn't. That one nicked my spinal cord. And once they could see what was going on, they found so much scar tissue and so many adhesions, the prognosis was clear. Between the old injuries and the new, I can never carry a child anywhere near to term."

"What does Riva have to do with this?"

"I had appendicitis as a child. Do you remember?"

"Not really."

"I guess you were just a baby. We were between nannies, and I was sick for a week. I kept telling Riva I didn't feel well, and she said it was a silly bug, that I would be fine. She kissed me, then she went off to her parties. And finally, when my fever got so high I was delirious, the housekeeper rushed me to the hospital. My appendix had ruptured. I nearly didn't make it."

Jamie was silent.

"When I woke up after *this* surgery, Isaac told me what the doctor had found. Isaac said it didn't mean anything—that we were lucky having children wasn't a priority."

"He sounds like a good man," Jamie said.

"Or one without a heart. I'm not sure anymore. We haven't talked about it since. As far as I know, it was a blip on his personal radar."

"But not yours."

"I don't know what to think."

Jamie got to her feet and walked a few steps to the railing, but she didn't light another cigarette. "So here I come. Two children I didn't plan for. I don't set strict rules. I don't always get them to bed on time or feed them the moment the first hunger pang hits. I roll around on the ground with them. I shout when I'm mad and hug them to death when I'm not. I'm not you. And if I were, I'd be asking myself why the world is so unfair."

"I try to avoid that. It's been hard today. I'm still angry at you. For a long time you were all I had. And you walked out on me. Now you're back, toting precious cargo." Kendra looked at Jamie, her lovely profile now a shadow against the soft light from the cabin window. "Why are you really here?"

Jamie reached over and touched Kendra's arm. One brief, featherlight touch. "So we can both begin to heal."

"I'm not sure we can."

"I'm sure we have to try."

CHAPTER NINE

Kendra hadn't expected to have a good night, but despite everything, she slept particularly well, not waking as she usually did when tree limbs rustled in the wind or a horned owl shrieked.

By the time she awoke, sun was streaming through the cabin's narrow windows. The prediction had been for rain, and she had dreaded a gray day indoors with two rambunctious, easily bored children. She doubted that Jamie had come prepared for such small quarters.

Aware that the only bathroom in the house was in the bedroom wing, she rose and showered quickly. She had told Jamie and the girls to troop through whenever they needed to, but if they had, they'd done it without a sound—which was unlikely.

She crossed the porch and opened the door into the living area. The air mattresses were gone; the room looked as untouched as a museum, and the little table in the kitchen area was set with crockery and pottery for one. The saucer held a super-size muffin—chocolate chip, from the look of it. The bowl held fresh strawberries, obviously meant to go with the plastic bag of low-fat granola beside it. Coffee warmed on the counter to fill her sunflower mug.

She was touched. Despite herself. Despite every instinct that told her to be careful, that her sister was a talented liar, that Jamie had managed to elude her, ignore her, forget for years to mention a daughter. Jamie was not the sweet-faced cherub who had clung to her older sister like a shipwreck victim clinging to a rock in treacherous waters.

And still, she was touched.

She poured coffee and retrieved milk from the refrigerator. She ate the granola and thought she might manage one bite of the muffin. Five minutes later she was carrying dishes, without so much as a crumb, to the sink.

She washed up to the chirping of birds,

wondering as she did so where Jamie and the girls had disappeared to. She stepped out on the porch and she listened for children laughing, then descended the stairs and turned to skirt the house and head toward the old apple orchard. She found her sister and nieces running through the tall grass, hiding among the gnarled old trees.

"Kendra!" Jamie's face was wreathed in a smile. "Don't run. Just stay there and grab one of these little monsters if she sails by."

Kendra was glad the girls were dressed in jeans and sweatshirts. She didn't know when this area had last been mowed. The trees were so old that some had fallen, yet she saw now that buds were beginning to form on the closest, despite its proximity to the ground. Undoubtedly the grass harbored ticks, snakes, any manner of varmints, but Jamie had foreseen the possibilities.

"We saw a snake!" This morning Hannah was less a princess than a tomboy. Her bright little eyes gleamed as she ran past Kendra, laughing when Kendra pretended to make a grab. "A big, big, big, big snake!"

"Back Booty." Alison scurried by. "Name's Back *Booty.*"

"Black Beauty," Hannah articulated carefully.

Kendra was sticking with Slithering Godzilla. "Under the porch?"

"You've seen him?" Hannah said.

"Sis, you knew?" Jamie bent over, resting her hands on her knees, to gasp for a breath. "My Lord, you knew that snake was there?"

"Trust me, I'm not real fond of him."

"I nearly jumped out of my skin. He went slithering by at about forty miles an hour. We were headed out to the van. I took the girls into town to use the facilities and have some breakfast so you could sleep."

"You didn't have to do that. But thanks. I haven't slept that late in a long time."

"Did you find your breakfast?"

"It was a treat. I appreciate it."

Jamie straightened. "We got the muffins at a bakery in Woodstock. What a cute little town. This whole area is so pretty. I think I'm in love."

"Tag!" Alison started to run again.

The familiar notes of "Egyptian" began to play.

"Darn," Jamie said. "Sorry girls."

"I guess it's hard to get away from real

life, even on vacation." Kendra told herself she wasn't prying. It was a simple, polite comment.

Jamie grimaced. "Tell me about it." She flipped open her phone and took it to a log.

Kendra could hear her voice, but not what she was saying or to whom. While Jamie finished her call, Kendra took the girls on an impromptu nature hike. They spotted a bluebird, an event that seemed to rival a day at Walt Disney World for Hannah, who proclaimed herself a nature lover.

"Rosario tells me about birds," she told Kendra. "He's one of Mommy's friends."

Kendra filed away "one of" and wondered how many men strode through the little girls' lives in an average month.

When Jamie finished her call, they wandered back toward the house, Alison riding piggyback and flogging her mother to go faster, and Hannah holding Kendra's hand. Hannah had slipped it there as naturally as if she had grown up with Kendra.

"What does Riva think of the girls?" Kendra asked after Alison and Hannah had gone to peer under the porch to see if Black Beauty had returned.

"You're not going to lecture me, are you?"

"Wasn't planning on it. Should I?"

"I won't let her see them."

This took Kendra by surprise. "You mean they haven't met their grandmother, either? Don't tell me you had to prove yourself to Riva, too?"

"Before I let her near them, she has to prove herself to *me.* She's off her medication again. Has been for a couple of years, as far as I can tell. But you probably know that. The girls wouldn't understand what was happening, and I don't think I can handle it. Even when she's stable, Riva's not good for me. But, of course, you know that. She can shred me into a thousand pieces in a matter of minutes."

Kendra knew Jamie didn't mean shred by criticism. She was talking about Riva's wrenching dramatic abilities. Riva could make a strong man weep by recounting a trip to the spa. Their mother could hold an audience in thrall or rally troops for war, and she could do it without a single genuine emotion. She felt everything and she felt nothing. She was the psychological equivalent of Typhoid Mary, a woman who could infect everyone in sight and continue undeterred.

"Maybe that explains why she's so quiet when your name comes up," Kendra said. "She doesn't want me to know that the girls are strangers to her, too."

"That's not the way I want it. But I've learned what I want the world to be like has very little to do with the way it really is." Jamie's phone sang again.

"None of these calls are from Riva, are they?"

"They're from a friend. And I have to take them. Excuse me."

Kendra was sitting on the porch steps and Jamie was still on the phone when a familiar pickup drove into the clearing. Kendra finished explaining to Hannah why crawling under the porch to leave a bowl of milk and Oreos for the snake was not an option. Alison was glued to Kendra's side, a dead weight against her.

"But you said he's not poisonous," Hannah argued.

"That doesn't mean he won't bite. Besides, I don't think snakes eat cookies or drink milk." Kendra raised her hand in greeting to Cash, who got down from the cab and started toward them.

Today Cash wore a dark green T-shirt

tucked neatly into khakis, and he carried a brown portfolio under his arm. As he passed, his gaze flicked appreciatively toward Jamie. Still on her call, she smiled at him, and the air warmed appreciably.

"How's it going?" Cash rested one foot on the bottom step and ruffled Hannah's hair.

"Do snakes drink milk?" Hannah asked.

"No, but they suck eggs."

"Aunt Kendra, can we—"

"Nope," Kendra said. "But I'll tell you what. We'll put a couple of eggs outside tonight, and then we'll see if they're gone by morning. But only if you promise you won't go outside and check when the lights go out."

Hannah considered. "Okay, but remember, I have not said a thing about the window." She took her sister by the hand and led her up the stairs into the house.

"Your sister?" Cash nodded toward Jamie.

"Yes." She thought how odd this was. For all practical purposes, yesterday morning she'd been an orphan. Today she was a sister *and* an aunt, plotting snake strategies with a child she had never been allowed to know or discuss.

She noted that Jamie was slipping her phone back in her pocket. Kendra waited until she joined them, and introduced Cash. Jamie held out her hand. Kendra had seen her mother make the same graceful gesture. Queen Riva acknowledging the knights of the realm. Queen Riva choosing which knight would wear her colors.

"I'm Jamie Dunkirk." She made no attempt to brush her hair off her face or straighten her plaid shirt. But all the same, she came on to him.

Kendra watched it happen, fascinated and appalled. She could not put her finger on exactly how the signals were sent. The way Jamie shifted her weight, perhaps. The way she thrust one hip forward, straightened her back so her small shapely breasts pressed against her shirt. Something about the way her eyes swept slowly across his face, lingering for just the tiniest part of a second on Cash's nicely formed lips. Maybe something about the way Jamie's own lips angled by degrees.

Kendra knew she was watching a master at work. She had been trained well.

"Pleased to meet you, ma'am," Cash said. "Were those your little girls?"

"Yes." Jamie looked over her shoulder. "Where have they gone?"

"Inside," Kendra said. "Probably to count eggs."

"They've talked you into something, haven't they."

"Hannah could talk a centipede into an extra set of legs."

"Her father's a defense attorney. You should see him with a jury. Alison will probably be every bit as bad. *Her* father can talk his way into any poker game in the world. Last I heard, he was making a lot of money doing it."

Kendra thought that had been neatly done. In her own way, Jamie had insinuated she was no longer with either man. She was free to pursue Cash, if she chose.

"They're real little beauties," Cash said.

She smiled as if he'd complimented her. "Smart, too, and sweet. I'm lucky."

"Looks to me like they're lucky, too."

Kendra could not stand another moment of this. "Cash and his father are going to do some renovation work for me."

"Really?" Jamie's smile widened. "You

mean you're not happy with the place just the way it is?"

"Not as happy as she's going to be once we finish up." Cash offered the portfolio to Kendra. "I've just put a few things together for you, and some rough sketches to go with them. *Rough* is the key word. This is just to get you thinking. But since time's a little short here, I wanted to get things rolling."

"Why is time short?" Jamie asked.

"We had a window in our schedule, but it closes soon. We'll still be working here, but our crews will also be working on other jobs."

"They're going to take down a barn a couple of miles away and use the logs to add on," Kendra said.

"Oh, imagine that." Jamie's eyes sparkled. "It's going to be glorious. I can't wait to see what you're planning."

Kendra honestly couldn't tell if Jamie was just trying to impress Cash—who was, she had to admit, worth impressing—or if her sister really was excited.

"The barn's coming down as we speak," Cash said. "They'll start hauling it this way come tomorrow."

"The girls will love that. Maybe we can drive over a little later and watch them take it down."

"You do that." Cash turned to Kendra. She thought he looked sorry to be pulling his gaze from Jamie's. "I ran out of time yesterday, but I've got what I need to finish up the railing. Mind if I do it now?"

"Of course not. And thanks, it's making things a lot easier for me already." Kendra stood to go inside.

"Why don't you send the girls out, Ken?" Jamie said. "We'll watch Cash work. They'll get a kick out of it."

Kendra wondered exactly who was going to enjoy watching him work the most.

Forty-five minutes later, she was working on the list of what she'd learned about Leah Spurlock, when Isaac called. Ten minutes ago, Jamie and the girls had followed Cash down Fitch Crossing to see the barn being dismantled and loaded on trucks. Tomorrow the logs would arrive. Considering the way Jamie and Cash had looked at each other, Kendra expected at least another hour of contemplative silence.

"How are you doing?" Isaac asked after a brief greeting.

"It's Friday. Aren't you at work?"

"I have a break."

Because hope is a hard emotion to banish, she waited for him to say he had missed her and needed to make contact. But she didn't wait long, because it wasn't going to happen.

"I'm doing fine." She put down her notepad, realizing how much easier it was to give her thoughts over to blank paper than to the man she had vowed to love, honor and cherish.

"It's been cold and rainy here. Are you having a decent spring?"

"It's fine." She pictured him deleting e-mail as they spoke. Isaac always did at least two things at once. Maybe he was signing letters, or penciling in appointments on his desk calendar.

"Is anything new?"

"You might say that."

He answered right away, as if he really *was* listening. "What's up?"

"Jamie's here."

For a moment he didn't respond. Then he made a noise deep in his throat, almost a laugh. "You've got to be kidding. You invited her?"

"No, I must have left a trail of bread crumbs."

"You're supposed to be taking it easy."

"She's here to take care of me."

There was a silence. She could almost hear him thinking.

"What's she like?" he asked at last.

"Beautiful. Charming. If I wasn't such a cynic, I'd say she's sincere."

"You're not a cynic. You've been burned."

"She has *two* daughters, Isaac. And she's a college student. The children are just . . ." She didn't know what else to say.

"Pretty messed up?"

"No. Amazing. A peek into eternity."

This time the silence spoke volumes.

"You need to come and meet them," Kendra said. "This might be the only chance you'll ever have."

"If it's the only chance, then it's hardly important."

She felt as if he'd hit her with both fists. "Fine."

"I didn't mean that the way it sounded. That's part of why I was calling, anyway. I wondered if you wanted company this weekend."

There were many things that could be said about Isaac, but he was not a liar. He didn't stretch the truth, and he didn't bend it to make life more palatable. If he said he had planned to come, he'd planned to come.

"I'd like you here," she said.

"Then I'll be over in the morning. Tell me what you want me to bring."

She'd been making a mental list. She checked it off now. A box of clothes she'd left in her closet. Another set of sheets. The few antiques she had bought could wait until the renovations were over. She recited the full list.

"I guess Jamie and her kids are keeping you busy," he said.

"That and the renovation."

"So you're going through with it?"

"You might be lucky tomorrow and see the barn logs delivered."

"That sounds like a good reason not to come."

"I've been visiting people, too. And I've found out some things about your family."

No response. She pressed on. "Your

grandmother sounds like a remarkable woman." She decided not to repeat the accusations Rachel had made to Manning. "A hard worker, a good person. Your mom sounds like she had her share of problems, chiefly that she didn't really fit in here. I think it was probably the times. It was hard for a young woman to find a place for herself in a small community like this. Unless she wanted to marry and raise a family."

"I don't know why this fascinates you so."

His tone bothered her. He sounded as if he were addressing a child who had an unreasonable interest in fairy tales or superheroes.

"It fascinates me so," she said carefully, "because it might be the only way I'm allowed into your life. From everything I can tell, all the other routes are completely sealed."

She was sorry the moment she'd finished her sentence, but she refused to take it back. She had spent too much of their marriage edging around the truth, which was that she wanted more than this man was ever going to give her.

"If you think that's a route to anything, you're mistaken. My birth family has nothing to do with who I am. You're welcome to peel and probe, just don't involve me. You're the one who's interested."

"The fact that you're not speaks volumes."

"The fact that you're pushing me when it's *my* family and *my* life speaks louder."

They never fought. Even now, both of them sounded reasonable and calm. No one listening would have understood the nuances.

"I'm living here," she said. "And the cabin is filled with ghosts."

"Just don't expect me to rub shoulders with them tomorrow."

"You're still planning to come?"

"I'll be there."

"Then do me a favor and pick up presents for the girls."

"Do I have the foggiest idea what little girls like?"

She waited, refusing to beg.

"How old are they?" he asked at last.

"Almost three, and six going on forty."

"Suggestions?"

"Yes, use your imagination."

She was still staring at the wall an hour later when she heard the slam of a car door.

As promised by the weatherman, the skies had darkened as the afternoon progressed. The girls were windblown and rosy cheeked. Alison looked as if she was two steps from exhaustion, rubbing her eyes with the back of her hand in a universal gesture even a woman without children understood.

"What fun," Jamie said. "And those logs? They're just amazing. *Country Home Magazine*, eat your heart out. You'll be a feature article once it all comes together. Which will be a very long time from now, by the way, no matter what these guys tell you."

Jamie swung Alison into her arm, and the little girl nestled her head against her mother's shoulder. "I've got a couple of pooped dumplings here. Even Hannah says she'd like some quiet time. Will it be a problem if I put them in for a nap? We'll blow up the mattresses."

Kendra was glad Jamie realized how tired they were. "Put them in my bed. They'll rest better there."

"I brought a plastic sheet. Just in case."

"Good thinking. And there's a Laundromat in driving distance."

"That's what we'll do, then. Hear that, girls? Off to bed you go. You'll be camping in Aunt Kendra's room. Very special, don't you think?"

The girls went without fuss.

After about ten minutes, Jamie returned to the other wing. "We had to have story-time," she said. "And it had to be a story about a snake. I considered Adam and Eve, but the introduction of evil into the world doesn't seem like the best thing right before a nap."

"What did you tell them?"

"Hannah decided she would tell the story. Something about eggs and milk and Oreos. It sounded like a recipe."

While she had been waiting, Kendra brewed tea. She remembered the way Jamie had liked it for their tea parties. Very sweet, diluted with milk. It brought home the distance between them, since she had no idea how this grown-up Jamie drank it.

Jamie lifted her mug in a toast. "To a few moments of peace and quiet. Tell me, are we wearing you down? Because that was not my intention. But I forget sometimes how exhausting children can be."

"It's wonderful to have them here." Kendra realized she meant it; when they were gone again, she would wonder about them all the time.

Jamie flopped into a chair. "So tell me more about the cabin and what you're planning to do."

Kendra gave her the basics, skipping over her developing obsession with Isaac's family.

"Have you looked at the stuff Cash brought you?"

Kendra hadn't even slipped off the elastic band. "No, would you like to see?"

"Are you kidding? This is what I live for."

Kendra rose to retrieve it. "You're studying architecture and interior design. What led you in that direction?"

"I won a scholarship based on a drawing I did."

For some reason Kendra hadn't considered the fact that her sister hadn't had clear access to their father's estate. The money had been put in trust for them, and neither Kendra nor Jamie were to be given control until their twenty-eighth birthdays. Jamie still had a year to go.

"Why did you need a scholarship?" Kendra asked. "Jimmy's trustees would have okayed educational expenses. Or I would have helped you. Even Riva would have done what she could."

"I didn't want anyone poking around in my life, setting conditions, keeping track of my friends or my grade point. Besides, if it had been that easy, I wasn't sure it would mean what it needed to. So I've done the education a little at a time, loans, scholarships. Of course, knowing I can pay everything back in one fell swoop next year is cheating a little. But I can't help almost being rich."

"You've been at this a while, then?"

"Five years. I have a part-time job and, of course, the girls. I took a year off after Alison was born. It all added up. Her father pays support and child care while I'm in classes. Hannah's father is even more generous, as long as he doesn't actually have to spend time with her. I rent a little house, nothing fancy, but it has a big yard and a playroom. Not the priorities I envisioned when I was a little girl yearning for a home of my own. I imagined wild seacoasts, crystal chandeliers, marble terraces. I got a jungle gym and chain-link fencing."

"Sorry?"

"Are you kidding? I know we're an unconventional family. I know so far I've picked men like Jimmy, daredevils, fast talkers, guys with short-term memory loss whenever it comes to really being there. I've got a way to go before I perfect the fine art of mate selection."

Kendra couldn't comment, since her own selection was now in question. Was the fact that Isaac was the polar opposite of their father what had attracted her to him in the first place?

"I like to think Alison was just meant to be, even if she wasn't in the plans," Jamie said. "If that makes any sense."

"I don't know what makes sense." Kendra took Cash's sketches and lists out of the portfolio. "But you'll get to see my choice tomorrow. Isaac's coming up for the weekend."

"Really? That's terrific." Jamie sounded genuinely delighted. "Let's do a cookout, Ken. Won't that be fun? The girls love to cook out."

"I don't have a grill."

"I'll buy a little one tomorrow, and steaks and stuff for salad. My housewarming present. But what you really need is a built-in barbecue. Add that to the renovations.

Maybe out that way." She gestured to the river side of the cabin. "Please tell me you're planning a series of decks? It's going to be the most wonderful place to entertain."

"Let's spread this out on the table." Kendra took her pile of papers and did just that. "Cash said they were rough." She smoothed one with the back of her hand. "Looks like he's right. But the general idea is here."

Jamie bent over to see what they had. "You're lucky they have time to do it. Isaac's on board?"

"Isaac would just as soon burn the place down as look at it. It's mine to do whatever I choose."

Jamie nodded as if she understood, which of course she didn't. But, wisely, she asked no questions.

"So, let's see." She took the first drawing and put it on top of the pile. "Okay, here we have a sketch of the cabin. Funky at best, and basically not a place you'll want to hang your hat very often once you move back to the city. It also doesn't begin to take advantage of the views or the river, particularly the river, and it's not historically important or interesting." She looked up. "You're sure you want to keep the cabin?"

"I'm sure."

"This land must be worth a small fortune. Let's make it worth more." Jamie put the first drawing at the bottom of the pile. "Okay, here's his first idea."

Kendra realized immediately that she had no ability whatsoever to look at a sketch and turn it into a house in her mind. She might as well have been looking at a geometry problem. She saw angles and shapes and lines, but nothing like a house.

"What do you think?" Jamie asked.

"I think you need to explain it to me. Apparently I'm spatially challenged."

"Oh, something I can do that you can't. A little sister's fondest dream."

Jamie began to explain. This was a porch. This was a deck. This was the addition overlooking the river. This was some kind of channel down to a catch basin on the side.

"Very perfunctory, very ordinary," Jamie decreed once she had finished her explanation. "Just the kind of thing someone would come up with on short notice. Let's talk atmosphere. What exactly will you want when you come up here for the weekend? Not rooms or laundry facilities. But what will you need right here?" Jamie put her fist over her heart.

"Peace. Contemplation. A place to breathe."

Jamie continued to ask questions, sifting through the drawings as she did. She found one she liked better and held it up for Kendra's inspection, pointing out all the salient features.

"Now this one does Cash credit," she said. "This is probably his dream plan, the one he'd like to build but assumes you won't want to commit to. He's giving you options."

"So this is the most daring?"

"Not nearly daring enough. Come on, let's tramp through the undergrowth before the rain starts in earnest. Pray Black Beauty is off taking a snakey nap somewhere in the woods."

By the time they returned half an hour later, the rain had begun, and Kendra had realized her sister had genuine talent and imagination. The house Jamie envisioned took full advantage of every view and mood, a side porch with a view of the woods for peace, a series of decks overlooking the river for contemplation, a pond and stream where Cash had merely planned drainage and Jamie envisioned a quiet meditation area. A wall of windows with nothing but sky and water beyond and light filtering inside. A master bedroom and bath that Kendra would never want to leave. A study with vistas that would make writing a secondary activity to pondering the universe.

Jamie flopped on the sofa as thunder rumbled in the distance. The storm promised to be a good one.

"The trick is to blend the old with the new. I think you need to give a sense that the cabin has been here from the dawn of creation and that the finished house will be here into eternity."

Kendra sat down beside her. "Pretty lofty."

Jamie gave Kendra a spontaneous hug, then immediately moved away. "I have a vested interest, of course. You have to expand so we can come and visit and I won't have to worry about the effect we'll have. I have a personal interest in the guest suite, which is what this room should be. Once you open up the back of the house, you're not going to care about this porch, but your guests will have their own retreat."

Kendra could almost see it. Jamie and her daughters, welcome guests, the family Kendra had never really had. A chance to see the girls grow up. A chance to know Jamie again.

"Egyptian," a song Kendra had loved as a teenager, began to play. She was beginning to despise it.

Jamie didn't look happy. "I'm not a big fan of cell phones."

"Can't you just turn it off?"

"The real world is still out there." She stood and carried the telephone toward the door.

"Go ahead and take your call in here," Kendra said. "You'll get soaked on the porch."

"This could go on. I'll stay close to the house." She snapped the phone open and spoke into it.

Jamie was almost at the door when there was a lull, one of those charged moments before the next fusillade of thunder. Kendra heard her sister's softly voiced words.

"I don't care what kind of crank you can get hold of tomorrow. That's a day away. Tomorrow's definitely not the deal we made. You want to be the one to disappoint Rosario?"

The door closed behind her; the thunder broke.

Kendra asked herself how she could have been such a fool.

CHAPTER TEN

Kendra didn't sleep well. In an early morning dream, she relived a scene from her childhood. She was seven again, and Riva had promised to take her to the circus at Madison Square Garden. Even at that young age, Kendra had learned not to believe anything she heard, training that would serve her well in her chosen career.

When Riva saw that her daughter didn't believe her, she took a knife, sliced the tip of her forefinger and made the sign of the cross in blood on the inside of her wrist as a solemn promise.

Then she left the house and didn't return for a week.

The dream was a faithful rendition of history, except that after Riva disappeared, the dream child nailed all the doors and windows of the Manhattan brownstone shut.

Kendra awakened with a pounding in her head.

She knew why the memory had surfaced. Yesterday Jamie had come inside from her telephone call and started a pot of homemade chicken soup. Watching her chop celery, onion and garlic, Kendra had wondered where her sister had learned to cook. Did Jamie hawk quarts of chicken soup along with meth and crack? Did she sell apple pies like the one she produced later in the evening to heroin addicts craving sugar with their drug of choice?

She tried to imagine her sister with such a dire need for money that she was organizing drug deals on the telephone. Her conclusion was twofold. Either she had misunderstood her sister's words—possible with the storm overhead—or Jamie was involved with a man named Rosario who was trading her need for drugs, money and love by having Jamie do some of his dirty work.

Kendra didn't know the sum of Jamie's moral lapses. After Hannah's birth, Kendra had considered hiring an investigator to find her sister. In the end, she had decided against it. If Jamie had discovered that Kendra was keeping tabs on her, any hope of a reunion would have died. She did know it was likely Jamie had been involved in the drug scene in Brooklyn. Rumors had surfaced, and although she knew better than to believe them outright, that didn't mean she discounted them.

She hadn't asked Jamie about the call. There were two little girls involved now. Did she want her sister and her nieces to disappear forever? Or did Kendra want to be the first person Jamie thought of if the children ever needed help or a place to live?

She woke, slept, woke. When she woke for the last time and found that the sky was bright outside, she also discovered she had company.

"There is only one egg now," Hannah said from her perch at the end of the bed. She was dressed in yellow flannel pajamas, and the top was inside out. "And there were two last night when we went to sleep. How does a snake suck eggs? Does a snake have lips to suck with?"

Kendra sat up and threw her arms out in a good morning stretch. Alison, in blue, was settled in beside her sister. "I've never gotten close enough to a snake's mouth that I could tell you," Kendra said.

"Something else might have taken the other egg. I think we must stand guard tonight."

"I think we must get a good night's sleep," Kendra said. "Some things have to remain a mystery."

"When I grow up, I plan to solve every mystery."

"Mz-ree," Alison said, with a decisive nod. "Me too."

"A pair of sleuths." Kendra leaned forward and gave them both a quick, sleepy hug. "Where's your mom?"

"She was up late."

Kendra suspected the cell phone had gotten some serious usage. "How did you sleep?"

"I never sleep. Alison snores."

"Is that true, Alison?"

"Schnore." Alison made a noise like a donkey snuffling.

"Yikes. I wouldn't sleep, either," Kendra said.

"Alison would like a story. I am neutral."

Kendra managed not to laugh. "What kind of story?"

"She's partial to fairy tales. But the ending has to be happy, or she cries."

"I know how she feels. Do you like the story of the ugly duckling?"

Hannah crawled across the bed so she was sprawling beside Kendra, and, not to be outdone, Alison took the other side. "Tell it and we'll see."

Ten minutes later, after adding a wealth of detail Hans Christian Andersen had never intended and downplaying the way the poor baby swan had been treated, Kendra wrapped it up. "So the poor ugly duckling wasn't a duckling at all, but a beautiful swan. And all the swans were so glad to see him, he had friends forever."

"End!" Alison shouted.

The door opened and Jamie stuck her head inside. "Someone kidnapped my little girls. Their beds are empty."

"Mommy!" Alison slid down and ran to Jamie, and Jamie swung her up in her arms, planting a resounding kiss on the little girl's cheek.

"How's my dumpling?"

"Ducks is bad!"

"That wasn't quite the message I intended." Kendra watched Hannah join the tableau in the doorway for a hug.

"Did they wake you?" Jamie asked.

"I think they sneaked in to use the bathroom and couldn't resist watching me sleep."

"I'm going to follow their path—unless you need it first?"

"Go ahead."

Jamie stopped on the way across the floor. "It's nice seeing the three of you that way. The girls need family."

Kendra wondered exactly what the girls might need from her in the future. It hardly bore thinking about.

A burgundy minivan had just pulled out of the cabin's drive when Isaac arrived. He glimpsed the silhouette of a woman and a child sitting high in a car seat before the van turned away from him on Fitch Crossing Road.

Kendra's sister and her children.

He hoped he hadn't missed the party.

He'd always been curious about Jamie. He knew the basics. Younger, pretty, confused, amoral, gone. Kendra had said Jamie looked a lot like Riva and seemed to be following her path. He'd met Kendra's mother twice. His own mother had been docile enough to seem comatose. She had worked hard to appear dowdy so she could forestall his father's accusations that she was trying to attract other men.

The last time he'd seen Riva Dunkirk, she'd been arrayed in leopard-print silk, black leather and rhinestones, and her laughter—not warranted by anything happening at the table—had filled the room. The eyes of every man in the restaurant had been riveted on her, either in horror or frank admiration. No one was ever lukewarm about Riva.

Kendra rarely talked about Jamie. He had never encouraged revelations, but not because he wasn't interested. The fact that Jamie had hurt his wife infuriated him, and that distressed him. Having spent his formative years with a man for whom anger was a way of life, repression seemed the wisest course.

When the van no longer blocked the driveway, he pulled into the clearing and parked. Nothing seemed to have changed, except that now there was a railing along the steps, something he was relieved to see. Since Kendra's departure, he'd had two breath-stealing, heart-stopping nightmares about his wife, and both of them involved her lying on the ground in this very place, with no one nearby to help her. If he continued that train of thought, the anger he felt over her decision to live here would ruin this visit. And sending their marriage whirling further into a downward spiral was not the point of his trip to Toms Brook.

He didn't get out of the car immediately. Despite himself, he sat behind the wheel and wondered about the woman who had given birth to him. What had it been like for Rachel Spurlock to grow up here? To his eyes, the cabin and surrounding land weren't picturesque but blighted by poverty and gloom. Was it any wonder Rachel had abandoned Virginia's rural countryside to find another life? Had Leah Spurlock Jackson really been surprised to lose her daughter?

Leah was more of a mystery. Kendra swore she was well thought of here. Yet no one seemed to know where she had come from, or why. Kendra's fascination with the subject troubled him, but apparently it had also reignited his own childhood fantasies, normal fantasies for an adopted child, particularly normal for a child in a difficult situation.

As a boy, he'd often dreamed about the people who had given him away. His father insisted his birth parents had been too poor and ignorant, too immoral, to raise a child. His mother—when his father was absent—explained that his father was mistaken. Isaac's birth parents surely had loved him and wanted the best for their son. Despite wishing for the latter, of course he had known better. If his birth parents had had his interests at heart, they wouldn't have sent him to live with Colonel Grant Taylor.

Now he was an adult. He understood that to anyone else his father had looked like an admirable candidate for adoption. He understood that women with no desire or means to raise a child sometimes found themselves pregnant, and in an era when abortion was clearly an option, his birth mother had chosen to give him life.

Those observations should have soothed the soul of the little boy inside him who had felt abandoned and trapped. Maybe they would have, if Kendra hadn't continued to ask questions, to come here to try to make a second home, to insist, without speaking the words, that he had to confront his past and somehow transform his life.

A door opened, and she stepped out on the porch wearing dark jeans and a rust-colored shirt over a black top with thin straps and a low neckline. His body stirred to life. Never really curvaceous, she was still so thin from the shooting and aftermath that now her figure was almost boyish. Shorter hair made her neck seem longer and emphasized the starker planes of her cheekbones and jaw.

And still, to him, she had never looked more desirable.

"You can come in," she called, leaning over the railing. "I don't bite."

He got out. "I was just admiring the view."

"That's certainly new."

"I don't mean the cabin."

"Compliments are in short supply around here. I like the sound of that one."

He started toward the porch. "Does your sister have a dark red minivan?"

"She just left. She forgot ice cream, and the girls were bereft. Jamie's determined this will be a celebration."

He tested the new railing and found it

sturdy enough to keep her safe. Up on the porch, he put his arms around her and pulled her close. He kissed her lightly on the lips. "You've gained a little weight, but not enough."

Her hazel eyes glinted with gold in the sunlight. "How can you tell?"

"I know every inch of you."

Her eyes searched his. "Not lately."

His heart was beating too fast, but his voice was steady. "Long-distance sex is hard to manage."

"Jamie's coming back in a few minutes."

He hadn't made love to her since before the accident, and now, despite wanting her—the proof was probably evident—he was also relieved that it was going to be impossible today as well. In subtle, indefinable ways, Kendra was a stranger to him now. And a man did not take a stranger to bed unless he was sure of the ground rules. At least this man, forever cautious and analytical, didn't.

"I wanted to stay tonight," he said, "but I'm leaving for Philadelphia tomorrow morning. I have to go home after dinner and pack."

"Conference? Business meeting?"

"A meeting. Someone cancelled and stuck me with it."

"Ouch." She slipped her arms around his neck and kissed him quickly again before she stepped away. "You've been working too hard."

"How can you tell?"

"Honestly? You don't look rested. I'm guessing maybe you're staying up until midnight and getting up by six. And I've called a few times on weekends—you haven't been home. You're going in to the office?"

Some part of him was aware how odd this was. Two weeks had passed since he'd seen her. Yet they were acting like friends instead of lovers. He wondered if she felt as at sea as he did, or if this was just the natural progression of a marriage that would end with a whimper someday in the not-so-distant future. They talked about sex, but he wondered if she was as confused about the etiquette of the separated as he was.

"There's no reason to stay home with you away," he said. "Last Sunday I biked part of the C&O Towpath."

"How far did you get?"

"Just Great Falls and back." It was the first time in a long time he had pushed himself hard enough to chase away everything except the sting of sore muscles, the roar of blood through his veins.

"I love that trip." She smiled sadly. "I wonder if I'll ever be able to make it again."

"How do you feel?"

She folded her arms over her chest. "A little stronger, I think. I'm doing my exercises religiously, walking as much as I can. I have a referral to a local therapist to oversee the recovery. The limp is no better, but then, it might never be."

"And resting? Eating?"

"Both. My neighbors have kept me fed. I've never seen so much food. And Jamie's a good cook. She's been cooking up a storm for tonight. I'm not sure where she learned it. Not from Riva, that's for sure." She inclined her head toward the cabin door. "Let's go inside. Would you like something to drink?"

He noted that she seemed steadier, even if her foot still dragged. Not too many weeks ago he had wondered if she would ever walk again.

"I'll make iced tea." Kendra went straight to the kitchen, and he followed, leaning against a counter to watch her. The kitchen area was so small that he took up far too much of it.

He tried to make himself smaller, pulling his feet closer to the counter. "So, before she gets back, tell me about Jamie."

"I want your opinion, and I don't want to contaminate it." She tossed him a lemon from the refrigerator. "Knives are in the drawer to your left."

He set the lemon on a cutting board and fished for a paring knife. "What can we talk about, then?"

"I thought you might like to see some of the ideas for the renovation."

"Did the logs ever arrive?"

She filled cobalt-blue glasses with ice from a freezer tray and tea from a matching pitcher. "They've postponed delivery until tomorrow. Some snag with removing the final few feet."

He presented her with lemon slices, and she added them to the tea, along with several spoonfuls of sugar. "From what I hear about building projects, there's *always* one snag after another."

"Make yourself comfortable. I'll get the plans."

He didn't want to start a fight by pointing

out that he couldn't be less interested. Clearly this was a major undertaking for Kendra. What faster way to doom their future than to refuse to see what she was hoping to do here?

She returned and spread papers on the coffee table. "Jamie is studying architecture and interior design, and she's really got a good eye. On the other hand, the drawings are Greek to me."

He sat quietly while she explained the possibilities, the choices, the potential. His discomfort grew. He saw immediately that Kendra was not simply planning to add another bedroom and a larger living area. This house promised to be a showplace. For her, the Foggy Bottom condo would never again be more than a convenient place to sleep. Home would be here.

"What do you think?" she asked at last.

"Are you planning to move here permanently?"

She looked up from the plans. "I'm just taking everything a step at a time. Does it seem that way to you? That I'm doing this to get away from you?"

He never answered those kinds of questions. "It doesn't feel like it has anything much to do with me."

"It's your land. I've always wanted you to be involved in everything we do here."

He was saved from answering by a clatter on the porch. Two little girls burst into the room. "We have peanut butter chocolate and blueberry sundae," the older said. "Are you Uncle Isaac?"

Isaac stood and watched a graceful young woman who looked nothing like Kendra and everything like Kendra's mother walk into the room.

"Yes, you have to be Isaac," she said, following up on her daughter's words. "Of course I'm Jamie. The munchkin with the ice cream is Hannah, and the urchin with the curls is Alison."

The munchkin and the urchin looked friendly enough, although he knew little about children and had thought even less about them.

Until recently.

Jamie held out her hand, and he shook it, murmuring all the acceptable responses. She flashed dimples just like her mother's, but not with the coy and somehow predatory expression that accompanied Riva's.

She looked genuinely happy to meet him, as if something good had just walked into her life.

"There is a snake under the house," the munchkin said. "His name is Black Beauty, and he is to be admired from a distance. He sucks eggs but does not eat Oreos."

Isaac looked at Kendra, who was watching him. "Snake?"

She shrugged.

"Black Beauty?" he asked Hannah.

"If I were a snake, I would marry him."

"If you were a snake, he would be lucky to have you."

Hannah smiled, and dimples flashed. "Alison and I can show you where he lives. You must hold her hand, though. She is still a little girl."

Jamie tried to intercede. "Uncle Isaac just got here, Hannah. He's probably tired from the trip."

Isaac held out his hand. "Not too tired to see if Black Beauty is visiting."

"Oh, he doesn't visit," Hannah said. "It's his house. We are the visitors. He was here first."

"BB's a black rat snake," Kendra assured him. "Not poisonous."

Isaac had a little girl holding each hand now. He felt like a giant. "We'll be back in a few minutes. Jamie, I'm looking forward to hearing all about your trip down here."

"And probably a lot more," she said.

His eyes met hers. He nodded. She smiled again. He was a cautious man who had every reason to distrust Kendra's sister.

He found himself smiling back.

CHAPTER ELEVEN

Kendra had dreaded Jamie's reunion "celebration." She'd imagined Isaac stiff and unnatural with the girls and suspicious of her sister's motives. Instead, he seemed entranced by her nieces, particularly Hannah.

As a gift, he presented Hannah and Alison with a bright red bag filled with bubble wands of all shapes and sizes, then taught them to make bubble solution with dishwashing soap and the addition of glycerin. Clearly, somewhere in the midst of a busy day, he had read up on the chemistry of this particular childhood pleasure.

Outside in the sunlight, the girls spent the better part of two hours creating bubbles. Or, more accurately, Hannah produced and Alison chased. While he watched, Isaac assembled the new charcoal grill and set it far enough away from Bubble Central for safety.

Jamie was tireless. She prepared a pasta salad with a balsamic poppy seed dressing she made herself, shucked sweet corn from Florida, and snapped the ends off Michigan asparagus. She baked a hot-water sponge cake to top with fresh whipped cream, then sliced strawberries and lightly sugared them to draw out the flavor. She answered her phone at least twice, although Kendra couldn't hear the conversations. Jamie made sure of that.

Kendra settled herself on the new porch furniture with a tall glass of Jamie's homemade lemonade and a book on signature quilts. She didn't get far. She was distracted by the sight of her husband with the girls. Isaac, the same man who had sidelined discussions of raising a family by saying he knew nothing about children and sworn he didn't have time to learn.

He would make an excellent father. She saw that now. The girls already adored him. He was patient, but, even more so, fascinated, as if he had discovered a new species in the most remote corner of the

Amazon rain forest and was determined to preserve every chromosome strand.

The irony wasn't lost on her. Isaac would make an excellent father. She was fairly certain she would make an excellent mother. Unfortunately, children were no longer an option.

"I think everything's almost done." Jamie came out to the porch, wiping her hands on a checkered dish towel. She had flour on one cheek; she wore another dish towel as an apron, tucked into a peasant skirt. Kendra almost expected her to yell for Laura, Mary and Pa. Time for supper at *The Little House on the Prairie.*

"Come sit with me," Kendra said. "You've been working too hard."

Jamie perched on the edge of the porch and leaned against a post. "Cooking's recreation for me. And let's face it, children aren't the best critics, so cooking for you is a treat. Hannah wants everything exactly the same way every time. Add a quarter of a teaspoon of something as exotic as oregano, and she'll starve herself out of spite."

"Where did you learn to cook?"

"I began by doing food prep at a chain

restaurant and worked my way to line cook before I started back to school. I even thought about pursuing cooking as a profession, then I won that contest I mentioned."

"I wonder what Jimmy would say about his daughters? Me in the same business he couldn't wait to get rid of. You chopping veggies and broiling fish."

"At least newspapers are in the bloodline. I doubt any other Dunkirk or Delacroix ever went to bed with the stink of raw onions and garlic on her hands."

"Can you see the horror on Riva's face?"

Both women burst into laughter, and it was cleansing. That they could laugh at anything about their childhood was a beginning.

"What's so funny?" Isaac came up to the perch to sit next to Jamie. The girls were on their final wand. Their attention spans were admirable but soon to be exhausted.

"Our mother," Jamie said. "Have you met her? And, yes, I know she's not a healthy woman. But we can laugh at the parts of her that are purely perverse, can't we? Lord knows we've cried over them."

"I've met her." Isaac's voice vaulted

higher. " 'Kendra, darling, is this mar-r-r-r-velous creature really your choice for a mate? And to think I believed you had never learned a thing I tried to teach you. And here is this man, this gorgeous, gorgeous man!' "

Kendra was astonished. She had been married to Isaac for six years and she'd never realized what a mimic he was. He had captured their mother exactly.

Jamie was laughing again. "Oh, she didn't! Wait, of course she did. Does she proposition you when Kendra leaves the room?"

Kendra answered that one. "We agreed to synchronize our bladders when Riva's in town. Isaac heads for the bathroom when I do and waits by the ladies room door until I come out."

"Poor Isaac." Jamie wiped her eyes. "And here comes the moment when I'm supposed to say maybe Riva's crazy, but she's really good-hearted underneath. But of course it's not true. She's just who she is. One of a kind. Completely unaware there's another person living on this planet."

Kendra wasn't shocked at the sentiment, but she *was* surprised Jamie was so comfortable with this sad truth. There was no blame in her voice, no self-pity. She wasn't sure that at Jamie's age she had been so aware or forgiving.

"So tell me about your job," Jamie said to Isaac. "I just know a little, and it's fascinating."

Kendra watched Isaac launch into an abbreviated version. He was enjoying himself. Isaac never flirted. Not precisely. But when he liked a woman, he was capable of giving her his undivided attention. Jamie had it now.

Jamie was even more interesting to watch. Despite the jokes at Riva's expense, Jamie had learned a few things from their mother. Although her response to Isaac was subtler than her response to Cash, like Riva, she gloried in male attention. She didn't bat her eyelashes, but she leaned forward, flashed her dimples, used her hands in ways that were almost provocative to illustrate a point.

Kendra wondered if Isaac recognized what was happening.

The girls broke up the conversation. Isaac's wands had worked a miracle, but the miracle had ended. Jamie took them inside to get drinks and celery and carrot sticks so they wouldn't fall apart while the steaks were grilled. Isaac got up to light the coals.

"She's not what I expected." He dusted his hands off on his jeans.

Kendra descended the steps to join him. They walked slowly toward the grill. "No?"

"I like her. I wasn't prepared to. But she's great with the kids. Take it from me, that's the best way to figure out true character."

"She's doesn't believe in rules."

"Sure she does. She just doesn't go around spouting them. Look how well behaved the girls are. The rules are part of the way they live."

They were arguing about how to raise children. She felt a stab of anger, one she didn't want to examine too closely. "Sorry, but the girls rule the roost. Jamie goes along."

"I think you're filtering some of what you see through the lens of your past."

"Oh? Then how's this? I think she's selling drugs." She told him what she had observed and, finally, what she had heard last night.

He was silent until they reached the barbecue grill. "There could be another explanation."

"Isaac, don't you get it? Jamie knows how to make you like her. She was flirting with you. And apparently it's working."

He frowned. "She wasn't flirting. She was being friendly. Don't you think I can tell the difference?"

"Jamie's determined that both of us will like her. She's doing everything imaginable for me. But I've been around people like Jamie before. You can't trust them or anything they say. I was on my way to forgetting that until last night. Then I heard her on the phone."

"So why don't you just have it out with her? Tell her what you heard and ask her what it means."

"I don't want to alienate her. I don't want her to walk out of my life again, not when I've just gotten to know the girls. I need to be there for them. It's a familiar story, isn't it? Families all over the world putting up with things they shouldn't have to, solely because children are involved."

"And now you're going to say she *had* the girls so she could use them as weapons?"

"No, she loves them. I know that. But

what's going to happen to them when she's caught selling meth or crack or angel dust? And if she's selling, is she using? What if one morning Hannah goes in to wake her mother and finds her dead?"

He rested his hands on her shoulders. "I can only tell you what I see. A young mother working hard to raise her children well. A sister trying to reestablish a relationship that means something to her. A vibrant, interesting woman you've missed like hell all the years I've known you. And my wife, who still wants to take care of her baby sister."

"Jamie's the same woman who walked away ten years ago and until now hasn't given me the time of day."

"Is that what this is about, K.C.?"

She changed tack. "Where does the K.C. come from, Isaac? That's what you called me in the early days."

"In the days where we weren't certain of anything except that we couldn't keep our hands off each other?"

"We seem to be doing that part well enough."

He was silent for too long. "I've been afraid of hurting you," he said at last.

"A legitimate fear."

* * *

"Well, I think that went well, didn't it?" Jamie looked tired from an afternoon of cooking, cleaning and managing her daughters. After a truly delicious dinner, Isaac had left for D.C. He had attained favored uncle status. The girls even tried to block his exit.

"Everything was great." Kendra was still simmering, but she refused to examine the reason too closely.

"Are you and Isaac okay, sis? I know it's not my place to ask, but I sensed tension. You can tell me to butt out."

Kendra answered more sharply than she had intended. "I guess if we were okay, I wouldn't be living here."

"I thought you came to get away from the city and recover?"

"That's certainly part of it."

Jamie changed tactics. "I like him. He's pretty buttoned down, but I sense a lot under the surface. Am I wrong?"

Kendra surprised herself by wanting to admit the truth. She took a chance. "I don't know anymore. When we married, I thought that was the perfect combination. Someone who didn't make demands. Someone who would reveal himself a little at a time. Only the last part hasn't turned out to be true."

"Jimmy and Riva did a number on us, didn't they? I looked for love in all the wrong places, and you looked for it in acceptable doses."

Kendra thought that was surprisingly insightful. "Apparently both of us got what we wanted."

"I sure did, but I have the girls, and that makes up for the mistakes. Although it doesn't make up for the people I hurt along the way." She put her hand on Kendra's arm as if she planned to say more. Her cell phone played its tune. "Damn."

"Don't answer it," Kendra said.

"I have to. I'm sorry."

Not as sorry as Kendra was. Clearly nothing was as important to her sister as the person at the other end of the line.

Jamie got up and started down the steps for the clearing. "I'll have a cigarette while I'm at it and kill two birds with one stone."

The expression seemed apt. Kendra felt her anger growing. She wasn't sure at whom it was aimed. Isaac, for discounting her so easily and in so many ways? Jamie, for ably presenting one picture of herself and living another?

Jamie disappeared behind the van. That seemed to be the end of it until a little voice called from inside the cabin. "I don't feel so good. . . ."

Kendra went inside just in time to find Hannah getting off her air mattress.

"Bathroom," she said, hand over her mouth.

Kendra opened the doors and quickly escorted Hannah into the bathroom, and just in time. With efficiency, the child vomited Jamie's excellent meal into the toilet.

Once she finished, Kendra wet a cloth and wiped the little girl's face, then she helped her rinse her mouth in the sink. Hannah was perspiring and trembling, and Kendra put her arms around her. "Feel better?"

Hannah nodded. "Too many strawberries."

Kendra hoped that's all it was. "Do you feel good enough to go back to sleep?"

"Where's Mommy?"

"Outside. I'll tell her you're sick."

Hannah nodded. "Okay."

Kendra knew better than to lift a six-year-old so soon after major surgery. Instead, she guided her across the porch. Jamie was nowhere in sight. She tucked Hannah back into bed and covered her with a light blanket. The little girl's eyelids fluttered shut. Alison was snuffling away.

Kendra waited by the door, but Hannah didn't seem to require anything else. In fact, she looked as if she had already fallen back to sleep.

Outside, Kendra cautiously took the steps and went to find her sister. She could hear Jamie's voice as she approached the van. It hadn't been her intent to eavesdrop—at least, she told herself as much. She wasn't using Hannah's illness as an excuse, but she slowed as she neared the van, and Jamie's words became audible.

"Come on, we've been through that. Either you're with this or you're not. Nobody's going to let you out gracefully. You know darn well what the consequences are if you screw up."

There was silence, then Jamie spoke again. "Fine, that's what you want me to tell Rosario? That you refuse to come through? That you're holding on to the stuff you got and hoping for big money? And you think, for some reason, this has nothing to do with your deal with us?"

Another silence. "Honey, I've been where you are, and I can assure you that all the tears in the world aren't going to make him change his mind. You can't sob your way out of this, and you can't beg. Either you make good on your promises or your life won't be worth living. I can tell you right now, Rosario will turn this over to the big boys, and they don't have his patience or forbearance."

Kendra had heard enough. She rounded the van. "Hang up," she said.

Jamie was startled. Her eyes widened. "Hold on," she said into the telephone. She covered it with her hand. "What's going on?"

"Your daughter's sick. She's back in bed now, but she vomited up her dinner."

"Alison?"

"No, Hannah."

Jamie bit her lip. "Strawberries. Darn it. This happened last time I made shortcake. She doesn't know when to stop."

It all seemed so strange to Kendra. Saint Jamie, of the split personality. One moment threatening someone's life for not turning over drugs to Rosario, the next trying to figure out the cause of her daughter's nausea.

"I'll finish and be there in a minute," Jamie told Kendra.

Kendra snapped. In the split second before she grabbed her sister's cell phone and hurled it into the undergrowth, she realized she was angry at a lot of people, most notably the man who had gunned her down in a parking lot, a man with a list of arrests for drug offenses as well as car theft. A man who had changed the course of her life.

"Don't you think I'm smarter than that? I heard enough of this phone call and another one to know what you're up to. And you will not spend another moment on my property selling drugs or whatever part you're playing in the drug scene now! I've tried to ignore it. I've tried to stay out of it for the sake of your girls. But no more, Jamie! My God, you're as bad as Riva."

Jamie's complexion was pale in the moonlight, but her eyes blazed. "Shouldn't you check out what you think you heard?"

"I know what I heard."

"Funny, as a little girl I remember you telling me never to believe my ears—that I'd be less disappointed that way."

"So what would I have discovered if I'd asked you to explain yourself?"

"That the woman on the other end of the phone was an outpatient in a drug treatment program, and I'm her caseworker. Her name's Trudy. She's relapsing. Our director, Ron Rosario, told me to cut her loose, that she's not ready to quit using for good, but I'm bullheaded, because I used to be right where she is. She told me yesterday she'd bought some stuff on the street and planned to sell it for more money. Even so, I thought I could save her."

Kendra knew what she'd heard. "Rosario will turn her over to the big boys?"

"Yeah, Kendra, the cops. She'll go to jail, and when Rosario finds out she's selling, he'll be the one to turn her in. Trudy knew if she got caught she'd go down. It's the only deal we'll make in the program. We're the final stop, the last hope, and we make sure everybody knows it when they sign on."

Kendra wanted to believe her, but at the same time she was leery. She was also beginning to worry that she, not her sister, had screwed up. "Then why didn't you just tell me what was up?"

Jamie was silent.

"You thought I should just trust you?" Kendra demanded. "Despite all signs to the contrary? You're a virtual stranger, Jamie. You walked out ten years ago. You threatened to disappear forever if I tried to find you. You didn't even tell me about Alison. What was I supposed to think?"

"I'm going to check on my daughter. Then we'll finish this. In the meantime, if you have a flashlight, you can find my phone. I'm not rich yet, and I can tell you that helping addicts put their lives back together doesn't pay nearly as much as I used to make out on the street."

Kendra watched her sister stalk back to the house. Jamie was furious, and if she was telling the truth, Kendra could understand.

If she was telling the truth.

Kendra still couldn't believe her sister. Suspicion was a job hazard, as well as a trait that had been instilled one lie at a time by their mother. And she was running on adrenaline. Her hands were shaking; her heart was pounding too fast. She went to the bushes where the phone had landed and stood at the edge. She had no idea what might be lurking there. With a sigh, she parted the closest ones and began to search.

A few minutes later, with neither snakebite nor rabies to show for her trouble, she located the phone. But she wasn't done. As she had searched, she'd made up her mind. The night was dark, but with the moonlight and a diffuse glow from the porch, there was enough light for her to locate the buttons. She found Call History and pushed "send" to reconnect with Jamie's last caller.

A woman who sounded young and out of breath answered and didn't give her time to speak. "Jamie, my God, what happened? I thought you gave up on me. I'm sorry. My life's a mess. I know it is. Don't abandon me. I've got to make it this time. I know it's my last chance to get clean. Tell me what to do. Tell me how to fix what I've done."

Kendra didn't know what to say. She spoke at last. "Look, this isn't Jamie. It's her sister. Jamie's little girl is sick, but she's going to call you in a while. Hang in there."

The woman began to sob. Kendra closed the phone.

She was staring up at the stars when Jamie came back.

"Hannah's sound asleep," Jamie said.

Kendra held out the phone. "She's waiting for you to call her."

"Trudy called again? You talked to her?"

"No. I called her."

Jamie took the phone. "And?"

"You're telling the truth."

"How nice I passed your test."

" 'Sorry' doesn't begin to cut it, does it?"

"Since I got here, I've tried to tell you in a lot of different ways that I'm sorry for my sorry little life. It doesn't seem to have made much of an impression."

The day had tired Kendra; the anger had tired her more. Her head felt too heavy for her neck. "Call Trudy. I'll be in the bedroom. Come find me when you're ready."

While she waited, Kendra took a shower. As she stood under the water, she remembered the many nights during her childhood when getting Jamie showered had been her responsibility. They were only ten years apart, but Jamie was the closest thing to a child she would ever have. And ever since Jamie's arrival, she had treated her sister like a child, a naughty child who had to be observed, controlled and punished. A child who was going to disappoint her yet again.

She hadn't wanted to let go of the little

girl she'd loved more than anyone in the world. She had been afraid to see the woman.

Kendra was dressed in a long nightgown when Jamie came in.

"Is Trudy going to be okay?" she asked.

"I don't know. Maybe tossing the phone in the bushes was a good thing. She thought I'd finally abandoned her. I'm the only person who hasn't, and she knows it. She says she's flushing the drugs and attending a meeting."

"Meeting?"

"Narcotics Anonymous. I called her sponsor, and he promised to pick her up and make sure she goes. He's going to watch her flush the drugs so I can make sure that's true. But I have to get back to Michigan. I want to get her in our residential program for another stint, and it won't be easy. Rosario's not nearly as squishy as I am."

"Are you going back to help, or are you going back to get away from me?"

Jamie sat on the bed, and Kendra joined her. "Both," Jamie said.

"I can't believe I blew things this badly."

"You're human. You have a lot you can honestly hold against me."

"But I'm your sister. I practically raised you."

"That's where we have a problem. You feel responsible for me. And you're not. You were never my mother. You were a kid, too."

Kendra wondered when she had last felt like a kid.

"We were both victims," Jamie said.

"It's just been so long. Then you show up claiming you want to take care of me. Not much in the way of explanation for all those years away—"

"You want to hear the explanation?"

Kendra wasn't sure anymore.

"I guess I need to tell you anyway. After Brooklyn, I fell about as low as I could and not die from it," Jamie said. "Drugs, booze, sleeping around, selling drugs, selling my body."

Kendra's eyes closed. "Jamie . . ."

"You have no idea what you can do when drugs are the only thing that fill that huge void called life. Once I found myself in a strange house in upstate New York, dumping somebody's trea-sures into a plastic trash bag. It was like I came to for a moment and I couldn't figure out how I had gotten there. I looked inside the bag, and I saw jewelry and what was obviously an incredibly valuable coin collection. Even photographs in sterling frames. I took out one of the photos, clearly old and probably priceless. I still remember it. Two little boys in sailor suits with a schnauzer on the bench between them. And I knew that somebody was going to feel awful about losing that photo. The thing is, I don't remember anything else from that day. I'm sure I just put the frame back in the bag and continued stealing everything that wasn't nailed down."

"You must have been desperate."

"I was arrested. Hannah's father was appointed to represent me. Larry's really not a bad guy. He got me off on a ridiculous technicality and tried to straighten me out. Once the charges were dropped, I conned him into bed, thinking he'd be good for a few weeks of food and lodging while I hustled more drugs. Getting pregnant was nobody's idea. Larry was up front about not wanting to be a father, and he warned me against trying to be a mother."

"But you had Hannah anyway?"

"I went into treatment the day I saw those two lines forming on the test-kit strip. I was pretty far gone, but not so far gone I didn't realize my choices. I could have drugs, or I could have the baby. Larry agreed to pay for the program, but he told me if I failed, he'd make sure I went home from the hospital alone. Luckily, I didn't."

Kendra mulled over the story. "Why didn't you come to me?"

"So you could take care of me? I knew better, Ken. Nobody could rescue me except me. Hannah was a hundred percent healthy when she was born. I won't tell you I didn't try to score drugs in the treatment center, because I did. Lucky for everybody, I failed. By the time I got out, I was on recovery road. I still walk it. It'll never be easy."

"Hannah's six, Jamie."

Jamie traced a line of stitching on the old Lover's Knot quilt that Kendra had brought to her bedroom for safekeeping. "And where have I been? Afraid to let you know how low I sank, and afraid I'd relapse. I had to prove myself. I needed to be sure I was standing on my own feet." She looked up. "And you know what? After tonight, I'd say that was wise."

Tears filled Kendra's eyes. "You didn't

give me a lot to go on. How was I supposed to know?"

"I realize that. But I didn't want to go into my sordid past, not right away. I wanted you to get to know me again and trust what you saw. Then I was going to tell you about the drugs and rehab and my commitment to this program. Every single person on our staff is an addict. Rosario served ten years in prison for dealing."

"I wish you'd told me sooner."

"Maybe I should have, but I came to help you. I thought it would be the right way, the right time, to start a new relationship. And here's the thing I figured out. You don't want *anybody's* help. You've been the big sis too long. You can't let go and let anybody else pitch in. So you found a reason to keep me at arm's length. If I'd been anyone else, wouldn't you just have confronted me and asked what was going on?"

"That's not fair."

"Maybe it's not the whole story, but it's part of it. I hope we can be equals someday." Jamie covered Kendra's hand. "It's all out in the open now. We'll let it sit there, and maybe someday soon, we'll try again."

Kendra turned her hand palm up and

caught her sister's. "You'd better mean that."

"Just once in your life, try believing what you hear."

CHAPTER TWELVE

Isaac arrived home on Saturday night to find his trip to Philadelphia had been cancelled. His cell phone had been out of range; he supposed he would have to choose another provider if he was going to continue to visit Kendra. He wasn't sure how he felt about his needlessly early departure.

Sunday morning, he woke up in a room that echoed with silence to a day with nothing planned. With nothing better to do, he decided to stop by the office to get a stack of documents to work on. At breakfast, he scanned the *Post,* sorry as he did that there was nothing with Kendra's byline. She took her talent for granted, but he had always felt lucky to be married to a woman with both brains and insight.

The drive to ACRE was easy, except for the occasional knots of churchgoers. He watched mothers shepherding children into stone and brick buildings that had stood for decades, even centuries. As a child, he had spent his Sunday mornings at whatever church his father decided they would frequent. As an adult, he hadn't even been willing to walk into one to marry his wife. He and Kendra had been married on the banks of the Potomac by a justice of the peace.

At his desk, he spent an hour answering e-mail, then gathered up his papers. On the way out, he retrieved a can of cat food that was one of a dozen residing in his desk. The chewed-up ginger tabby hadn't exactly become a friend, but he accepted Isaac's offerings as if they were his due. Isaac supposed coming into the office had been as much about feeding the cat as anything.

Usually the cat came out when Isaac called. He never came close, but he made himself known. Today there was no sign of him. Isaac knew better than to be concerned. The cat was a veteran of city streets. Perhaps the pickings here had diminished in proportion to successful hunting. The old guy had probably found a better alley, or was simply making his daily rounds.

He decided to open the can and leave it behind the Dumpster where the cat seemed to hang out. That way, if he returned, the food would be waiting—if some other critter didn't get it first. Tomorrow he would check again and bring another can. If the cat wasn't back in the next few days, Isaac would give the food to Craig, ACRE's vice president of marketing, whose partner John fostered cats for a local rescue operation.

The alley wasn't the most pleasant place to spend a Sunday morning. The odors from the Dumpster suggested more than leftover coffee grounds and stale pastries. Rainbow oil slicks adorned last week's puddles. A frustrated artist had sprayed graffiti on the brick wall but needed help with spelling. Isaac picked his way between parked cars and over concrete barriers. He didn't see the cat until he bent over to shove the can behind the Dumpster.

The tabby was sprawled crookedly in a position no cat would willingly choose. Isaac's stomach knotted. He was sure the animal was dead—until he opened his eyes.

The cat managed one pathetic screech that warned Isaac to keep his distance.

Isaac backed away. He didn't know how the tabby had managed to drag himself to shelter. For that matter, he didn't know how this wily alley resident hadn't dodged the car that hit him. He wondered if someone had purposely run him down.

The cat didn't have long to live—Isaac could see that—and moving him would surely finish the job. Sometimes it was kinder to let nature take its course. Isaac had done what he could, maybe too much. If he hadn't fed the cat, maybe he would have moved to a safer place.

"What in the hell do I do with you?" He realized he had spoken out loud.

The cat opened his eyes again. They were glazed with pain, but Isaac thought he saw something behind them, and it wasn't resignation.

"You'll scratch me into a million pieces, won't you?" But even as he asked the question, Isaac was taking off the ACRE sweatshirt he'd zipped over his T-shirt.

The cat didn't move as he approached. With just a few feet to go, Isaac pulled out his cell phone and called information.

* * *

The gray-haired vet at the emergency clinic was experienced and kind. From the looks of him, he had saved the lives of thousands of animals and ended the lives of more than he wanted. He sedated Isaac's sweatshirt-bound prisoner immediately, then shook his head over the cat's multiple injuries.

When the exam was over he shook it again. "He's a stray?"

"The proverbial alley cat," Isaac said.

"We need to put him down."

Isaac had expected to hear this. But the confirmation finished tying the knot in his belly. "He doesn't have a chance?"

The vet removed his stethoscope. "Maybe, with a lot of care. We'd have to do emergency surgery. There'd be at least a week of hospitalization while he heals, then a lot of care at home. That is, if he'd let you take care of him." His gaze flicked to the scratches on Isaac's arms. "You'll need a tetanus shot. Did he bite you, too?"

"He has a lot of energy for a dying cat."

"If he was someone's beloved pet, trying to save him would make sense. But he's not."

Isaac knew the right answer. By bringing the cat here, he had saved the poor guy hours of misery. He was sedated now. He simply wouldn't wake up. The vet was kind; he would do it immediately and make sure the cat didn't suffer.

"What will the treatment cost?" he asked instead.

"Thousands. And what will you have to show for it when he's healed? If he makes it, that is. What will you do with him?"

"How old is he, do you think?"

"I'm guessing two or so."

"I thought he was a lot older."

"Don't let age make your decision. This cat's lived nine lives already."

Isaac couldn't believe they were still having the conversation. "You've told me everything you responsibly should. Now, if you were me, what would you do?"

The vet was silent. Then he sighed. "If he doesn't make it through alive, I'll donate my fee for the surgery. Will that help?"

Isaac was embarrassed he couldn't seem to let go. "This is crazy. I could send that money overseas and feed a batch of hungry children."

"You can do that, as well. All creatures great and small . . ."

Isaac felt the knot slowly coming untied. "Where do I sign?"

Kendra had never been much of a churchgoer. Nominally she was Catholic. The Delacroix grandparents had made sure she and Jamie were baptized, then washed their hands of their daughter's children, duty done. Kendra was fairly certain they'd found limited interaction with Riva was easiest. That way they couldn't witness closely the damage she wrought.

Riva avoided Mass even more efficiently than she avoided mothering her children. There was no First Communion, no lessons in catechism, no holy day celebrations. Kendra's real religious education came early in her career, when she served a stint on the religion section of a medium-size daily and learned too much about the issues and scandals of religious life.

Once she became dissatisfied with her marriage, life's unanswered questions loomed larger, and she'd searched for a church that would help make sense of them. She'd been surprised to find sustenance at the Shenandoah Community Church where Sam Kinkade was minister.

Early on Sunday morning, she waved goodbye to Jamie and the girls, and when the resulting silence made the house almost unbearable, she knew the time had arrived to make her first Sunday morning appearance since the shooting. She'd made friends here, and she wanted to renew those bonds.

The parking lot was crowded, but she pulled into a space in the farthest corner and took her time getting to the front door. She was greeted by strangers, but Elisa saw her almost immediately. She came over to hug Kendra and ask her to sit in her pew.

A choir from an African-Methodist church in D.C. was visiting, and they performed a rousing gospel medley that had the mostly white SCC congregation on their feet applauding by the end. Sam's sermon on racial justice was nearly as exuberant and well received.

Once the sermon ended, Kendra was greeted warmly. Helen spotted her just as she and Cissy were leaving the church, a squirming Reese imprisoned on Cissy's hip.

Kendra took Helen's hands and leaned over to kiss her cheek. Helen harrumphed.

"When are you going to visit me?" Kendra asked.

"I was thinking this afternoon, 'less you got other ideas or better ways to spend your time?"

"I'll be glad for the company."

Helen frowned. "This quiet life's not setting too well?"

Kendra realized her mistake. "No, I'm fine."

" 'Cause we always need more quilters in the bee, and that's a fact."

The SCC Bee met weekly on Wednesday mornings. The women were delightful, but Kendra wasn't a quilter.

"You don't want me." She pulled a long, sad face. "I'm hopeless."

"No chance of that."

Kendra tried to change the subject. "I'll look forward to seeing you this afternoon."

"You think we're finished with that other conversation, but we just started." Helen left for the door, and Cissy, who was trying to untangle Reese's fist from her hair, aimed a sympathetic smile in Kendra's direction.

A man spoke somewhere behind her. “She’s up to no good, isn’t she.”

Kendra turned to find Sam. “She thinks I’ll be joining your quilting bee.”

“You’re doomed. Words I don’t often say, by the way.”

She smiled, the first natural, easy smile of the day. “She’s met her match.”

“You wouldn’t care to make a bet, would you?”

“Cash beat you to it.”

He took her arm and steered her out of traffic and into a quiet corner.

“So how are you feeling?”

“A little stronger every day.” She told him about her work in Leah’s garden. “I’m doing better, but I’m preparing to limp for the rest of my life.”

“I imagine you remind yourself every day that limping, under the circumstances, is a blessing.” He smiled at her cautious nod. “And I imagine that kind of Pollyanna wisdom isn’t helping as much as you’d like.”

“I’m not asking myself why this happened to me. That’s where you come in, right?”

“Sometimes.”

“And what do you say when you’re asked?”

"That I've never known a good parent who put a child in harm's way just to make a point. People attribute acts to God that a normal father would be arrested for."

"But bad things happen."

"Good parents can't protect children at all times and in all places. But they can give them the tools they need to move forward through adversity or accept the inevitable with grace."

She thought this was one of those simple explanations it might take a million incarnations to understand. It also brought Jamie to mind. In a few sentences, she told Sam about Jamie's reappearance in her life.

"So let me get this straight," he said when she'd finished. "She disappeared for all those years, and you knew she'd been into some pretty heavy stuff. And you didn't accept her without a qualm?" He paused. "Welcome to the human race."

She was trying to figure out how to answer that when he continued. "But we're not going to let you off that easily. I hear you saying that part of the reason you didn't want to trust her was that you might have to admit you need her."

Sam was too good at this. It was true that

the only time recently she had admitted she needed somebody, he'd failed her.

"You're thinking about Isaac, aren't you." He made a casual assessment of the space around them and saw no one was approaching. "If things had turned out differently the night you were shot, let's say you'd gotten your pills, gone home, taken them and crawled into bed, would you still be angry with him?"

"I'm trying to figure things out. I'm not angry."

"Of course you are. He failed you. It's in your voice, in the way you're holding your head, the way you're gripping your purse."

She relaxed her fingers. The head seemed locked in position. "He didn't fail me. He was playing by the rules we made."

"Apparently you think the rules need to be changed. Have you told him?"

She searched for an answer that didn't involve laying her soul bare to a husband who had shown no signs of wanting to see it. "I'm not very good at doing that."

Sam's expression softened. "Isaac may pay the closest possible attention to everything you do, and he may care a great deal.

But if he doesn't think that's important, then why would he risk letting you know?"

When she didn't answer, he went on. "Here's the great thing about marriage. It only takes one person to change it. Change, not fix, of course, but sometimes change is the first step in that direction. You've changed what you want out of your marriage, but now you have to let Isaac know. Unless you're sure it's too late."

Was she sure? She didn't think so. But was she courageous enough to tell her husband the things she could so easily tell Sam? Because if Isaac really wasn't interested, if he was too busy to pay attention to her concerns, then her marriage really would be over.

She glanced past Sam's shoulder and saw with some relief that a group of men was bearing down on them. "I have to give this some serious thought."

"No platitudes on this end. This may not turn out the way you want it to. You need to be prepared. And if it does turn out well, you need to be prepared for that, too. You really aren't used to needing someone else. It's going to take some serious adjustment."

She thought of her sister, on the highway back to Michigan. "Then I'll adjust."

"I'll see you next Sunday?"

"I think you'll be seeing a lot of me. I *need* this place."

He leaned over and kissed her cheek. "That's a good start."

Helen arrived at about three, carrying a discount store shopping bag. On the porch, she thrust it in Kendra's direction with complete lack of ceremony. "Something for you. Call it a housewarming present."

Kendra pulled a quilt from the bag and shook it out. It was a log cabin in scrappy earth tones—browns, beiges, grays and olive. The large center squares were a sunny gold, and the light and dark halves of each block had been laid out to resemble furrows. Best of all, names were penned in the center squares. Kendra recognized the names of the SCC quilters she'd met.

She cleared her throat, which felt as if it were suddenly stuffed with quilt batting. "I don't know what to say. It's just so beautiful. And perfect."

"Log Cabin seemed appropriate, considering this useless pile of timber you're calling home now. And we knew you liked friendship quilts."

"It's a treasure." She held it to her cheek.

"Well, all of us know what you did for Reverend Sam and Elisa and that brother of hers. They might not be with us here, if it weren't for you."

"I was doing my job."

"So we did ours, and here it is."

Kendra rubbed it against her cheek once more, then clutched the quilt to her chest. "Thank you, Helen. I love it."

"You'll need it come winter, if you're still here. Manning Rosslyn's the best around, but he's not fast, no matter what he tells you. You'll need something to snuggle under while they tear this place into matchsticks and reassemble it. I'm counting on watching for entertainment."

"The show starts tomorrow. They're delivering the barn logs and starting the foundation."

With the quilt under her arm, Kendra ushered her guest inside. Reluctantly, she draped the quilt over the armchair and went to get the iced tea she'd prepared. She returned with it, along with some of the cookies Jamie had baked. Helen was already examining the Lover's Knot quilt that Kendra had folded over the back of the sofa.

"Well now, this surely is something else," Helen said. "You say Leah Spurlock made this?"

"That's what we were told."

"Well, I've seen a heap of old quilts in my time, made a heap, too, as you know. But I've never quite seen a sight like this one. You're right about the pattern, but it can be called Rose Dream, too, or True Lover's Knot. I've heard 'em all. Called lots of different things, like a lot of quilts."

"I'm no expert, but even I can tell the quilting's not the best—if you compare it to the others I've collected." Kendra picked up the small pile of quilts and set them next to Helen. Then she perched on the sofa beside them and unfolded the top one, a simple two-color pattern of bright pink and white that had twenty-five signatures. "Look how small these stitches are."

"Yes, indeed. That's Big Dipper, by the way. Works as a signature quilt, particularly sashed like that. My mama and her friends made one like this when our preacher moved away. That was almost expected, you know, giving a quilt to mark a preacher's years. Of course, that particular time nobody much liked the man and we were glad to see him go. So the women put together all the scraps they didn't like, although nobody said as much. But there were some shameful colors mixed together in that quilt, let me tell you."

Kendra wondered if the poor preacher had realized he was being well and truly dissed by his flock. She smiled as she traced the perfect parallel quilting lines on the Big Dipper.

"I wonder about the women who made the quilt." She pointed at one name. "Lizzie Hemlock. What do you suppose she thought about while she was signing this? Was she worried about a child who had whooping cough? Was she looking forward to a trip to see her family? Was she married to a man who paid too much attention to somebody else?"

"You got imagination, I can see that for sure. A good thing in a quilter."

Kendra pretended to ignore that. "I guess that's part of the reason Isaac's quilt intrigues me. It must have meant so much to Leah. She left it for Isaac, even though she had no idea where he was or if a quilt was something he'd care about."

"And does he care about it?"

"No, but I care for him."

Helen thumbed through the rest. There were only four, two fairly worn but with no large stains or tears, two that looked as if they had been packed in a trunk since the day the last stitch was sewn.

"Well, these others are pretty, all right. This Basket quilt's a real keeper, even if it's worn at the edges. The Chimney Sweep's a classic. And this Churn Dash was a fund-raiser, I'll just bet you. Too many signatures to be anything else. Some church or school made a little money from this one. But not a one of these is as interesting as Leah's. Or as odd. And that's the only word for it, you know. Just plain odd."

Kendra thought she knew what Helen was referring to, but she waited for her to go on, the student at the feet of the master.

"Now take the Lover's Knot pattern, for starters." Helen removed Isaac's quilt from the sofa back. "It's true any pattern can be a friendship quilt—that's what we usually called them when I was growing up. That or album quilt, too. Anyway, no question any old pattern could be used, as long as there's someplace in the block light enough to sign or embroider. But it's also true that some just lent themselves to writing on, and those are the ones people signed most of the time. This quilt don't look like it was made to be signed. The white patches are odd shapes. Signing won't do a thing for the pattern, if you see what I mean."

"I do. And there's no rhyme or reason to the way it's signed."

"That would be the next thing. See, most friendship quilts—" Helen pointed to the four folded beside them "—the signatures are in the same place in each block. Oh, maybe not every block gets signed, but there's a plan to the pattern. Maybe every other one. Or the signed ones make a cross through the center of the quilt. Or the signed ones are placed inside the border or smack in the middle. Depended on how many blocks and how many people signing. But likely there was a plan and a purpose."

Helen held up the Lover's Knot. "Now see, on this one? Signatures scattered all over it. And some of them are over the colored pieces."

The quilt was a mixture of white muslin

and a variety of prints that twined throughout like knotted ribbons. And Helen was right. There were places where the embroidered names lapped over into the prints.

"See what this means," Helen went on, "is that when Leah made this top, there weren't no signatures. And that's not the way it's usually done. Most of the time people sign blocks, then they get laid out in some pattern or other and sewn together. But that didn't happen here. Look at this." She pointed to several different areas. "Do you see that? The signatures go across one block and into another? So the top was made first."

"And that's unusual?"

"Some. And just as unusual, there wasn't a bit of thought given toward making the signatures look like they belong together. Some are turned this way, some that. This one here's practically upside down. It's higgledy-piggledy. And you know what else? Every single one of these signatures is in the same handwriting. Now, what do you think of that?"

Kendra had noticed that all the embroidery thread outlining the names was the same color, but she hadn't really noticed that all the letters looked the same. Now she saw that Helen was right. "They used to teach penmanship in schools, and handwriting was more uniform. I thought that's why they looked so similar. But you're right, one person probably did them all. And that would be odd. Because why would one person scatter names across a quilt top that way?"

"And you know, don't you, what's just about oddest of all?"

"Tell me."

"I don't know a one of these names. I was right here in Toms Brook the whole time Leah Spurlock lived here, and I can tell you I knew almost every single person in this county, one way or t'other. But I don't know a single one of these folks." She squinted over the names. "Not a single one."

Kendra sat back. "So the names come from somewhere else."

"Or she made 'em up—and what would be the point of that?" Helen was turning the Lover's Knot quilt around and around. "You know most of the colored fabrics are feedsacks, don't you?"

From her reading, Kendra knew that feed, flour and other staples had once come in colored cotton sacks so that women could take them apart and use them for household needs and clothing. She hadn't been certain how to identify them, though. Helen clearly was.

"This here's what they call a conversation print," Helen said. "See the little houses, the animals? Some good old prints in this quilt. And there was an eye for color. A lot of trouble went into choosing them. See the way the colors fan out? Reds in the center, purples moving into blues, until we get these greens at the border? Scrap quilt, yes, but planning went into it."

"You don't think Leah made it?"

"She wasn't much good with a needle."

"I can relate."

"Not for long you won't. But Leah, well, my mama said she was pretty much hopeless. And see the way every single seam matches? Takes a bit of doing to make that happen."

Kendra could only imagine.

"But the quilting." Helen shook her head. "No, Leah did the quilting. I'd believe that. Never saw such a job of quilting in my life."

"I noticed it's uneven."

"Uneven don't do it justice. There's not a

bit of thought to where the lines are going. Some lines that ought to be parallel cross, and everybody knows that's not the way it's done. Quilt's lumpy 'cause here there's a mess of quilting. Here there's hardly any. So I'd say from what I know of her skills that Leah did quilt this, even if someone else pieced it."

"That's what my quilting would look like."

"I'm aiming to fix that, only I won't be around for the next week or so to do it. Going down to Richmond to see my daughter, then we're coming up through Harrisonburg and stopping by the quilt museum to have a look at a few things."

"You've got a quilt there, don't you? Your Shenandoah Album quilt?"

"Never have figured out why they're so excited about it. But they want to interview me on videotape. The way some people spend their time . . ." Helen picked up her tea and took a long sip.

"I'm looking forward to seeing that quilt myself."

"I got to go in a minute," Helen said, "but we didn't tackle the biggest question this quilt of your husband's brings to light."

Kendra knew what Helen meant. "Why Leah left this quilt to Isaac?"

"That would be the one."

"Why did she, do you suppose? Because it was the only one she ever finished and she was proud of it?"

"She was a smart woman. She wouldn't be proud of this. She might not sew well, but she had eyes."

"Because she wanted her grandchild to have something she'd made for him?"

"A signature quilt? With signatures that make no sense to anybody else?"

"Do you suppose these are names from Isaac's family?"

"Don't see no Spurlocks here—do you?"

Kendra had considered that already. "Spurlock was probably her married name. We don't know a thing about her before she arrived here, and we don't know her maiden name."

"Seems like you could dig that up somewhere. State's got to have records of a Leah Spurlock someplace."

"I can look into it." Kendra felt the thrill of a reporter tracking down the first real lead on a story. She was more than curious about Leah Spurlock. She was determined now to find answers. Leah's was a life she wanted to understand.

"Well, you got to promise to keep me up to date." Helen stood. "You got the quilt bug, you know, only you're looking at things from the outside in. I'm fixing to change that."

Kendra was afraid that before too long, despite all her protests, she was going to be buying Cash Rosslyn a very expensive six-pack.

CHAPTER THIRTEEN

Blackburn Farm
Lock Hollow, Virginia
November 29, 1932

Dear Puss,

I hardly can beleave I will be married tomorrow without you standing right beside me.

Of course you cannot travel with little Alice so sickly. You are wise to use Troutman's Cough Syrup, though I think boiling cherry bark with mullein and mixing that water with honey will do better. I have sent you some to try and how to do it is clarely marked.

Also inside the box is boneset. Devide into three parts, then mix one part with two cups boiled water. Give it just warm, a sip at a time. Keep her well covered.

Birdie seems happy, her knowing that Jesse will be with us taking care of the farm. She quilted a Lover's Knot as her present, and has pieced one just like it for her hope chest.

Jesse says for you not to worry about the park talk. He says what with this Depression, the government won't have money for such happenings, and if they do, we will be outside it anyhow.

Still your best friend even when I get married,
Leah Blackburn soon to be Spurlock

Out of respect for Leah's parents, Leah and Jesse waited until Thanksgiving to marry. Even so, the news traveled quickly, and women from the hollow and beyond came to visit before the wedding, bringing small presents for the bride-to-be. Sauerkraut carefully fermented in oak barrels, wild muscadine jelly, pickles as sweet as candy.

All were cherished at a time when money was scarce and food a family didn't need was exchanged for due bills at Grayling's General Store.

Leah received a Bible from Jesse's oldest sister and snow-white petticoats from his youngest. His middle sister embroidered a nightdress of filmy white cotton with bits of lace at the neck and sleeves. Ginny Collins, Jesse's mother, brought Leah a brand-new featherbed she and her own sisters had made from goose down and feathers. Best of all, Birdie stayed up late every night quilting, and finishing one of the two Lover's Knot tops for their marriage bed.

On Thanksgiving morning, Leah awoke with the knowledge that today her life would change forever. She could hardly wait.

Birdie was still sleeping, so Leah was careful not to shake the bed when she slipped out from under the pile of quilts. She tiptoed barefoot into the kitchen and reignited the fire in the cookstove. Then she lit the woodstove that sat on the hearth of the old stone fireplace. It began to warm the room immediately, but she hugged herself as she waited, dancing from foot to foot.

New brides usually moved from their family homes, but to Leah it seemed right to be staying here. She loved this house, particularly this cozy room where she had spent so many evenings. The logs were newly chinked and whitewashed. The roomy loft where she and Jesse would sleep looked down on the fireplace, but there was a railing for privacy and a window beside their bed to let in the light. She wanted a window in the roof. She wanted to lie with her husband and ponder who lived on the moon and stars, and what they thought about when they looked down at her. She planned to see if Jesse could add such a thing. She thought if anyone could, it would be her Jesse.

The kitchen was large enough for eight at the table and more if people kept elbows to their sides. When more came to dinner, her mother and father had pulled in a work table from the porch and set it in front of the black walnut china cupboard. Of course, Mama had been sure to remove whatever dishes she needed first. There was no getting them after the table came inside.

Now Leah would be the one to bring out Mama's dishes. They were not elegant, but many a good meal had been eaten on those chipped surfaces. Memories lived in every spidery scar.

She had tried to talk to Birdie about the dishes, about who would take them out, who would decide when to invite neighbors for meals and where they would sit. Birdie was the older, of course, and it seemed right that she should have a say. But Birdie only laughed.

"If I wanted the things that come with marriage, I would have found myself a man to have me. Maybe you get some of the good things as come with being wedded, but me, I get the things that don't. Like not having to decide who best to pamper and cultivate. Now you and Jesse, you'll have to make those decisions and leave me alone to do whatever I like."

What her sister liked, Leah knew, was cooking meals, baking whatever the cupboard allowed, sewing clothes and making quilts. Birdie also liked listening at night when Leah read aloud from whatever book she managed to get from Aubrey Grayling, Jesse's best friend and the son of the man who owned the general store. Aubrey, who these days did most of the work there, kept two shelves with books to borrow, as long as borrowers left something precious behind as ransom. Her grandmother's seed-pearl brooch resided behind a counter at Grayling's more often than it resided in Leah's own dresser.

"Now here's the bride turning as white as a snowstorm," Birdie said from the doorway. "If you want to call off this wedding, I reckon you just have to say so. But you're fixing to make yourself sick."

In a rare moment of open affection, Leah ran to her sister and wrapped her arms around her. "Birdie girl, I was just warming the house for you. The last time it'll be me doing it."

Birdie felt as fragile as a young sapling, but she put her arms around Leah for a quick hug before she pushed her away. "Me, I don't see nothing to be sad about. I'll have a whole bed to myself, and you can sleep a mite longer every morning, because Jesse will be the first up to get the fire started."

"Well, *I* won't have a bed to myself." Even all these weeks after Jesse had proposed marriage, Leah was still pondering that. Sleeping with Birdie, who never moved and took up only a fraction of the space, was one thing. But sleeping in a bed with Jesse, who took up room just by breathing or smiling? It was something to consider.

"No need to dwell on that," Birdie said. "It will happen soon enough."

Leah wondered exactly how much sleeping she and Jesse would do, and the thought pleased her. "You still aim to go and stay with Etta after the dinner?"

"You're no help to me with my quilting. Etta'll help me finish two tops I promised I'd put in Grayling's before Christmas."

Leah felt such fondness for her sister. Although it was painful for her to travel, Birdie was leaving for the rest of the week to give Leah time alone with Jesse. Of course, Birdie had found a way to pretend spending time with their cousin Etta was exactly what she wanted.

From the moment Leah had told her sister she and Jesse were going to be married, Birdie had been particularly thoughtful, as if she felt she needed to take their mother's place. In her sweet distracted way, she had made Leah look at all the ways life would change. And when Leah had firmly declared her intentions, Birdie had promised to welcome Jesse into their family. There had been no talk of her moving away for good, though. Even if they had wanted it that way, there was no place for Birdie to go.

"I'll make us some coffee," Birdie said. "It'll chase away the cobwebs in my head. They're thicker than snow clouds in a blizzard."

Leah walked with her toward the kitchen. The house was already growing pleasantly warm. "Didn't you sleep, Birdie?"

"I did."

"Did you have good dreams?"

Birdie shook her head. "I saw terrible things."

"What kind of things?"

Birdie considered. "Maybe I shouldn't say." She paused. "Or maybe I *should.* Etta says if you tell a bad dream before breakfast, it cain't come true."

Leah laughed. "You're a goose. Go ahead, then, tell me."

"I dreamed you was running down the mountain, just as fast as your legs would carry you, Leah. So fast that before I could call to you, you were gone. Then I heared you falling. And falling . . ."

Leah shivered. "You only dreamed such a thing because I'm getting married today.

Just remember, I'm not running away from *you.*"

"Jesse was trying to run after you, and he couldn't catch up."

"Well, see? Now we know for sure how foolish a dream it was. There's nowhere I could ever run that Jesse Spurlock couldn't run faster."

"Well, I'm glad I told you, just so's it won't come to pass."

Leah was glad, too. Today she wanted Birdie to be as happy as she was. If it made her sister feel better, it was a small thing to listen to some of her worries.

Leah gently squeezed Birdie's arm. "I'm going to dress and do the chores. Then I'll come inside and we'll eat breakfast."

"Don't dawdle," Birdie said. "We have pies to bake for dinner. And Jesse'll be over to get us midday."

"I'll have a lot to be thankful for today." Leah paused. "I wish Mama and Daddy were here."

"I'll be there," Birdie said. "You just remember that. I'll be there for you. And from this day on, I'll be there for Jesse, too."

* * *

The Spurlock house was larger than the Blackburns', the first story built of carefully mortared stones, the second of logs that fit together so perfectly there was little need for chinking. The house was the finest in the hollow. The front porch was wide enough for chairs against the rail and walls, and the paneled door had been deeply carved with scrolls by Jesse's father, who had been the hollow's most talented woodworker. In the summer, yellow roses bloomed along the front, accompanied by bridal wreath and snowball bushes. Mountain laurel and flame azalea preened on the shadiest side of the house.

Leah, in her best print dress, the palest of blues sprinkled with tiny red roses, was greeted enthusiastically by Jesse's mother, Ginny, and stepfather, Luther Collins, as well as all the family and neighbors who had been invited to share Thanksgiving dinner and witness the wedding. She wore her grandmother's seed-pearl brooch, ransomed back for the occasion, and carried an embroidered handkerchief her mother had carried on her own wedding day.

Because the afternoon was unseasonably warm, tables had been placed outside to take advantage of the extra space. Three turkeys raised in a pen on corn and cheerful anticipation had met their fate. Now they fed the Thanksgiving gathering, along with platters of harvest vegetables, dried beans cooked with sausage and ham, mashed potatoes, sweet potatoes, hot bread, cornpone and pies made from every type of fruit growing in the mountains. Mrs. Collins had made three apple spice cakes with boiled frosting. The preacher blessed the food and reminded them how lucky they were in a time of want to have such bounty before them.

As the afternoon passed, children finished quickly and chased one another around the tables. Babies cried and were taken inside to be fed. The oldest men and women napped in the sunshine.

Leah and Jesse were put at opposite ends of the largest table. She ignored the quips of the old men, the way they poked Jesse in the ribs and wiggled their eyebrows when they looked at her. The women were just as bad, although Jesse's sisters took pity and placed the preacher beside her so she would have someone sensible to talk to.

When the meal ended, homemade peach brandy was served, and although no one in Lock Hollow paid much attention to Prohibition, the fact that the twenty-first amendment might soon be repealed pleased them all.

The preacher, a beefy man who fed his brood by chopping trees and hauling them down the mountain, was as pleased to see brandy as anyone at the table. Pipes were lit, more brandy was poured and the women began to clear. When Leah and Birdie tried to help, they were told to stay put.

In truth, Leah was sorry to be the honored guest. Though they were still sitting outside, the smoke of Virginia's own tobacco made her eyes water.

"So what do you hear, Aubrey," one of the men asked, "about this here park they're trying to shove down our gullets?"

Aubrey Grayling was not as handsome as Leah's husband-to-be, but he was easy to look at, with chestnut-colored hair and bright blue eyes. He was slight, befitting a storekeeper, and not as strong as a man who fed his family by laboring in the fields. But Leah knew looks were deceptive. In a fight, any man in Lock Hollow was glad to have Aubrey Grayling on his side.

Aubrey sat back in his chair, happy to be the center of attention. Since sooner or later everyone visited Grayling's and stayed to swap stories, Aubrey always knew the most recent news, far and near. "I reckon they want to move us out of our houses, all right, but nobody in charge has got the time or money to do it."

"Took the government more than a decade to figure that Prohibition wasn't gonna stop men from drinkin'," one of Jesse's cousins said. "Give the men in charge a cane pole and a washtub of trout and they still wouldn't know enough to put a worm on the hook."

Leah knew too well what the men were discussing. For many years there had been talk that the United States government was going to build a park in Virginia's mountains. Laws had passed; officials had appeared and disappeared; boundaries had been discussed, drawn and redrawn. The federal government couldn't buy the land, but the State of Virginia seemed willing to buy it or steal it for them. A condemnation order had been issued. Landowners had sued and sued again, tying up the process in courts.

But the prospect of the government taking over what the mountain people had worked so hard to attain was still just a topic for discussion. Remote Lock Hollow was on the fringes of the acreage to be set aside, and as yet no one had come knocking on their doors. Like most residents, Leah didn't think a park would come to pass in her lifetime.

Of course, one year ago ground had been broken for Skyline Drive, a road that would wind along the highest ridges and let travellers view Virginia's scenic beauty. The first section was due to open in two years, bringing with it a host of strangers. And no one had thought that would come to pass, either.

"We're boring the ladies," the preacher said. "And there ain't no call to have this discussion on a day when we come together to give thanks." He paused long enough to stir a little guilt; then he grinned. "So who's got a coonhound that can beat my old redbone?"

By the time the dishes were cleared and the tables returned to the house, the sun was on the wane and the air had grown cooler. Leah still wanted to be married outside, but she knew they had to get to it soon. Some of the men had brought instruments, and furniture had been moved to the sides of the rooms so people could dance. She and Jesse would slip away when no one was paying attention. She was pretty sure no one would follow them and try to disturb their first night together, not with death such a recent visitor to the Blackburn home.

There was a flurry of activity on the porch; then Jesse's sisters came down the stairs, surrounding Leah and Birdie and bringing them inside. Suddenly everyone was fussing over the Blackburn sisters. A cousin had powder and lipstick and a comb, and proceeded to use them with abandon. An aunt had picked the remnants of the season's chrysanthemums and tied the bouquet with a pink ribbon. Ginny Collins presented Leah with a white hat, the narrow brim accented with the same ribbon.

Leah was touched by all the attention. She knew the women were trying to make up for her mother's absence.

She was walking down the steps before

she had time to think about what was coming. Birdie, in her red and white checked dress, went first, taking the steps slowly and leaning against the rail. Leah stepped out on the porch as soon as Birdie made it safely to the ground.

Jesse was standing at the bottom of the stairs waiting for her, handsome in a dark suit that had probably fit his stepfather better than it fit him. But it didn't matter that the suit was a little short and a little tight. This was Jesse. Leah waited for Birdie to move away, patient as her sister stopped for a long breath, then took the time she needed to get past Jesse, who gave her a warm smile. Finally, with Birdie safely clear, Leah walked down to meet him.

The ceremony was short. While some had helped her primp, the other women had arranged dried flowers, twigs and leaves in jugs, and set them in a wide semicircle in the clearing just beyond the house. She and Jesse followed the preacher and Birdie. When they were settled, the preacher pulled out his Bible and read Psalm 128, then began to preach.

Leah tried to listen, but afterwards all she could remember was Jesse's expression.

His eyes were warm, his lips turned up in a smile, but three sentences into the sermon, his foot began to tap. As the preacher droned, it tapped faster, and faster. Jesse had more energy than any man Leah knew, and standing there with nothing to do was surely driving him crazy. Despite the smile, she knew he was about to burst.

Just as she was afraid he was going to bolt, the preacher asked them to repeat their vows. She wasn't sure what she said, but whatever it was, she did it correctly. In a moment the pronouncement was made, and she and Jesse Spurlock were married and kissing.

As the last person finished congratulating them, the music began. People brought more gifts and piled them on the porch for the new couple to take home. Birdie had even brought the Lover's Knot quilt to show it off.

"We have to stay a little while," Jesse said, "but just before it gets truly dark, you meet me on the back porch, and we'll go out that way without saying that's what we're doing."

She liked that. She was already exhausted, and she wanted to be alone with him. They went inside hand in hand, and she was whirled from one set of arms to another as two fiddlers and Aubrey Grayling on the banjo filled the house with music. Two of Jesse's tiniest nephews clung to her dress, and she lifted them up to dance, one in each arm. The family applauded when their mothers finally came and took the little boys away.

Birdie had her own admirers. Old men graciously took her in their arms and, barely moving, took her through the dance steps. Puss Cade's mother told Leah how sorry she was that Puss and her brother had not been able to bring his family home for the wedding.

"I sent a right smart bunch of yarbs to help little Alice," Leah said. "I surely hope she stops feeling poorly."

"We depend on you the way we depended on your ma," Mrs. Cade told her. "Nothing we buy at Grayling's helps half so much as what your ma would give us."

An hour later, Leah saw that the sun had almost set. A quick scan showed that her new husband was nowhere in sight. Unless he was out in the barn sampling some of the whiskey his own corn had made possible, he was waiting for her on the back porch. She fanned herself as if she were too hot and smiled at the women who had engaged her in conversation.

"I think I'll just go get a little air." She waved her hand harder. "All that dancing has me as hot as a chimney fire."

One of the women winked. "We'll see to it that nobody comes after you."

Leah winked back.

She made her way through the room as unobtrusively as she could. In the kitchen, she pointed to the door when Mrs. Collins asked if she needed anything. "Just some air," she said.

Mrs. Collins winked, too, and went back to washing dishes with two of her aunts.

Jesse wasn't on the porch, so she descended the steps into the shadows. An arm snaked out and grabbed her, but before she could screech, Jesse's lips silenced her. She put her arms around him and kissed him back. She could taste whiskey and warm-blooded male, and she liked the flavors very much.

Finally she pulled away. "You like to have scared me witless."

"You witless is a sight I'd like to see."

She giggled. "Can we get away now?"

"The wagon's all ready."

She wished they had a car. There were some in the mountains, but only where roads were good enough to warrant. The roads in this hollow were made for walking. Even the wagon was a bone-jolting ride.

She had an idea. "Let's not take the wagon. Let's walk. We can go through the woods."

"I got it loaded up with all the stuff folks give us today."

"We can get that later in the week. I don't want to start my marriage all shook up like a beehive in a bear's paws."

"Then come on." He pulled her behind him, but she dug in her heels.

"Jesse—" she kept her voice low "—let's get Birdie's quilt."

"And carry it all the way back?"

"I want to sleep under it tonight."

She could hear his snort, but he started in the other direction. In a minute they were at the wagon, and he lifted her up to find it. She took the quilt and folded it under her arm; then she let him lift her down.

"C'mon," he said. "Or somebody'll figure this out."

"Leaving the wagon will fool 'em for a while."

"It might at that."

He led her through the farm, sure of every step. The sun was gone, but the sky was still light enough that they could find their way. Soon the moon would come up, and they would be able to see it from the window in the loft.

Things took a bad turn when they got to the woods that ran between the Cade and Spurlock farms. Leah had not considered that her best shoes might not stand up to a walk through the darkening woods. She stepped over a log and her foot twisted. In a moment she was facedown on the forest floor.

She'd hardly had time to cry out before Jesse gathered her in his arms and helped her up to sit on the log. "Are you all right?"

"I just . . . I cain't . . ." She tried to catch her breath and couldn't.

"Don't get all tightened up. Put your shoulders and head down. Let 'em droop. Now see if you can breathe."

She did as he'd said, and air filled her lungs again the moment she stopped fighting it. "How'd you know that?" she asked when she could talk.

"I been in enough fights to know what it feels like." He slipped off her shoe and felt her ankle. "How's that?"

Nothing hurt. She realized she was lucky. She was clumsy, not injured. Her laugh was shaky and low. "I feel about as silly as I can."

"We were going too fast. It's my fault."

"I was in a hurry, just like you."

He laughed. "Well, we got to rest a spell now. I'm not fixing to risk another fall on the way home."

She could see the sky through the canopy of leafless tree limbs. It was indigo verging on black now, and she could see the stars appearing one by one. "It's getting cold, but look at them stars come out, Jesse. You ever seen anything prettier in your life than stars?"

"Just when I look at you."

"I must look a sight right now." She started to brush off her dress, but he swiped her hand away.

"I can see better."

She sat still as his hand traveled over her breasts, lightly brushing away leaves and tiny branches, and puffs of rich, dark dirt. His hands felt as if they had always belonged there, yet she was certain they would always feel unfamiliar and wickedly forbidden, too. "You getting it all?"

"I don't know. Maybe we ought to slip you out of that dress, Leah. You know, so's we can shake it out real good."

"Jesse!"

"Why not? We just got married. Nobody said nothing about not being together out under the stars, did they?"

"I'm sure the preacher said that very thing." She let him know she was teasing by lifting one of his hands and kissing his fingertips.

"You weren't listening to that preacher and neither was I."

"I was too listening! He said something about me being a fruitful vine and having some olive plants."

"I don't aim to raise olive plants. Got too much to raise as it is. But children? Someday. For now, I want you to myself for a while." He began to kiss her neck, the place just under her ear, her earlobe.

"Then maybe we ought to wait a while on this," she said, her breath coming faster.

"Or maybe, since there's not a lot we can do about having babies, we ought to do this a whole lot while we still can."

She could feel him unbuttoning her dress, and his hands against her skin were better than against the cotton. Oh, so much better.

Just as she was about to strip off the dress herself, he stopped and moved away.

"Where are you going?" she demanded.

He rose and picked up the quilt, which she had dropped as she fell. He shook it out; then he moved away to a small space where the ground was deep in fallen leaves.

When he'd spread the quilt, he turned and opened his arms to her.

Leah stood on shaky legs; then, as Jesse watched, she wiggled the dress from her shoulders and let it float silently to the ground.

"Don't you worry about getting cold now. You come to me," he said in a husky voice. "And I'll keep you warm. Me and this wedding quilt."

And in no way did he disappoint her.

CHAPTER FOURTEEN

Two weeks later, Kendra wasn't thinking about quilts or Isaac's family. Noise was the issue. Noise, and men streaming on and off her property. Noise and trucks and power saws and backhoes and excavation equipment for which she had no names. She was amazed at how quickly permits had been granted, crews assembled, initial plans drawn up. There were a million fine points to be discussed and decided upon, but all had agreed that Jamie's ideas were sound and should be incorporated.

The first order of the day was to excavate a portion of the hillside behind the house for a second guest suite and family room. The space was there, and although Kendra saw no reason to finish it immediately, roughing it in would add valuable square footage to the house were it ever needed.

Cash joined Kendra on the front porch, where she had gone to get farther away from the grinding whir of a cement mixer. "You having second thoughts?"

It was eight a.m. and she was already fanning herself with the Outlook section of last Sunday's *Washington Post.* She smiled up at him. "Absolutely not. I'm having fourteenth thoughts. Fifteenth, maybe."

"It'll all be worth it. You'll have central air."

"I tell myself that a lot."

"I'll tell you how to keep yourself cool without it. Simmer a pot of water with lavender and rosemary, then strain it and put it in the refrigerator. When the weather gets hot like this, you dab it all over you, then sit out on the porch with a big glass of cold mint tea. It's all anybody needs."

"And that's what you do?"

"Me? I sit inside where I've got ceiling fans and air-conditioning and open a six-pack."

She laughed. "Any other tips for the less fortunate?"

"I know a bundle of folk remedies. That comfrey you got in that pot on the porch, for instance. You can use that to help heal broken bones. Did you know that?"

She was delighted. "I *thought* that was comfrey. I dug it out of the garden and put it in that pot. It looks like an illustration in one of my herb books, but I wasn't sure. I should have shown it to you. Nobody else has been able to tell me."

"Called it knitbone in the old days."

"How do you know this stuff?"

"My granny. She was a dowser, too. She didn't exactly take to anything new. Whenever she could get me to sit still, she taught me the old ways."

"Well, I guess someday we'll see if she taught you anything helpful."

"When it's time, I'll figure out where to drill a better well. You don't have to worry."

Cash was just getting up again when they heard a shout from the back of the house. The machinery ground to a halt. A stream of profanity filled the silence.

"I guess I'd better see what's up." Cash strode back through the dogtrot. Since she had nothing better to do, Kendra followed.

Behind the house, where a gaping hole abutted the structure, she saw the problem. Black Beauty, who hadn't been spotted since construction began, had reappeared. One of the men had him cornered against two boulders that had been excavated and set above the new hole in the ground. The huge snake was coiled as if to attack. As Kendra watched, the youngest of the workers, a skinny man with long stringy hair under a lumberyard cap, came striding over with a rifle. He motioned with his head for the other man to move away.

"Let him go. He gets away from those rocks, I'll shoot."

The other man stepped back, and the snake began to wriggle away.

Kendra didn't have a moment to think. She flashed back through time to the night when she had cowered in a dark parking lot, terrified she was about to die. She saw a handgun swinging up, heard the loud report of the bullet that had nearly severed her spine. Then she felt nothing but fury.

She jumped off the porch and took three steps toward the young man, knocking the rifle out of his hands just as he braced it against his shoulder.

"The hell, woman!" The man, red faced with anger, bent down to pick up his rifle. "That could have gone off!"

She stepped on the barrel so he couldn't retrieve it. "Don't you dare pick that up! Who told you it was okay to bring a gun on my property?"

He straightened, and his eyes were angry slits. "I carry it to protect myself!"

Cash was between them. He put a hand on Kendra's shoulder. "Randy here was trying to help."

"Help? That's not a poisonous snake! You told me yourself it kills rats and whatever else. And that has *nothing* to do with my point. Nobody but *nobody* sets foot on this property with a gun. I don't care if that's not the norm around here, do you understand?"

Everybody stared as if she were having a psychotic break right there at the construction site.

"It's a friggin' snake," Randy muttered. "I didn't want you being scared every time you saw it."

She tried to take a deep breath, but oxygen didn't help. She was shaking all over, and her leg was threatening to buckle. She needed to sit. For a moment she was afraid she was going to pass out.

Cash took her arm, as if he knew he had to steady her. "You all listen up, okay? Ms.

Taylor has about the best reason out there not to like guns. She got shot by some nut-case in the city, and you scared her half silly just now. Okay? You understand what I'm saying?"

She saw six sets of eyes sizing her up, trying to figure out exactly who they were dealing with and whether they wanted to continue. A lot rested on her response. No one here was a gun-wielding maniac like the man who had shot her. These were men who were used to guns, who saw Randy's response as nothing more than chivalry laced with a smidgen of bravado. She could let them know she understood and keep their respect, or she could disregard the obvious facts and flog her self-righteousness.

She lifted her foot off the rifle barrel. It took every ounce of strength. "I guess I scared you half silly, too."

"Somebody should have told us," Randy said, half under his breath.

"Well, you know," Cash said, his tone changing to something a little less friendly, "I don't half expect my crew to get gun-happy on me. So if I didn't say anything, that's why. Maybe I better think of anything else I need to warn you about. You know, the stuff I thought good sense would cover."

Kendra knew it was up to her to salvage the situation. She didn't want the men who would be here every day to take a dislike to her. She wanted them to like their job and do it well. She held out her hand, even though it was visibly shaking.

"In the city guns only mean one thing. I guess it's different out here. I appreciate you trying to protect me, Randy. But nowadays I'm a lot more afraid of guns than I am of that snake. And my nieces love him. I don't know what I'd tell them if somebody shot him."

Randy took her hand, because there was really nothing else he could do. He mumbled his response. "I'm sorry. I didn't mean to frighten you."

"I appreciate that. Thank you."

"You oughta post your land, though. You don't want hunters, you got to put notices all around your perimeter. Come fall, you'll wish you had."

"I'll make sure that gets done." She looked around. "Anyone see where my snake went?"

Randy answered. "Ma'am, that snake's

long gone. But if he comes back, we'll be sure to leave him alone." He glanced at the other men. "You want we should protect the rattlers and copperheads, too?"

Somebody laughed. Kendra could feel the tension ease. She managed a brief smile. "Can we tackle that later?"

The men peeled off to do what they'd come to do. Cash clapped Randy on the back to show there were no hard feelings. Then he stepped up to the dogtrot and held out his hand to help Kendra back up. "That leg of yours okay? That was a big leap for you."

She realized her bad leg was throbbing. A lot. "It's okay, but I'd better take it easy for a while."

He walked her to the front. "If you're going to live in the country, you got to understand country people. We don't have much in the way of animal control out here. We have a problem, we take care of it ourselves."

She countered, "And *you* have to understand we don't live in the kind of world where you can shoot anything that moves. Randy's not Daniel Boone."

"You know what I think? People like him

and people like you probably got a lot more in common than you imagine. It's too bad somebody doesn't sit down and explain it in a way that makes sense to reasonable people on both sides. Because gun control is one of those issues that's going to define the twenty-first century."

Over the weeks she had become even more aware that Cash was both intelligent and educated. "You were good back there. They listen to you. They like you."

He grinned. "What's not to like? I'm just a simple country boy."

Hours later, Kendra sat on the front porch, watching darkness steal across the clearing. All the lights were off, although the first mosquitoes of the season were finding their way to her anyway. She had done research and found that a variety of herbs were supposed to repel them. Catnip oil, lemon grass, pennyroyal, rosemary. Skeptical, she settled for spraying DEET on her arms and legs, although she had citronella candles ready if needed.

She was exhausted, and her leg was throbbing relentlessly. She still felt unsettled from the morning's confrontation. As she faced off with Randy, she had relived the parking lot scene, and several times, as the day progressed, she had flashed back to the shooting. Those brief interludes had taken a toll. Now, when she thought about guns on her land, she felt light-headed with both anxiety and fury.

More than once since moving here, she had sensed someone on her property and sloughed it off as imagination. Now she wondered if poachers were stalking prey in her woods, although she'd heard no gunshots nearby since moving in. Spring was definitely not deer season, but she knew some hunters paid little attention to the calendar. And what could she do to protect herself? Get her own gun? Wasn't it a gun that had caused all her problems?

She closed her eyes and tried to let her mind drift to something pleasant. Thunder rumbled in the distance. Rain was expected later, and the local farmers would be happy, since spring had been dry. She would lie in bed and listen to the drops thrum against the tin roof.

Lie alone and worry about poachers.

She forced her mind in a different direction. The renovation was a hassle, no question, but the result? The result was going to be glorious. She could imagine just how lovely the house would be once it was finished. Though living right at the worksite was challenging, traveling back and forth to make decisions when she resumed her job was going to be more so.

Just the thought of moving back to the city made her heart speed. And what *didn't,* this evening? She couldn't think about her job, her husband, her sister and nieces, her injuries, the future. . . .

In frustration, she opened her eyes and there, at the clearing's edge, stood three deer: two does and a young buck. They were about forty feet away. As she watched, they drew closer.

She held her breath and waited as they approached the porch. She knew this was a common enough sight here, that her neighbors would probably shout or fire shotguns to send them into the woods. Vegetable gardens needed protection; so did azaleas and hydrangeas.

She preferred the deer to anything planted in the clearing. Against all odds, traffic, hunters, encroaching civilization, the deer were testimony to Mother Nature's resourcefulness.

The buck raised his head and stared straight at her. She stared back, curious what he would do. The standoff lasted for seconds. Then he turned and leapt toward the woods. In a moment, his female companions followed.

"Goodbye," Kendra whispered. "You're welcome anytime."

The sky was growing darker. She would have to move inside before the rain arrived, but the deer had worked a bit of magic. She felt comforted. She would fix a simple dinner, maybe drink a glass of wine with it, and afterward she would write to her sister. She would tell Jamie what had been done so far and explain that what was now the cabin's living area would be a wonderful guest suite, just the way Jamie had suggested. Kendra would ask her to bring the girls and be the first guests to use the suite the moment it was finished. She would install bunk beds along one wall.

She got to her feet and squinted into the purple-tinged twilight, hoping to get one last glimpse of the deer. At first she saw nothing but trees and shadows. Then she saw movement.

For a moment she thought the deer had stopped just inside the woods, planning to return to the clearing after she went inside. But as she watched, she saw a slim figure move from one tree to another.

A man.

Without thinking, she slipped behind a porch pillar, her breath catching in her throat. She could see he was moving farther into the woods. If he'd been watching the house, now his attention was elsewhere. She was fairly certain she knew the cause. Three deer, and the hell with hunting season.

The fury she'd felt that morning returned. Someone was stalking the lovely creatures that had visited her clearing. She felt impotent. Who was she to go up against a man who was probably carrying a rifle? Hadn't she already gone up against a maniac and almost been killed?

But what if she could scare him away? What if she went into the woods and shouted that she'd seen him and called the sheriff? What if she let the man know he'd been spotted and ought to leave before someone arrived? Would he know the threat was bogus, that the sheriff's department probably didn't have the manpower to follow up on this kind of call, and that if they tried, it might be hours before anyone arrived?

Even if *he* wasn't frightened away by her shouts, the deer certainly would be.

She was no fool. She had no business in the woods at night just before a storm, facing off with a poacher. But even as she considered it, she was moving away from the pillar and toward the steps. The bullets that had lodged inside her had clearly destroyed more than tissue; they had destroyed her ability to be rational in the face of danger.

Anger carried her forward anyway. "Hey, get out of there! Leave those deer alone. I've called the sheriff's department, and they're sending somebody."

She limped toward the edge of the woods. She thought she saw a figure farther ahead. She moved beyond the perimeter, hobbling slowly from tree to tree.

"I'm serious. Get out of here! It's not deer season, and this is private property. This is my land and you're trespassing!"

She was breathing hard now. Suddenly

she realized the man she'd seen might be Randy, exacting revenge for the way he'd been treated in front of his coworkers. Maybe her attempt to make amends hadn't helped. Maybe he had more on his mind than hunting deer.

She stopped, aware that she had clearly lost her mind. Someone was out here, and she was shouting like a maniac. Logic threaded through rage. She wondered if she wanted to die, if in the wake of a difficult and painful recovery she had become so discouraged that she was begging someone to finish her off.

Logic, having made inroads, was now a flood.

"Lord . . ." She put her hand on her forehead and leaned forward, trying to catch her breath.

Nothing she'd done was rational. She was identifying with deer. She had transferred her feelings to them. *For the second time that day she was challenging the man who had shot her in a dark parking lot, even though he was safely in prison.*

She listened. Somewhere in front of her, a twig cracked. She wondered how she could have been so foolish, made herself so vulnerable.

She had moved farther into the woods than she'd realized. The clearing was well behind her. She knew the way out, but could she get out, without attracting more attention? By now the deer were long gone. The hunter had no good reason to stay. Night was falling fast, and unless he was equipped with night-vision goggles, he'd missed his chance for fresh venison steak.

She waited and listened. She heard another twig snap, but she thought the sound was farther away. The man was either continuing his hunt or heading through the woods, back to a truck, perhaps, or over the hills.

She could hardly catch her breath. She felt sick and shaky, and her leg was throbbing as badly as it had that morning after she'd jumped off the porch. The thunder rumbled, and she knew the storm was moving closer. She began to wonder how she would make it back to the house without collapsing.

She heard more noise beyond her. In the past few minutes, crickets had begun their nightly serenade, and somewhere in the distance, crows cawed good-night. But over the sounds of a Virginia spring evening, she heard brush rustling, as if someone was passing through it just ahead of her.

She had to start back before the forest grew so dark that she lost her bearings and the storm arrived.

She moved slowly, feeling her way. The ground at her feet was shrouded by brush and vines. With sunlight filtering through the trees, it was easy enough to pick her way through it, but now she had to test each step before she gave it her full weight. Brambles snagged her jeans and she stopped to untangle herself. She thought about Black Beauty and wondered if he was nearby. A black snake would be the least of her worries, but she didn't want to encounter him in the darkness. She doubted his mood was any better than hers.

She inched along, wincing every time she put her weight on the injured ankle. She was silently berating herself for setting back her recovery, when she stepped into the hole. One moment the ground was firm as she tentatively shifted her weight, the next it fell away. Pain shot through the injured ankle, and she fell forward. She managed to catch herself as she hit the ground, but her right hand slammed against a rock. The pain in her wrist rivaled the pain in her leg. She was stunned by it.

The forest went suddenly silent. She realized she had cried out, temporarily interrupting the twilight symphony. She bit her lip, trying not to moan, but the pain was fierce. Tears filled her eyes, and despite all efforts, she began to sob.

Moments passed while she gave in to her misery. Then, choking back tears and using her good hand, she managed to sit up. When she inched her injured foot from the hole and pressed it against level ground, agony shot through her.

She couldn't imagine how she was going to get back to the house. Clearly she couldn't put weight on the ankle now. Whatever damage she'd done to it that morning had just been made a hundred times worse. And who would guess she was here? Tomorrow was Sunday and no one would arrive to work on the house. When she didn't show up at church, no one would give her absence a second thought, assuming she just wasn't up to it.

She had no choice but to drag herself

back to the cabin, sparing the ankle and wrist as much as she could. But she knew better than to think that could be accomplished quickly. Dragging herself with one hand and leg, resting, starting over, would take half the night. And a storm was on its way.

She was such a fool. Isaac was right. She had no business being out in the middle of nowhere. Her friends and neighbors had been kind, but it wasn't their job to keep watch over her. Jamie had tried, and Kendra had chased her sister away.

"Ma'am?"

She gasped. The voice came from the darkness. "Who's there?"

"Did you hurt yourself?"

"Who are you?" She wiped her nose on the back of a hand grimy with forest soil and peered into the darkness.

A figure materialized. The boy—and he was just a boy—appeared almost like a ghost in the shadows. But as he stepped closer, he formed into flesh and bone.

"Name's Caleb."

"What are you doing out here?" She looked for his gun. "You're hunting, aren't you? You're the one I saw."

"I don't hunt."

"Then what are you doing?"

"Watching."

"Watching me?"

"The deer."

She tried to take this in, but the pain was more immediate than his words. "You've been here before?"

He stooped beside her. She saw that his hair was light, and his face still had the rounded cheeks of childhood. She guessed he might be as old as fourteen or as young as ten.

He didn't look her in the eyes. "Never meant any harm. Can you stand?"

"No chance of that."

"You got to go back inside before the rain comes."

"You're the one I shouted at?"

He was silent for a long time. Then said softly, "Didn't mean to scare you."

"Well, you did."

He nodded, as if accepting that. "I'll help you up."

"You can't manage my weight."

"I can." He got to his feet and held out his hand.

"I injured my ankle."

"Got another one, right?"

Despite everything, she found that funny. The laugh was closer to hysteria than pleasure, and she hiccuped. "For the record, I injured my wrist, too. And yes, I have two of those, as well."

He didn't smile. He was a somber boy and he'd yet to meet her eyes. He dropped his arm and drew closer, stooping again.

"Put your arm 'round my shoulder."

She was taller than he was, and he was slender. "I'll pull you over." She weighed her choices. "Considering you got me into this, you deserve to be pulled over."

"Yes, ma'am."

She gathered what was left of her strength and put her arm over his shoulders. Then, using her good hand and leg, she pushed hard as he stood. She realized she was now upright, but dizzy from the pain.

"Wait a minute," she gasped.

He stood perfectly still while she took deep breaths, willing herself not to faint. Even with his help, she wasn't sure how she was going to manage this.

"You lean hard," he said. "I can take it."

They did manage somehow. She almost blacked out once. The boy was stronger than he looked and he kept her upright, although there were several close calls. What seemed like hours later, he helped her lower herself to the porch steps. She gritted her teeth and used the railing to jack herself up until she was sitting on the porch itself. From there, Caleb helped her stand again, just long enough to get inside and into a chair near the telephone.

"I'll be going now," he said, heading for the door.

"Wait, you haven't . . . told me anything about yourself."

But by then he was gone, the door closing softly behind him.

CHAPTER FIFTEEN

"What a mess." Elisa knelt at Kendra's feet, gently feeling her friend's ankle. Outside, lightning still shattered the darkness, but at longer intervals.

When her friend moved the ankle to the right, Kendra gasped. Elisa continued to probe. "I'm guessing it's a really nasty sprain. But you have to get an X ray in the morning. No arguments. Ice tonight. Twenty minutes on, twenty minutes off. I brought a couple of packs. And four ibuprofen for pain and swelling. Now, let's see the wrist."

Kendra held out her arm. Elisa made tsking noises under her breath, then went for a washcloth and basin to clean it.

"Not as bad as the foot," she said, peering at her handiwork when she'd finished. "But you will have a nasty bruise on the heel of your palm. You'll probably need a simple splint to keep the wrist from bending while it heals."

Kendra was bleary-eyed with misery and exhaustion. The moment Caleb left, she'd called Elisa. Now Elisa emptied the basin and returned with an ice pack, carefully wrapping it around the injured ankle and fastening it in place with what looked like strips of an old towel. Then she handed Kendra the pills and a glass of water.

Kendra swallowed them gratefully. "I can't thank you enough for helping me."

Elisa patted her shoulder. "So, you've met Caleb."

"I'm pretty sure he's been in my woods before."

"He's Cissy's brother. He lives with her in-laws, the Claibornes."

That much sounded familiar. "She did mention him."

"He hasn't been here long. It's complicated." Elisa pulled the coffee table closer to Kendra's chair and gently propped her leg on a sofa pillow.

Kendra closed her eyes. "How fast do you think the Advil will work?"

"Not fast enough, but it's the best I can

do until I'm licensed to practice medicine again."

She wanted to concentrate on something other than her ankle. "Tell me about Caleb."

"Well, Cissy hadn't seen him in years. In fact, she thought she would never see him again. When she was a girl, her mother was declared unfit, and Cissy went to live with her grandmother. But the grandmother didn't have the strength to take them both, so Caleb was put up for adoption."

"What happened?"

"Once Caleb was in state custody, the authorities discovered he had a heart defect. He had several surgeries, spent a lot of time in hospitals and special group homes. By the time he was well enough to live a normal life, he was too old to be easily adoptable. An enterprising social worker looked up his records and discovered he had a sister who by then was old enough to take him in. She tracked down Cissy, who was thrilled."

"But he doesn't live with her?"

"Cissy's awfully young, and she has Reese and Helen to worry about. So the Claibornes stepped up to the plate. They'd already raised three boys, but I think their house was feeling too empty. So they volunteered. Cissy spends every minute she can with Caleb, and the Claibornes take up the slack."

"Is it working out?"

Elisa was silent.

Kendra opened her eyes. "No?"

"Caleb has led a troubled life. He's a loner. He refuses to make friends or spend time with kids from school. He rarely smiles or says much. He does what he's told without complaint, but he's just going through the motions. He has had therapy, of course, but that doesn't help much if your life is unstable."

Kendra had seen a different side of Caleb. "Apparently he loves animals. He was following a group of deer. And he came to my rescue, even though I'd yelled at him to go away. That's not going through the motions. A lot of well-adjusted teenagers would have run for cover."

"It is a good sign."

Kendra shifted her foot, and pain shot through it. She winced. "He reminds me of Isaac. Isaac was also at the mercy of people who didn't love him. It's like this ankle. Everything's just fine until I make the slightest change. Caleb and Isaac are careful not to change a thing, because they're afraid that however bad things are, they *really* won't like what comes next."

"I called Isaac, Kendra."

Kendra sat forward, and regretted it immediately. "When?"

"I called before I came. Because you can't stay here alone. You have to have somebody helping you for the next few days, and I have interviews in D.C. and Charlottesville tomorrow and the next day. We can find somebody from the church to stay with you, but Isaac deserved the right of first refusal."

"You should have asked me first. I can manage—"

Elisa cut her off. "No, you can't. There are some things you can't do alone."

Kendra started to argue, then fell silent as she remembered her talk with Sam. There was a common theme here. "What did he say?" she asked at last.

"He's on his way. He should be here before too long."

"I'll bet he wasn't happy."

"He didn't tell me his feelings. He just said he would come. Without hesitation."

"You know I'll never be able to trust what he does. Is he coming because he feels guilty he let me down the night I was shot? Or is he coming . . . ?"

"Because he loves you?"

Kendra shrugged.

"Why don't you just dispense with the tests and ask him?"

Kendra heard the gentle censure. "Because I'm afraid to hear what he'll say."

"But once you know for sure, you can move forward."

"Right now I can't move at all."

Elisa rested her hand on Kendra's shoulder in comfort. "Good. That means you can't run away. And if he is the decent person I think he is, neither can he."

The last time Isaac had driven this fast, he'd been following Kendra's ambulance to George Washington Hospital. That night would haunt him forever. There had been a moment that night when he had considered driving past the hospital, out of Foggy Bottom, abandoning the District forever. He had imagined himself driving through Maryland and Pennsylvania into the flat prairies of the Midwest. He'd wondered how far he could drive before exhaustion claimed him. And what would he do when he reached the West Coast and there was only the Pacific Ocean crashing in front of him?

He had told Kendra not to move into the cabin. He'd warned her that she might encounter problems living alone. The woman he married could have survived alone in a Bedouin tent or a thatched hut on the Amazon. But this new Kendra, this fragile creature who had come so close to death, had too few resources and too many needs. He had told her, and she had refused to listen.

He was angry. He could feel it boiling up inside him. Kendra had placed herself in danger, almost as if she were thumbing her nose at him. *You won't take care of me, so I'll take care of myself.*

Now he wondered how badly she was injured. What would he find when he got there? A false alarm and a wife on the porch to greet him? An empty cabin with a note telling him where another ambulance had taken her? He had planned to visit her again, but he'd found one excuse after another to delay.

But if he'd come, if he'd just come . . .

He banged his palm against the steering wheel.

No matter what he found, it was time for Kendra to come home. He'd had enough of worrying, of wondering, of his hand poised over the telephone as he debated whether to call, just to hear her voice. She had insisted she wanted solitude, but now he was going to insist she abandon it.

He arrived in the final whimper of the thunderstorm and saw Kendra's and Elisa's cars. He pulled in and sprinted toward the porch. Something too much like a river ran along the side of the cabin, washing away soil as it flowed. He didn't bother to knock when he entered. He pushed the bedroom door open, but no one was there. He crossed the dogtrot and opened the living room door. Kendra was sitting in the armchair, her foot propped on a pillow. Elisa was walking toward her with an ice pack.

"How are you?" he asked his wife without preliminaries. He fixed his gaze on Elisa's hands as he spoke.

"Better than I have a right to be."

Kendra managed to sound nonchalant, but he could tell she was in pain.

"I don't think anything is broken." Elisa

pressed the pack against Kendra's ankle and tied it in place. "But she has a nasty sprain. She will need X rays tomorrow, wrist and ankle, just to be sure."

"Thanks for calling me."

"She needs to stay as quiet as possible. That means she will need help."

"That's why I came."

"I'm actually sitting right here," Kendra said. "In case anyone's forgotten."

Elisa straightened. "You may have four more Advil in three hours. You will call your doctor first thing in the morning?"

"Good thing I found one in Woodstock."

To Isaac, the fact that Kendra now had a local doctor was one more sign she intended to stay in Toms Brook. He felt anger slice through him again, even as he told himself that having a doctor nearby only made sense.

"I can take over from here." Even to his ears, his voice was too gruff.

Elisa took her purse off a chair. "She's had a hard evening."

He heard the warning. *Don't make it any harder.* He gave a curt nod. "I'll take good care of her."

"I like to leave my patients in good hands."

"I'll walk you to your car." He glanced at his wife, something he had tried not to do. Her complexion was drained of color, and her freckles stood out in sharp relief. Her expression was haunted. "You'll be okay?"

"I'm not going anywhere."

That was debatable.

He opened the door for Elisa. Outside, the storm was now a drizzle. She stopped at the edge of the porch and drew a deep breath. "It's cooler. I was afraid it might just be more humid."

The temperature had dropped, although he hadn't cared enough to notice. "Watch where you step. There's a stream flowing past the house."

They descended together. Now the drizzle actually felt good, balm against his heated skin. He slowed his pace to match hers.

"Kendra would like us to think she's recovering on schedule," Elisa said. "But she won't recover fully until she faces the damage she has suffered."

"What in the hell was she doing out in the woods with a storm coming? And with the threat of poachers? It's a terrible idea for her to stay here. I hope she'll see reason now."

Elisa was silent until they reached her car. Then she faced him. "I have to disagree."

"With which part?"

"It's a *good* idea for her to stay here. Too many people use work, exercise, useless activity to keep from asking themselves questions about their lives. She has made a commitment to ask. What she hasn't yet done is listen to the answers."

"You're talking in riddles."

"You will have to find the answers together."

"That's pretty hard to do when she's so far away."

"You're here now. She's here."

He watched her get in the little Honda and drive away; then he took a deep breath. Things were better than he'd feared. Kendra was in pain but otherwise all right. There was no emergency.

Minutes passed before he went inside. Kendra's eyes were closed, so he examined her in the lamplight. Her breathing was too fast and her lips were drawn down in pain. Her expression and bravado reminded him of the alley cat he'd rescued. Somehow, despite all predictions, the cat had survived surgery and had been released from the animal hospital to recover at the apartment of ACRE's vice president of marketing. Kendra would recover, as well.

Kendra opened her eyes. "Make yourself at home. There's a container of chicken soup in the fridge. Did you eat dinner?"

"I'm not hungry."

"I think there's beer. I know there's half a bottle of wine on the counter."

"Would you like something?"

"A new start to the day. I'd do it a little differently."

"I imagine." He went into the kitchen to rummage through the refrigerator. He found four bottles of beer squeezed behind cartons of milk and orange juice, and took one. He recognized it as a leftover from their barbecue.

He found an opener; then he poured Kendra a glass of wine. She took it gratefully.

"If I pass out right here, just leave me. I'll never know the difference."

"How long do I leave the ice pack in place?"

"Twenty on, twenty off."

He took the seat across from her. “How does it feel?”

“Like I stepped in a hole and nearly separated the foot from the ankle.”

He didn’t know where to go from there. He sipped his beer as if that took great energy and concentration.

“You’re dying to ask me what happened, aren’t you,” she said at last.

“I got the basics from Elisa.”

“I didn’t ask her to call you.”

“I’m sure you didn’t.”

“What does that mean?”

Anger flared again, despite all his earlier attempts to dampen it. He set the bottle on the table with inordinate care. “It means I know you’d rather drag yourself through the forest like a wounded animal than ask me for anything.”

Her eyes widened. “Well, that’s true enough.”

“You sound surprised. Maybe you think I haven’t noticed?”

Something sparked in her eyes, either pain or anger that was rising to match his. “Well, now that you mention it, I wasn’t sure. There’s not a lot you notice about me. I’ve become a piece of furniture in your well-ordered life."

"A piece of furniture conveniently removed to the country house?"

"More like a piece of furniture being refinished."

"Why don't we stop talking about furniture and talk about us?"

"We *are* talking about us."

He carefully spaced his words. "I have never stopped noticing you."

"And what does that mean, exactly? That you recognize my existence? Well, thanks a lot."

A familiar whisper in his head told him to call this quits right now. *Isaac, don't push him. Don't get him mad. You know what he'll do. Just let it go. Let it go. . . .*

"This is no time to argue," he said after a moment. "You've already had one hell of a day."

"I don't need a good ankle to get this out in the open."

"Get *what* out in the open?"

"Isaac, can you really be that clueless? Do I need to spell out everything? Okay, here I go." She leaned forward, although judging by her wince, the move cost her.

"I am less to you than your job. I am at most a convenience, somebody who pays half the mortgage, somebody you can take out to dinner and have sex with, or at least somebody you *used* to. I'm fine in my place, but that place doesn't include anything resembling intimacy. And when I become an inconvenience, I'm easy to sweep under the rug."

His mother's whispers died. He heard his own voice on the day he had taken Kendra home from the rehab unit. *I think Kendra and I can work things out together. We always have.*

And Dr. Gupta's response. *Have you? I wonder. Or, like most people, have you merely ignored the fragments that don't fit into the picture you hold of your marriage?*

"Why am I here, then?" he asked. "Why did I come all this way? Or am I too clueless to understand that, as well?"

"You came because you're basically a good person, and even you can't ignore the fact that the last time I needed you, you were too busy to help."

"I dropped everything after your phone call that night and drove like a maniac to get to the pharmacy." He leaned forward, too.

"And how was I to know you'd behave like an idiot and try to get the prescription when you should never, *never* have been behind the wheel of a car?"

"You really don't know me very well, do you? Do you have *any* idea how much it cost me just to ask for your help? I mean, this isn't a relationship where we really reach out to each other, is it. We're fine as long as we're both pulling equal weight. That's the way we wanted it."

"*We.* You said it. *We* wanted it that way. Apparently that was the deal we made."

"And what a deal, huh? All the good stuff and none of the bad. Did we take for better or for worse out of the vows we made? I can't remember. Of course, the ceremony was so casual, I don't think there was much in the way of vows. We pretty much just signed our names. Symbolic, isn't it?"

"I tried to help!"

"You were just a little late. How many times that night did you think of me at home, sick as a dog? None, right? None until I called that last time and made it clear I'd had it with your excuses. So you got in your car, just like you got in your car tonight. Not because of love, Isaac. Because of guilt.

And I don't want your guilt. And I don't want a marriage where the real vow is that we'll enjoy the better times and ignore the worse. I don't want it!"

"Great. Fine." He leapt to his feet. "You've made that clear a couple of times now. You don't want the marriage, you don't want me. Who starts the paperwork?"

"No, it's not going to be that easy. You can pretend you don't hear me, but I'm going to make this *perfectly* clear. I don't want this marriage the way it is. I've never said I don't want *you.*" Her face grew paler. "I will not divorce you over a misunderstanding. So let me lay it out. I need somebody I can count on, somebody who isn't a stranger to me. All these years I was willing to settle for whatever part of you I could have. But not anymore!"

"This is so much psychological claptrap." He was furious now, so angry that he couldn't even sort through her words. "You don't want me, you want a perfect man who doesn't have a life."

"No, I want a man who has both. A life *and* a marriage, with one enriching the other!"

"What do you want me to do? Hang on your every word?"

"I want you to share what's in your heart. I want you to share what's in mine."

"Oh, that makes it a lot clearer!" He was shouting now, angrier than he remembered being since adolescence.

"You want an example? Here's one. I'd like to know why this is the first time in all the years we've been together that we've had a real fight."

"We've argued plenty of times."

"This is not an argument!"

"What, do you want me to analyze myself right here and now? Share every little suspicion and inkling?"

"Damn it, yes, I would!" She was shouting now, too.

"Okay, because I am not my father! I will never raise a hand to a woman, not as long as I live! I will never hurt you the way he hurt my mother!"

She stared at him.

He was breathing hard now, and his hands were balled into fists. But he hadn't moved closer to her. A minute passed, then two. Little by little his fists uncurled and his breathing slowed.

"You are *not* your father," she said softly. "You are *nothing* like him and never will be. And I will *never* have any reason to be frightened of you, no matter how angry you are. Apparently I trust you more than you trust yourself."

He felt as if someone had cracked his chest and laid his heart out to be clinically examined.

He was outside before he even realized he was on the way. He took the porch steps two at a time and strode the distance to his car, then he leaned against the hood and crossed his arms over his fantasy wound.

"You'd better not hurt her."

Isaac whirled and saw a slim figure in the darkness. The figure moved closer. Isaac saw it was a boy in his early teens, a boy holding his hands away from his sides like a gunslinger about to draw a weapon.

"You hit her?" the boy asked.

Isaac stared up at the stars. "Of course not."

"You're sure?"

As odd as the question was, Isaac thought about it a while. "No, I would never hit her."

The words were strangely freeing. He had

not so much as grabbed his wife's shoulder. As furious as he had been, he had never considered touching her. He wasn't stupid. He knew his childhood had deeply affected him. But had he ever fully realized how terrified he was that any display of anger would turn him into Colonel Grant Taylor? That this distrust of his own emotions was part of the legacy his adopted father had left him? Fear that at every disappointment, every misstep, every missed opportunity, he, like the colonel, would strike out at the people he was supposed to love?

"She okay?" the boy asked.

"You're Caleb, aren't you," he said, remembering the name Elisa had mentioned on the telephone.

"So?"

"Thanks for helping Kendra. I'm Isaac, her husband. I don't know what we would have done without you."

"You were shouting at her."

"We're angry at each other right now. Very angry."

"No call to shout at a woman."

"Sometimes people don't know how else to get things said."

"How come she lives here all alone if she's got a husband?"

He weighed his answer. He didn't know this boy, but he sensed no harm in the question. After the evening's episode, Caleb had elected himself Kendra's protector. Instinctively, Isaac knew that this boy saw himself as a protector of all things weaker. He also guessed there had been far too many times in Caleb's short life that there hadn't been anyone weaker than himself.

Isaac could recognize a kindred spirit.

"I work in the city," Isaac said. "She came out here to recover from an injury. I'll be coming and going."

"She needs somebody to help her."

"I'm staying until she can get around on her own."

"Staying and shouting." It wasn't a question.

"It's late, and somebody somewhere's worried about you. Do they know you're gone?"

Caleb didn't answer.

"I'll take good care of her," Isaac said at last. "I promise."

"You'd better."

Isaac watched the boy fade back into the

shadows. Until he could summon the strength to go inside and face his wife, he stood perfectly still and remembered himself as a boy like Caleb, disappearing into the shadows of a world where he had been powerless and alone.

CHAPTER SIXTEEN

The next morning Kendra woke up alone. Isaac had carried her to bed, but after their fight, conversation had been perfunctory. He had helped her into a nightgown and performed his nursing duties like a pro. In the middle of the night, when she had woken in pain, he'd gotten up to give her more pills. At that point he'd been sleeping beside her. She did remember that much.

Now, as she levered herself to a sitting position, both the ankle and wrist throbbed unmercifully. Isaac chose that moment to return with a tray.

"Hey, I was going to help you."

She was wary. "It's okay. I made it. I wasn't sure—"

"If I was here? Of course I'm here. I'm

staying until you're on your feet again. That's that."

She didn't want a repeat of last night's fight. She had criticized him for not talking about the things that mattered, but she wasn't much better at talking than he was. She was emotionally drained.

"What about work?" she asked.

"I can do some here. Heather volunteered to bring anything I need. I made breakfast. You don't have many groceries."

"I planned to shop this morning. Are the workers here?"

"Not yet."

"That smells good."

"Coffee. Toast. Yogurt. No wonder you're so skinny."

She raised a brow. "Skinny?" He'd said it almost playfully. And how long had it been since they'd teased each other about anything?

"I'm going to fatten you up. I remember a more well-rounded woman. I plan to find her."

"The neighbors have been stuffing me like a Thanksgiving turkey."

"They've been bringing you food, but have you been eating it?"

"Some."

Isaac set the tray on the bed beside her. "You have a doctor's appointment at nine-thirty. Elisa persuaded him it's an emergency."

"Okay. I'll be ready."

"I know. I'll make sure of it."

He did. She ate; then he helped her into the bathroom again, helped her dress, helped her to the car. He sat patiently in the waiting room, helped her into an examination room, then took her over to the hospital for the X rays the doctor agreed that she needed. Afterward he took her back to the office to have her wrist and ankle wrapped and crutches issued, then to the pharmacy.

By the time Isaac had scooped her up and carried her up the stairs of the cabin and into the living room, the workers were busily excavating the hillside, and Kendra was so tired she could hardly keep her eyes open.

"One of these should help." Isaac stood in front of her with a glass of water and a pill. "It must hurt like hell."

She swallowed the prescription painkiller greedily.

"I'd ask if you want a nap, but you won't

be able to sleep with that racket outside. Let me know when you're ready for lunch."

"Not for a while."

Someone knocked at the front door, interrupting any new forays into polite chitchat. She was supremely grateful. The effort of pretending everything was fine was exhausting her.

Isaac went to the door and let Sam in. He was wearing shorts and a T-shirt with "Blessed Are They Who Can Laugh at Themselves, for They Shall Never Cease to be Amused" written across the front.

"I got the blow-by-blow from Elisa," he said, bending over to kiss her on the cheek. "How are you doing?"

"Elisa had it nailed. No broken bones, just sprains. Rest, painkillers and immobilization for a while. But I'll be fine."

"Good. Do you two need anything?"

"Isaac's promised to get some groceries later."

"How much later?" Sam asked him.

"I thought I'd go this afternoon," Isaac said.

"Feel like going for a run with me in the meantime? It's my day off."

Isaac looked as if somebody had just offered him a gold mine. Then, carefully, he shook his head. "I'd better—"

"You'd better go," Kendra said. "Or I'll get up and shove you out the door with my crutches. I need some time to moan without anybody listening."

"You're sure?"

She wasn't sure which was harder. Saying all the things that still had to be said or politely dancing around them. She only knew she was so worn out that having Isaac gone for a while was the antidote. "Go."

"I'll change and be right with you." Isaac left for the bedroom.

"How's it really going?" Sam asked once the door had closed behind Isaac.

"It's going to be a long road or a short side trip. I don't know which." She was sure he knew what she meant.

"It took you a long time to get where you are. It'll take a long time to go somewhere else. 'The journey of a thousand miles starts with a single step.' "

"Straight from one of your T-shirts?"

"From Lao Tzu by way of a T-shirt. I'll take care of Isaac, you take care of yourself."

The two men left together. Kendra could hear workmen shouting in the back and the incessant drone of heavy machinery. But the painkiller had begun to do its job. She felt almost comfortable for the first time since she'd fallen. She closed her eyes.

Another knock sounded. Her eyelids flew open and she called, "Come in."

Helen stepped into the room. "What's this I hear about you getting hurt again?"

"Is there a neon sign by the roadside?"

"Now you're getting smart with me."

"I just feel pretty stupid, that's all."

"From what I hear, you surely ought to." Helen came in and made herself at home in a chair. "The Claibornes told Cissy. I guess they drug it out of Caleb last night. The boy's not much for talking."

"If it weren't for him, I might still be lying in the woods."

"You'd have got yourself up here some way or t'other."

Kendra appreciated that no-nonsense statement of confidence. She noted Helen was carrying a grocery bag, but she knew better than to ask what was inside. Helen would tell her when she was good and ready. She settled for gossip instead.

"Elisa told me Caleb's story. How long has he been here?"

"Let's see, it's May now. He come just after Christmas, from over Norfolk way. Cissy, well, you never seen anybody as glad as she was to see that boy. Of course Caleb doesn't remember her. He was too little when they were separated."

"Is he doing okay with the Clairbornes? Elisa said he's having problems adjusting."

"Marian and Ron, well, I never seen people try harder. I think if he burned down their house, they'd just ask him to help build another one. Not that he'd do a thing like that, mind you. But that's just to say they'll stick with him, no matter. They have three sons. They know what boy trouble looks like."

"They sound like good people."

"Cissy worries about him."

Kendra understood that too well. She was going to worry about Caleb, too. She searched for a less emotional subject. "How was your trip? Did they treat you well at the Quilt Museum?"

"They like to have sucked every single thing I know about quilts out of this brain of mine. I'd be surprised if anything's left."

"That's the best way to keep history alive."

"I brought *you* a little history. And a

casserole, too. Don't you dare fuss over it, either. It's just macaroni and cheese I made first thing after I heard, but the quilters'll be coming by with more. So you won't have to worry about cooking for a while."

Kendra reached over and squeezed Helen's hand. "You're all so good to me. I think I owe you about a hundred meals."

"Give or take."

"My husband's here, and he'll be taking care of me, but he can't cook worth a darn."

"Time he learned." Helen took a plastic storage container from the grocery bag and set it on Kendra's lap. "These are for you."

Kendra could see fabric inside, but she was mystified. She unsealed the top and pulled out a stack of quilt blocks, setting them on her lap. "Well, would you look at these."

"They been cluttering up my sewing room for longer than you've been alive. If I haven't got to them by now, I never will."

Kendra thumbed through the blocks. They were shades of brown, dusty pink, blue and plain muslin. Best of all, they were signature blocks. Names were penned somewhere on the muslin, each with a short

Bible quote above it. Each quote was different, and so was each pattern.

She looked up. "Where did they come from?"

"My mama sewed a little for money. I think somebody gave 'em to her to put together and quilt, although these were already old by then. From the colors and all, I'd say they're from the early 1900s. I recognize most of the names, folks from over near Strasburg. Used to be an old German church between here and there. I'm guessing the blocks came from them. Anyway, Mama took sick, then she died. Nobody ever come bothering us about them after that, and I was too busy to go searching up names. These women who signed this, they were old as the hills when I was still a girl. Maybe they were making it to give somebody who died before Mama could get to it. Whatever happened, there's nobody left to ask."

"You're not going to put them together?"

"I don't have the time. I have a hundred quilts of my own to make and probably no time left to make ten. I can give them to the rummage sale at church. Or I can give them to somebody who thinks they're interesting."

"You're giving them to me?"

"On one condition."

"Oh, no . . ."

"That's right. You have to sew them together. What good will they do anybody in a paper sack? Surprised they look as good as they do, aren't you?"

"You are much too trusting."

"You make a mistake, you can always tear it out."

"I don't have a sewing machine."

"Old fabric. It will do better to sew it by hand anyway."

Kendra knew she'd been bested. She was not going to let these beautiful blocks go to the rummage sale. "I just sew them one next to the other?"

"We'll talk about that at your first lesson."

"Lesson?"

Helen gave a definitive nod. "We can do it at the bee some Wednesday."

"You're good, you know?"

"Oh, I'm the very best." Helen took the casserole out of the bag and trudged into the kitchen with it. Kendra heard the refrigerator open and close, and Helen returned.

"One more thing, and then I'll go."

"You don't have to rush off," Kendra said.

"Cissy will be on her way back about now. No, I just wanted you to have those. See, the thing about those blocks is that I know facts about the people who signed them. Emma Haff? Hers is blue, one of those about in the middle of the stack. She grew sunflowers in her garden, right betwixt every cornstalk. People called her the sunflower lady, on account of her sunflowers growing tall every year and her corn being right spindly."

"The sunflower lady." Kendra liked the sound of that.

"And Melissa Putzkammer? Well, hers is pink, if I remember correctly. She was an old maid and mean as a scorpion. Come Halloween night, her outhouse was always the first to get tipped. She'd load her shotgun with rock salt and shoot anybody who come up her drive if they couldn't give a good enough reason to be there."

"But she made a block?"

"I'm thinking maybe she wasn't as bad as I remember. See, the thing is, quilts can teach you a lot of history."

"Uh-huh." Kendra knew more was coming.

"And I ran into some history at the museum. I wish you'd been there with me."

"Why?"

"Because I saw fragments of a quilt, just like your Lover's Knot. Almost exactly like it, I think."

Kendra was wide-awake now. "Helen, really? Where? What were the circumstances?"

"Well, that's the thing. It's not a pretty story."

"I don't care."

"Seems about a year ago they found two skeletons in a cave inside the park. They'd been there a long, long time. And they were wrapped in what was left of this quilt I mentioned. If I'm not mistaken, the quilt's a twin to the one your Isaac inherited."

Isaac usually ran alone, so he was surprised by how comfortable it was to run with Sam and two of the ugliest dogs he'd ever seen. The huge wolflike monstrosities, Shad and Shack, were every bit as friendly as they were ugly, and one of them—he wasn't sure which—had assigned himself to be Isaac's canine bodyguard, running right beside him.

"How often do you run?" Isaac asked.

"Three, four times a week. More if I can manage. How about you?"

"To and from work a couple of times a week when I know I'm staying in the office. On the treadmill a couple more. Kendra and I usually bike or hike on weekends if we're not working."

"My weekends are tied up, but I make sure I get outside on Mondays no matter what."

"Kendra says for a small church, yours is the busiest she's seen."

"We're calling an assistant minister. That'll give me more time for my prison ministry."

"You expect that kind of activism in the city," Isaac said. "Not out here."

"We have our share of problems with it. But I think the church is stronger for talking about issues."

"They used to talk about issues at the churches I went to as a boy. Mostly who they could target that week. Politicians, usually, who didn't see the world the way they did."

"Condemning people isn't our style. You ought to come with Kendra sometime and see."

"Is this a conversion speech?"

"Nothing like it. I think you'd find friends and a place to think."

"I've had enough church to last a lifetime. I saw what it didn't do for my mother."

"Your mother was a churchgoer?"

"My father chose our churches, but we went as a family every Sunday. Religion was just one of the ways he kept us in line. He used to quote scripture while he beat us. He was the master of Biblical excuses."

The moment he'd admitted this, Isaac wondered why. The fight with Kendra last night? A heavy-handed stab at Sam's own faith? A warning that religion was a closed subject?

"I'm sorry. Did your mother ever leave him?"

"She found a lump in her breast and didn't see a doctor. I think she was hoping she would die, and she did. Nobody cried harder than the colonel."

"He's still around?"

"Somewhere. Mother's dead, and now

that I'm bigger than he is, the thrill's gone out of having a family."

"No hope of a reunion, I guess."

"Don't tell me you think people like Grant Taylor actually change?"

"I've seen it happen." Sam paused. "But a man with a taste for blood rarely loses it."

"When I was twelve, my mother went to our preacher and told him what was going on at home. She wanted him to help us get away. He said it was her duty to keep her husband happy, that somehow it was her fault."

"Isaac, surely you don't believe there's a Christian conspiracy to oppress women like your mother? Your father scouted for preachers who affirmed his twisted beliefs. Don't tar us all with the same brush."

"You've never counseled a woman to stay with a man?"

"I take marriage vows seriously, but I'm nobody's fool. I've taken women straight from my office to safe houses."

"I guess you weren't reading the same Bible passages my father was."

"The gospel of John says, 'God is love.' Twice. Talk about hammering home a message . . ."

Isaac fell silent. He admired Sam for living his principles, even when it had cost him a lot. But now he realized he liked him, too.

After two miles they turned around and started back, running on the shadier side of Fitch Crossing Road. Back at the cabin, Sam piled the dogs in his car, told Isaac to call if he or Kendra needed anything, and drove away.

He did some stretching exercises to cool down, exchanged a comment or two with a couple of workmen, then went inside. The logs kept out some of the encroaching heat, but the temperature was beginning to rise.

Kendra was still sitting where he'd left her.

"How are you doing?" he asked.

"It's going to be a scorcher, isn't it."

"Why don't we move you out to the front porch, where there's shade and a breeze? I'll get you something cold to drink and your sandwich."

"You'll find a casserole in the fridge and more food on the way. Helen Henry came by and dropped it off."

He helped make her comfortable on the porch, then went to pour soft drinks. In minutes they were both settled with sandwiches they'd bought in town on her trip to see the doctor.

"Ms. Henry must have come and gone quickly," he said.

"She left me with the casserole and something to think about."

He settled himself beside her. The view wasn't the best, since they were looking out over their cars and two pickups. For the first time he felt a glimmer of excitement about the renovations and the resulting view of the river.

He unwrapped his sandwich. "What stirred your interest?"

"Isaac, have you ever paid any attention to the Lover's Knot quilt your grandmother left you?"

He was sorry the conversation had taken this direction. "Not much."

"Helen came over a couple of weeks ago to see it. You remember she's something of a local quilting celebrity, don't you?"

He listened with one ear as she told him all the strange things about his grandmother's quilt. Some part of him was still thinking about his conversation with Sam.

"I thought I'd do some research into the names on the quilt," Kendra finished.

"Looking into birth or social security records, maybe, to get some idea where those people lived."

She had his attention now. "There have to be more interesting ways to spend your time."

"I guess I thought so, too, because I didn't get around to it. The renovations started and I've been busy dealing with that. You have no idea how many decisions I have to make. Fixtures, windows, lighting, flooring."

"Uh-huh." She was right, he had no idea.

"Turns out I was wrong."

He frowned. "About what?"

"Apparently the quilt's a lot more interesting than I'd guessed. Let me back up." She unwrapped her sandwich and set the two halves on the plate he had provided, but she didn't take a bite.

He guessed she was stalling.

"Okay, here's the story the best I know it right now. About a year ago, some hikers were up at the Shenandoah National Park. They had a dog, and they'd taken him off the leash to let him run ahead. After a while he disappeared. They searched for an hour, and eventually they heard him barking, but they couldn't figure out where the sound was coming from. Finally one of them realized it was coming from some boulders a fair distance from the path they were on. Apparently the dog had been chasing something and managed to chase it into a small cave. But then the dog couldn't figure out how to get out."

"I thought this was about a quilt?"

"I'm getting to that."

"Eat something before you start in again."

She took two big bites. He was already on his second half.

"Anyway, even together, they couldn't move the key boulder, because another one was right up against it. So one of them hiked back to get a ranger, while the other stayed to be sure they could find the cave again. It took most of the day, until a couple of men came to help."

"I imagine the dog wasn't happy."

"The dog survived without a scratch. Anyway, with the four of them working on it, they managed to move a boulder and expose the cave. The dog bounded out, and that should have been that. But the two rangers were interested. Neither of them knew the cave was there. So one went to the mouth and shone a light inside."

"And?"

"He saw bones. Human bones." She paused. "Wrapped in a quilt."

She had his attention now. He crumpled the sandwich paper into a ball and dropped it on his plate. "I think I remember reading about this. You say it was a year ago?"

"Almost exactly. The local sheriff brought in a forensics team and removed the bodies. Turns out there were two. A man and a woman. Dead from a single bullet each. They were wrapped in what remained of one quilt. The authorities estimated that they died somewhere around seventy years ago. The cave was well sealed, which is the only reason any part of the quilt was still intact. But of course only fragments remained."

"What does this have to do with my grandmother's quilt?"

"Helen saw some of the fragments at the Virginia Quilt Museum. The authorities hoped a historian would be able to help figure out where the fabrics came from, how old they were. Somebody there showed what they had to Helen, and she recognized them. She thinks the quilt that wrapped those bodies is virtually identical to the one your grandmother left you, although there's no trace of signatures, not that she saw, anyway."

"How can she tell? You said yourself the quilt was in fragments."

"The authorities put the quilt back together as best they could and took photos before they sent a few of the fabric scraps to the museum. Helen had examined yours just a week or so before she saw the photos. And when it comes to quilts and fabric, her memory is faultless. If I asked her to describe your Lover's Knot without looking at it, every detail would be perfect."

"Where's all this leading?"

She tilted her head. "Are you kidding? It's odd enough that your grandmother left you that quilt. It's not a perfect specimen by anybody's standards. But now we discover it's identical to one that wrapped a couple of bodies buried in a cave? Don't you think there's a story here? Or an answer to questions about your family's past?"

"I *have* no questions about my family. You're the one with the questions. And why do you care if I don't? My mother died in a fire. My father could have been any one of dozens of men. My grandmother may or may not have been married to my mother's father. I was dumped with a sadistic Air Force colonel and a woman he ground under his heel so long that she couldn't stand up for either of us. And now a couple of dead bodies to boot." He got to his feet.

She stopped him with a hand on his arm. "Two things, Isaac. One, it's the story of real people who had hopes and dreams just like people everywhere. And apparently one of your grandmother's dreams was to give you a connection to them."

He didn't look at her. "You said two things."

"Don't you think it's time to stop assuming the worst? The truth can't possibly be any more sordid than your imagination. Your father made sure to rub your nose in the few details he had. But he was wrong about everything else, so why would he be right about your family? Don't you want to know?"

With effort, he kept his voice steady and low. “No, I don’t.”

She dropped her hand. He stood still, looking out over the woods and his grandmother’s herb garden.

“Okay,” she said at last. “I’m sorry. And you’re right, it’s your past, not mine. I feel a bond with Leah Spurlock, living in her house, working in her garden. I’ll admit it. I almost feel her presence sometimes.”

“Please.”

“But it is your life,” she continued. “I’m sorry. I won’t go looking for answers if you don’t want me to.”

He gazed down at her. “Is this just another story? You can take the reporter out of the job but you can’t stop her from investigating?”

He watched her consider this. Kendra weighed every fact, a hazard of the job or maybe a trait she’d picked up in childhood, when facts were in short supply.

“No,” she said at last. “That’s not it.”

“And don’t tell me you want to pursue this because you want to know me better. That makes no sense at all.”

“Two new reasons, then,” she said.

“Again?”

"Just these last two. I want you to know *yourself* better, Isaac, because I think you'll be happier. That's the first thing. And here's the second. I love you. And love is easier to share when it's not all tangled up with everything else in your heart."

The heart in question seemed to constrict. He looked down at this woman who had recently suffered so much and always demanded so little. They rarely talked about feelings. They were simply two private souls who had chosen with little fanfare to spend some part of their lives together.

Yet gazing at her face, he could not imagine a time when he would want to be with anyone else, when he would want to wake up and know Kendra had disappeared from his life. He didn't trust words like *love* or *forever,* yet hearing her say that despite his failure to meet her needs, she still loved him, changed everything. One moment he was angry. Now he realized exactly what the anger covered.

"What will happen, K.C., if you find out my family story *is* even worse than I think it is?"

She frowned, as if she couldn't imagine

what he meant. Then she tilted her head. "Don't you know it won't make the slightest difference to me?"

He looked out toward the woods. He wondered what Leah Spurlock had thought about when she stared at this view. And Rachel, his mother. In that moment he felt the faintest tug of connection with the two women, and with the lives they had led here.

"Leah left you the quilt for a reason," Kendra said. "It begins and ends there."

"Go ahead, then." He touched her shoulder; then he lifted his hand to push a lock of her hair over her ear.

She reached for his hand and brought it to her lips. "You're sure?"

He gave a short nod before he could change his mind. "I'm going to dig some holes."

"What?"

"You've got a drainage problem. I'm going to see if there's any system in place. I'm just going to check it out. I'm sure your workers plan to bring in a backhoe at some point to fix it."

"Jamie thought we ought to build a pond."

"Jamie is welcome to come back and do it." He ruffled her curls.

"Thank you, Isaac."

He left before he could say anything more revealing.

CHAPTER SEVENTEEN

Two weeks later, Kendra was standing on her own feet in every possible way. The ankle and wrist had healed, and Isaac had moved back to the Foggy Bottom condo. Although he didn't complain, she knew he was putting in extra hours to make up for the time he had missed. He still managed to call almost every night, a change from her first weeks at the cabin. There was a new intimacy when they shared the details of their days. The calls lasted longer each night.

She wasn't foolish enough to think that one fight or one conversation could change a marriage. But she did remember Lao Tzu's T-shirt wisdom.

The weeks had been clear, and cooler than normal. She knew this was a blessing that wouldn't last. As the ankle and wrist improved, she had gone back to work in Leah's garden, perching on a stool and managing longer stints each day. She corralled Cash for a tour, and he pointed out the remnants of a few plantings. Through the years, tansy and peppermint had been victorious against weeds and formed determined, impenetrable mats. Horehound and lemon balm were vying for attention in patches all over the garden. She was fascinated by the array. She cleared with care, several reference guides beside her as she worked, imagining Leah cautioning or prodding as she moved between the rows.

When she woke up on Saturday morning, staying at home had no appeal. A cement mixer was on its way, and she knew it would earn its keep throughout the day. The attending noise wouldn't be good for anything except a headache.

Quickly she showered and dressed; then, after greeting the crew, she headed for her car. She'd had an idea brewing, and this was clearly the day to see if she could make it happen.

It was just past eight when she knocked on Helen's door. No one slept in at Helen's, not with Reese in residence. Only seconds passed before Cissy flung the door open, Reese on her jeans-clad hip. She gave Kendra a big smile.

"Those workmen chase you out of your place?"

Inside, Kendra followed Cissy to the kitchen. "They're working on the foundation for the addition. It seemed like a good day to disappear."

"Reese and I are glad you disappeared this way—aren't we, girl?"

Reese held out her arms to Kendra, as if begging to be released from the clutches of a torturer.

"I'm trying to get her to eat something besides Cheerios for breakfast," Cissy explained. "So far she don't—doesn't much care for scrambled eggs."

Kendra took the little girl and balanced her against her side. "You're a drama queen, aren't you."

"Me a queen." Reese nodded, clearly aware what it meant.

"Maybe you'll have better luck," Cissy said. "She always has to remind me who's in charge, in case I forget."

Kendra smiled down at the cherub in her arms. Something fiercely and forlornly maternal stirred inside her. "Do you like ketchup, Reese?"

Reese sized her up, pursing her lips in thought.

"Can she have ketchup?" Kendra asked.

"Sure. She likes it, too. I never thought about putting it on eggs."

"My little sister ate it on everything." Kendra settled Reese in an oak high chair that looked as if it had already served a dozen children. Cissy produced scrambled eggs and ketchup, and let Kendra do the honors. Kendra tasted them herself and realized she was hungry.

"Yum. If you don't eat this, I will," she told Reese, setting the plate on the tray. Then she turned her back as if she wasn't interested.

Cissy took the cue and ignored her daughter, as well. "I've got cinnamon rolls Marian brought over last night. Ms. Henry's bound to be down in a few minutes. I'll put some coffee on."

"I'd tell you not to go to any trouble, only I'd be happy if you did."

"Take a seat at the table."

Kendra squeezed past the high chair where Reese was trying to decide which was more important, proving independence or diving into the ketchup-splattered eggs. By the time Kendra was settled, the eggs had won. No one mentioned the victory.

"Ms. Henry will be glad to see you." Cissy finished setting the table.

"I'll be glad to see her, but I'm really here to see you."

Cissy looked pleased. "Me?"

"I'm taking a trip up to the Shenandoah National Park, and I want to see if Caleb is interested in riding along. I hope you and Reese will come, as well. And Helen, if she's interested."

"What am I interested in?" Helen came into the kitchen.

Kendra stood to greet her, but Helen waved her back into the chair. "I've just been finishing the binding on a quilt for the church fair next weekend."

The fair was a fund-raiser for the church's outreach ministry to prisoners. It promised to be a bit of excitement in their quiet community. "What kind of quilt?"

"It's an old pattern my aunt Mavis made once upon a time, called Cactus Bloom. I still have her templates, cut from Cream of Wheat boxes after she traced the pattern from some newspaper or booklet. We thought maybe it was a good one for this. They say even a prickly cactus can flower if it's given the chance. Not that I'm sure that's true, mind you. But the ladies in the bee each made three blocks, some better than others, but it's not going to shame anybody."

"It's a sight," Cissy said. "Golds and oranges and reds on a pale blue background. People are coming from all over to bid on it."

"She's making that up," Helen said. "They're coming on account of there's going to be a big rib cook-off, and the fire department's standing by with their trucks, just in case, and giving rides to the children once the fire's out."

Helen lowered herself into the chair across from Kendra's. Cissy brought cups and saucers and the cinnamon rolls, giving Reese one on the way, since the toddler had almost finished her eggs and was pounding a fist on the wooden tray.

Kendra brought Helen up to speed on her plans. "I want to see if I can find out more about the bodies in the cave and the quilt fragments."

"You could just make a phone call. You don't have to go all that way."

"I thought about it. But I'd rather go myself and just see what I can. And it's a beautiful day for a drive."

"I've got to finish that quilt. But you all go on. Give me a day's peace and quiet. You go with her, Cissy."

"There's a fiddlers' contest somewhere or the other, and Zeke took some of his instruments to set up a booth. He left early. I don't see why we couldn't go."

"Do you think we can persuade Caleb?" Kendra asked.

"Getting up into the mountains for a day would please him a lot. I'll call Marian." Cissy brought a pot of freshly brewed coffee to the table and set it on a trivet. After a quick phone conversation, she took a seat next to Helen and snagged a roll.

"Marian says he'd like to go, and she volunteered to watch Reese. Does anybody want scrambled eggs?"

Kendra, who had a clear view of the pulverized ketchup- and orange juice-laced remains of Reese's, politely declined.

* * *

Twice since the night of the storm, Kendra had caught glimpses of Caleb. She'd sent word through Cissy that he was welcome to enjoy her woods anytime, and she had seen him the previous Sunday afternoon, working his way into the heart of them, perhaps tailing deer again or simply enjoying the way the trees were coming to life as summer officially approached. Another time she'd spotted him in a cornfield beside the Clairbornes' small ranch house, standing beside a tractor, talking to Ron Claiborne. She had been tempted to stop and offer her thanks again, but she knew he would be embarrassed.

She wanted to reward Caleb for helping her, but this was the first good solution she'd thought of. Money was out of the question, inappropriate and she suspected, insulting. Caleb had helped because she'd needed him, the way neighbors usually helped neighbors in this part of the world.

But Caleb was fourteen—she'd learned as much from Cissy. Young teens were not always aware of a community's rules or interested in participating. Caleb might be having problems adjusting to his new life, but she was convinced he could have a worthwhile future, in spite of a difficult past. She wanted to make sure of it.

Now he passed Cissy and Reese on their path to the door. He wore brand-new jeans that were stiff enough to stand alone and a dark green T-shirt with a 4-H logo. She got out to greet him and saw that his eyes were the same dark green as his shirt. His reddish blond hair had been recently cut, and his skin was lightly tanned. He still had boyish features, a softly formed nose, chubby cheeks, but a square chin and jaw were signs of the man to come.

She extended her hand. "Hi, Caleb. It's good to see you again. The circumstances are a lot happier this time."

He didn't smile. She thought smiles were probably a rarity in his life. But his face lightened a little, as if he had jumped some imaginary hurdle, and he shook her hand briefly.

The others joined them as Kendra struggled to think of a conversational topic. Reese was snuggling in her grandmother's arms. Marian was medium height, with salt-and-pepper hair and a no-nonsense perm. She had probably never been a pretty woman, but she moved with a vitality that was both attractive and hard to ignore.

"I've got a whole day ahead of me with nothing much to do," she said. "I'm glad to have this little one."

Cissy took out the car seat in case Marian needed it later in the day. Caleb climbed in as soon as the backseat was clear. Cissy said goodbye to her daughter and joined Kendra in the front.

"The sun rises and sets on that little girl, but a day apart won't hurt either of us one little bit." Cissy didn't sound completely sure.

"She'll appreciate you even more by the time you get home," Kendra promised.

She estimated the trip would take at least an hour and a half. She wanted to travel Route 11, a scenic byway through pastoral Shenandoah Valley fields and towns. And once she made the turns to Skyline Drive, which ran through the park and eventually connected to the Blue Ridge Parkway, the speed limit changed to 35 mph.

Once they were really under way, Cissy settled back into her seat. "I'm so glad we're going. I love the park. Caleb, have you ever been there?"

A "no" came from the backseat, the first word he'd spoken.

"Did you know some of our people come from up there?"

He was quiet so long that Kendra wondered if he would answer. Finally he said, "Up where?"

Cissy didn't seem disturbed at the length of time it had taken him. "I'm not sure where, exactly. Granny told me stories, though. I'm glad you're going to see it."

Kendra slowed as they drove through Woodstock, past attractive shops and the imposing Massanutten Military Academy. "What kind of stories?"

"About the way people were moved out of their homes to make way for the park. She was just a little girl when it happened. As far back as anyone could remember, her family had lived on land way up in the mountains. Then the government decided they had to have it all for a park. So they moved people out of there and left it for the hikers."

"Just like that?"

Caleb's question had come so swiftly it surprised Kendra. But she said nothing, listening to the brother and sister converse.

"That's what she told me."

Caleb was clearly interested. "Where'd they get moved?"

"I don't know. She said they lived on a farm for a while, but they moved again after a time. I think they just didn't know how to make a new life. They were basket-makers. Made and sold baskets, she said. I do remember that part. And once they left the mountains, they couldn't get what they needed to make good ones. And they didn't know how to make a good living farming. So they moved on."

After a while Kendra filled the silence. "The government has the right to take over land it needs for the public good."

"Some right, pushing people out of their homes," Caleb said.

It was about the longest speech she'd heard from him. She encouraged it. "I know, on the surface it doesn't sound fair, does it."

"Sure doesn't," Cissy said. "Granny said her mama and daddy hardly ever talked to each other without fighting after that. He took to drinking and never gave it up. Her mama got old before her time and died too young. Granny struck out on her own after that and married a man she shouldn't have, just so she'd have a place to go."

Kendra knew that the effects of a forced move like the one from the park could destroy lives.

"Some people did okay," Cissy said, as if she'd read Kendra's thoughts. "Granny told me that, too."

"Probably made her mama and daddy feel even worse," Caleb said. "Them not being able to make it themselves."

Kendra thought that was insightful. "There's a lot of talk about this issue right now. The Supreme Court just ruled that cities can take over land to build shopping malls and office buildings if they benefit the economy."

"You don't move people just because you can," Caleb said.

Kendra wondered how many times Caleb had been moved "just because you can." Her heart went out to the boy who until now had never had a home he could really call his. She wondered if he felt he had one now.

They drove in silence for a while. As she made the turns that would get her to Skyline Drive and into the park, she told them about her Lover's Knot quilt and Helen's story of the cave. Cissy, who was as good at expressing her feelings as Caleb wasn't, said she was happy to be coming along to investigate.

The scenery along Skyline Drive was beautiful, but to make sure they saw the best of it, Kendra pulled over at several scenic overlooks, so they could stretch and take advantage of the breathtaking vistas. They'd all been fairly quiet for the past half hour, but at the second one she asked Caleb if he'd ever done any wilderness hiking.

He shook his head. "No, ma'am."

She wondered if there were any remnants of the heart problem that had affected his life. She remembered that he'd had surgery, but he seemed to have no limitations.

"Isaac—that's my husband—loves hiking. I hike, too, although I get tired a lot faster than he does. The Appalachian Trail goes right through here." She glanced at him and realized he didn't know what she meant. "It's a hiking trail that extends all the way from Maine to Georgia. Isaac and I did a weeklong hike along a section in New Hampshire several years ago." She tried to read Caleb's expression. "Does that sound like fun?"

She thought he nodded.

"We hiked with friends," she said, "but you don't see many other people along the way. It's pretty special."

"You probably didn't see many people up here before the park took over, either."

He sounded nostalgic. She wondered if Caleb could ever be convinced that people were worth getting to know. Being a teenager was a lonely business anyway, and experiencing those years without at least a few friends to help was going to be lonely indeed.

Two hours had passed before they reached the visitors center at Big Meadows. It was an attractive building, with what were probably spectacular views through wide windows. They parked in the lot, but Kendra knew better than to suggest they go inside immediately after the long ride. Instead, she took out her day pack and suggested they hike a nearby nature trail.

Both Caleb and Cissy instinctively slowed their steps to hers, so the short loop took twice as long as it might have normally. Neither seemed to mind, but Caleb, in particular, was fascinated with every new view, as if he were framing and snapping photographs in his mind. On a bench near the end, Kendra offered them bottles of water from her pack, and they rested.

"How's your ankle?" Cissy asked.

"A lot better than it ought to be."

"Maybe you shouldn't be walking so far?"

"This is as far as I'll go today. But it's feeling good. I'll probably always limp a little, but that's from . . ." She took a deep breath. "From the carjacking."

"Carjacking?" Caleb said.

She told the briefest possible version of the story.

"How come nobody's there taking care of you?"

She tried to think of a quick way to explain something she didn't quite understand herself. "I need to prove I can do it alone. Although I haven't done a bang-up job so far. The whole county seems to be taking care of me."

"Seems only fitting," Cissy said. "From what I hear, the woman who used to live in that cabin took care of everybody in the county."

Kendra got to her feet. "And she's the

reason we're here. Let's go and see if there's anybody we can talk to and find out more about the quilt."

The views inside *were* lovely. The building was open and breezy, with stone slab floors that brought the outside indoors. Best of all, there was a hallway beyond the reception area that featured an in-depth display about the evictions. They took their time reading the history and looking at photographs. When she had completed the circuit, Kendra went to the reception desk and waited for the ranger to finish with a young couple looking for information about hiking trails.

Kendra introduced herself and pointed out Cissy and Caleb, who were still looking at the displays. "Do you have a little time to talk to us?"

The young man in a khaki ranger's uniform maintained a pleasantly attentive expression, but she suspected he would rather be outside doing something physically challenging than answering tourists' questions.

She favored him with her most winning smile. "I understand the park service found a couple of skeletons in a cave about a year ago."

He was no longer as relaxed. "They weren't hikers or climbers. Any place can be dangerous, but the park is no more dangerous than any wilderness area."

She sympathized, sure he'd answered too many inquiries about park safety since the bodies were discovered. She launched into her story and reasons for being there. She told him what she knew about Leah, which didn't take long. She ended with Helen's trip to the Virginia Quilt Museum.

He seemed interested. "I don't know a lot about quilts, but didn't lots of people make the same patterns over and over?"

Cissy had wandered up to listen. "Even in those days, there were a lot of fabrics available. So if there was a wide selection to choose from, having the very same fabrics in the very same places on quilts made from the same pattern, well, that surely does mean something."

"By any chance did you bring the quilt?"

"It's in my car," Kendra said.

"Why don't you bring it in? I'll see if I can find Hank Armstead. He's our history buff.

And he was one of the two men who found those skeletons."

"I'll get it," Cissy told Kendra after the ranger had gone. "No call for you to be running off to the parking lot."

Kendra gave Cissy her keys. Caleb joined Kendra, and she explained what was happening.

"Did you enjoy the exhibit?" she asked.

"Doesn't say enough."

She was pretty sure that wasn't what most boys his age would think. "I notice they've got books for sale. Why don't you pick out the ones that look most interesting for me. I'd appreciate your help."

Something close to a smile crossed his face. She watched him head to the racks. Spending so many years with Isaac had taught her to look for small signs. She suspected enthusiasm.

The young ranger returned with another and left them together. Kendra introduced herself, and Hank Armstead shook her hand. Judging from the silver hair paired with a still youthful face, Hank was in his late fifties. He wore round glasses like a grown-up Harry Potter, and twice before the introduction was completed he pushed them up his nose.

"Jake told me about your quilt."

"Here it comes." Cissy was just coming through the doorway with a black plastic garbage bag. Caleb looked up from the bookracks, and Kendra motioned for him to return.

Hank seemed pleased. "Let's go in the back, where we can spread it out a little."

"May Cissy and Caleb come? They're descendants of people who lived here before the park was created."

"Is that so?"

Hank waited while Kendra introduced Cissy. Caleb had joined them by then, and Kendra introduced him, as well.

"Where did your family come from?" he asked. "Do you know?"

"I think I might recognize the name if I heard it," Cissy said.

"Then we'll put you to work with a map," he said. "I've got a big one on the wall in my office."

They followed him to a small room that was normally off-limits to the public. He guided Cissy to the wall map, which filled a space the size of a large dining room table.

While Cissy looked it over, he cleared a utilitarian fold-up table along one wall so that Kendra could open the quilt. Off went a stack of books, a three-tiered letter tray and a stapler that looked like it could secure a loose-leaf manuscript of the Bible.

"Okay, set it there," he told her once the table was bare.

She removed the quilt from the bag, unfolding it until the whole top was revealed and draped over the four sides. She didn't say anything. She just waited.

Hank bent over the quilt. "Jake didn't say how you got this."

She told him about Leah, about Isaac's inheritance and the fact that no one could understand why Leah had worked so hard to make certain he got this quilt. "It's not a beauty," she said. "Not by artistic standards."

"Hmm . . ." Hank was studying it carefully, inch by inch.

"Do you happen to have the photos of the quilt fragments you pieced together?" she asked.

He straightened. "You bet I do." He left for the filing cabinet in the corner and returned with a folder. He pulled out four photos and spread them on top of the quilt. "What do you think?"

She thought it was possible the quilts had once looked alike, but it was nowhere near as certain as Helen had claimed.

"That's all you have?"

"That and the fragments."

"Do you have any here? I know some of what was left ended up at the Quilt Museum."

"Not right here I don't. But I can tell you this . . ." He pointed at one block of stained muslin paired with a red print sprinkled with tiny white and green windmills. "We have that." His finger moved. "And we have that," he said, pointing to a blue fabric with green and red roses. "And this one." He pointed to a green fabric laced with spidery white and blue lines. "There are fabrics here we don't have, but that doesn't mean they weren't on the quilt. Our quilt was in that cave a lot of years, and some of it just disappeared."

He straightened, and turned to Kendra and Caleb. "There's not a fabric I do remember that's not on this quilt of yours. I'm sure of that."

Kendra said a silent apology to Helen for ever doubting.

"Corbin Hollow," Cissy said from the other side of the room. "That's where our family lived. Leastwise, I think it is. Caleb, come and see."

Kendra had forgotten that another mystery was being solved. She followed Caleb and looked where Cissy was pointing.

"Cissy told me her family made baskets," Kendra told Hank.

"That fits," Hank said. "Corbin was the closest hollow to Skyland, which was built as a resort in the late 1880s." He moved his finger to the left and let it rest on another area. "The folks who lived near here made their incomes working there, or selling crafts to visitors. Baskets were a big deal. Some of the finest craftsmen lived near Skyland in Corbin and Nicholson hollows, although the folks at Nicholson were farmers, too. But there were whole families famous for the baskets they made."

Hank continued, telling Caleb and Cissy more about that area and the hikes they could take to see it up close. "There's still an old cabin standing, a fairly primitive example that's been renovated. One of the ways officials talked the public into voting to remove residents from the park was to make them sound too ignorant to take care of themselves. You're too young to remember Li'l Abner, but it was a comic strip about a bunch of hillbillies in a place called Dogpatch. The trick was to turn this area into Dogpatch in people's minds. We were in the middle of the Depression, and the folks in Corbin Hollow, who'd depended on tourism for their income, suffered the most. So they were the ones the government trotted out as examples."

Cissy was drinking it all in. "My granny said that her mama and daddy just didn't know what to do with themselves afterward."

"I've heard it was particularly hard for the basket-makers," Hank said. "They went from being honored craftsmen, with all the white oak saplings they needed right there for their use, to begging farmers in the areas where they were resettled to let them scavenge for trees. There just weren't enough materials to do what they did best."

"I'd like to go there," Caleb said.

Kendra was pleased. Like Isaac, Caleb had few reasons to feel tied to his family. But the more he understood them . . . It was becoming a common refrain in her life.

Silence fell. She knew it was time to change the subject. “Hank, while we’re staring at the map, can you show us where the bodies were found?”

Hank moved back a little; then he put his finger on a spot south of Corbin Hollow and close to the park’s boundary. “Right here.”

Kendra’s gaze fell to that section of the map. She bit her lip as she stared.

“Surprise you?” Hank asked. “You thought it might be in another part of the park?”

“I didn’t have any idea where it was.” She stepped forward and traced a line. “These blue lines are rivers?”

“Not all of them are what you’d think of as rivers, no matter what they’re called. More like creeks.”

“And these are hiking trails?” She traced a series of dotted lines.

“Uh-huh, but some of them have been there since Native Americans peopled these mountains.”

“So some of these would have been trails or footpaths before the area became a park.”

“Definitely, though I can’t tell you the history of each one.”

Kendra cocked her head and squinted. The moment she'd looked at them, the lines of rivers and trails had seemed oddly familiar, but now, as she stopped and silently repeated a name on the map, she understood why. "Lock Hollow?"

"This little area right here. This is Little Lock Mountain." He pointed. "Not a big mountain, as they go, and not particularly good for hiking. The cave where the bodies were found is at the base of the mountain. There used to be a small community there with a little store. Good land for farming."

"Lock for Spurlock," she said.

"What makes you think so?"

"The lines on my quilt? The quilting lines? I think they're a map of Lock Hollow. And I bet if you have a list of the residents who were forced off their property in that area, we'll find Spurlocks on it. Maybe that's what Leah Spurlock Jackson was trying to tell her grandson."

Hank marched over to the quilt and studied it. He spoke after a moment. "Maybe she was trying to tell him more."

Kendra pulled her gaze from the wall, although she was still fascinated that Isaac's grandmother, a mediocre needlewoman, had managed to render this map in thread. "What else?" She crossed the room, and found that Cissy and Caleb were already flanking him.

"See these lines here?" He pointed to a section in the right-hand third of the quilt, about halfway down. They stood out from the others, tiny and even, in thread that seemed to be thicker and darker, as if particular care had been used when stitching them. Kendra had never noticed it before.

She gazed at the spot, then back up at the map. "There's nothing on the map that corresponds to that intersection, is there?"

"Not on the real map. But where these two lines cross? That would be the cave where we found the bodies."

CHAPTER EIGHTEEN

Isaac had a theory that sometime during the wee hours of every morning, a bevy of elves tiptoed into the ACRE offices directly to his desk. Instead of leaving a tidy bare surface for him to admire in the morning, the elves left extra work. Mountains of extra work.

Victimized by lazy elves. He would have preferred a fire-breathing dragon or a wicked snow queen in his personal fairy tale.

"For someone who's about to close the biggest land deal of his career, you're looking a little glum."

Isaac glanced up to find Heather standing in his doorway. It was after five p.m. on Monday, but she looked like an advertisement from an Eddie Bauer camping catalog. Khaki cargo shorts, blue microfiber shirt, Nikes and sport socks.

He leaned back, head in hands. “Did you come to work like that and I just missed it?”

“I changed. It’s too pretty to stay inside this evening. I’m going for a long bike ride. Want to come?”

“I promised John I’d drop by to talk about Ten.” Ten was now the name of the cat he had rescued. Ten because the cat was clearly blessed with at least one more than the traditional nine lives.

“How is old Ten?”

“Beating up John’s cats. I think he’s being evicted.”

“You’re taking him home?”

“No cats allowed in our condo. I’m hoping I can talk John into keeping him until I can find another home.”

Heather gave a snort. “Isaac, what are the chances?”

Isaac didn’t know. Not everyone appreciated a down-on-his-luck alley cat with homicidal tendencies.

“Anything new on Pallatine Mountain?” she asked. “You haven’t brought it up lately.”

“Dennis says the money’s in place.” When Gary Forsythe had finally gotten back to Isaac and promised to sell the land to

ACRE if they could come up with another half-million dollars, Dennis had promised to find it.

"Do you know how he's raising it?"

"Not yet."

"Because I heard a rumor . . ." Heather looked down at her nails; then she polished them against her shirt.

The gesture was so unlike her that Isaac was instantly alert. This was not a casual conversation. "What?"

She stepped inside and closed the door behind her. "I hear Dennis isn't averse to selling some select acreage on Pallatine to raise the necessary funds. Not to developers, but maybe to people who've done favors for ACRE."

"We can't develop it. That's part of the deal with Forsythe."

"But can we sell the right to build a few houses? With conservation easements, of course."

Selling with conservation easements meant that theoretically the land was still protected. Restrictions were written into the deed. Among them, no one could log the land. Nothing could be built near sensitive areas like streambeds. A limit was set on the square footage of any buildings.

Isaac knew the way this usually worked. The land was sold to a few buyers at a price severely reduced from what ACRE paid for it, but by then the land, with all the attendant restrictions, was worth less. At that point the buyers would give a significant donation to ACRE, which they could deduct from their income taxes. ACRE would still realize enough money to offset some of the cost of preserving Pallatine, and the buyers would both lower their tax indebtedness and own property on a pristine mountainside.

Or a *formerly* pristine mountainside.

Isaac picked up a pencil and did a fair imitation of a snare drum solo on his blotter. “I’ll ask Dennis.”

“Other organizations have done it. Some of them say it works to everyone’s benefit, that the owners are people with a personal stake in sound and careful management, and the land is better off with a few occupants.”

Occupants in mini-mansions. On a formerly pristine mountainside.

Isaac dropped the pencil. “Those organizations caught a lot of flack and lost a lot of donations. They've changed the way they do things."

"Well, I'm sure Dennis won't fall into any traps that have already been sprung by others." She paused. "In other words, he'll find some way around the finer points of the contract."

"You don't like Dennis, do you."

Heather polished her nails again—the most attention she had ever paid to personal grooming in his presence. "He's a lot like you. He tunnels ahead without looking from one side to the other. Luckily, I usually admire your direction. I'm not sure about his."

"We're meeting tomorrow."

"Really? I'll be waiting to hear what he says."

She left, nails shining, and Isaac knew it was time to call it a day.

He was still thinking about their conversation when he knocked on the door of the row house in Glover Park where Ten had a temporary home. John had promised to lavish tender loving care on the recovering cat. But after their phone call today, Isaac was pretty sure Ten had outstayed his welcome.

John answered the door looking nothing short of harried. He was a short man, with dark hair bleached bright gold at the ends. He sported a diamond in one earlobe and an unbuttoned aloha shirt adorned with hula girls.

"He's a rascal, and I'm a wreck."

Isaac shook his head. "I'm really sorry, John. You should have called me sooner."

"He did okay at first. He was still recovering. But he's not a team player, your boy. He got out of his cage last night and terrorized my little gang. And he nearly cut me to ribbons when I tried to put him back in."

"I really am sorry."

"You're here to get him?" John sounded more than hopeful. He sounded desperate.

"Thing is, I don't have a place for him to go. I worked on it today, but—"

"Isaac, honey, he just can't stay. I don't know what to tell you. I called a couple of other rescue people, but none of them has a place for him right now. They all have cats. He has to go to somebody without a cat. There shouldn't be another cat for about a hundred miles."

"I don't know a place like that."

"Someplace out in the country? Maybe

somebody with space, so he can roam a little? He'd probably stay nearby if somebody was feeding him. I don't know what else to say. Just that he can't stay here."

"Not one more night?"

John put his hands on his hips. "Don't do this to me!"

Isaac was ashamed. "I'm sorry. I'll take him."

"You're not taking him to the pound, are you? They'll put him down without thinking about it."

"No."

"He's in his carrier."

That was the ultimate sign of John's desperation. Isaac scrambled for a solution even as he followed him toward the bedroom where Ten had been deposited.

"Someplace in the country," John said. "You must know somebody in the country who'll take this cat. Somebody with a soft heart." He stopped and faced Isaac. "You *must* know somebody like that."

The construction crew left about three, claiming they had to wait until the concrete dried before they could move forward. Kendra knew them all by name now, and although she suspected they were still taking her measure, most were friendly. Randy was the only one who didn't speak.

Kendra relished the thought of silence for the rest of the afternoon. Two hours and a brief nap later, she sat looking over the woods with a fresh glass of spearmint tea from Leah's garden. The spring had been surprisingly pleasant. She wondered if she could tolerate the hot weather, which was undoubtedly going to make an appearance soon. She wondered how Leah had managed without so much as an electric fan, at least at the beginning.

Leah was pregnant with Rachel when she arrived in Toms Brook. A dilapidated cabin, at first no indoor plumbing or electricity, no husband to help or support her. She had probably come out to the porch when she could to catch a breeze, exactly the way Kendra had.

She sipped slowly, enjoying the peaceful vista. Earlier she'd heard movement deep inside the treeline. At first she'd suspected it was Caleb, who she was hoping to see; then she'd glimpsed the soft gray-brown coat of a deer.

Ah, country life.

She was ready to go back inside when she heard another noise, this time from somewhere down her driveway. A dog's howl.

She walked to the edge of the porch and waited. At times neighboring children used her woods to hike down to the river, although it was not one of the better ways to get to the riverbank. Since she wasn't expecting anyone, she guessed this might be more of the same.

But this time the noise *was* Caleb.

"Hey!" She waved. "Who's your friend?"

The friend was a mutt the likes of which she'd never seen before. She suspected even the most astute dog lover wouldn't be able to guess the totality of this puppy's parentage. At least she thought it was a puppy, judging by the size of its feet, although it already came halfway to Caleb's knee.

Part hound, she theorized, from the length of the body and that one pitiful howl. The spectacularly matted coat was the mottled blue merle of a purebred collie or Australian shepherd. The head was squarish, like a lab or, worse, a pit bull. Early in her career she'd been forced to cover a week-long dog show. So she knew her breeds. This was a dog only Sam, whose dogs defied description, would love.

"Want a soft drink?" she asked when he was nearly to the porch. "And some water for your friend?"

"Just water for her."

"Looks like you've got a new pal." She stuck out her hand for the dog to sniff. The dog ignored her. It had the sad expression of a bloodhound.

Caleb chewed his lip and didn't look at her.

Kendra had learned to read body language at a young age. Her heart sank. "Caleb, what have you done?"

"This dog, well, she's got no home. Someone dropped her off at the Clairbornes'."

Her heart hit bottom. "Caleb . . ."

"They already have a dog."

"And they won't let you keep her?"

"Can you get that water?"

Vacating was an excellent idea. She would take her time filling a bowl for the dog and prepare a gentle letdown speech. Because she knew what was coming. The air was thick with it.

By the time she returned, boy and dog were sitting on the porch. The dog still looked dejected, as if she had figured out that this home, too, wasn't going to work out.

"Did the Clairbornes ask you to find her a home?" She had already set the bowl on the ground for the dog, who ignored this, too. Now she handed Caleb a can of Pepsi he hadn't requested and watched him pop the top.

"Not exactly," he said after half the can was gone.

"And?"

"She's got a brother."

"And?"

"And, well, they told me I could keep him."

"So you've got a new dog all your own."

He finished the cola before he spoke again. "They told me I could keep this one, too."

She felt her heart lodge firmly in her chest again. "Aren't those Claibornes great?" She said it with even more enthusiasm than it deserved.

"But, see, I want you to have her. I gave her a bath and everything. I got a dog now.

And you, well, you got nothing. Look at this. You're all alone out here with no protection. And this dog barks at everything—don't you, girl?"

The dog, who had been lying lethargically at his side, didn't even wag her tail.

"Well, she does," he said.

She was impressed with the speech. "I'm sure you're right—"

"And the thing is, you could train her. She'd be a help. She can fetch, chase rabbits out of your garden. You need that."

She was stumped. Caleb had appointed himself her guardian. She realized it was a good sign that, despite the number of upheavals in his young life, he could still care about the well-being of others. He had been at least partly responsible for the injury to her ankle and completely responsible for helping her to safety afterward. In his mind, that made him responsible for her into the future.

She stalled. "What's her name?"

"She's *your* dog."

She opened her mouth to tell him he was wrong, that the dog needed a better home than she could give it, that her future was too uncertain for her to take on a pet. Caleb was watching with troubled eyes, and she realized he was worried he had made a mistake. She imagined he worried about mistakes a lot. He had dared to reach out, and now he was afraid he'd been wrong.

"How about Blue, for the silver color of her coat?" she heard herself say. "Or Dusty? Or maybe Patience, since she looks like the most patient dog in the world."

He relaxed visibly. "I named mine Rusty. He looks like her, only his coat is red."

"Then she has to be Dusty. You can bring Rusty to visit."

He looked so relieved, she wanted to hug him—but knew better. Being his mom was Marian's job. Hers was just to be his friend.

And the patsy who couldn't say no.

She had a sudden insight, and not a positive one. "Have you taken Rusty to the vet yet, you know, to have him checked over and get his shots?"

Caleb gave a shake of his head.

She wondered if Dusty's sad demeanor was due to illness. "Tell you what, since you've given me such a nice present, why don't we go together. I'll make the appointment for one afternoon this week."

"Mr. Claiborne said he'd give me some chores to earn the money I'd need for that."

"Good. But let's go as soon as we can, and you can pay me back later. Deal?"

"Okay." Caleb ruffled Dusty's fur and patted her head; then he stood. "Well, I guess I ought to go."

"Caleb . . ."

"Uh-huh?"

"Well, you've done a lot for me, and don't say you haven't. I've got something for you. It's a thank-you present."

"I don't need a present."

"I know you don't. But I have something anyway. Will you wait a minute?"

Warily, he lowered himself back to the step to pet Dusty some more. The dog still hadn't moved.

Kendra returned in a minute with a shopping bag. "I noticed something about you Saturday. You have a great eye for detail. I'm a reporter, and I've worked with a lot of photographers. They all look at things the way you do. Kind of framing them in their minds."

She held the bag out to him. "I hope you like it."

He was frowning, but he took it and

looked inside. Then he set it down and took out a box. "A camera?"

"It's a digital. You don't need film. You can download the photos to a computer, then print them out if you like."

He turned the box over in his hands. She hadn't bought the cheapest model, but neither had she bought the best. It was a good sturdy starter camera, capable of photographs he could be proud of.

"It's for me?" he asked at last.

"All yours. And if the Clabornes don't have a computer for downloading the photos, you can come over anytime and use mine. Pretty much everything's digital now, and I didn't want you to worry about buying film."

"I never had my own camera."

"Well, you do now. But there's a condition."

That seemed to make him feel better. "You need me to do something?"

"I'm interested in what we learned up at the park. I've been looking up the history on the Internet this afternoon. I want to do some more research, maybe even write some articles about what happened and the aftermath, the way lives are still affected.

And having photos will be a big help. So I'd like you to be my photographer. Would you be willing?"

"I never had a camera, and now you want me to take pictures for something like that?"

His speeches were getting longer. She was delighted. "I know you can do it. For practice, there's the Community Church fair coming up this weekend. I thought maybe you could go and take photos, just to get used to it."

"I'm not much for churchgoing."

Cissy had told Kendra she wished Caleb would get involved in the youth program at Community. There were a number of boys close to his age, and Caleb needed friends. Kendra waited and hoped.

"But I guess I could," he said.

"Terrific. I can pick you up. I'm going in the morning."

"I guess I'd better go back to the Claibornes and read up on how to use it." He held up the box.

"Need a ride?"

"Nope." He started down the steps; then he turned. "I never had a camera," he said again, then paused. "Thanks, Ms. Taylor."

She smiled. "It's Kendra, and you're welcome, Caleb. And thanks for Dusty. I'll take good care of her."

"I know."

He nearly smiled. She could see it in his eyes, and that was good enough for now.

He'd vanished into the distance before she looked down at the dog. "What in the name of heaven am I going to do with you?"

Dusty still looked dejected. Kendra doubted the dog was capable of any other expression.

"Great, a depressed dog. I'll be taking care of *you.* Some protector you'll be." She considered what to do with the dog now. She didn't want to tie her up while she made supper, but she knew if she left her alone, Dusty might wander off. And how would she explain that to Caleb?

She didn't want the dog underfoot while she cooked. She decided to imprison her in the bedroom. With some coaxing, Dusty followed her inside, and Kendra installed her in the bedroom, along with the water bowl. A quick investigation for fleas and ticks turned up pink skin under the tangles and snarls, and nothing creepy-crawly. The dog's nose was cool and moist, and her eyes, though droopy, were clear.

Dusty flopped down on the rug, and Kendra left her to her own devices.

She was chopping mushrooms for pasta sauce when she heard a car honk outside. For a fleeting moment she hoped the dog's real owner had come to get her. Someone who trained service dogs, maybe. Someone genuinely tearful. Someone who wasn't looking for Rusty, too.

"Right." She rinsed her hands and grabbed a dish towel, drying them as she walked outside.

Isaac was just getting out of his Prius.

She was so surprised that for a moment she didn't know what to say.

"I know you weren't expecting me," he said.

Her hand went to her hair, the dish towel flapping against her shoulder. "You don't need an invitation."

"You may change your mind about that." He slammed his door; then he opened the back door before she could ask what he meant. Isaac was still wearing his work clothes. A blue Oxford cloth shirt, charcoal-colored trousers, polished loafers.

When he didn't reappear immediately, she called to him, "Don't tell me you brought me a present. You're not the first."
He reemerged, and her eyes widened when she saw what he had in his hands. "You're kidding, right?"

Isaac held the cat carrier straight out from his side. She could hear the cat yowling loudly as Isaac walked toward the porch. And Isaac? Her self-confident, unemotional husband had never looked so sheepish.

He set the carrier down at the bottom of the steps. "I didn't know what else to do."

She stared down at the cat inside, then up at her husband's face. He looked sheepish, yes, and something else. Confused. Isaac could not figure out why he had done this. It went against everything he believed about himself.

"This isn't happening," she said.

"I never planned to bring him here."

"Isaac, what is that . . . that thing?"

He looked away, as if anything else would be easier to stare at. "It's kind of a long story."

"We don't have time for a long story. That monster's going to claw its way outside and take over the universe."

He shoved his hands into his pockets and rocked back on his heels. A lock of hair fell over his forehead, and he didn't even brush it away. "K.C.—"

"Don't K.C. me."

"Okay, here it is. I found him dying in the alley across from the office. I, well, I rescued him, and the vet saved his life. John—you remember John, Craig's partner?" When she didn't nod or encourage him, he sighed. "John nursed him back to health after his surgery."

"Surgery?"

"Quite a bit, actually."

"Isaac. That's an alley cat."

"I know." One hand snaked out of his pocket to push through his hair. "I just couldn't let him die. I thought he would calm down after he was all fixed up, that I could find him a home. But he's a mess. He attacked John's other cats. He wants to be free. He wants to roam, but I couldn't just stick him back in the alley. He'd get hit by a car again, or Animal Control would catch him."

She stared at her husband. This was not the man she thought she knew. She would have bet money Isaac wouldn't rescue this cat. That instead he would call Animal Control and hope for the best and quickest end to the story. He wasn't one to spend money freely. He wasn't stingy, but he knew how to be frugal. She could only imagine the vet bill.

Or maybe this was the real man, the one locked inside him.

"I gather this isn't simply show-and-tell?" She was still trying to sound stern.

"I'm in a real bind here. I know it's asking a lot."

"What'll I do with him?"

"Well, I think the best thing would be to put him inside for a few days. Then you can let him out and see what he does. When he feels at home—"

"Feels at home? Would you like me to throw fish bones on the floor and park cars by the sofa?"

"It's been a while since he's been in the alley."

"You never told me a thing."

He smiled. "I was embarrassed."

His smile totally melted her resolve. She remembered this smile too well. He used it rarely, but when he did . . .

She tried not to let him see she was relenting. "Then what would I do with him? You know, after I've made him feel at home?"

"By then maybe he could go in and out. I think he'll stay close by if you feed him. He likes tuna, by the way. And his name is Ten."

"You *should* be embarrassed."

"I know. I'll owe you big time if you do this."

Then, and only then, did she remember Dusty. The irony of being presented with two misfit pets in the same day wasn't lost on her.

Isaac came up the steps. "K.C., you always said you wanted a cat. Well, I listened."

"I *never* said that."

"Okay, but you were thinking it. Who knows you better?" He rested his hands on her shoulders. "But if this is too much to ask, I'll understand."

He never asked for anything. That had been their bargain. "Did you rescue alley cats when you were a little boy?"

"Not successfully."

That spoke volumes. She stood on tiptoe and kissed him. He returned it doublefold.

She wrapped her arms around him and leaned closer.

They were interrupted by a series of furious yowls from below.

"What was the other present?" he asked, his arms still around her.

"What?"

"When I got out of the car, you said this wasn't your first present of the day."

"Um . . . Caleb brought me some surplus . . . from the Clairbornes' farm." She only wished it had been that simple.

"I have a nice roomy cat kennel in the back of my car. John loaned it to me. You couldn't keep Ten in the carrier for long."

She was disappointed when he moved away, but resigned. She didn't want Isaac walking into the bedroom right now, anyway. The moment he saw Dusty, he would disappear with his favorite alley cat, and her chance to help him would be over. For now, the existence of the dog would have to remain a secret.

"You can put the kennel in the main room," she told him.

"I can see why you wouldn't want him in your bedroom."

He didn't know the half of it.

She helped him set up the cage by the door, with a small litter box, water and food; then she watched as he brought in the carrier, positioned the doors so one opened into the other and jostled Ten into the cage. He slammed the door in the nick of time and fastened it.

"This will do for a day or two."

Kendra had already crossed the room to pour them both half a glass of red wine, finishing what was left of a bottle. She didn't even ask. She handed one glass to him, and he took it gratefully. She hoped Dusty would remain true to form and comatose.

"To Ten," she said. "May he like his new home."

"To everything that moves within two hundred yards of the house. May they escape while they can."

"To my husband, who thought I wanted a cat."

"To my wife, who always comes through in a pinch." They sipped.

"I've got to get back tonight," he said at last. "I wish I could stay."

"How about some dinner first?"

"I have a meeting at eight. I'll pick up something along the way."

She was just as glad. As unlikely as it seemed, Dusty might bark and spoil the moment. "Finish your wine and I'll walk you to the car. I have something to tell you."

He did, and they went outside together after he'd said a gruff goodbye to the cat, who was hissing and glaring at them from the kennel. A cool breeze rustled through the leaves. It was going to be a beautiful evening.

"I went up to the park on Saturday." She stopped beside his car, and he folded his arms. Then she told him what they had discovered.

"You had to pursue it."

He didn't sound angry, and she was relieved. "Isaac, don't you think if your grandmother had killed two people, giving away the location of the bodies would be the last thing she'd do?"

"We don't know anything about my grandmother other than a few reminiscences. And the fact that she probably had some connection to a place called . . . what?"

"Lock Hollow." She hesitated. "There's more to the story. After we realized the quilting stitches were a map of the area—"

"A map that emphasizes the location of a cave where two bodies were found."

"Okay, but *afterward,* Hank found a list of people who lived in that area before they were removed. There was a farm right there in the hollow that belonged to a Jesse and Leah Spurlock. And Hank says it's some of the nicest land there."

"Sounds like you got your answer, then."

"Isaac, all the names embroidered on the quilt were on his list. Every single one of them. It's more proof that Lock Hollow is the place where your grandmother came from."

"Okay. So?"

"Hank told me about a group that meets monthly. It's made up of people who were evicted or are related to people who were. The evictions were in the thirties, so most of those people are gone now, but not all. Turns out they have a meeting this week."

"Something tells me you're not done investigating."

"Do you want me to be? So far it's not a happy story, and I'm afraid it's reinforcing all your stereotypes of your family."

He pondered that. She could see him turning it over in his mind. Somewhere nearby a dog barked. She was afraid she knew where.

Isaac was lost in thought and didn't pay attention. "You've gone so far already that I'll just wonder now. I guess you should go on and find out what you can. But don't expect to have this story handed to you. Either nobody knows the answers, or nobody's going to tell you."

"And if I do find out, I've made things worse, haven't I."

He considered that, too, then gave a single shake of his head. "No."

"No?"

"It's always been a shadow hovering over my life." He touched her hair, winding a curl around his forefinger. "Go ahead and let in the light, K.C. It can't be any worse."

She looked up at him, at this man whose heart and soul had been buried under emotional debris for far too long. She thought that with each newly exposed layer, a new man, a man she could love even more, was emerging. "Come back this weekend, Isaac? There's a fair at church. We'll have fun."

He smiled at her, a slow, lazy smile. "Can I sleep here?"

She sent him the feminine version of his smile. “You’d be welcome.”

“If I don’t get here in time, go on to the fair without me. But I’ll be here by the afternoon. You can count on it.”

“Okay.”

He kissed her, a gentle, searching kiss that promised more; then he got in his car and drove away.

He hadn’t been gone more than a minute when another car replaced his. Kendra recognized Marian Claiborne’s Buick. Marian rolled down her window.

“Caleb’s got something for you.”

Caleb got out of the passenger side and opened the rear door. He pulled out a huge sack of dog food. “You’ll need this.”

She wondered what the boy would do if he saw Isaac’s cat. Ten would take all the pleasure out of giving her the puppy. “Of course I will. What a good idea.”

“I’ll just take it in the house.”

“Um . . . Don’t do that. Just put it on the porch. I’ll keep it outside for the time being. I’ll probably feed her out there.” She manufactured a big smile.

“Some animal or t’other might get into it,” Marian warned. “You’re sure you don’t just want Caleb to carry it inside? It's heavy as a sackful of rocks, and he's strong."

"I'll find something to put the food in. I have a nice new trash can that nothing can get into. But there's no room for that bag in my kitchen."

"You'll have lots of room once they finish, won't you?"

Room enough for a freaked-out feline and a comatose canine? Room to hide one or the other from the two males in her life? Kendra wasn't sure there was that much room in the whole world.

"I'll be thrilled when the renovations are done," she said, as Caleb climbed back into the car. "Come back for a tour when they're finished."

She watched as Marian turned the car and headed out the way Isaac had just gone.

Then, with no one to hear her, she began to laugh.

CHAPTER NINETEEN

As expected, Dusty clearly had never received veterinary care, and after the first barrage of shots, Kendra left with a variety of treatments and the name of a groomer who could tackle the knots in the puppy's coat. Rusty, a sleeker red-coated version of his sister, got the same treatment. Kendra told Caleb his portion of the bill would be fifty dollars. Like most kids, he had no idea what the trip had really cost and told her he would pay her as he earned the cash.

"The vet liked Rusty," he told Kendra as she took them home. The two dogs were settled on the back seat. Rusty had given up trying to get Dusty to play with him.

Kendra wasn't sure what the vet thought of Dusty. The puppy's initial exam had turned up no signs of life-threatening infection or disease, which was a relief, although they had to wait for lab results. "She might perk up once she's wormed" was the most she'd gotten out him.

Kendra's only consolation was that Dusty seemed to be housebroken. Used to living outside, the pup preferred grass to Kendra's floors. Still, Kendra knew better than to risk an accident while she was away. After she dropped off Caleb and Rusty, she made another trip to the home improvement center and ordered a roomy doghouse. The young man in charge promised to deliver it on his way home that afternoon.

She was dressing to go out again when he arrived. The young man and a friend had brought a bale of straw for the floor and chicken wire for a fence around it. Once the setup was complete, she tipped them generously. They had placed it behind some trees on the side of the house where it wouldn't easily be seen, although she knew better than to think Isaac wouldn't notice if the dog barked. She would need another plan for that.

Installed in her new home, Dusty lay down on the ground outside the arched door and went to sleep.

The next pet wasn't as easy to please. Ten, who hadn't taken well to his newest quarters, tried to make a break when Kendra opened the door to feed him. She managed to shut the door in time, but she pondered her options. One, let the cat out and hope he wouldn't destroy the room while she was gone. Two, keep him inside with no food.

Ten's expression was the cat equivalent of a dirty old man's. She was positive he was leering at her. *Let me out of here, baby, and just see what I can do.*

She laughed. "I'm a heck of a lot bigger than you are, buddy. I'll step on you if get out of line." She opened the door and stood back. He streaked under the sofa. The Road Runner of cartoon fame was slow in comparison.

"Well, you're clearly on the road to recovery, aren't you." She set a fresh bowl of food on the floor beside the cage and another of water. She pulled out the litter box and emptied it, filling it again and stashing it in the corner.

"When you're ready to brave your new world, tough guy, everything's here for you."

Back in the bedroom, she finished getting

ready for another trip. Tonight was the bi-monthly meeting of The Way We Were, the organization Hank had told her about. Kendra's research had turned up an active group whose goal was to make certain their story was told with honesty and integrity. They had already been instrumental in the removal of an inaccurate and unflattering interpretive display at the park visitor center.

To prepare, she'd called the contact number listed on their Web site and spoken to a young woman named Jennifer, who told Kendra that her great-grandfather, Aubrey Grayling, would be at the next meeting. Mr. Grayling was a rich source of information about the area called Lock Hollow. The name was familiar to Kendra. Aubrey Grayling was on her quilt, as well as on the list the ranger had given her. It was the best luck she could imagine.

The meetings were held in different locations, and luckily this one was only an hour away, at a church outside of Luray. Kendra had asked Cissy if she wanted to come, but Cissy and Zeke had made plans to visit his cousin who lived nearby. "They have a little boy Reese's age," she'd confessed. "Last time Reese sat on his chest and decorated Ryan's face with chocolate pudding."

Kendra had tried not to laugh. "An artist in training."

"Either that or she's taking after one of those big old Japanese wrestlers. You know, the ones that look like they're wearing diapers?"

Kendra was afraid she might never look at Reese the same way again.

The drive was pleasant, corn sprouting in roadside fields, bright blue chicory waving along the shoulder, small houses on hillsides sheltered by century-old trees. She could brave the Interstate now, but she still preferred taking her time. She wondered how much scenery had gone unnoticed while she pursued her career with single-minded intensity.

She arrived at St. Joseph of Cupertino with just a few minutes to spare. She found the basement meeting room, a pleasant space with blue industrial carpeting, acoustic ceiling tile and gray metal columns. Religious art adorned the walls, and folding chairs were placed between columns in front of a lectern with a small microphone. No one was yet standing in front to conduct the meeting, so she wrote her name in a guest book and took a nicely printed brochure. The meeting began before she could introduce herself to anyone. She counted eighteen others in attendance.

Like every meeting of its kind, the first part was business. Her mind wandered as the hospitality committee discussed cards to members who had been ill. She tried to guess which of the older men, three of them, might be Aubrey Grayling. She hoped it was the white-haired gentleman wearing red suspenders over a crisp white shirt. He had ruddy cheeks and laughed easily. She thought he might be willing to talk to her.

When the program turned out to be a presentation on an archaeological dig in Corbin Hollow, she was sorry Cissy hadn't come along. The presenter told them a number of interesting facts about the way people there had really lived, including foods they had consumed, patent medicines they had used, even the toys their children had played with. The dig overturned the notion that all the people of Corbin Hollow had been so isolated and backward that they had needed the government's intervention to bring them into the twentieth century.

Afterward, she listened with interest to the discussion. Several attendees were descendants of Corbin Hollow families and repeated tales they'd heard while growing up. One had brought a large photograph of her family's farmhouse, which she held up for everyone to see. Lilacs and snowball bushes in front of a wide front porch, two stories covered in clapboard, with a stone chimney rising above them. A house no different from many in rural Virginia.

The meeting ended with an invitation for the attendees to stay and chat over coffee and cookies. Kendra stretched before starting toward the table set up with a coffee urn and platters.

Almost immediately, she was greeted by a pretty young woman in her late twenties, with blond hair sleeked into a high ponytail and a friendly smile. "Are you Kendra Taylor?" She stuck out her hand.

"You must be Jennifer." They shook.

"Paw-paw's looking forward to meeting you. That's him sitting over there." She pointed.

Kendra saw that the man with the suspenders *was* Aubrey Grayling. "I'm so glad he came."

"He doesn't get out much these days, but these meetings mean the world to him. He turned ninety-two last month, but he's still sharp as a tack. Especially when it comes to things that happened when he was young."

"Most of the adults who lived in the mountains before the park are probably gone now, aren't they?"

"That's right. Most of those coming to our meetings were pretty young at the time their families were evicted. Though you'd be surprised. We're hardy stock. Paw-paw's not the only one in his nineties."

"My husband's grandmother would be eighty-nine, if she were still alive."

"Come talk to Paw-paw and see what he has to say."

Jennifer introduced Kendra to a couple of other people before she led her to the row of chairs where Aubrey was sitting. He had just finished a conversation, and the seat beside him was now empty. Jennifer gestured for Kendra to take it. "Paw-paw? This is Ms. Taylor, the woman I spoke to. Remember me telling you about her?"

Aubrey looked at his great-granddaughter

fondly. "You think I'd forget something like that?"

"Just reminding you. I'll leave you two alone now."

Aubrey Grayling looked younger than ninety-two. Hardy stock indeed, and a tribute to Darwin. Kendra supposed that for many years before penicillin, tetanus shots and central heating, only the strongest had survived in Virginia's mountains. His hair was thin but still covered most of his head. His eyes were a blue so pale and cloudy that she suspected cataracts. She wasn't sure how well he could see.

"So, Ms. Taylor, tell me why you're here again?"

She wasn't sure, but she suspected he knew *exactly* why she was there. "Call me Kendra, Mr. Grayling."

"Then I'm Aubrey."

"I guess Jennifer told you I've recently discovered that my husband Isaac is the grandson of a woman who might have lived in Lock Hollow."

"Well, that's right. She did now."

"And you lived there?"

"I did. For the first twenty-two years of my life. I was one of the last to leave. Until they came in and burned our family store right in front of me. Had to be sure we didn't come back, they said."

His expression was still pleasant, but she could only imagine the emotion behind his words. "I don't think you can really get over something like that," she said.

"You figure it's best not to gnaw on it too much. You try to find a life somewheres else. I did, after a while."

She noticed that he hadn't asked her the name of Isaac's mother. She waited to see if he would continue.

"I knew Leah Spurlock," he said after a brief silence.

So he *had* remembered Leah's name. But just to be sure he knew details, she told the story again—inheritance, quilt, trip to the park. She left out the cave.

"A ranger gave me a list," she finished. "Leah and Jesse Spurlock were on it. That's how I found you."

"I knew them both. And Leah's sister, Birdie. Birdie Blackburn, she was. Even prettier than Leah, some thought, though I never did. She never did marry. She lived with Leah and Jesse on account of her being crippled."

Clearly Kendra had stumbled on a wealth of information. “So Leah’s name was Blackburn before she was married.”

“That would be right.”

She filed that away. “All this came to light because the quilt I mentioned is identical to—” She backed up. “First, do you know about the bodies they found in a cave in Lock Hollow?”

“I heard tell of it.”

She waited, but obviously that was all he planned to say. “Well, the quilt I mentioned? The one Leah left my husband? It’s nearly identical to the one they found there. Or as far as we can tell from what’s left of it.”

“Now ain’t that interesting?”

“And the quilting pattern is a map of Lock Hollow. Except for one thing. Two lines cross at that cave, almost as if Leah was marking the spot with an X for someone to find later.”

“Now that hardly seems likely.”

“Aubrey, would you know anything about this? Would you have any idea who those bodies were? Because I think Leah was trying to tell some kind of story, and maybe the bodies are the final paragraph.”

There was a long pause, as if he was considering what she had said and searching his memory. But when he spoke, he surprised her.

"I read the newspaper. Or did, when I could still see good enough. I'd read it from cover to cover near to every day. The *Richmond Times-Dispatch,* the *Washington Post.*" He smiled. The teeth weren't his own, but they were good ones. "I paid attention to just about everything I read. And I used to like the articles I read by somebody with your name."

She sat back. This was a man who had probably never had the wool pulled over his eyes. "I do write for the *Post,* but this is personal."

"I always say you can pinch the wings off a butterfly, but that don't turn it back into a caterpillar."

Since she'd thought about pitching a series of articles to her editor, she couldn't lie. "I don't know what I'll do once I have my answers. But surely there can't be anybody left who would be hurt if the truth came out now."

"Well, that would depend on the truth, wouldn't it? But it don't matter. I'm just having fun with you. See, I don't know a thing about those bodies. Not one blessed thing. Or could be I misplaced what I did know. If I'd known about the bodies back when, maybe I'd remember something to help you, some little detail I forgot 'til now. But you don't remember what's not important."

How was she reading the eyes of a man who was nearly blind? She was almost positive Aubrey Grayling was not telling the truth.

She tried a different tack. "Can you tell me about Leah, then? I can't figure out why she went all the way to Toms Brook, and alone, besides. Do you remember? Or what happened to her husband? Why he wasn't with her?"

Aubrey shook his head. "Can't rightly say. See, at the end there, it was pretty bad for everybody. People coming and going, the government sending workers to make threats and buy people out. I was awful busy just trying to find a way to stay myself. We didn't live so close together, you know. People just up and left, and nobody heard from them again. Some went this way, some that." He lifted his frail shoulders. "Up and gone."

She sat back and pondered this. She was

face-to-face with a master storyteller, only she couldn't get him to tell the stories she needed to hear. She realized she had gone for the big facts before he trusted her. Her personal stake had clouded her judgment.

"Well, that's too bad," she said. "I feel like Leah wanted Isaac to know something. But I think she also wanted him to know her better."

"Might have," he agreed.

"Are there any Blackburns or Spurlocks living? People who knew her well? Or their descendants?"

"I couldn't say. So many are gone now."

More stonewalling. In fact, Aubrey was building the wall of secrecy so high she was afraid she wasn't going to be given so much as a peek over it.

She switched tactics again. "On that map at the park, the farm closest to the Spurlock place was owned by somebody named Cade. Any chance there are Cades still living?"

"Well, that's something I can tell you."

She smiled in encouragement. "Yes?"

"The original generation, they're all gone. But their young 'uns are still around. Puss Cade? She was Leah's best friend growing up. See, when Leah and Jesse got married, they took over the Blackburn place, so it was Leah's home-place where they settled, not his. The Cade farm was right in between the old Spurlock place and the Blackburn place. Puss got married and had a daughter name of Prudence. Prudence Baker, I think. She lived over Flint Hill way. Probably still does. She don't come to these meetings."

Kendra felt a splinter of victory. "I'll see if I can find her."

"Some folks got relocated over that way. Her mama was one of them, her and the whole Cade family."

"Well, maybe Puss told her daughter something about Leah."

"Might have at that, seeing's they was that close and all."

"Can you tell me anything else about Leah, Aubrey? Anything you remember?"

"Oh, I remember a lot."

She was sure he did, a lot more than he'd told her so far. She decided to go for background, something small she thought he might part with. "Why did Jesse and Leah live on *her* family's farm? I didn't see any Spurlocks embroidered on Leah's quilt, or any other ones besides Jesse and Leah on the list the ranger gave me."

"That's easy. The Spurlocks, now, they were one of the prime families in Lock Hollow. They had a lot of good land, a house they could be proud of. The Blackburns were the other family who did just fine, come what may. The Spurlocks, though, they had this problem. See, they was always giving birth to girls. More girl Spurlocks than you can imagine. Jesse finally come along just about when everybody thought the name was going to die out for good, and Essie and Grover Spurlock, well, they was as happy as they could ever be. Then Grover died, and Essie remarried a man name of Collins."

Kendra remembered the name Collins on the ranger's list and the quilt. "I see."

"So Jesse's mother and her new husband, they kept the old Spurlock place. Jesse would have got it eventually, you know. But when he married Leah, she and Birdie were all alone on account of their parents dying of typhoid fever."

"So I guess it only made sense for Jesse to move to the Blackburn place and farm

Leah's land while his mother and stepfather were still alive."

"That's right. Leah's folks left the place to her. See, they knew if they did, Leah would always take care of Birdie."

"You said Birdie was disabled?"

"Polio. You young folks just don't know how it was back then."

"We do take immunity for granted."

"You go someplace like India or Indonesia, you still see it."

She was reminded yet again that she was dealing with a man who was well read and intelligent.

"I like the story so far," she said. "What were Leah and Jesse like? And Birdie, too?"

He crossed his arms over his suspenders and shut his eyes. At first she thought he was telling her he was tired. Then he smiled. "I lived as close by as anyone, you know. I saw a lot in those days."

"I'm listening."

He smiled again. "Good, 'cause I'm about to start talking."

CHAPTER TWENTY

Blackburn Farm
Lock Hollow, Virginia
February 18, 1934

Dear Puss,

I do not know why the doctor there at Skyland cannot ease Miss Lula's rhumatism. I know she is good to work for, and I am sorry she is too often puny. It beats all that the doctor told her to sweat it out, since even without his kind of schooling, I know that will not do a thing.

I am sending dried poke berries. She should swallow one a day, and work her way to six, if they do not make her sick. She should spit out the seeds if she can and never chew them, since they are dangerus. Fresh berries would be best, but you cannot find them until summer. I also beleave that white willow bark eases the pain. You know how to use it. Some is with the poke berries here.

I do not know a remedy for keeping the government of Virginia away from these mountains. I surely wish I did. I am sorry the gentlemen at Skyland think the government stealing what belongs to us is a good idea. I wish you would come home.

The friend who misses you,
Leah Spurlock

A year after her marriage to Jesse, Leah had two sorrows. The first was that she hadn't gotten pregnant. From the moment of Jesse's proposal, she had hoped not to have a baby right away. As she'd provided nursing care to her neighbors, she had seen how too many children in a family tired a woman. She hoped to be blessed with only the number she and Jesse could love and care for. But when a year had passed and there was no sign of a child, she began to worry.

The second sorrow was more insidious and even less likely to be favorably resolved. The decision to build a park in Virginia's mountains seemed to be moving forward at a rapid rate, despite all the reasons against it.

The country was in a terrible state. In cities, people stood in breadlines. Millionaires jumped from skyscraper windows, and widows sold apples on street corners. In some places families lived in caves or sewer pipes. President Hoover, who had built a private presidential retreat not far away on the Rapidan River, had been voted out of office, and the new president, Franklin Delano Roosevelt, seemed more determined to improve the lot of ordinary people. But how would giving people's homes to the deer and buzzards help anyone?

Some families who thought the park would happen also believed they would be allowed to continue living on their land afterward. There had been assurances along the way. And who would force a thousand people from their homes just so trees could grow untended?

Still, the evidence that their futures and farms were at stake was mounting. Some mountain people had simply packed and gone, accepting the inevitable. The amount of acreage for the park had been reduced, as expected, but Lock Hollow was still just inside its boundaries. The residents could no longer ignore the fact that their lives were about to change forever.

In February, Leah was helping Birdie prepare blackberry pies when Jesse stalked in, ushering in the chill of winter with him. The year hadn't brought prosperity to anyone, but that summer, as if in sympathy, the blackberries had doubled their yield. One of these pies was to go to an old woman who lived alone on the next ridge.

"Now they've gone and done it. Really done it."

Leah dried her hands on her apron and went to take Jesse's coat and the bundle he carried. He had been gone all day, helping the Cades repair their roof, the victim of a tree that had toppled in the last storm.

"There's snow coming," she said. "I can feel it in the air. I'm glad you made it home before it started."

"I wish I hadn't gone at all."

"What are you talking about? Who did what?"

Jesse sat on the kitchen stool and removed his boots—boots that needed replacing, like almost every item of clothing he owned. In better times Leah was paid for tending the sick and for the remedies she made using her mother's recipes. Jesse sold milled lumber, and the shakes and shingles he hewed, along with corn and the exceptional apples that grew in the Blackburn and Spurlock orchards. Even Birdie made quilts to sell at Grayling's Store.

But these days people were making do with whatever they had, and the past summer Jesse had quietly sold his corn crop to a "stiller" in Free State Hollow. Even though Prohibition had finally ended, corn liquor was still the most profitable use of the crop and the cheapest way to ship it out of the mountains.

He finished removing his boots. "The government's saying they won't accept title to our land from the State of Virginia 'less all of us are off it. So they'll be coming after us now, every last one of us."

Leah looked at Birdie, who was staring out the window as if the outline of leaf-bare trees against the darkening sky was more important than the conversation.

"Jesse—" Leah lowered her voice "—what about the lawsuits? Don't the courts have to decide whether they can do it or not?"

"You're not listening. They've just gone and done it!"

"Are we really going to have to leave? Can they make us?"

"They try, there'll be some fighting up here. You know there will."

"Not you." She put her hand on his arm. "What would that accomplish except separate you from your land *and* your family?"

"They say they'll be coming right quick to look at each farm in the holler and see what they owe for it. You think they can pay enough for what this holler means to us? My family's been here for nigh two hundred years. And yours nearly as long. These mountains belong to us. We bought what we own with the blood of the people went before us."

Leah felt that, too. It was disgraceful that the State of Virginia could walk into their homes, calculate their worth and pretend to pay them enough to start again somewhere else. How did you pack up generations of memories, friendships with neighbors, a way of life that had kept their stomachs full and houses warm while the rest of the nation suffered?

"You ought to see what they're saying about us out there." Jesse got to his feet, and started toward the living room and the warmth of the wood stove. "They're saying we're nothing but a bunch of ignorant hillbillies, that not a one of us won't be better off if the government roots us out of here. We'll go down below, get an education, learn how to eat with a fork, and say 'please' and 'thank you.' As if we don't do that now! They say someday we'll realize how lucky we are this happened."

Leah followed him. "I don't hardly know a single family anywhere that wouldn't send their young 'uns to school every single day if they could."

"Not according to the newspapers. They say there ain't enough schools here because we don't want 'em. Don't matter how many times we've asked the county and the churches to help. Don't matter how many times they've had to say no because they don't have the money to build more."

"Why do people say those things?"

Instead of warming his hands over the stove on the hearth, Jesse reached for the German Luger on the fireplace mantel. It had been his father's, a memento of service in the Great War, and Jesse had placed it there for their protection when he moved in, along with his father's medals and a German spiked helmet. The collection seemed at home now, a part of Jesse's past, but seeing the pistol in his hands when he was angry made her uneasy.

He sighted down the barrel, pointing it toward a window. "To make it easier to force us out of here, that's why. People in the cities think too hard, they might sympathize and work to stop the park. This way, nobody thinks twice. They think they'll be doing us a favor."

"If this happens, where will we go?"

"Aubrey's coming by after supper."

Aubrey Grayling had been Jesse's constant companion since childhood. Even now that Jesse was married, Aubrey was a frequent visitor. Leah liked him well enough, although sometimes, like any new bride, she resented the time her husband spent with his friend. But Aubrey was good-natured and smart. When he was younger, he'd been sent to live with family in Luray to receive more education, and he was always reading.

Leah put her hand on Jesse's shoulder, and he let the gun drop to his side. "You let us finish these pies, then we'll get supper on the table. You go and put your feet up a while."

Leah watched as he replaced the gun and collapsed into the rocking chair. Judging from his expression, his burden was every bit as heavy as when he'd walked through the door.

"He's worried," she told Birdie in a low tone. "And that worries *me.*"

"Jesse won't allow anything bad to happen," Birdie said. "God sent him to take care of us."

"You ever think maybe God sent him to help us pack up and move?"

"If that's His will. But it ain't."

Leah wished her faith was as strong as her sister's, but she was worried. She had only rarely ventured out of the mountains. Her mother had hoped to send her to Hagerstown, Maryland, for nurse's training, but the Depression had made it difficult to put money aside. Then Flossie's death had made it impossible. Leah had yearned for more education, but even more, for a chance to see a little of the world.

For a moment she imagined what life might be like somewhere else. Jesse was smart and a hard worker. He could get a job, even if the government didn't pay them enough to buy another farm. Perhaps down below she could train as a nurse after all. Together, couldn't the three of them have a good life? Surely they would make friends, become part of whatever community they went to. If they were ever blessed with children, it would be easier to educate them.

"It would be a different life," Leah said. "But maybe not a worse one."

"You oughtn't to let Jesse hear you talk that way," Birdie said. "He's planning to stay here, and he don't need you a-tugging at him and saying different."

Leah wondered if her sister was right. But if they were forced from their home, they would need to prepare. And preparation meant not only packing and taking what they could, but finding something good about the situation to hang on to.

As if Birdie were trying to cheer Jesse,

supper was even better than usual. The corn bread was laced with cracklings, and the poke salit was cooked with onions from the root cellar as well as side meat. The blackberry pie was topped with heavy cream and served with a flourish.

"You feed us so good, Birdie girl, no one'd ever know there was a problem in the world," Jesse told her.

Birdie smiled. "As hard as you work, Jesse, you need to eat well and often."

Leah knew Birdie was just trying to make Jesse feel better, but the compliment annoyed her. She helped her sister clean the kitchen and wash the dishes, going out to the pump twice for pitchers of fresh water. In truth, she went out to see the sky and to look for more signs of snow. She could smell and taste it in the air. The hair on her arms stood up in anticipation, and she could feel her cheeks and nose turning red.

She hadn't heard the door open and close, but by the time she registered footsteps, she felt Jesse's arms slip around her. "You really need all that water just for a few dishes?"

She leaned against him, happy for the first time since he'd come home that evening. "We did all that baking before supper. So you could eat *well* and *often.*"

He chuckled and his arms tightened around her. "That's not the only thing a man has to do *well* and *often.*"

"I can surely testify to the *often* part. You just cain't seem to leave me alone, Jesse Spurlock."

He laughed again and turned her to face him. "And would you want me to?"

She kissed him in answer. "As for *well?*" She stepped back to see his face in the moonlight. "I guess that all depends on how much of a hurry you're in."

"That's why I aim to do it often. So I won't be in a hurry."

"Now I see how it is." She smiled; then she sobered. "I just wish all that well and often would bring us a baby."

"Don't you go getting worried about it. It's a gift not to be burdened with a young 'un right off in a marriage. And with this problem with the park waiting just around the corner . . ."

She wished she hadn't said anything. She had ruined the moment.

"I just want you to know that whatever happens," she said, "we have each other,

Jesse. We can face anything together. We can go anywhere and make us a good life."

"This is where I belong." There was no room to argue. She heard absolute conviction in his voice.

There was no *time* to argue, either. A light appeared just beyond their barn, and as they watched, it moved closer.

"That will be Aubrey," Jesse said. "He ate supper with the Cades."

"He's spending a lot of time over there. Do you reckon he has his eye on Mary?" Mary was Puss's younger sister. Puss herself was cleaning rooms at the Skyland resort now that her brother in Stanardsville had remarried. She got one day a week to herself, but it wasn't enough time to come home.

"He hasn't said anything about Mary," Jesse said. "More likely he wants it to look that way, so he'll get a good meal now and then."

Aubrey's mother had passed on two years before. Aubrey was always looking for a home-cooked meal, and Birdie fed him regularly. Sometimes Leah wondered if Aubrey might settle down with Birdie just for her cooking. That way he and Jesse would be brothers-in-law, and he could spend even more time with her husband. So far, though, neither Aubrey nor Birdie seemed interested in that prospect.

Leah went inside and left Jesse to greet his friend. She poured water into the dishpan and used it to rinse the last of the dishes. Birdie was in the bedroom the two of them had shared as girls, most likely piecing another quilt.

Leah dried what she'd rinsed and had finished setting the kitchen to rights by the time Aubrey appeared with Jesse.

Aubrey removed his hat. "I reckon you're doing well?"

"Nice to see you, Aubrey. Let me take your hat and coat." She did, and hung them on a peg. "We just finished some blackberry pie. Would you like a slice?"

He refused, claiming he'd eaten two helpings of apple cobbler at the Cades'.

"Well, I'll just be with Birdie helping her make a quilt top," Leah said, turning to leave the men to their conversation.

"I think she oughta stay," Aubrey told Jesse. "It's her land and all."

Leah looked at her husband.

Jesse gave a short nod. "This land belongs to you. When they come to tell us how much they're planning to pay, you'll be the one they want to talk to."

Leah was glad to be included. It was easier than worming the conversation out of Jesse. They all took seats near the woodstove, Leah on the horsehair sofa that her father had brought in by mules and a wagon as a gift to her mother, the two men in hickory rocking chairs.

"Here's what I know—" Aubrey said.

Since it was unusual for anyone visiting to go straight to the heart of a matter, Leah knew how important this was.

"—and the news ain't a bit good."

"Just pass it on," Jesse said, his voice tight and low. "And get it over with."

"The state's already made a blanket condemnation of our land, and none of the challenges that's been made against it have borne fruit. What that boils down to is now they're saying all this land belongs to them, and we got to get off fast. They say they'll pay fairly, even help folks move someplace just like this and start all over. They'll be buying land for resettlement."

Jesse's tone was bitter. "You mean they don't think the mountains are good for us, but they don't plan to move us out of them. Mountains over yonder somewhere are better for us than *these* mountains."

"There's no call to try and make sense of it or to believe anything they say means what they say it does," Aubrey said. "It's a legal situation. The State of Virginia's slicker'n red clay in a spring rain. Now they've condemned it, they can say a pig is a cow, and as far as that goes, it will be. They'll claim the land's not worth much. And they're right, since nothing's worth nothing with this Depression hanging over us. They want it for recreation use, but they don't price it that way. Nobody's looking at a mountain view and saying it's worth anything to anybody."

"So what's going to happen?" Leah didn't look at Jesse but at Aubrey.

"It's a legal situation, so we have to get legal real fast. We have to band together, all of us in the holler, and hire somebody to represent us. First we'll see if there's anything left to challenge in court and stop it for a while. But I'm afraid it's just a matter of time. They'll move us whether we want it or not, so it's up to us to make sure we get everything we can first."

"Won't that cost money? None of us has anything put away."

"Oh, they'll be counting on that," Jesse said. "Aubrey's right about the way they'll do it. They know we don't have ten cents to hire a lawyer."

"I'm working on that," Aubrey said. "I just need to know if you're with us."

"Us?"

"The Cades, your ma and Luther Collins." He named four more families in the hollow.

"You talked to all them before you talked to Leah and me?"

"I just saw them first, that's all. Every single one came into the store this week. Saw the Cades tonight."

Jesse got to his feet. "They're all giving up. Just like that?"

Aubrey got to his feet, too. "What do you mean, giving up? We're fixing to find a way to get what's ours. Don't matter if you want this or not, Jesse. Just 'cause you say they can't do it, don't mean they won't. Everybody hereabouts knows you're the last Spurlock of Lock Holler, but when they come around with trucks and rifles and tell us we have to be gone, there won't be any use in telling *them* so. They won't care, and the people who did'll be on their way somewhere else."

Leah saw her husband's hands ball into fists. Jesse was hot-tempered, but he also knew how to control himself. Taking his anger out on Aubrey was a measure of how distraught he was.

She slid between the two men and held up her hands. "Everybody knows you two always fight on the same side. You got no reason now to change that. Aubrey, you delivered your news. I were you, I'd take my hat and coat and get myself on down the road before this snow falls. We need some time here to sort this out. You can understand that."

Aubrey looked as if he wanted to say something; then he shrugged and started for his coat. When Jesse started after him, Leah grabbed his arm.

"You let him go," she said softly. "Or you'll be sleeping by the fire tonight."

At the doorway, Aubrey turned. "I don't aim to sit still on this. If you're in, we're glad to have you." The door shut behind him.

Leah slumped in relief. "What call do you have going after him that way? He was here to help us."

Jesse shook off her hand. "Help? There's not enough money in the whole country to pay what this land and the Spurlock land is worth to us."

"And how will scrapping with Aubrey change that?"

He didn't answer.

"Some things happen and we can't change them," Leah said. "Last month I did everything I could for poor Mary Hamm up near Stony Man, and not one thing I tried could help her. She died while I was wiping her forehead. Just up and died, and I knew then there wasn't one more thing I could have done to change it. You got to realize sometimes, Jesse, that no matter how bad you want something, you got to give it up."

He turned to stare at her. "You want *me,*" he said at last, "I'll be sleeping out here by this fire. It'll be warmer than your bed."

She put her hands on her hips. "That'll be just fine. Why don't you let one of the dogs in, while you're at it. Maybe they'll be better company, too."

She left him to consider that. But once in the loft, she stood at the window after she had undressed and wondered how she could bear to sleep without him.

CHAPTER TWENTY-ONE

Dusty was beginning to take an interest in her mistress. Kendra sensed the puppy's eyes following her when she moved around the bedroom. If she stepped inside the closet, Dusty scooted closer to be sure Kendra hadn't disappeared, although when Kendra backed out, the dog always looked elsewhere. Rather than subject the poor animal to Ten, Kendra had taken to leaving Dusty loose in the dogtrot when she went into the living area. As if she needed to prove how aptly the porch had been named, Dusty trotted back and forth outside the door until Kendra came out. As the door opened, Kendra always heard the dog plop into place, head angled away as if she had never even noted Kendra's absence.

This, she supposed, was progress.

Ten, on the other hand, remained hidden, although from time to time she saw his tail. Judging by the rapidly emptied bowls of cat food, he ate well, and he certainly used his litter. He never once tried to make a break for the door, but the catnip ball she'd bought him was always somewhere new when she entered the room.

She felt like a psychologist in a pet psychiatric facility. She wasn't sure she was up to psychoanalyzing Dusty and Ten, but she was perfectly happy to feed them and watch what they did next.

On Saturday morning she led Dusty out to her car and settled her in the passenger's seat. As she started out the driveway she explained her plan.

"Now listen, I'm taking you to the groomer. She's a very nice lady who has three dogs of her own. She's busy, so she's going to keep you overnight. That way she can take her time. Once she gets you washed and brushed and all the knots cut out of your fur, maybe I can keep up. But I'm coming back for you." She paused. "Just as soon as Isaac leaves tomorrow."

She didn't think it was necessary to explain that Isaac was the biggest reason for the overnight stay. She still hoped he wouldn't discover she had a dog. As perverse as it was, for the time being she wanted him to believe he was the only one for whom she would make this kind of sacrifice.

She glanced at the puppy. Dusty's eyes were closed. "I can see how worried you are."

The groomer was a pretty dark-haired young woman with two little boys who tried unsuccessfully to get Dusty to play with them.

"She has a clean bill of health, but she's the original droopy dog," Kendra apologized.

The young woman tried to coax Dusty to sniff her hand. "I've seen this before. Once she gets used to her new life, she'll be a good companion. Dogs are like people. They stop trying if they don't see any point in it."

"I have a cat that needs therapy, too."

"You got your hands full, don't you?"

Kendra wasn't sure, but as she pulled away she thought Dusty looked sadder. Not that it was easy to tell. She hoped whatever progress they'd made wasn't going to evaporate.

Last night she had dropped by to firm up the trip to the fair with Caleb. Marian had confided that Caleb still hadn't made friends at school. Although his teachers were impressed with his intelligence, they were concerned. Too many bright students dropped out if they felt they had no stake in what happened there.

Today Kendra had plans for Caleb he didn't know about.

He was waiting on the stoop when she drove up. Marian came out of the house wiping her hands on her apron. "You've got a perfect day. We're going over to my oldest boy's for supper tonight. You'll have Caleb back by then?"

"I'll have him back after lunch."

Marian patted his shoulder. "You take some good pictures, son. We're counting on you, since we can't get there ourselves."

Kendra heard the "son" and wondered how Caleb felt about it. "Son" was certainly used by adults for children who weren't one's own, particularly in the South. But she thought Marian hoped that in the ways that mattered, Caleb would become a real son.

She and Ron had welcomed the boy into their lives and, from all signs, their hearts. Now it was up to Caleb.

"Have you taken any photos yet?" she asked, once Caleb was settled beside her. The last time she'd asked, he had explained with heartbreaking gravity that he needed to read the instructions and really understand them before he tried. She knew he was worried he would do something wrong.

"A few," he said.

She was relieved. She'd been afraid she might have to stand behind him and position his finger on the shutter button. "How did they turn out?"

"Couldn't get them to work on Mr. Claiborne's computer."

"You can bring them to my place next week, and we'll download them and see what you've got. You'll have all today's photos, too."

"What do you want me to take pictures of?"

"Anything you want. Anything that looks interesting."

"I guess I can do that." He didn't sound sure.

Kendra didn't know how to help him. She

just hoped that finding a tool like the camera to bring people closer would make a difference.

Marian was correct. The weather was perfect—although too dry to suit the local farmers—and apparently everyone for miles around had come to see what was happening. Kendra parked on Old Miller Road behind a line of cars some distance from the church. Clearly this was *the* event of early summer.

"If you want to go off on your own, feel free," she told Caleb. "I'll find you when I'm ready to leave. But let's plan to eat here. The food's going to be great."

His expression said she might as well issue the orange jumpsuit and leg shackles now. He stayed with her as they walked along the roadside, but once people began to greet her, Caleb wandered off.

She was impressed by the work that had gone into the fair and sorry she had been so little help. On Thursday she had come by to design and print menus. Afterward she had spent hours feeding onions and garlic through an industrial-size food processor for the vats of chili. But some people had worked for most of the year to get the fair organized.

Striped tents were set up all over the grounds, although Kendra noted that Sam's prized rose garden had been spared. The children had been given their very own activity space at La Casa Amarilla, just a short walk away. La Casa, once the church's parsonage, was now a community center that welcomed and worked with the county's Latino population, tutoring children and, most recently, providing English classes for their parents.

Today, at the cheerful yellow house, all the children would be treated to pony rides, face painting and a craft center where they could create projects to take home. During the afternoon, Elisa's good friend Adoncia Garcia would tell stories in Spanish and English, treating the children to painless lessons in both. Meantime, their parents could shop without them.

She toured the grounds, admiring what had been accomplished by so many volunteers. A fifteen-foot barbecue had been erected for grilling chicken quarters, and earlier the volunteers had started a fire so the coals would be ready in time for the lunch crowd. Tables were set up under a tent and elsewhere under shady trees. Kendra knew the menu well. Chicken, vegetarian chili, ham potpie, salads for the health conscious and a baked-potato bar. Another tent would serve nothing but strawberry shortcake, made with the last of the valley's spring crop, and fresh whipped cream.

She saw tables of baked goods and headed for another smaller one filled with jams and jellies, which glowed like rubies and amethysts in the June sunshine. She was considering a half-pint jar of strawberry rhubarb jelly, when someone tapped her on the shoulder.

She turned to find Gayle Fortman, former president of the board of deacons and one of the members Sam could always count on. She was blond and slender, somewhat older than Kendra, judging by the equally blond teenage boy at her side, who looked so much like Gayle he could only be her son.

"I've been looking for you to say hi," Gayle said. "I hear you're coming to services, but we never cross paths."

"I've noticed." Kendra smiled at the

young man at her side. She extended her hand. "I'm Kendra Taylor."

"Jared Fortman." Jared had a strong handshake and didn't seem embarrassed by their exchange. He looked as if he might be in his final years of high school. He had his mother's gray eyes and aquiline nose, but the chin was square and masculine, and the forehead broad. Kendra imagined the girls in his class were more than aware of him.

Kendra didn't know Gayle well, but she liked everything she did know. Gayle ran a local bed-and-breakfast, and she managed to do a number of things well. Gayle had been the member most instrumental in obtaining a congregational vote of confidence for Sam when he'd needed it last year.

Jared excused himself and took off for more interesting pursuits.

"Are your other sons here?" Kendra asked.

"Dillon's at a Boy Scouts campout for the weekend. He's the youngest, thirteen. Noah—he's my middle son—is here somewhere with Leon."

Kendra remembered that story. Leon Jenkins was the son of a former troublesome deacon. George Jenkins was an alcoholic, and last year Leon had moved in with Gayle. He was probably about sixteen, and Kendra suspected he would still be in residence at Gayle's when he graduated from high school.

"I need a favor." Kendra picked up another jar of jelly and started toward the checkout line. "You're the resident expert on teenage boys."

"I'm not sure how that happened. I intended to have nothing but girls."

Kendra knew better than most how decisions about children could be taken out of one's hands.

She explained briefly about Caleb, and Gayle nodded. "I'd heard some of the story. How's he doing?"

"He's a good kid, but he spends too much time by himself. I don't think he's ever had the chance to make friends, so he probably doesn't have a clue how it's done."

"Would you like me to talk to my boys? Noah's the most likely candidate. He just turned fifteen, but he's easy to know. Leon's sixteen, but after everything he's gone through, he's a sensitive soul. He'd be the best one to watch out for Caleb and try to steer him toward the right crowd."

"That's beyond my expectations. Thank you."

"Let's see if we can track them down. If you have time?"

"Now is perfect."

They strolled together, lingering at Granny's Attic, with its collectibles of old rhinestone jewelry, mismatched china and vintage tablecloths. Gayle bought a crocheted one to cover a table in one of her B and B's bedrooms.

They admired tables filled with books, plants and handmade crafts. Apparently the crafters had decided to specialize in clothes made for American Girl dolls, because there were dozens to choose from. Kendra bought three outfits and mentally earmarked them for Hannah's Christmas present. She looked forward to choosing a doll to go with them. While she was at it, she made a mental note to have Jamie's doll collection shipped to her this week. With that in mind, she bought three more outfits.

They found Noah Fortman and Leon Jenkins at the photo booth. Some creative volunteer had painted plywood cutouts, so fairgoers could pay generously to stand behind them to have their photos taken. Participants could be General Stonewall Jackson or St. George the dragon slayer, career choices that in the Valley were considered to be one and the same. Joan of Arc and Scarlett O'Hara were available for females who weren't feeling Stonewallish. There was a generic superhero cutout, too. Most likely the artist was avoiding the possibility of copyright infringement.

No one was in line at the moment. Noah and Leon had been tapped to collect money and operate an impressive digital camera. The boys sat behind a card table looking important. Noah had chocolate-brown hair, but the nose was definitely his mom's. He stood when Gayle introduced Kendra, and Leon got to his feet, as well. Leon's hair was a paler brown, and he was thinner than Gayle's stocky middle son. But both boys had an air of confidence, as if they knew who they were and where they belonged. Kendra chalked up a parenting point to Gayle and her husband.

As they'd looked for the boys, Gayle had obviously considered how best to broach the subject of Caleb. She explained the situation with a minimum of fuss, and the boys listened politely.

"We can do with some help over here," Leon said. "Caleb can use the photo printer. We're going to get backed up later when everybody starts coming. We can show him how to do it."

Kendra was delighted. This would be easy to explain to Caleb, and a natural way to introduce him to the other boys.

"Your sons are so nice," she told Gayle before she split off to coax Caleb into giving the photo booth a try. "You and your husband have done a great job with them, and Leon, too. I know he's had a tough time."

"Eric's not on the scene very often." Gayle waved to someone under the white elephant tent. "We divorced when the boys were little. So I'll take the credit."

The name clicked for Kendra. "Eric Fortman? The television journalist?"

"Of course you'd know him. I never thought of that."

Kendra backtracked. "I don't really know him. We've been at events together a few times." Eric Fortman was a correspondent who had reported for several of the major networks. He was known for a certain recklessness that led to assignments in the world's hot spots. The last she'd heard, he was in Afghanistan with a team of reporters trying to track down former members of the Taliban.

"You never forget Eric once you've been introduced." Gayle smiled, to show there was no malice in her words. "Lord knows I never have, but being a single parent is easier than being married to Eric."

Kendra wondered how Gayle had managed so well. Were some marriages, even marriages to good men, harder than they were worth?

On her own, she set off to find Caleb, but as she started back to the food tent—first choice when searching for a teenage boy—Helen Henry stepped forward to block her path. She was dressed in a blue and green plaid blouse, with a blue skirt and matching tennis shoes. Her hair had been freshly cut and curled. Kendra bet Helen's daughter or granddaughter had been in town recently and forced her to shop.

"You buy your quilt raffle tickets yet?"

Kendra had only seen the Cactus Bloom quilt from a distance, but she was satisfied it was a stunner. "I'll buy a bunch. I promise."

" 'Course this one doesn't have anybody's signatures. Like the ones you like so much."

"Diversity is my middle name."

"You learn anything more about that quilt of yours?"

Kendra filled her in on the visit to the park and her trip to Luray to attend the Way We Were meeting.

"Well, you're making progress, I'll give you that," Helen said. "Now, what kind of progress have you made on those blocks I gave you?"

Kendra tried to figure out how to say "none" in a way that wouldn't bring Helen to her front door to snatch them back. But she had reached the final exit. There was no escape. "None, but I'm willing to learn."

"That's what I wanted to hear. You come to the next bee. Wednesday morning. Bring those blocks. We'll have everything else you need." Helen nodded as if the matter were settled, and marched off.

"She looks happy. Was it something you said?"

Kendra turned to find Elisa coming up behind her. They exchanged quick hugs, and Kendra told her that she had just given up the fight to avoid learning how to quilt.

Clearly Elisa had expected this. "I'll probably see you on Wednesday. They have me working on a new quilt. Something for the church nursery, although I think they're hoping Sam and I will need it ourselves."

Kendra's throat tightened. "You're not . . . ?"

"No, I'm still trying to work out a residency, but we're not getting any younger while I do."

Kendra and Elisa were about the same age. Kendra knew that time was a factor for her friend. In three more years, getting pregnant would be less likely.

"But we will adopt, if that's the best way to make our family." Elisa's gaze settled on her husband, who had just joined the crew at the grill and was setting chicken quarters in place. Sam wore a chef's apron that read "May the Forks Be With You."

"You'd be okay with that?"

Elisa turned back to her. "Absolutely. We've talked about it even if we have babies. We'd like more than one or two. There are always children who need families. My own country has many."

Kendra thought of Colonel Grant Taylor. "Any child you adopted would be lucky."

"No, we would be the lucky ones. It's a wonderful way to make a family."

Kendra heard the unspoken message. A way she and Isaac might want to consider. Only she and Isaac weren't discussing children.

Elisa left to take her place beside her husband. Kendra felt a twinge of sadness as she watched Sam put his arm around his wife's shoulder and squeeze in the seconds before Elisa set to work. Kendra wished she and Isaac had that same unquestioned affection, that easy level of comfort that Elisa and Sam probably already took for granted.

She went to look for Caleb, a child whom adoption had failed. Only with Caleb, there was still time to help turn things around. Caleb, unlike Isaac at the same age, had people who wanted the best for him.

She was fast becoming one of them.

Isaac felt odd about going inside the cabin without Kendra. He'd arrived at noon, expecting to find her back from the fair, but fifteen minutes later he was still alone on the porch. The cabin had belonged to his grandmother, yet he was the stranger here. Kendra had taken his inheritance into her heart. He still felt like a trespasser.

He checked his watch and debated what to do. She would be back. He had no doubt about that. And it was silly to wait outside. He wanted to check on Ten. He wanted a drink of water.

Aware he was acting like a fool, he retrieved a bag from his car; then he strode up the steps and opened the door into the living area. Inside, he stowed the bag in the refrigerator, then went to the sink and filled a glass. As he drank, he leaned against a counter, searching the room for the cat. In one of their phone calls, Kendra had told him that Ten was still skulking under furniture and generally hiding his existence. Isaac was sorry he couldn't reason with the cat. He would explain that everyone had Ten's best interests in mind. They would shake, paw to hand, and Ten would stroll outside for a look at the new world that was his to explore.

That being impossible, he wished his personal alley cat would deign to show a paw or the tip of his tail. Just for reassurance.

As if on cue, Ten peeked out from under the sofa. Isaac didn't move, all too aware that Ten might disappear again.

Ten looked right at him. Then, with his gaze riveted on Isaac, he slipped out and padded slowly to the bowl of food Kendra had placed about six feet from where Isaac was standing. Ten glanced down at the food, then quickly up at Isaac again.

"I'm not going to snatch it away," Isaac said quietly.

As if the sound of his voice reassured the cat, Ten bent his head to the task and began to eat. When he was satisfied, Ten looked up again. Isaac squatted slowly and held out his hand. Ten didn't move. For a moment the cat and the man regarded each other with the intensity of rival gang leaders. Then Ten turned and streaked back to his hideout under the sofa.

"Progress is progress." Isaac rose. He understood only too well how slowly trust had to be acquired.

He didn't know when Kendra might return, but he did know he didn't want to spend more time inside. He and Ten were facing the same problem. Neither of them was willing to admit that life as they'd known it had changed. Ten still believed the world outside these doors was a maze of mean streets, and Isaac still believed that the cabin where his mother had been raised could harm him. Neither he nor Ten seemed capable of reason.

Despite Isaac's promises, Kendra hadn't been sure when he would arrive. From experience, she knew he became absorbed in his work; hours could pass before he realized he had another commitment. She didn't feel guilty when she arrived home at two to find Isaac's car already in the driveway.

After she dropped her purchases inside and combed her hair, she went outside to look for him. She found him calf-deep in a hole where there had never been a hole that size before. He was just downhill from the house, level with what would be the bottom section when it was completed. He was digging exactly where Jamie had said they needed a meditation pond.

For a moment she just watched. Having Isaac involved in the renovations was more than she had hoped for. Yet here he was, either preparing to make supersize mud pies or fulfilling her sister's vision.

When he stopped to wipe sweat from his forehead, she spoke. "You didn't even hear me coming. What if I'd been a bear or a bobcat?"

He looked up and flashed a smile just faintly tinged with fatigue. "How long have you been standing there?"

"Long enough to think you need a cold glass of lemonade."

He leaned on the shovel and gestured to what he'd done. "What do you think?"

First she admired the way his navy blue ACRE T-shirt stretched across his chest. "New family graveyard? Rumors of gold?"

"Rainwater drains down that slope." He pointed above him. "And it pools here before it spills down the hill. The force of the flow carved an indentation, so it's constantly marshy. You need to either fill the hole and channel it past this point, or dig a deeper hole and make a small pond."

"Let me guess which I'm doing."

"Not necessarily. I can fill it with rock and build it up for better drainage. Either way's better than mud, which is what you have now."

"Which would you like to see?" Though the question sounded simple, she was asking Isaac to choose, to stamp this renovation with his own preferences. She was asking him to help make the cabin and land into a home.

He tossed off his answer. "You're the boss lady. I'm just the hired help."

"No, you're not."

He was silent a moment; then he shrugged. "Digging is therapeutic."

She felt a rush of pleasure. "A pond not a lake, right?"

"This may look simple, but since you've been light on rain lately, the ground is as hard as rock. Actually, too much of this ground *is* rock. It's going to take me a long time just to get this hole deep enough for goldfish."

"Fish?"

"Intellectual stimulation for Ten. He can sit at the edge and plot the best way to catch his supper."

Clearly he'd given this some thought. She was encouraged. "Just so I don't have to perform fish rescue missions."

"Deep enough for fish safety, shallow enough for cat fantasies."

She noted the way his hair glinted with gold highlights in the sunshine. "Sounds perfect. What about that lemonade?"

"I'd love a glass, but then I'm going to work a while longer. I have a rhythm going."

"I'll make a pitcher. Then I think I'll change and work in the garden. Somebody at the fair told me it's not too late to put in tomato plants."

"Right before they sold you a couple?"

"Six big ones. And a pot of basil." She headed for the house, calling over her shoulder, "I'll yell when the lemonade's ready."

In the house, she changed into denim shortalls so she could hook her hand hoe to the belt loop and fill the deep pockets with other gardening paraphernalia. In the kitchen, she prepared a pitcher of lemonade, cheating by using a mix and squeezing only two lemons. She sliced the last one and added half the slices to make the pitcher more appealing.

Isaac didn't seem to mind that the lemonade wasn't one hundred percent authentic. After washing his hands, he joined her on the porch and finished a glass before she'd taken more than a few sips of her own.

"Hot work." He smiled his apology.

"That's why I made a pitcher. The pond's going to be beautiful."

"We'll see."

Throughout their marriage, they had avoided household proj-ects. In their first apartment they'd hardly taken the time to unpack and fill the closets. She wondered if she'd just been waiting to make sure her marriage survived. Had she subconsciously determined that the odds weren't good enough for much of an investment?

Isaac reached over and pulled the bib of her shortalls away from her chest so he could see the T-shirt underneath. His fingertips brushed a breast as he did, and fire streaked through her.

"Farmer Taylor? A Toms Brook fashion statement?"

She gazed down at his hand. "Aren't I cute?"

"I was just thinking that." His hand slid up to her neck; his thumb caressed her chin. "You can hoe fields and pick cotton for me anytime."

Her eyelids drifted shut. “Corn. We’re too far north for cotton.”

“I’ll take whatever you give me.”

She wondered.

She felt his hand move away, and she opened her eyes.

“Right now you can give me a refill,” he said. “But later will be a different matter.”

Kendra weeded a new patch of the garden and got the plants in the ground before she called it quits for the afternoon. Inside, she took a long shower to ease the knots in her neck and back. Every day she seemed to grow stronger. The physical therapist she now saw biweekly was pleased with her progress. The irony of using a garden once filled with healing herbs as a way to restore her own health wasn’t lost on her. Leah would have approved.

She set out fresh towels for Isaac, and he arrived soon after, sweaty and dirty and altogether appealing. She was standing in front of the refrigerator, taking stock, when he emerged from the shower wearing clean shorts and his favorite generic green shirt. Isaac shopped for clothes with only two criteria. Easy care and no advertisements.

He stood behind her and rested his hands on her shoulders. "Hoping the ingredients will assemble themselves?"

"I should have done some shopping. I guess we'll have to go out for dinner. I'm afraid I eat very simply."

"Example?"

"Sandwiches. Yogurt. Fruit. Sometimes a salad, if I'm feeling energetic after an afternoon in the garden. I don't eat a lot of salads."

"I have groceries in the car."

She faced him. "Really?"

He turned her toward the open refrigerator again. "And there's something in there behind the milk and orange juice."

She pushed aside a milk carton and saw a bag. "I didn't notice."

"You're going to relax, and I'm going to take care of everything."

"What have you done with my husband?"

"What have you been hungry for since you got here? Something they don't have right around the corner."

She chewed on her lip. "Nothing you have in a bag in your car, I'm afraid."

"What?" he repeated.

"Thai food."

"How does shrimp pad thai sound?"

"You brought takeout all the way from D.C.?"

He rested his hands on her shoulders when she faced him again. "K.C., you're refusing to get it. That's a pound of Gulf shrimp in the fridge. I'm going to make shrimp pad thai. Right here, in your kitchen."

"You don't cook."

"I do now."

She tried not to smile, but she wasn't successful. "Since when?"

"Since my wife moved away. The Food Network keeps me company late at night."

"You've started cooking? Food Network recipes?"

"More like I'm going to start right now. How hard can it be? I did the shopping. I've seen it made. I have the recipe. I have the perfect victim."

"You're experimenting on me?" She leaned over and kissed him. "I'm enthralled. Cook away. Can I help?"

"You can pour the wine. I brought a very good merlot. I'll bring it in."

She was still mulling over this miracle when he returned with two brown grocery bags and set them on the table. "A large glass for the chef, please. I'll be chopping for a while."

She found the corkscrew and took down two glasses from the cabinet. Then, as he got out what looked to be half the wares of an Asian market, she opened the wine to let it breathe. The vintage was indeed a good one. Wine important enough for serious seduction.

Isaac examined everything he'd laid out. "Looks like I'll be chopping for, oh, about three days. Stay nearby and talk to me."

Part of her wanted to rescue him, and part of her wanted to see exactly what he had in mind. She could feel anticipation stirring. Anticipation of the wine, of the conversation, of the meal . . . of the aftermath.

He filled the teakettle and set it on a burner, turning on the heat beneath it. "Tell me what you've been doing since the last time I was here."

She lounged against the counter and eliminated Dusty as a topic. "Trying to lure Ten out from under the sofa."

"He came out to see me."

"He didn't!"

"Came out, ate his fill, then went back to hide. But it's a start."

"Then he's alive, and it's not mice eating his food."

"More likely Ten's eating the mice."

"I saw Black Beauty yesterday. He hasn't abandoned the cabin. He just leaves earlier every morning. Before the men arrive."

"You're blessed with pets."

More than Isaac knew, of course. She wondered how her three living, breathing charges would get along when they finally confronted one another. She wasn't sure she wanted to be there.

"I went to that meeting I told you about," she said. "Over in Luray."

"I wondered."

She was encouraged by his tone. Had there been even a note of censure, she wouldn't have continued. But Isaac sounded almost . . . interested?

"I met a man who knew your grandmother as a girl. And your grandfather."

Isaac looked up. "Really?"

"Aubrey Grayling says he was your grandfather's best friend. It's pretty amazing."

He took carrots and a red pepper to the

sink. She wondered if he knew the carrots needed to be scraped. He returned to slice the pepper, and she was impressed with how well he managed it. How many television chefs *had* he seen?

"Do you think he's for real?" Isaac asked.

"I do. He's in his nineties, but he remembered so many details. Your grandfather was named Jesse Spurlock. His family owned apple orchards in Lock Hollow, the biggest and best. Leah's family, the Blackburns, had fewer acres, but Aubrey said the Blackburn farm was a gem. They grew corn, mostly, and vegetables. They had animals, a two-story log and frame house, a chestnut barn. They weren't rich, but they had a good life. Both families were well thought of."

Isaac finished chopping the pepper into matchstick-thin slices before he spoke. "I've spent my whole life trying not to think about my birth family. Now I'm imagining the Waltons." He paused. "The Waltons with inconvenient secrets."

"Aubrey's story brought them to life for me. Leah had hair the color of yours, Isaac. He said she was particularly pretty, with green eyes and a slender figure, but she was the picture of sturdy good health. Not like her sister."

"Sister?"

"That's right. Birdie. She was dark-haired and blue-eyed, very delicate featured. He said in some ways she was even prettier than Leah, who was younger. But Birdie was frail and in constant pain. She had polio as a child and nearly died. She was also so nearsighted that she had to squint to see anything more than a few feet away. Aubrey said both disabilities gave her a narrow focus, that she was content to live her life no farther away than the circle of her arms."

"Aubrey sounds like something of a poet."

Kendra went to pour the wine, and waited until Isaac had scraped the carrots—he *had* learned a lot from television—before she handed it to him. "He didn't say too much after that. He got tired, or so he said."

"So he said?"

"I don't think he was being completely straight with me."

"Maybe he likes the attention and wants you to come back."

"I didn't get that impression. In fact, he pointed me toward the daughter of Leah's best friend. He said she might be able to help me." She peeked over his shoulder. "Are those shiitake mushrooms?"

"You're going to love this."

She watched with awe as he wiped the mushrooms clean with a damp paper towel. The kettle whistled, and he turned off the burner, measuring water and pouring it slowly over rice noodles he'd placed in a bowl. "Five minutes," he said. "Time them for me?"

"You bet."

"So that was the end of your conversation?" Isaac asked.

"He did say the marriage of Jesse Spurlock and Leah Blackburn was as expected and natural as the coming together of two royal families."

"Except they all *didn't* live happily ever after . . ."

"Maybe that's the next installment."

"You're going on with this?"

"I'm hooked."

He diced tofu. Tofu? She wouldn't have guessed he even knew where to find it in a store. He minced garlic, chopped peanuts, sliced green onions on the diagonal, squeezed a lime into a cup. Her mouth was beginning to water.

She watched as he combined a variety of things, all aromatic and wonderful, in another bowl and set it aside. She issued a warning. "If you have anything else to combine, you're out of luck. You're now officially out of bowls. And it's been five minutes, by the way."

"Drain the noodles, K.C., and let me cook."

She laughed and did, setting them aside in the colander.

Isaac stood back and raised his hands dramatically, as if he were about to conduct a symphony. "Now you get to watch the real fun. Master chef at work."

"I am just so impressed."

"Tell me about the fair."

She did, ending with the story of Caleb and the camera. Isaac had heated two kinds of oil in her largest saucepan, and now, with one last flourish, he added shrimp.

"The camera was a good idea. How are his photos?" Isaac began to stir as the shrimp sizzled.

Over the noise, she explained about his

lack of a computer on which to view the photos. "But I invited him here to use mine. Meantime, he might have made a start on finding friends today. But it was hard to watch him with the other boys. He's so quiet. He hardly said a word."

"Do you think he enjoyed himself anyway?"

She watched as he dumped all the vegetables he'd assembled into the pan with the shrimp, which had turned a lovely pink. "I hope so. Leon and Noah were friendly. Maybe Caleb will loosen up eventually."

"I was just about that quiet."

Isaac always seemed comfortable in social situations. He was reserved, but he always contributed. And the fact that he didn't chatter worked well for him. When he spoke, people hung on his words.

"Were you?" She moved closer to inhale what was now definitely the aroma of excellent pad thai. "You're so confident now."

"Confidence took a long time and a lot of work." He flipped vegetables and stirred like a pro. Finally he turned off the heat under the pan and, in a surprise move, put his arms around her, pulling her close. "Maybe

I haven't done enough work, K.C. Maybe I still keep too much to myself."

"Like what?" She could barely find the breath for the words.

"Like not telling you how much I miss you. Not telling you how hard it is to have you so far away."

"Then why haven't you come to see me more often?"

He touched her cheek. "Did you want me to? You came here without me. You're making a home without me. You're making a life I have no part of."

"You're a part of everything I do, Isaac. Whether I want it that way or not. Whether you're with me or somewhere else."

"Did you come here to change that?"

"I came here to see if I could live without you." She saw the pain in his eyes. She leaned closer. "Because I thought it was inevitable."

"Thought?"

"Now I think we'll both suffer if we let this relationship die without a fight."

His arms tightened. "But I don't want to fight. Not tonight."

She looked into eyes as dark as the doubts that had tormented her since the shooting. She had always found them nearly impenetrable. For too long she had wondered what was behind those eyes, what feelings were hidden there. Now she knew better than to wonder. She knew she had to be sure.

"If we make love tonight, I want it to be a new start, Isaac. That means both of us have to try to find our way to something better. I'm not sure how we do it, but I know we have to make that commitment."

He smiled a little, and suddenly she had no trouble reading his thoughts.

"I know how we can find our way to something better," he said. "But not right here."

"And what about my special dinner?"

He scooped her into his arms, as if she were a new bride about to cross a threshold. "I told you I've watched a lot of cooking shows?"

"Isaac . . ."

"Reheating is going to be my specialty."

CHAPTER TWENTY-TWO

Kendra liked to sleep with Isaac. Awake, he was energetic but contained. He had learned to be careful about the space around him, only allowing his restlessness to boil over into prolonged bouts of exercise. In sleep, there were no restrictions. If she happened to be in the way, he incorporated her easily, pulling her close, wrapping arms around her, settling her against him. She liked to think that the affection he felt for her was most in evidence then, that in sleep he could express his longing for intimacy.

On the nights they'd slept together since the shooting, he had stayed on his side of the bed. Kendra had told herself he was afraid of hurting her, but the distance had stretched more than inches. In the end, she had been hurt because of him.

Early Sunday morning, she awoke with Isaac's arms around her. Last night he had been careful when making love, still clearly afraid she was too fragile for more energetic sex, but once they were asleep, he had relaxed into old habits.

Viva old habits.

She snuggled deeper into his arms and felt him kiss her hair.

"You doing okay?" he asked.

"Not as good as I could be." She turned, her nose just a fraction of an inch from his.

"What's wrong?"

"I'm thinking last night was a practice session. To make sure we remembered what we were here for."

"How'd I do?"

"You still seem to have the hang of it. But I think you need another session, just to make sure."

"You're okay?"

"Better than that."

"You're sure you don't want to get up and have a big country breakfast? Seems to me you were half starved last night. You ate every bit of your pad thai."

She pushed his hair off his forehead and wiggled her arms around his neck. "And some of yours."

"I wasn't going to bring that up."

"Did you learn to cook a big country breakfast from the Food Network?"

"Not yet."

"Then I guess we'll have to settle for this." She nudged his head down, his lips toward hers.

"K.C. . . ."

"Uh-huh?"

His hand slipped between them, sliding over her abdomen and up to her breast. "I love you."

He said those words so rarely. She knew what they cost him. Her breath caught. Her throat seemed to close. She cleared it. "It's mutual. You know that."

"How do things get so messed up?"

"Let's just spend some time straightening them out."

"I like the sound of that." Then he kissed her.

An hour later, Isaac was sleeping so soundly that Kendra was able to slip out of bed and shower without him so much as moving. She grabbed her keys and went out into the clearing to her car.

When she returned half an hour later, coffee was brewing in the kitchen, and judging from the discordant rattle of the old water pipes, Isaac was in the shower. She set the table, and laid out the coffee cake and newspaper she'd purchased. When he came in, hair wet and shirt unbuttoned, she was lounging at the table, reading the headlines.

"Not the *New York Times,*" she said. "I know you need the comics."

He kissed the top of her head before going to the counter to pour his coffee. "The *Post?*"

"Uh-huh."

"My favorite journalist hasn't written anything in a while."

"Nor has she had much desire to."

"You don't miss the job?"

She had asked herself that every day, so the answer was easy. "Eventually I'll feel the pull again. Just not yet."

"You were so devoted."

"It's easy to get stuck in one track. When something tosses you out of it, you begin to realize there's scenery you haven't noticed."

He joined her at the table and took the front section. "I'm not so sure you've moved that far out of it."

"Why do you say that?"

"You're going about the search for my past the way you used to go after stories for the paper."

"You're not the first to make the connection." She told him what Aubrey had said. "I think my job's one of the reasons he's reluctant to talk to me."

"You say he's in his nineties? And he remembered your byline?"

"I doubt he had much education, but his mind's as focused as a laser beam. He remembers details most of us would never notice in the first place."

"I'd like to meet him."

She found that encouraging. "I'd planned to call Prudence Baker today, visit her if she's free. Her mother, Puss Cade, was your grandmother's best friend. The Cades lived on the farm between the Spurlocks and the Blackburns."

"Puss?"

"Short for something, I'm sure."

"And Puss is dead?"

"Yes, but Aubrey thought she might have

told her daughter a few things. Sunday seems like a good day to visit her." She paused. "Want to come?"

"I have to get back in a little while." He folded his paper. "There's a situation at work."

Talking about the coming day felt like old times. She went for more coffee. "What kind of situation?"

He was silent for a moment. She almost thought he'd ignored the question in favor of something he was reading, but finally he looked up. "Something I need more information about."

"Want to tell me?"

She listened as he explained to her about the purchase of Pallatine Mountain. "But why do you sound so cautious?" she asked, when he'd finished telling her how he had gotten Gary Forsythe to sell his land to ACRE. "Normally you'd be thrilled. It's a big deal." She filled his cup and set the pot on the table. "So what's up?"

"There's some debate about how we're going to finance it. Our budget's stretched, and people aren't donating as much as they once did. Gas prices, the war . . ." He shrugged.

She tried to feel her way through his explanation. "For an organization that specialized in smaller properties, that wasn't as much of a worry. But now that you're moving into larger parcels, I guess it's a bigger one."

"And Dennis is determined to find ways to cope."

Kendra didn't particularly like Dennis Lavin. Her husband ignored personality in favor of results, but from their first meeting, she had been put off by Dennis's narcissistic charm. ACRE's new CEO reminded Kendra of her dental hygienist, a young man who talked incessantly about himself, secure that his patients were physically unable to respond. Dennis seemed to feel that same sense of power, only he didn't need sharp instruments to enforce it. He had his position and his right to fire anyone who seriously disagreed with him.

"Are you worried about the methods he's considering?" she asked.

"One of the possibilities is selling some parcels to ACRE supporters. We would put covenants on them, of course. But I've seen what's being proposed."

"And you don't like the idea?"

"It's not what I expected when I talked Forsythe into selling to us. He's picturing no development. So was I."

"Where is the land, exactly?"

"Not far from the Shenandoah National Park."

"Wow . . ."

"It's nothing to worry about. We're meeting tomorrow to consider all the options. It's always a balancing act."

She thought that this particular act bothered him more than most. "Tell me about Pallatine. You've been there?"

"I hiked nearly the whole thing when you were in Guatemala researching Elisa's story."

"And?"

"It was logged back at the turn of the twentieth century, but that's hardly evident now. Hunters are fond of it, so hiking it isn't as hard as it sounds. They keep the trails passable for ATVs. But other than that, it's a different world."

"One you'd like to keep for posterity."

"I'd like to see the land used for the public, but government budgets are tight for the same reasons donations are down. We have a lot to consider."

She was surprised he hadn't mentioned Pallatine before. In too many important ways, their lives had grown separate.

"I'd like to see it," she said.

"You're going to have to ease back into long hikes. Pallatine isn't the best way."

"Then I'd like to do some hiking in the park. The trails are well marked, and there's a lot of information about them."

"Maybe we could arrange that." He looked up. "If you'd like to go together."

She put her hand over his. "Who better to go with?"

He raised her hand to his lips and kissed it.

They finished breakfast in a companionable silence, breaking it only to read little snippets of articles to each other, the way they'd always done. She was sorry when he stood to pack the few things he'd brought. When he'd finished, she walked him out to his car.

"Maybe you could plan a whole weekend here," she said, as he threw the pack into the backseat.

"Maybe you could plan a weekend at home." He straightened to face her. "Are you ready?"

She didn't know. She did know it wasn't fair to expect Isaac always to come here. But this was home now, in a way the condo never had been. She wasn't ready to leave.

"I have this cat," she reminded him. "Maybe when Ten's going in and out the cat door successfully . . ."

"Cat door?"

"Cash promised to install one."

"We'll have to figure out what to do with him when you move back to the city."

She was spared an answer by the shouting of children. She couldn't see them, but she could hear them moving through the woods. From experience, she knew where they were and where they were going.

"There's a path at the far edge," she told Isaac. "Just a little footpath down to the river. It's not a thoroughfare, but now that it's warmer, they go down to tube. I can see them from the back of our house once they get down to the bank. I'm pretty sure they live nearby, because there's a more direct pathway down the road a ways. I think our woods are just closer for this gang."

"As long as they're not up to mischief."

"Not so far." She hesitated. "I like to hear them laughing. It's a sound I always expected to have in my life. I don't want to give it up just because I can't have kids."

"From what I hear, having teenagers is highly overrated."

"Like all good things, I'm sure it has its moments."

"What would we have done with teenagers? Or infants? We're both so busy. Our lives are too complicated. Once you come back home, you'll immerse yourself in the paper again. We'll have to schedule every minute together."

She was stunned that for Isaac it all came down to time. *You can't have children, Kendra? No reason to worry. It would be hard to fit them into our lives, anyway.*

It was as simple and as basic as that. Isaac hadn't said it was better this way, but he'd certainly implied it. As if the most emotional, even traumatic, moments of her life, of the past months, were merely blips in her personal radar.

She tried to sound calm. "You're assuming a lot."

He misunderstood, or he chose to pretend he did. "I know we have to keep work in bounds. But even if we work half as hard as we did before, it would be tough to fit children into the mixture."

"Things turned out the way they were supposed to, then?"

"You know I don't believe in that kind of logic. But we can be reasonable and say that since we rarely talked about having children, we must not have wanted them very much."

It was so cold-blooded, so rational—and so very wrong. Without even asking, he had made assumptions about her feelings. He had taken the loss in stride and assumed that, given their history, she was taking it in hers, as well. Her presence here, her reluctance to return to their home and her job, seemed not to have entered into his thinking at all. Those were bumps on the road to success, an odd little detour, and surely a temporary one.

She couldn't speak. She was afraid to—afraid she would say something that sent him away for good. Conversely, she was afraid that she would not adequately convey, yet again, just how wrong he was and how devastated she was not to be able to share their deepest feelings.

She wondered if he had any inkling that there was anything to share.

Isaac glanced at her face, then down at his watch. “That wasn’t much breakfast. I have time to take you out for lunch before I head back.”

“No, you go ahead. I’m going to call Prudence Baker and see if she’s willing to talk to me this afternoon. She’s some distance away.”

He looked relieved. Perhaps offering lunch had been something of an apology. Maybe he realized he needed to back up and really talk to her. But she didn’t want to talk about children now. Not when anger was the only emotion she could tap.

“I don’t think there’s anything on my schedule next weekend,” he said.

He was waiting for her to ask him to come back. She could not find the words. “You know where I live.”

“It’s been a good weekend.”

She nodded and managed a smile. “Yes.”

He leaned over and kissed her; then, without looking at her again, he got into his car, backed around and drove away.

She took her time walking inside. She could feel tears threatening, but she wouldn't give in to them. She went into the bedroom to get her purse and the phone number that Aubrey's granddaughter had given her for Prudence Baker.

On the neatly made bed was a single sheet of paper. Isaac had drawn a cartoon of them embracing. It was both romantic and sexy. Her knee was nestled between his legs, her face turned up to his, her hair a mass of untamed curls. In a few simple strokes he had captured the essence of her features and a perfect come-hither expression. She read the words scrawled below it in Isaac's forceful script.

Love is the shortest distance between two hearts.

She rested the paper against her chest and closed her eyes.

"Except sometimes," she said softly, "even the shortest distance is too far to travel."

Prudence Baker lived just outside Flint Hill, about forty-five minutes away. Kendra took the interstate most of the way to make sure she didn't get lost. She arrived at three, exactly when Prudence had told her to come.

On the telephone, Prudence had sounded as if she might be in her sixties, a number that jibed with everything Kendra knew. Had Puss Baker been alive, she probably would have been just a little younger than Aubrey. Prudence had sounded pleased Kendra was coming. She'd been told of the impending visit by Aubrey.

Kendra wasn't sure whether Aubrey had called Prudence to smooth her visit, or for other reasons. She was certain his memory hadn't faltered at the end of their conversation. He knew more than he'd let on, and if he wanted to keep a secret, he might well have called Prudence to tell her so. If Prudence knew the secret, of course . . .

Kendra wondered whether the secret might have something to do with bodies in the cave on Little Lock Mountain.

Flint Hill was a picturesque country town with a few small businesses. Nearby, the world-famous Inn at Little Washington had its own heliport so the rich and famous could fly in and out without having to brave the narrow country roads. But Rappahannock County had a mixture of residents, escapees from the city as well as people with roots sunk deep in Virginia's soil. Locals could choose barbecue over the gas-station counter or organic Kobe beef burgers at the farm store of a retired AOL executive.

Prudence's house was more the gas station end of the county, a cozy brick bungalow with a carport that had been given over to grandchildren. Kendra noted half a dozen riding toys, from tractors to smiling bananas, and a race course outlined in chalk that zoomed down the driveway.

She parked on the road beside another SUV and heard the sound of children in the backyard. Although at first she wondered if anyone would hear her, Prudence came to the door right away, introducing herself and briskly extending a hand. She was just a bit overweight with steel-gray hair cut into attractive layers, and gray eyes behind narrow copper-rimmed glasses.

"Just call me Prudence. My grandchildren are about to go home. Will you mind if I see them out?"

Kendra followed to meet the flock, three boys, one lone girl and Prudence's daughter, who was a younger, more harried version of her mother. She was trying, with only moderate success, to dry off the two younger children, who had obviously been playing in the sprinkler.

The flock, ranging from perhaps seven to two, disappeared after a few raucous minutes, driving away in their Ford Explorer.

"I had my children late. She did the same, and so did my son." Prudence shook her head. "It's a wonder any of us survived it."

"Judging from all the drawings on your walls, you're loving it."

"The spirit loves it. The flesh is tired. May I offer you a glass of tea?"

The kitchen was small and spotless, adorned in fingerpaintings, plaster casts of tiny hands and framed inspirational poems. The windows had frilly curtains, and the tablecloth was flowered plastic—a sensible choice for cleaning up after spills and sticky peanut butter and jelly sandwiches.

"Have a seat," Prudence said. "Would you like a cookie to go with it?"

"Tea'll be fine."

"Aubrey tells me you're a reporter."

Bingo. Kendra could almost hear the words that had come after that. *This Taylor woman's a reporter. Don't tell her anything you don't want the whole world to know.*

"I'm on a leave of absence," Kendra said.

"I'm living in the cabin Leah Spurlock left my husband. Isaac is her grandson." She explained the circumstances as briefly as she could; then she waited.

Prudence held up the pitcher. "Lemon? Sugar?"

"Just lemon, thanks."

Prudence busied herself finishing the tea, while Kendra tried to decide how best to find out what she wanted to know. Prudence finally came back, setting a frosted glass in front of Kendra before she dropped into the seat across from her.

"Aubrey told me your mother and Isaac's grandmother were best friends," Kendra said, after thanking her hostess.

"Mama talked about Leah quite a bit. I grew up on those stories. She made it seem like it all happened just a week or two ago, like it was that real."

Kendra was encouraged. "Leah didn't settle that far away, you know. Of course, it was harder to travel back then, but Flint Hill and Toms Brook were within driving distance."

"Times were different, I guess."

"Your mother . . . Puss, right?"

"Short for Prudence. Same as me."

"Puss came here right after leaving Lock Hollow?"

"Not right off, you understand. She was working at Skyland—that's a resort up in what's now the park—to save money to help her folks. She stayed on a while, until she could afford to join them here. Mama wasn't married at the time."

"So her family came here to start over?"

"The government bought more than six thousand acres in the surrounding counties so they'd have a place for people to go. Took them some time, though, to build houses. Flint Hill was one of the places where people were settled. Our family got a house, a barn, and a chicken house and some other buildings, on about fifty acres. Mama said the house was fancier than anything her parents had ever seen. Running water, electricity, real appliances. Of course, some people said that was too much to give us hillbillies. I guess they thought stealing the land was good enough for us."

One generation removed and Kendra still heard the resentment. "It must have been a painful time."

"Mama said her own mama took a while to get over it, but Grandpa liked the new place right off. Mama got married after she'd been here for a few years, and she and my father took over the farm when my grandparents died. She was some homemaker. You never saw anyone half so committed to keeping house. Came from losing the first home she'd ever known, I guess. My brother took over that land until he died a few years ago. It's sold now. Kind of a shame. But I was a widow by that time, and nobody in my family had any use for it."

"Toms Brook wasn't one of the places where people were resettled. At least not from anything I've read."

"I don't think it was."

"I don't know why Leah went there. Did your mother ever mention where she'd gone or why?"

Prudence swatted a fly. "Not that I remember."

"Can you tell me anything she said about her?"

"People have a lot of reasons for asking questions, don't they."

Kendra had expected this. "I know Aubrey's worried I'm doing this just so I can write about it. And I can't promise I won't. It's an interesting story, but it's also very personal. I think my husband needs to know where he came from. His life's always been a mystery. Answers might help."

Prudence searched her face. "Aubrey tells me you were asking about the bodies in that cave."

"Leah left Isaac a quilt almost exactly like the one those bodies were wrapped in. It was the only thing besides the cabin and land she left him. She must have thought it mattered somehow. And names are embroidered all over it, including 'Cade.' "

"Now that's interesting."

"It's more or less a map of Lock Hollow. But two lines meet where the bodies were found, as if Leah was connected to it in some way."

"People have different ways of revealing things. I've seen it all my life. Some people just blurt out whatever goes through their heads, and others, well, they move slowly into it, just a little at a time. Sometimes that's because they aren't so sure the people they're talking to want to hear what they have to say."

"I've noticed the same thing."

"Mama used to tell stories about Leah. I told you that already. Mama wasn't around much, but when she was, she watched the way Leah and Jesse acted after they were married. She wasn't jealous, mind you, but she said watching them made her want the same things for herself that Leah had. A man who could be her world. It's an old-fashioned notion, but she found that same kind of love with my father. She died of a broken heart after he passed on. I'm convinced of it."

Kendra almost couldn't imagine that. "It sounds like they were lucky."

"And if Mama hadn't come here, she never would have met him. So some things work out, even when you think they won't. Which reminds me, I got something your husband might like to have."

Prudence rose and went to a bookshelf that held a variety of cookbooks. "I said Mama was some housekeeper? Well, she kept notes, pages and pages of them, on how to clean everything. She kept quilt patterns from the newspaper, put them in this. . . ."

She held up a thick bound notebook. "Recipes, household hints. Anything she could find in the paper or from neighbors. It's a real piece of history. I treasure it."

"Of course you do," Kendra said.

"After you called, I got to thinking about your husband. And I remembered there's a section in here on sickness and what to do. We would call that first aid these days. The thing is, Leah wrote Mama whenever she was away and told her how to cure little things that were wrong with her or other people wherever she was. And Mama kept them all. She fixed them to the pages here. And I still have them."

Kendra was intrigued. "That really is a treasure trove, isn't it."

"I can't give you the originals, because they're glued tight, but I thought maybe your husband would like to see some things his grandmother wrote. Folk medicine, mind you, but there's probably some truth in all of it. Anyway, I gave it to my daughter, and she took it in to work and had these pages copied." She slipped a stack of papers out of the book and held them out to Kendra.

Kendra took what looked to be about two dozen pages. A glance showed that the handwriting was round and childish, but legible. "This is so wonderful. You don't know how glad I am to see these." Briefly she told Prudence about Leah's garden.

"Then you'll enjoy them that much more."

Kendra tucked the papers into the side pocket of her purse. "You talked about how things worked out for your mother and father, partly because Puss was inspired by Leah's marriage. But apparently things didn't work out for Leah and Jesse. She moved to Toms Brook without him, even though she was already pregnant."

"Down the road, I'm afraid there were problems in that marriage." Prudence picked up her heretofore untouched glass and sipped.

"Do you know what kind?"

"Everybody had problems once it was clear the park was going to happen whether the people living on the land wanted it to or not. You can just imagine, can't you? And it took its toll. I remember my grandmother telling me that when she realized my grandfather was going to be happy with the new place, she stopped speaking to him. For one whole month. Just to make a statement."

"Do you think the problems between Leah and Jesse were related to the park?"

"It's a good guess."

"They must have been serious. She left

her husband. And so far, I haven't found any information about where he might have gone."

She waited, but when Prudence didn't speak, she continued. "Aubrey said Leah had a sister, too. Birdie Blackburn. And I haven't found anything about her, either. It's like she and Jesse disappeared from the face of the earth. . . ." She let her words trail off and locked gazes with Prudence.

"That would take some doing."

Kendra was frustrated, but she had expected to be. "Did your mother ever say anything about Jesse or Birdie?"

"She did speak of them."

Kendra waited and hoped.

Prudence looked away. "It's not a pretty story."

"I'd like to hear it."

"Some people thereabouts said Jesse and Leah had a falling-out, a big one. Afterwards they thought maybe he and Birdie ran off together. That the two of them just up and left Leah to find a new life by herself. Anyway, that's what they said."

This was new information. Kendra pondered it. "People really believed Jesse and

Birdie fell in love? Did your mother think so?"

"She wasn't clear. She loved Leah, you know. All those years later, she still loved and admired her. But I think there may have been more to it than she knew back then. Don't you? Considering . . ."

"The bodies?"

Prudence smiled sadly. "That's right. Because two people disappeared from Lock Hollow. Just up and left, and no one ever saw them again. Of course, homesteads were isolated. Nothing more than footpaths between some of them. Mama told me they'd go visiting at night with coal oil lanterns to light their way over rocky trails that were miles long. Hard to imagine, isn't it?"

"Very."

"But even then, people knew what was going on. They checked on each other, visited, had work parties to shuck corn or string beans for drying. One day Jesse and Birdie were living at the Blackburn farm, the next they disappeared. And Jesse's own mother never heard from him again."

Kendra remembered that Jesse's mother and her second husband had still lived on the farm just beyond the Cades'. The old

Spurlock place, which someday would have belonged to Jesse.

Prudence nodded in emphasis. "Not a word, and from what I remember my mama saying, Jesse had sisters, and none of them ever heard what had happened to him, either."

"What do *you* think happened?" Kendra asked.

"Me? I think maybe somebody was angry enough with Jesse Spurlock to kill him. Maybe Birdie got in the way. And if that's true, wouldn't it explain those bodies?"

"Somebody?"

Prudence looked straight at her. "That would be my guess. *Somebody.* That's as far as my guessing goes."

Kendra couldn't let that be the final word. "Prudence, are you saying you think Leah killed her husband and sister?"

Prudence's gaze didn't waver. "I wasn't there, was I."

"It's a terrible thought, isn't it? That Leah might have been a murderer?"

Something about the way she said it must have touched the other woman, because her expression softened. "My mama thought the world of Leah Spurlock. She always said folks had jumped to the wrong conclusions. Maybe I can't tell you what happened at the very end, up in that hollow, but I do know a little more about what caused the troubles between Jesse and Leah. Maybe that will help."

CHAPTER TWENTY-THREE

Blackburn Farm
Lock Hollow, Virginia
April 4, 1934

Dear Puss,

I understand why you have to stay at Skyland now. Your family will be glad for that money when they are forced to move. I am still hoping for a miracle, but God don't seem to here any of us in these mountains now.

I am sorry you have trouble falling to sleep. The best cure would be for the government to leave us alone, and that is a fact. Miss Lula might think putting the Holy Bible under your pillow will give you better dreams, but I would not depend on gitting anything but a crick in your neck. I am sending catnip for tea. Drink it before you go to sleep. If that don't work, try warm milk, if they will let you have some. A shot of Free Hollow whiskey in it would not hurt one bit, but most likely Miss Lula will say no.

I wish I had a cure for what ails Jesse. I have not seen him smile for nigh two months. It worries me more than I can say.

Wishing you were home for good,
Leah Spurlock

The government arrived at the Blackburn house one morning when Leah was alone on the farm. Birdie was spending a few days with Etta and wouldn't arrive back home until that evening, and Jesse was helping his stepfather rebuild the Spurlock chicken house. That he and Luther Collins would stubbornly improve any structure on the farm was a testament to their unwillingness to face facts. Luther was certain the city lawyer Aubrey had hired to represent Lock

Hollow would work magic. Jesse was determined to stay and fight.

Leah opened the front door to find a tall, broad-shouldered man with curly copper-colored hair and pink-toned, freckled skin to go with it. He took off his hat, while a younger man—no, a boy—with his back to them, held the farm's three snapping hounds at bay.

Leah admonished the dogs, who backed away at the sound of her voice.

"I'm right sorry," she said. "I didn't hear you coming, or I would have called them off. I was in the chicken yard."

"Ma'am, my name is Daniel Flaherty, and this is Charlie Thompkins. He helps with the surveying equipment." Flaherty gestured behind him to the teenager, who was dark haired and lanky. Both were dressed in black pants and shirts that were clean enough, but rumpled.

Leah felt as if someone had a palm flattened hard against her chest, because suddenly she understood why the two were here.

"We're with the government," Daniel Flaherty said. "We're here to work out what your land is worth."

"Everything." She lifted her chin. "It's worth everything and then some more."

"Ma'am, I know how you must feel."

"You couldn't possibly." She took a deep breath, surprised the air passed through her lungs as naturally as always.

"Is your husband in?"

"He is not, and you should be glad of it." She considered closing the door, but unlike Jesse, she knew there were no gestures of protest powerful enough to keep the government away. And hospitality was ingrained in her.

She sighed and opened the door wider. "Come inside."

The two males looked at each other. Thompkins, who looked younger than she, perhaps sixteen to Flaherty's twenty-eight or so, shrugged.

Leah turned away but left the door open. "I reckon you'll be thirsty. I'll get you some fresh water." The two followed her inside and waited on the sofa in the sitting room as she went to the pump.

"Sit," she said when she returned. They did, and she handed them glasses before she perched on the edge of a rocking chair across from the sofa.

Flaherty was clearly the one in charge. He sipped, then set down the glass and leaned forward. “You understand about the park, don’t you?”

She examined him, curious about the man who would put her family out of their home. “Can you sleep at night? Doing what you do?”

He looked genuinely unhappy. “I sleep knowing I have a job to go to in hard times. And Charlie and I, well, we do the best we can for people. We try to get them the most money the government will allow. Isn’t it better people like us do the job than people who don’t care?”

She couldn’t fault him. Thompkins looked as if he wanted to be anywhere other than where he was, but Flaherty seemed truly concerned. He had an appealing face, with sincere hazel eyes. He was a man most women would be attracted to, a man who projected both gentleness and strength.

“We don’t want to go,” she said.

“You have a beautiful place here. I wouldn’t want to leave it, either. But it’s not up to you and me. People you’ll never see made this decision. My job is to help you make the best of it.”

"My husband says he won't leave."

"Our records say the property belongs to one Leah Blackburn."

"It's Leah Blackburn Spurlock now, and you're speaking to her."

The two finished their water; then Flaherty stood, and Thompkins, taking his cue, got to his feet, as well.

"I'm going to tell you something in confidence, then," Flaherty said. "Your husband can fight this a while. It's likely no one will come and drag him away. Not for some months, anyway, or maybe longer. It's even possible you could get on the life list."

She rose to follow them to the door. "What's that?"

"There's a chance some people will be allowed to stay, but I don't want you holding out hope. If the park officials decide to do that, mostly it'll be the oldsters who get that privilege. And why would you want to? Those people won't be allowed to clear more land or cut trees for firewood. They can't add on to their houses, since they would belong to the government. They might not even be able to graze their animals. It won't be a good way to live, and their children won't be allowed the same privilege once they're gone."

She tried to imagine this, being a prisoner in her own home, with the government watching everything she did, every blade of grass she disturbed. Her eyes closed, and for a moment she could visualize everything he had said. Their hollow filled with ghosts and old people waiting to die. It would be worse than moving away.

"Ma'am, you'll be better off if you start making preparations."

She opened her eyes and saw he believed everything he said. At that moment she realized that Daniel Flaherty, a complete stranger who represented a government she had grown to hate, was more concerned about her adjustment and future than her young husband.

They stared at each other for a moment. Something inched along her backbone, something not quite sexual attraction, not quite a need to cry on this man's broad shoulder.

"We're camping not far down the road. We'll be walking your land, looking it all over carefully," he said at last. "I hope your husband isn't thinking about doing anything foolish."

"I'll make sure he don't," she said softly.

"Thank you."

She saw them to the door, but when they were halfway between the house and fence, Flaherty turned to regard her. His eyes were filled with compassion . . . and something else. "You take care of yourself, Mrs. Spurlock. God bless."

And she knew, without knowing how, that he wanted to say more.

Birdie was exhausted when she returned from Etta's in the wagon driven by Etta's father. Leah made her a cup of valerian root tea sweetened with honey and gave her sister a biscuit with huckleberry jam.

"Do you feel all right, Birdie girl? You're looking peaked." Leah knelt in front of the rocking chair where Birdie had collapsed. "I got some Red Liniment. I could rub your legs and arms."

"I reckon I just need a rest."

Birdie kept her feelings to herself. Leah suspected she was afraid complaining set her further apart. Even Leah wasn't always sure what was on her sister's mind.

"I'm making us some supper," Leah said. "Jesse should be home soon enough. I made squirrel stew and dumplings, but it don't taste as good as when you make it."

"Where did Jesse go?"

"Back home to help his step-daddy." She paused. "I was glad to have him go. I'm ashamed to say so, but it's the truth. It's so hard to get along with him, I only feel I can breathe right when he goes out that door."

"He does take it all to heart, don't he."

Leah sat back and crossed her legs under her dress, gazing up at her sister. "He's not the same as he was. He hardly says a word to me, Birdie. I talk to him and he looks at me like he don't remember where I come from. Like I don't belong to him anymore." She didn't recount the worst, that Jesse turned away from her every night now, no longer taking pleasure in their marriage bed.

"He does have a lot gnawing at him."

"But why cain't he talk to me about it? I want to make him talk to me, but I reckon I don't know how to do it."

"The Spurlocks get these sorry spells. You know they do. That's how Jesse's daddy was. Maybe you cain't remember, you being younger and all. But I do. He'd have dark times, just like Jesse's having, and he'd sit in the corner when company came and say nary a word. He'd stare at the wall, and he'd stare some more. Then the next time he was about, you'd think he was pert near the friendliest man in the holler."

Leah didn't remember this. All she could remember about Jesse's real father was a grin and a whistle.

"What should I do about it? Should I try to make him talk to me?"

"You'd best just leave him alone. You cain't make him talk if he don't want to. But you sure can make him angry."

Leah wondered. If she was feeling as bad as Jesse, she would want to talk about her feelings. She would want to know someone cared enough to ask and listen. But Jesse was a man, and in her limited experience with that breed, talking wasn't what men did best.

"I have something to tell him, something he don't want to hear." Leah explained what had happened that morning, describing the two men. "Those men, especially the one name of Daniel, they really cared how I saw it all. They don't like doing this. I could see that, clear as a poor man's window. Daniel, he said they want the best for us."

Birdie's eyes had fallen shut, but now they flew open. "You gonna tell Jesse they was *here?*"

"I have to tell him. They got a camp up the road. He'll see them walking over the place making notes, or one of the neighbors'll mention it. He has to know. I don't want trouble."

"You liked them?"

"It's not their fault. They have a job and they're doing it, that's all."

"You better tell Jesse that they're good men and mean no harm, then."

"Won't he think I'm some kind of traitor?"

"He'll know it's better to be set off our land by good people than bad."

Leah didn't know what to think, but she was glad her sister was there to give advice. Birdie might live in a limited world, but she was queen of it. She saw everything, knew everything. And unlike Leah herself, Birdie had less invested in the outcome. No matter what happened, she knew that she would be welcome wherever Leah and Jesse went.

"I'll talk to him." Leah nodded to confirm it.

Birdie smiled, as if she was glad her advice had been taken. "Just don't say too much. Let him come to you whene'er he's ready."

That night, Leah waited until Birdie had gone to her room at the back of the house before she joined Jesse in the sitting room where he had been whittling all evening.

"What are you making, Jesse?"

He looked up and turned his head to gaze around the room. When he seemed satisfied, he spoke in a low voice. "Got some good oak boards for a new quilt frame for Birdie. She's got a birthday coming up soon, don't she?"

She was greatly encouraged. This was the first time in weeks Jesse seemed to be thinking of something other than the park.

She rested her hand lightly on his shoulder. "She needs a new one. She's about wore out Mama's."

"I'm whittling clamps to keep the quilt stretched tight."

"You're as good at carving as your daddy

was. Do you ever wish you could just do that?"

"From time to time. But folks up here don't need fancy carving. And most of them can make what they need to get by."

"Down below it might be different."

He only paused a heartbeat. "We'll never know."

"I got something to tell you, and you won't like it."

"I don't like it already."

She squatted in front of him, her dress floating like a lily on the floor around her feet. "Don't be like that, Jesse. I got to be able to talk to you, don't I? What's the reason for being married if we cain't talk?"

He looked up, hand poised as if he planned to start right back to whittling. "Just say it, then."

"Two men come by while you were over to your mama's house this morning. They're gonna be up and down the holler surveying the farms and land, and deciding what they're worth."

He froze. Seconds passed; then his hands began to move again, the scraping of his knife against the block of wood the only sound in the room.

"They seem like good men," she said. "They seem powerful sorry to be doing this, but Mr. Flaherty, he's the one seems to be in charge, he says that he's going to do everything he can to get us a good price and a good place to live when we leave here."

He looked up. "Who's leaving?"

"He says *we* are. He says we need to be prepared. Jesse, I'm scared. If we don't do what they say, how can we keep them away? Nobody else up here is talking about staying to the bitter end. Nobody's going to declare war on the government just so we can keep this place. When it comes time to go, you'll be standing in front of this house by yourself."

"You're saying you won't be standing beside me?"

She didn't know how to answer that. "If I do, there will still only be two of us. And there will be as many of them as they need to make us go. Won't it be better to get ready? Maybe go in on that lawyer Aubrey and the others have hired? To make sure we get what's our due? Mr. Flaherty says—"

"I don't care what he says!" Jesse slammed the block of wood down. "I don't want you caring what he says, either. I don't want you listening to anybody but me."

Anger filled her. She sat back on her heels and stared at him. "How can I listen when you don't even talk to me? I might as well be one of the dogs lying on the porch for all the words you send my way. Even my mama and daddy talked to me before they expected me to do anything difficult. They explained what was happening, and if I had feelings about it, they listened."

"Then they spoiled you. And it's time somebody unspoiled you."

Now she was furious. She got to her feet with one push. "No, they just treated me like a human being. And that's the way you were raised, too, don't tell me it wasn't. Nobody in your house taught you to be as stubborn as a mule and as mean as a rattlesnake! You learned that all by yourself!" She turned on her heel and headed straight for the door.

Before she could even think about grabbing her shawl, she was walking down the road in the chilly mountain air. Luckily she had pulled on shoes earlier in the evening to take scraps to the hogs, and had yet to remove them. She was used to bare feet, but the road was soft from spring rain, and the mud would be icy against her soles.

"Jesse Spurlock, somebody's got to talk some sense into you, but it won't be me!" She paused outside the gate, trying to decide which direction to take. She wished Puss was living at the Cades' place again. Even on a dark night, she knew the way so well she would probably be safe without a lantern. But Puss was at Skyland, and there was no one to run to. She turned right and started up the hill. At least on the road she wouldn't get lost. When she got too cold to go farther, she could turn around. Maybe by then Jesse would be in bed and she wouldn't have to see his face.

She wasn't out of sight of the house when she saw the silhouette of a man just yards away.

Startled, her hands flew to her mouth. "Oh!"

"Don't worry. It's me, Daniel Flaherty. I'm sorry I scared you. You're all right?"

He materialized out of the shadows as he approached. He was smoking a cigarette, and the small flame illuminated his face. He was dressed the way he had been that morning, but he wore a heavy coat over the rumpled shirt.

"What are you doing out here?" she demanded.

"We're camped that way." He stomped out his cigarette, then pointed over the hill. "Nobody lives there."

The land he spoke of had been abandoned last year when an old couple without children died within four months of each other. It was hardscrabble land, steep and rocky, and no one had claimed it, despite views that could set a heart pounding.

"Then what are you doing *here?*" she asked.

"I was out for a walk. Looks like you were, too."

"I just needed to do some thinking."

"No place to be alone, is it? I mean, you surely know your way, but don't you worry about running into something or someone you don't want to see?"

She shivered, and as quickly as if he were trying to save her life, Flaherty stripped off his coat and draped it over her shoulders. "And it looks like you ran off without thinking about the weather," he added. "It turned cool this evening after the rain. Very cool."

The jacket felt good, heavy and warm, and she wrapped it around her for a moment, although she knew she needed to give it right back.

"You ever just find yourself somewhere you didn't plan to be?"

"You mean like you right now? What made you race off?"

There was only one man she should be telling her feelings to, and it wasn't Daniel Flaherty. Unfortunately, the man who should be listening wasn't interested.

"You told your husband about our visit, didn't you," he said when she didn't answer. "And he wasn't happy. I'm sorry we put you in that position."

She couldn't discuss Jesse with him. "Tell me what it's like where you live."

He laughed. "Right now I'm living up here, and it's cold and wet, and I'm tired of taking a bath and doing my laundry in a stream."

"How about the rest of the time?"

"I live down in the Valley. In a place called Harrisonburg. You've heard of it?"

"I know where it is. What's it like living there?"

"Not as quiet as this. Flatter, because we're down below, but you can see the mountains, and there's plenty of farms and land around us."

"Us?"

"Us who live in Harrisonburg. I have a small house on the outskirts. My mother lives not far away. It's easy to go to church and school, but people still help each other."

She tried to imagine this. She had never been that far, but she thought it was possible she might be happy in a place like that.

"I didn't see any other Blackburns on my list. Are you alone up here? Do you have anybody you can talk to about what's happening?"

"It's not something people want to talk about."

"That makes it hard on you, doesn't it."

"Are there jobs in Harrisonburg? For people like us who had to walk four miles to school every day and couldn't get there as much as we needed?"

"I think you could learn anything you needed to know very quickly. Some men are getting jobs with the park, helping to put in the roads and clearing the dead chestnut trees. They'll be replanting, doing all sorts of things. Your husband could apply."

"When our old hog flies south for the winter."

He laughed, his teeth white in the moonlight. "What would you do if you could, Leah? What kind of job would you like to have?"

"A job?" The thought wasn't so strange. Puss was cleaning rooms at Skyland. Other women sold crafts or pies to visitors there. Her own mother had always been paid for helping the sick.

"I would be a nurse. I'm the one they all come to now for help anyway. I'm the one here that knows the old ways and some of the new."

"Nurses are always needed. You could get some training."

The thought excited her. With Jesse earning money to put food on the table, Birdie keeping house, she could get the education she needed. She knew she was smart enough. They could do it.

She fell back to earth. "I'd better be going." Reluctantly, she removed the coat and handed it to him. "I shouldn't be out here like this."

"I think you need somebody to help you feel better." He left the rest unsaid, but Leah knew what he was thinking. *Because your husband isn't doing it.*

"Jesse's a good man. He'll come 'round. He has to. But this is his life."

"I would think *you* would be his life. He's a lucky man."

For a moment she was afraid to breathe. He hadn't touched her. He hadn't moved a hair closer, but suddenly the space between them seemed too small.

She stepped away, but her eyes sought his. They were concerned, as if he wondered what she might face again when she went back inside.

"Good night, Mr. Flaherty."

"Daniel," he said.

She knew better than to call the man who was evicting her family by his Christian name. But she nodded anyway. "I'm Leah."

"Good night, Leah."

She hurried back the way she had come. The temperature was dropping steadily, and by the time she got inside, she was shivering again, but from exactly what, she couldn't say.

Jesse was waiting by the door. "What call you got to run off that way and scare your sister? I know she's been staring out her window wondering where you went to and worrying!"

For a moment Leah couldn't speak. Had she been standing close enough to the house that Birdie, even with her limited vision, had been able to see her from her bedroom window? Had Birdie seen her with Daniel Flaherty, and would she tell Jesse?

"Jesse, I told you she was all right," Birdie said, coming to her doorway.

Leah whirled and saw Birdie nodding. "She was just outside looking at the stars. I seen her from the window. Just looking at the stars on a purty April night. You be good to her now, and don't you be angry."

Leah watched her sister go back inside her room.

"What do you think them stars is going to tell you?" Jesse shoved his hands in his pockets as if he were afraid what they might do. Then he started toward the loft.

She waited until he was up the ladder before she closed her eyes in relief.

CHAPTER TWENTY-FOUR

Early on the Wednesday morning after Kendra's visit to Prudence Baker, Manning paid a scheduled visit to the worksite. The sun was just beginning to glow through the trees that surrounded the clearing, and a fine blue-gray mist rose from the ground around them.

"It's going to be a fine house once it's finished," he said as he climbed out of his pickup.

Kendra was prepared with a cup of coffee that he took gratefully. "Which won't be as soon as you said, will it?"

"There's just no predicting the delays."

Kendra remembered her sister's warning. She and Jamie chatted several times a week now, and Jamie always laughed when Kendra bemoaned how slowly the work was going. Kendra was glad to be the butt of this particular joke. She had to overcome a lifetime of being the wise older sister.

They walked around the construction, which was nothing more than a foundation, a bare-bones frame and roughed-out plumbing. Kendra asked a few questions, satisfied each time with Manning's answers. Either Manning or Cash came by every week to see what their crew had accomplished and to consult with her.

"Your men are starting to feel like family." Kendra paused for effect. "Family I don't see often enough."

"Cash told me there was some trouble with Randy last month."

She was sure Manning had heard the entire story. "I haven't noticed him here for a couple of weeks."

"I have enough work to keep him busy elsewhere. He's a hothead, has something of a drinking problem, but he's a good enough young man under it, I think. I take on a man or two like that if I can. I was a hothead, too, when I was his age, and having a regular job and good people to work with settled me some. I try to return that favor."

"Maybe you could find a few more like Randy and let them work extra hours. I'd be happy to help them achieve patience and harmony in the name of getting my house finished."

He laughed. "You like my lady plumbers?"

Kendra was delighted that two women did all Manning's plumbing. "I do. Which is good, since I'll be seeing a lot of them one of these days. Soon, I hope."

"There's no rushing it. We're doing what we can. But with all this dry weather, we're scurrying around trying to get everyone's framing finished. And you've chosen some fixtures and other specialty items that are hard to get. Besides, working around the old cabin makes it that much harder to do right."

She *had* gone crazy choosing any number of things for the house that would make it take longer to complete. But how many times in her life would she be able to do this?

They completed their tour, and Manning made a list of questions he couldn't answer, saying he would have to get back to her.

Dusty, who had just realized Kendra was in the yard, came down to stand beside her.

The puppy didn't quite touch her, but the outer edges of her fur tickled Kendra's shin. Kendra reached down and petted her, and Dusty looked up as if to ask for more.

"That dog's the laziest thing I ever saw," Manning said.

"This is Dusty at her most active."

"Well, she seems happy."

Kendra looked down. "She does, more or less, doesn't she?"

"Like she feels at home. I'd say you're feeling at home, too."

Kendra was glad an opening of sorts had occurred. After she'd told Helen about Isaac's relationship to Leah, she'd taken Manning aside and explained the truth to him. He had seemed pleased to discover some part of Rachel Spurlock still existed. She hoped to introduce him to Isaac one day soon.

"Manning, I've been meaning to ask you about feeling at home in this house. I'm starting to find out more about Isaac's grandmother." As briefly as she could, she filled him in on everything she'd discovered about Leah.

He gave a low whistle that reminded her of Cash. "That's all news to me. The park, huh? I never heard anyone say that's where she was from. Of course, I was a kid, and kids don't listen all that well."

"I'm not sure anybody knew. But I suspect someone knew *something* about her past."

He waited.

"Rachel," she said. "I think Rachel knew something, and I think she might have told you what it was that night she called you. I don't want to pry. I know you didn't want to share it last time we spoke of this. But this is Isaac's family, and I think he deserves to know whatever we can find out."

He considered, crossing his arms over his wide chest and leaning against the door of the truck. "Sometimes it's better to just imagine what happened, that it was a prettier story than it really was."

"I understand, but *you* have to understand, my husband's always imagined the worst about his birth family. Knowing the truth will be better for him. Even if it's grim."

"It doesn't get a whole lot grimmer." He pushed away from the door. "Rachel said that her mother would burn in hell. And the reason was that she had killed Rachel's father."

Kendra had been afraid of this. "How could she know such a thing?"

"She used to wait tables over in Strasburg to make a little money after school. She'd hitch a ride over, hitch one back. She was required to wear a plastic nametag. One day some man who stopped in asked if she was related to some Spurlocks up in the mountains. She told him her father's name was Jesse. Then he told her that her mother had run away from wherever it was because she killed Rachel's father."

Kendra couldn't even imagine what news of this kind would do to an impressionable teenager, particularly one who was already desperately unhappy with her life. "Can you imagine somebody telling her that?"

"You have to question somebody who'd do such a thing, don't you? But he told Rachel he came from wherever Leah had lived, and everybody there knew she'd done it, only nobody could prove it because the body was never found."

"And Rachel believed him?"

"That's why she left Toms Brook and never came back."

"Before she died in that fire, she was planning to come home. Leah's stepson told us. It must have been well after that phone call to you. Rachel called Leah and told her she'd had a baby, then she promised to come back and see her. Maybe she wanted to find out once and for all if the man at the restaurant had been telling the truth."

"Leah never told me Rachel called her. I guess she thought it might make things harder, knowing she'd almost come back and died before she could."

"A pretty mess, huh?" She touched his arm in sympathy. "Thanks for telling me what she said to you."

"Do you believe it?"

Kendra didn't know. "Maybe people in Lock Hollow—that's the name of the place they were from—maybe they thought Leah murdered her husband and maybe even her sister. Does that mean she did? Not in my book."

"I think you're falling under Leah Spurlock's spell."

"Was there such a thing?"

"You'll have to decide." Manning tipped his Rosslyn and Rosslyn cap, then opened the door of his truck and drove away into the mist.

* * *

Every morning at eight, Kendra fed Dusty before she made her own breakfast. She'd been feeding the dog on the porch so that Dusty and Ten wouldn't collide, but this morning she didn't have the inclination to stand over the puppy and watch her eat. She was going to make good on her promise and attend the Wednesday Morning Quilting Bee. She still had to finish getting ready. For the first time, she let Dusty into the living room and went into the kitchen to prepare the puppy's meal.

Ten had not appeared for Kendra the way he had for Isaac, but several times she had caught glimpses of him. He no longer darted back under the sofa the very moment she came into the room. He moved more slowly, as if he were taunting her to catch him. When she showed no interest, he slowed down even more. Entire seconds went by when she could examine her new pet.

She poured the dry puppy food into a bowl and set it down for Dusty, but for the first time in their brief history, Dusty showed no interest. Dusty was lying on her stomach, legs splayed flat, peering under the sofa.

"I'll warn you," Kendra told the dog, "he's got a reputation. He could eat you alive."

Dusty took no notice of her.

"Don't say I didn't try."

Kendra popped a piece of bread into the toaster and snacked on a banana as it cooked. She was spreading the toast with jam when she heard footsteps on the porch. A knock, the door opened, and Elisa poked her head inside.

"Almost ready?"

Kendra hadn't expected to see her friend. She greeted her, toast in hand. "How did you know I was going to the bee?"

"Well, I didn't, but when I went to pick up Helen, she wouldn't get in the car unless I came over to fetch you first. She's waiting at home."

Kendra grinned. "I'll be ready in just a minute."

"You know, this fussing over you's a good sign. For years Helen was almost a hermit. Now she meddles, and it's an improvement."

"Want a piece of toast?"

"No, but do you have coffee?"

"Come and drink it with me." Kendra started back toward the kitchen. After just a few steps she stopped and spread her arms, and Elisa collided with her. "Look at that," she said softly.

Ten had slipped out from under the sofa and was inching sideways toward Dusty, like a crab on four paws.

"Are we about to have a fight here?" Elisa asked.

"You don't know this cat. If I intervene, he'll pin me to the ground."

With few choices, she started forward, but Elisa grabbed the back of her collar. "Let them work it out."

"You're kidding. I'll be cleaning up for weeks."

"You have to trust them."

"They have little brains."

"A hummingbird brain weighs about as much as a paper clip. But it knows how to fly forward, backward and sideways, things you can't do."

Kendra got the point. She waited, poised to interfere if necessary.

Ten sidled up to Dusty, back raised, hair on end, and hissing. Dusty lethargically wagged her tail. When that turned out to be too much work, she plopped down on her hindquarters and watched the cat moving closer.

Ten stopped just inches away and stared at the puppy. Dusty yawned.

"Anda despacio que tengo prisa."

"My Spanish isn't that good," Kendra whispered.

"It means, " 'Make haste slowly.' That's what your dog is doing."

Ten's head snapped around, as if he had just realized people were in the room. He looked at them, then at the dog. Dusty took that moment to stand, and before Ten could streak away, the dog's tongue shot out to lick Ten in the face.

"Yikes." Kendra started forward, but Elisa pulled her back.

Ten hissed and batted the puppy with a paw. Dusty licked again. Then, content that she had tamed the wild beast, Dusty shambled off to get her breakfast.

Ten, eyes wide, back still high, turned to look at Kendra as if to say, *You didn't see that.*

Kendra held up both hands. "I wasn't watching."

Ten headed for his retreat under the sofa. But with dignity.

"Ver y creer," Elisa said.

This one Kendra could figure out. "Seeing is believing."

"We'll have you speaking Spanish in no time."

The Community Church Beehive was a small room in the walkout basement that no other church group had claimed. The quilters had made it their home. There was just enough room for a large, sturdy quilt frame and some comfortable pieces of furniture. The group had grown since Kendra had first visited them, and now there was talk of knocking out a wall and expanding into a seldom-used storage room.

After everyone had settled in, the meeting began with a show-and-tell, and Kendra showed the signature blocks Helen had given her. She was encouraged to lay them out on the design wall—a piece of batting nailed onto the paneling—and the group discussed the best placement and what kind of sashing to use between blocks. Despite herself, Kendra was enthused about some of the possibilities.

"You have had it now," Elisa told Kendra when she was allowed to sit down. "There will be no turning back."

The official conversation meandered to other things, and finally Kendra was paired at the quilt frame with Dovey Lanning, who promised to help her take her first quilting stitches. The other women were cutting squares from brightly colored cotton to make Christmas quilts for the children at La Casa.

Kendra slipped a thimble Helen had provided onto her third finger. It felt like a lead weight. "I really feel I need to warn you. My high school had a class called Women's Studies—History and the Domestic Arts. We had to make an apron and write a paper on how the experience helped us grow. I nearly failed the semester."

"We called it plain old home economics and were lucky to have it." Dovey looked to be as old as Helen, with white hair scraped into a bun and a magnifying lens on a cord around her neck to augment the glasses she already wore. "One sewing machine among us, an old treadle. We had to make a dress, mostly by hand, and wear it to school the last day."

Kendra tried waving the thimbled finger, just to see if she could. "I'm sure yours was wonderful."

"When I sat down at my desk, one seam ripped. I spent hours trying to hide it, until the teacher found a large enough safety pin. When I got home, I looked down and saw that the hem had come loose and was hanging in three places."

"I feel better."

"Meant for you to. Now, watch the way I do this."

Five minutes later, Kendra had managed to get her needle through the quilt and bring it up again. An inch or farther away. "This won't do, will it."

"Not hardly. Take it out and start again. It's just practice you need."

Privately, Kendra thought her thimbled finger and thumb were going to need a stiff drink, a relaxing soak in a tub and at least six ounces of chocolate.

"How do you like living at the old Spurlock place?" Dovey asked.

"I love being out in the country. My husband's grandmother left him the cabin and land. Nobody's lived there for a long time."

Dovey didn't seem surprised. Kendra suspected the story had made the rounds.

"I knew Leah Spurlock. Knew her in the best possible way."

Kendra looked up. The new stitch was no better than the first. "What do you mean?"

"She took care of me when I was sick. During the war, it was. I had a stillborn baby, a little girl, and Leah stayed with me for a week while I recovered. My own mother was in Tennessee, and my husband was off in the South Pacific. My mother-in-law had five children still at home. Leah came without being asked, and nobody could have been kinder. That woman had gentle hands. And she knew just what to say to make me feel better."

Dovey looked down at the new stitches Kendra had taken. "Better, but take 'em out again."

"I have no aptitude."

"You have no patience. Take 'em out."

Kendra picked at the stitches with her fingernail. "Did Leah ever tell you anything about herself? We know so little."

Dovey considered that. Finally she looked up. "I was real unhappy. You can understand it. I'd counted on that baby to help with having my husband off in the war. I didn't think I'd ever get over it. One night Leah made me a cup of some herbal tea to help me sleep, and she told me that someday I would feel better, even if I didn't believe it right then. She said she had lost people she loved, so she knew what she was talking about. But she said that one day the pain would only be a dull ache, and I could learn to live with that. You know, if she had told me one day I'd forget that baby, then I wouldn't have thought much of her. But a dull ache? That was something I could believe. It helped."

Kendra knew this wasn't idle conversation. Dovey wanted her to know how much she had thought of Isaac's grandmother so that she would pass it on to him. "Was she right?"

"I went on to have two healthy boys and another girl. But I never forgot the first one. I never forgot Leah, either. I told people how much help she'd been to me, and she got some jobs because of it. I wished I could have done more."

Kendra wondered if a woman with hands that gentle could have used them to commit murder.

CHAPTER TWENTY-FIVE

An hour before sunset Kendra filled a saucepan with water for linguine and picked out a jar of sauce to pour over it. In a moment of creative whimsy, she decided to add new ingredients instead of serving it the way she normally did, unadorned and unappreciated. A search of the refrigerator turned up half a dozen possibilities. With nothing better to do, she took out a red pepper, half a zucchini and a carton of mushrooms, adding a chicken breast at the last minute. As she sliced and chopped, she thought of Isaac's gourmet pad thai and his quiet pride that he was mastering a new skill. Isaac, who had made no plans to see her next weekend.

She was sautéing the vegetables when she heard a loud explosion and the screeching of wheels. She turned off the burner and headed for the porch, wiping her hands on her jeans. Dusty wagged her tail as Kendra stepped over her.

She got there just in time to see a battered pickup making a circle in the clearing just outside her door. As the truck nearly missed a tree, she heard shouting from the occupants and glimpsed a cab crowded with bodies. A beer can soared from the window on the passenger side and bounced off the hood of her Lexus. The truck backfired, most likely the source of the explosion she'd heard, and, weaving from side to side, sped back the way it had come. A flurry of more beer cans bounced in its wake.

She leaned against the porch railing and stared into the clearing, willing the truck to stay away. She was afraid she had just been treated to one of the downsides of country living.

The clearing grew quiet. As if they sensed danger had passed, the crickets began to chirp, and, farther away, near the riverbank, she could hear the faintest croaking of a bullfrog.

Her heart was pounding too fast, but she

was aware of something else. She was anxious, yes. She didn't want the pickup and its occupants returning for more mischief. But she was anxious, not terrified. She was angry that her peace had been disturbed. Both were normal emotions under the circumstances.

Maybe she really was on the way to recovery.

As if to challenge that, lights peeked through the clearing. She leaned over the railing for one more look before she went to the telephone. But something stopped her. It was the absence of noise. The pickup had an engine that roared, probably tuned for that effect. The lights growing steadily brighter were accompanied by the chirping of crickets and nothing more. She only knew one person who drove a car that quiet.

She met Isaac in the clearing, puzzled by his sudden appearance and thrilled by his timing. He got out and slammed his door.

"Are you okay?"

She knew why he was asking. "Are *you* okay? Did you run into them on the driveway?"

"They were just coming out. I'm surprised

they made it, the way they were weaving, but they didn't hit me. What happened?"

"Nothing much. They came wheeling in, threw some beer cans, turned around and left. I heard either a gunshot or the truck backfiring. It was too dark to see a license plate, or I'd call and report them. But they'll be long gone before anyone can get out here."

He put his hands on her arms. "You're okay?"

Her smile felt genuine. "Yes, I really am. I didn't panic. I—"

His hands gripped her arms tighter. "Well, damn it, *I* panicked! All I could think was that somebody had hurt you again!"

"They didn't."

"What are you doing out here in the middle of nowhere? Do you see now why this is such a bad idea? What if those guys wanted more than a joyride and a garbage dump?"

This time she spaced the words. "They didn't."

He dropped his hands. "You still don't get it, do you."

Anger flared. This had been a milestone, but he saw it only as another excuse to prove a point. "Are you going to tell me how safe I'd be in the city, Isaac? Because we both know that didn't prove to be the case."

"Well, maybe it would have been if you'd used some sense."

She stared at him without risking a reply.

Moments passed as he considered his words. "Or if I had," he said at last.

She relaxed a little. "Coming here was my own choice. You don't have to feel guilty if anything happens to me."

"You think this is guilt?"

She searched his expression and saw everything but guilt. Concern bordering on terror. Anger at her stubbornness. And love. Plain and simple and utterly naked.

The anger disappeared, and she touched his cheek. "I'm sorry you were frightened, but I'm fine. And I *was* frightened for a moment, but not terrified. I'm recovering, Isaac. I'm starting to feel like myself again. That can only be good, right?"

He sighed; then he turned his head and kissed her hand before he took it and folded it into his own. "I worry, K.C. There are a lot of miles between us."

She knew he wasn't talking about highways and country roads. "You traveled some of them on a weeknight to see me. I have to say, I'm really surprised. What's up?"

"I'm taking the rest of the week off."

She wasn't sure she had heard him right. "You're doing what?"

"Time off. It's called using my annual leave."

She knew something was going on when he didn't say more. She also knew he would only tell her when the time felt right. "Well, I'm thrilled."

"I had another reason for coming, other than to see you. Something for Caleb." His bleak expression softened. "But being with you was the big one."

She had spent the past week wishing Isaac were different and wondering if she could live with the man he was. Now all the arguments seemed to melt away. He might be detached from his feelings, but the feelings were there, deep and powerful and worth the exploration.

"And I have enough supper for two. What a deal." She turned back to the house. "The water should be boiling. I'll put the pasta on."

She took a moment to breathe as she slid the pasta into the water, then flipped on the burner and reheated the vegetables. She was just putting the chicken into the oil when she heard Isaac's voice.

"Kendra, is this thing on the floor a dog or a rug?"

Caleb's eyes widened when he saw the computer monitor in Isaac's arms. Kendra had called first to check with Marian. The computer was Isaac's previous home computer, still powerful and up to date enough that Caleb could learn whatever he needed on it.

"You need one to download your photos," Kendra told Caleb. "And for schoolwork. Mr. and Mrs. Claiborne said it was all right to give this to you."

Caleb stepped aside, and Isaac carried the computer monitor into the boy's bedroom. Ron Claiborne followed with the processor. Kendra followed with a box of odds and ends.

The room was painted a masculine shade of gray blue, and the bedspread was a green and blue plaid. The furniture was old but comfortable-looking, not antique, but heavy dark wood. The most significant thing about the room was the complete absence of personal touches. The bookshelf was nearly empty. The walls had no posters. The bulletin board had one 4-H newsletter pinned in the middle. The dresser top was clear, and the desk Isaac set the computer on had two books piled neatly on one corner.

The institutional flavor was depressing.

"This is just what this room needs," Marian said, clapping her hands. "My sons were pack rats. You never saw so much stuff in one place. This will liven it up, make it more fun for Caleb to come in here in the evenings."

Caleb touched the computer monitor almost reverently. "I might mess it up."

Isaac seemed to understand. "It's yours now. You can jump up and down on it when we leave, and nobody will care. I don't need it anymore and it's just taking up space in a corner. So you can't do anything wrong."

"I never had a computer."

Again Isaac rescued him. "Mind if I stay a while and show you some things about this one? I have a lot of software installed. I'll show you how to download your photos if you have any."

The two males were plugging in the computer and fooling with an alarming number of cords when Kendra, Marian and Ron backed out and left them alone.

"I hope that does it," Marian said as she led Kendra to the kitchen for a cup of coffee. "You don't know how hard I've worked to get him to make that room his own. But there's never as much as a sock on the floor. And he won't put anything on the walls. Says it will hurt the paint."

"You're doing such a good job. It's just going to take him some time to realize this is home." Kendra paused, then decided she had to ask the next question. "It *is* home, isn't it? As long as he needs one?"

"As far as we're concerned, it's his home forever. We want to adopt him."

Kendra felt a wave of relief. "I am so glad."

"Cissy's in favor, and we've talked to his social worker. She thinks it will go through with no fuss if he wants it. But he has to agree. So far, we haven't brought it up. We're just waiting for him to give some sign he's comfortable here." Marian waved her to a chair and went to the counter to make a fresh pot. Ron had gone back outside to work on his pickup by porch light.

"Isaac understands Caleb," said Kendra. "He wasn't raised in the best circumstances, either. I'm glad they're spending some time together."

"The way some people treat kids . . . It's a crying shame."

The kitchen was seductively pleasant. The windows were open, and the smell of freshly mown grass lingered in the air. The wallpaper was blue and yellow; the white cabinets had blue ceramic knobs. A sign on the refrigerator read A balanced diet is a cookie in each hand.

Kendra enjoyed listening to Marian bustling around filling the pot, scooping the coffee and readying cups. Outside, Ron tried revving the ailing engine. Mild profanity punctuated the too-frequent silences.

Marian set cream and sugar on the table and brought the coffee once it had finished.

"It's nice to have you here," she said, sinking into the chair across from Kendra's. "I'm busy, but I always take time to sit when a neighbor visits."

"Maybe we ought to make sure somebody visits every day. I think you need time off your feet."

Marian stirred her coffee, but she smiled,

as if she appreciated that someone had noticed. "I was born not far down the road. The oldest of six. I grew up working hard."

Kendra hadn't realized Marian was that local. "Did you know Isaac's mother, Rachel Spurlock?"

"She used to babysit for us once in a while. She was just that much older."

"Do you mind telling me what you remember about her? Isaac knows so little—only what I've managed to find out."

Marian didn't seem to think that strange. Kendra wondered, if like Dovey, she had heard the stories.

"Rachel, well, she loved the outdoors, like our Caleb."

Kendra liked the sound of "our Caleb."

"You could hardly keep her indoors," Marian said. "Even when she was babysitting, we always went outside. Played ball or tag or something. Some people thought she was strange, but I never did. She had an imagination. She liked to pretend. Even when we played tag, it was always cowboys and Indians, or spacemen, or knights and dragons."

Although Isaac had a different kind of imagination, Kendra thought one reason he had climbed so far was his ability to imagine a multitude of solutions to difficult problems and choose the best among them.

"Once she told me her daddy was a prince," Marian said. "I never forgot that. For the longest time, I believed her. She said he had left her in Toms Brook because there were bad men in his kingdom who wanted to harm her. But one day, when he was king, she would go home, and her daddy would tell everyone she was his princess."

"How old was she then, do you think?"

Marian considered. "Fifteen maybe? I don't think she believed it, but she was a dreamer. I always wondered if that's why she left, you know, because she had all these dreams, and none of them were going to come true in this little town of ours."

"Were they practical dreams?"

"I don't think the girl had a very tight grip on reality."

Kendra wondered how tightly Rachel had gripped reality on the afternoon a stranger told her that her mother had murdered her father. Perhaps it had explained so much that there was no reason to question.

Marian changed the subject. "Caleb liked his trip up to the park. He doesn't talk much. You've noticed that. But he told me a lot about that day. He even had a few things to say about the fair. I'm grateful to you and your husband for the interest you've showed. It helps him."

"Have any of the boys he met at the fair given him a call?"

Marian brightened. "He went over to Gayle Fortman's house yesterday. They went on a hike, him and her son and that Leon Jenkins. I had to push, but he went, and I think he had a good time."

"That's great."

There was a whoop from the direction of Caleb's bedroom. "I think they got it hooked up," Kendra said with a grin. "But which one of the guys was that?"

"Beats me. But I think you'll be here a while. Want some pie to go with that coffee?"

Many things in life were overrated, but not make-up sex. Hours later, a deeply satisfied Isaac lay next to Kendra and listened to the roar of crickets outside the open window. Summer was rushing their way. The night air was cool, but the room felt still and muggy from the afternoon's higher temperatures.

"I can't wait for the house to be finished." Beside him, Kendra pillowed her head on her hands and stared up at the ceiling. Her slender body was an ivory statue in the moonlight, marred only by the scar across her abdomen. "I love this cabin, but I'm not going to love living here in July."

He didn't point out that she could come back to the city. He was finally beginning to understand why she had chosen to recover here. "It's peaceful. When I visit now, the tension drains away. There's a lot to drain away these days."

She propped herself up on one elbow and stroked his chest. "It's not like you to take off from work on a moment's notice."

He realized he wanted to tell her what was worrying him, that in fact he had only been waiting until he had time to tell this right. "ACRE's going ahead with selling portions of Pallatine Mountain. Dennis is sure it's the only way we can afford to buy it. Of course the covenants will be strict. But frankly, not nearly strict enough."

She traced a figure eight. "Like what?"

"Like the size of the houses they can build. And the clearing they'll be allowed to do. And the roads they'll widen so property owners can get in and out." He explained his reaction to the news from start to finish, and when he was done, he realized he had lightened his emotional load.

"I can see why you're unhappy."

"Things used to be easier. Compromises didn't bother me the way this one does. As long as a solution seemed ethical, I'd move ahead without looking back."

This revelation was so unlike him that apparently Kendra didn't know what to say. "Now I second-guess myself a lot," he finished.

"Why?"

He turned to look at her. "Because of you. Because of what happened to you, and your coming here."

Again, he could tell she didn't know how to respond. He reached up and touched her cheek; then he cupped it and brought her lips to his. After the kiss ended, she snuggled against him, head on his shoulder.

"When did life get so complicated?" he asked. "Or has it always been this complicated and I just refused to notice?"

"Maybe you noticed when you were a boy. But the only way to move ahead was to ignore the complications and the feelings that went with them. You made plans. You moved forward. You made more plans, and finally got yourself into a situation where you had some control."

He thought about that. "I guess that makes sense."

"Then one night a crazy man shot me. At first we blamed each other. But when it comes right down to it, Isaac, *neither* of us was to blame. The thing is, there's a lot we can't control. I've been thinking of the quilt your grandmother left you. Lover's Knot. Life's like that. It's a silk cord. Everything goes along smoothly, then, suddenly, there's a knot. Either you have to untie it and smooth the cord again, or you have to look closely to see why it's there. Because sometimes a knot holds a cord together and makes it stronger, and sometimes it's a hurdle that can't be overcome."

He stroked her hair, twirling a curl around his index finger. He asked the question that was uppermost in his mind these days. "Is our knot going to make our relationship stronger?"

"I hope so."

He took her hand and threaded his fingers through hers. They were quiet for a while. He could hear her soft breathing, but he knew she wasn't asleep.

"Do you want to hear about another knot?" she asked at last.

"Let's pile on the complications."

She laughed. "Maybe this should wait. It's about your family."

He could have predicted this. "What more have you discovered?"

He listened as she told him everything she'd learned.

"So far, I haven't heard a bit of proof your grandmother murdered your grandfather," she finished. "Or even that he was one of the bodies in that cave. All I know is that Leah became friends with a man named Daniel Flaherty, and some people in Lock Hollow believed that caused problems with Jesse. And that's as far as it goes."

"So are you at a dead end? No pun intended."

"Isaac, I've just told you a pretty sad tale. You must have some feeling about it."

He did feel sad. And he supposed that was one of the consequences of intimacy. "Haven't I 'shared' enough tonight?" He tried to say it lightly.

She punched his shoulder. "I'm panning

for gold here, and I'm working harder after that first unbelievable strike."

"It doesn't matter for me," he said. "But it mattered to Leah and Rachel, didn't it. It infected their lives."

"It infected yours, as well. If Rachel hadn't suspected her mother of murder, she might never have left here, never had you and given you away."

"You're determined to make what happened in that hollow seventy years ago relevant to my life, aren't you."

"Leah thought it was, Isaac. Don't you see? That's why she left you this cabin. That's why she left you that quilt."

"Then why didn't she just write down the story and leave it with her stepson to give me if he ever found me? Why this treasure hunt? With a prize I'm not too keen on accepting."

She pushed a lock of hair off his forehead. "I've thought about it a lot. Leah lost everything when she moved from Lock Hollow. She lost her husband and sister, although we're not quite sure how that came about. She lost her friends, her neighbors, her home and land."

"And?"

"The point is that she lost every connection she ever had. That silk cord that was her life? Severed beyond repair. And she had to come here and start all over again. It must have been so hard. Your mother suffered for it, too. So nobody understood better than Leah what it was like to feel alone, with no history, no roots. When she heard Rachel had given up a child for adoption, I think she was afraid that, one day, that child would feel the same way."

"That might explain why she wanted to find me, but not why she didn't just set all this down for me to read."

"Because she didn't know anything about you. I bet she hoped your life had been so happy you felt no need for your birth family. If so, the quilt would simply be a curiosity, the land a nice nest egg. But if it wasn't happy, if you needed the connections, then she made certain the clues were there to follow. All you ever had to do was the simplest detective work, and check out some of the names. They would have led you right back to Lock Hollow."

"Where I would discover that my grandmother was a murderer."

Kendra kissed him, as if to take away the sting. "You see, that's the thing. I don't think that's what you *will* find if you keep looking. I don't think Leah would have gone to so much trouble to lead you to that ending."

"Anyone who remembers the story will be dead soon. In another generation, Leah and Jesse Spurlock won't exist in anybody's memories. Why dig up the dead?"

"You have to answer that, not me."

In the end, if he was going to be truthful, there was only one answer he could give. "I guess I'd just like to know."

"As I was leaving, Prudence told me that Leah and Birdie had a cousin who's still living. Etta Norton. She lives in Luray, in an assisted-living facility. She's almost ninety, but Prudence says she's in good enough health to see you."

"Me?"

She lay back. "It was okay for me to go to Prudence and Aubrey. But Etta Norton is family. How would she feel if I showed up and told her about you, but you weren't there?"

"I have a cousin." He said the words the way a child tastes ice cream for the first time. Tentatively, but with growing appreciation.

"From now on, this has to be your search. I'll go with you, if you decide to do it. We could go tomorrow, if she agrees to see us. I have the phone number."

"About tomorrow . . ." He turned on his side toward her. "Let's go camping. I brought everything we'll need. I thought maybe we could go up to the park. Get off the beaten path a little and see what's up there." He paused, because until now, he hadn't even admitted the next part to himself. "Maybe find Lock Hollow."

Her eyes lit up, then grew cautious. "It's really off the beaten path. I'm stronger, Isaac, but I can't carry a pack yet. And you can't carry everything we'd need, can you?"

"No, but Caleb could."

"Caleb?"

"He told me about the hike he took yesterday. He spent a lot of time taking photos. He'd love camping even more, and we could persuade him to come if we told him we wanted pictures of my family home site."

"So we have enough equipment?"

"I brought the single and the double tent, so I'd have a choice if you didn't want to go with me. We could take both. I brought both our packs, easily enough food for three of us."

"What about a sleeping bag for Caleb?"

"Somebody in the Claiborne family's bound to have one he can borrow."

"I have a dog now."

"You insist on calling the rug a dog, do you?" He laughed when she narrowed her eyes. "I bet the Claibornes will take her while we're gone. And Ten will be fine alone."

She didn't consider for long. "If you're willing to work around a limp, and more enthusiasm than strength . . ."

He lay back, oddly excited. "Luray's on the way to the park. We could stop and see Etta Norton . . . I don't think Caleb would mind a short diversion. We'll call the Claibornes first thing in the morning."

She grabbed his hand and kissed it; then she linked her fingers with his. They fell asleep that way.

CHAPTER TWENTY-SIX

Luray was a small town in a small county. Given the choice to participate in the conversation with Etta or walk the streets of the quaint downtown, Caleb chose the latter. Isaac dropped him off at the visitors' center with instructions to meet them there in an hour.

They found Etta's address without difficulty. Maple Inn was a two-story white frame building shaded by large red and silver maples. It seemed more an old-fashioned boardinghouse than a serious medical facility. The porch was filled with residents in rockers and wheelchairs, socializing and enjoying the morning sun.

Isaac and Kendra chatted with the two men closest to the door until they could make their way inside. The entry was large and airy. The living area was decorated with a cottagey mixture of antiques and garage-sale bargains. Someone connected with the house had a green thumb, because even though the current drought was playing havoc with gardens, vases filled with flowers brightened tables and ledges.

An employee in a lemon-yellow smock pointed them to a room at the end of a first-floor corridor. Isaac knocked, and they entered when a quavery voice told them to come in.

Etta Norton was sitting in an easy chair looking through one of two windows. Her thin hair was tinted a soft peachy blond and carefully waved. She was tiny and gnarled, and Isaac had an immediate impression of a woman who had fought hard for everything she'd achieved.

She put her hand over her heart when she saw him. "I swear, if I didn't know better, I'd say Jesse Spurlock's come back from the dead."

Isaac hadn't expected the immediate rush of pleasure her words gave him. He introduced himself, then Kendra. "Thank you for seeing us on such short notice."

"Oh, not that short. After Aubrey called, I

figured you'd make your way here eventually. Glad I lived long enough."

"Aubrey gets around," Kendra said.

Etta had a one-sided smile that indicated she might have suffered a stroke. "Pull up a couple of chairs. Every time my daughters leave, they shove them against the wall."

"Do your children live around here?" Kendra asked.

"Not too far, any of them. I married a man who got a job with the park service, and eventually we settled here." She held out her hand to Isaac. "Let me look at you up close."

He obliged her, taking her hand. She leaned forward and squinted, examining him. "A bit of Leah, maybe, in the hair color. But mostly Jesse. Of course, his hair was black as coal. If that don't beat all."

"Why?"

"Because there were questions, you know, about that marriage. But maybe you don't want to hear about that."

Kendra had pulled two chairs closer, and they settled into them. "We've heard a little here, a little there. We were hoping you'd be able to add to it."

Etta looked pleased. Isaac thought being

needed was probably the best medicine the old woman would receive that day.

"So what do you know exactly?" she asked.

Isaac told the story the best he could. "There's been a hint that another man was involved."

"Daniel Flaherty. We all got to know him, you know. Him and his assistant . . ." She paused, staring off into space. "Charlie Thompkins was his name." She smiled, proud of her recall. "My little brother followed him all over the farm, that's how I remember. My father cut a hickory switch and taught Will to remember who his real friends were. I remember that, too."

As if she realized she was off track, she got back to her story. "Well, the two of them spent time with every family in our hollow, making notes, taking information, measuring acres. Daniel was conscientious, I will say that about him. He swore he was doing the best he could to help us. Of course, in the end, he destroyed a marriage while he was doing it."

"So Daniel Flaherty came between Leah and Jesse?"

"That's no way to refer to your grandparents, son. But then, I guess they don't feel much like grandparents, do they? You never having met them." She squinted at him again. "They'd have thought you were a marvel. I can tell you that."

"They aren't real to me," he admitted. He felt an absurd stab of pleasure, even so.

"Well, I'll tell you this. Jesse Spurlock was the best-looking man I've seen before or since. And smart? Lordy, he was smarter than any teacher that ever come to our little school. But he wasn't perfect. He had dark spells. We'd call that depression nowadays. Then, of course, we just thought it was sulking. That made him hard to live with. I can understand that now, even if I didn't then. At the time, I couldn't understand how Leah could look at anybody else, but I wasn't living with Jesse and going through what all she did. When you're young, it's easy to condemn folks. Not as easy when you've made mistakes yourself."

It was a long speech, and it left her winded. Kendra got up to pour some water from a pitcher and bring it to her. Etta took it gratefully.

She spoke after she'd sipped and rested a little. "If you get me that album over there,

I got something to show you." She pointed across the room.

Kendra got up before Isaac could, and got a photo album from the table beside the bed. She brought it back and rested it on Etta's lap. Etta thumbed through until she came to the page she'd been looking for.

"You want to know your grandparents better, you should know what they looked like. And see if I'm wrong about you looking like Jesse." She handed the album to Isaac. "Third photo on the right. That's them on their wedding day. One of the neighbors had an old Kodak box camera. We thought that was really something. He took that photo. That's me to one side, but that's your grandma and grandpa in the middle."

Isaac stared at the small black and white photo and saw himself, a little younger, hair that was a lot darker. But the resemblance was striking. Leah was as lovely as Kendra's contacts had said. He soaked in the sight of these people who were, for better or worse, his family. After a minute, he passed the album to Kendra.

She held it up to the light. "You do look like Jesse. Etta's right, it's uncanny. And I'm so glad to finally see Leah. But she was just a kid, wasn't she? I mean, we knew that, but it's sobering to see the proof." She looked up. "Do you have photos of Birdie?"

"Oh, Birdie wouldn't pose, not for anybody."

"When they disappeared, did you think she and Jesse had run off together?" Kendra asked.

Etta didn't look surprised at the question. "Birdie could always get Jesse to smile. She was the one who could coax him into a better mood. She used to tell me about it when we would visit. We were good friends. I knew more about her than anybody, even Leah."

"Do you feel like telling us a little?" Isaac asked.

She smiled and set down her glass. "Does it look like I have anything else to do?"

Blackburn Farm
Lock Hollow, Virginia
May 1, 1934

Dear Puss,

I am glad Miss Lula is feeling some better. But I doubt it is the poke berries. I think it is the warmer weather.

I am glad you wrote me. No, I do not reccommend eating the leafs of poison ivy so you will not git a rash this year. I think that will only make you sicker than you ever plan to be. I know some people do this. Those people don't have good sense.

If you can't stay away from the leafs and do git a rash, wash it good in cold water with strong laundry soap. Then rub it good with jewelweed every time it itches. You know where to look for it. Near the plants that got you.

Mr. Flaherty says we will get good money for our property. Jesse don't want to know about it. These days he don't say he is planning to stay at the farm no matter what. But he don't talk to me or anybody that much. So I cannot tell what he thinks.

I did not know marriage would be like this.

Fondly like a sister,
Leah

Leah was weary to the bone. Although she was convinced that they would be leaving their home, she saw no choice but to continue taking care of the farm and the animals that depended on them. Daniel had told her that they would be allowed to take their animals when they left. They could also take furnishings and personal belongings, although they could not remove anything that was part of the farm or house, not even the new fencing Jesse had installed last spring. She supposed the government wanted to have more to destroy once they were gone.

Although she had tried to convince Jesse to continue working until final plans were made, he refused. In a matter of weeks he had replaced defiance with lethargy. He rose late, ate only if food was put directly in front of him, spent his time whittling or walking in the woods. The only work done was done by her. After her parents died, the neighbors had pitched in to be sure the heaviest chores were completed by men strong enough to do them. Now that Leah had a healthy young husband, no one came around to help. She was struggling to do her chores and Jesse's, too. And the effort was wearing her down.

The only person who seemed able to reach Jesse was Birdie. Jesse always managed a smile for her sister and a response when she spoke to him. But Leah, who had tried and failed to push him to accept the inevitable, received little more than a cold glance.

Leah's only solace came during her increasingly frequent meetings with Daniel. They met at night, when skies were dark and they wouldn't be seen. She coupled their meetings with trips to the barn to feed the animals or other outside chores. He wasn't always there waiting for her, but often enough that they were able to talk about their days.

Leah didn't want to examine their friendship too closely. She knew she had grown dependent on Daniel for the small kindnesses her husband avoided, the way he listened intently when she spoke, the warmth in his hazel eyes, the concern for her feelings. She could talk to Daniel as she could no longer talk to Jesse.

On this night Daniel wasn't waiting near the stand of hickory where they usually met.

She leaned against a trunk and waited, the intoxicating scent of apple blossoms wafting on a light breeze from their orchards. Overhead, the full moon was like an extraordinary pearl.

She was later than usual, because she had needed to chop wood for the cookstove. She supposed Daniel had given up hope she would come. Their agreement was silent. There were no expectations, no whispered plans. She knew these meetings were more than an extension of his job and that he enjoyed being with her as much as she enjoyed him. When she thought about it—and she tried not to—she realized Daniel was attracted to her as a woman.

She was afraid she was attracted to him, as well. He was older than Jesse, with a thoughtful maturity her husband lacked. Jesse's intelligence and wit illuminated their little world like streaks of lightning. Daniel was steadier, less apt to make her laugh, but also less apt to criticize or infuriate her. She was aware of the irony. Daniel worked for the men who were stealing her farm and had driven Jesse into gloom.

When it was clear he wasn't coming, she made her way back to the barn and the chopping block, where earlier she had split seasoned logs into smaller chunks. Behind the barn, she located the wooden handcart and pulled it around the side to load the wood and haul it up to the house. A shape materialized out of the shadows. For a moment she thought Daniel had sought her here, in the heart of the farm, where anyone might see him.

But it wasn't Daniel.

"Looks like you could use some help," Jesse said.

She took a deep breath to steady her hands, another to slow her speeding heart. "I could always use help," she said at last. "Though I reckon I've forgotten what it feels like."

"I aim to fix that."

"You're like a man who misses his wedding and just comes for the party. I've already done the hard part."

"Party? You know how hard it is to stack this wood all proper in the cart?"

"Well, I've been learning real fast, since I'm the only one that does it anymore."

"I can see you haven't learned good enough. Let me show you."

"Jesse—"

He shook his head. "Hush now. The master's a-teaching."

She wanted to be angry. She had every right to be. But this was a quicksilver glimpse of the old Jesse, the man she had married, the one she had admired from afar for years before the day they hunted bloodroot together.

"First you choose the biggest pieces. Course, you hope that whoever did the splitting knew what she was doing and got them all even like."

"It's not my job!"

"But sometimes there's a complication. And beggars can't be choosers. So we'll go with what we got here."

"How very kind of you."

"Now, don't these look like the biggest?" Before she could answer, he began to juggle three large chunks. "Which is biggest? This one? This? This?"

She was mesmerized, although she wouldn't say so. "Maybe I ought to just go inside."

"And miss the show? That don't hardly seem right. How much entertainment do you get in a day? Watch this." Quick as a weasel, he grabbed a fourth piece and sent it into the air with the others.

"Now watch *this,*" he said, his eyes trained on the wood. "You might learn a thing or two."

"I'm learning what a sorry fool I married."

He laughed. It wasn't quite the deep-chested, rolling laugh she remembered from better days, but it sounded real enough.

"Here goes." He turned, and as each piece came down, he flicked it into the cart. In a moment, the four chunks of wood lined the bottom.

Despite herself, Leah was impressed, but she was determined not to show him. "I hear they got circuses where men like you entertain the crowds. 'Course, I don't see a crowd right here—do you?"

"Let's see you do the same thing."

"No thanks. I'll just finish doing *your* job, that's all. Like I been doing for weeks now."

"No call for that. Give me a chance and I'll teach you how to have some fun."

When she didn't move, he raised a brow. "Come here, Leah."

"Why should I do *anything* you ask me to?"

" 'Cause you're the wife of a sorry fool, but that still makes you a wife, don't it?"

"Jesse, you think this makes up for—"

"Come here." His arm snaked out, and he caught her around the waist. He inched her toward him, applying his strength, but he didn't hurt her.

With her back against his chest, he held her firmly, left arm clamped around her waist, right hand free. "Maybe we better start with something smaller'n them logs you think you split."

"I'd ask you to teach me to do it better, only you don't work that hard anymore."

"This little pinecone here, it's good for starters. See you throw it up in the air like this, and you catch it like that." He changed arms, his right clamping her to him, his left hand catching the cone.

"Now you try it," he said.

She wiggled against him, struggling to break free. Suddenly she was aware that her movements were not having quite the effect she had planned. She turned in his arms. "Jesse . . ."

He gathered her close, the cone thumping against the ground at their feet. "Everything's been closing in on me," he said.

She knew that was all the apology she would get, and more than she'd thought him capable of. "But you got no call to pull away from me. I'm the one loves you the most. I want what you want. Maybe we cain't exactly have it now, but we can have something good."

His hands threaded through her hair. "Everything. It's just everything going all at once."

"I know. I know." She rested her arms across his shoulders, righteous anger forgotten. "But it's not everything. You got me. We got Birdie. We'll have a little money and a place we can start again."

He kissed her. The kiss was hungry and demanding and still somehow despondent. She knew he was desperate to lose himself in her and take some solace in their marriage. She felt him lift her skirt. In just moments he was inside her, and in moments more, he was calling her name, as if it were the only name he knew.

Time passed. A whippoorwill called his mate in the moonlight. Their cow lowed somewhere in the pasture. "I didn't plan for it to happen like this." Jesse stepped back and fastened his pants as she pulled her dress down.

She couldn't analyze how she felt. Part of her was glad they had shared at least this much. Part of her felt as if she'd been used and now abandoned again.

That part was the stronger. "You didn't *plan?* You're sure? Isn't this why you came a-saying you were sorry?"

One of the dogs barked; then the brush lining the path in front of the barn rustled. "Jesse? Leah? Are you out here?"

"Birdie's looking for us," Leah said softly.

"We're over here," Jesse called. "You go on back inside now. We're just getting wood to bring in."

Her voice floated toward them. "No, I can help. I'm out here anyway. No call to go back empty-handed."

"You tell me before she gets here," Leah whispered. "Was this all about having what you wanted? Or was there more to it? Just tell me so I'll know!"

"You don't know, then I got no reason to enlighten you, do I? Because you won't believe anything I say!"

She grabbed his shirt as he started to turn, but at that moment Birdie came around the barn. Leah dropped her hands to her sides.

"I reckon you do all the hard work, Leah," Birdie said. "And you don't leave half enough for me. The least I can do is help. What with you doing all that negotiating with Mr. Flaherty, you hardly got time to do everything else."

Birdie's gaze flicked to Jesse, who had gone rigid with anger at the mention of negotiations. "Jesse," Birdie added softly, "ain't it your job to take better care of my sister?"

Jesse vanished so quickly that Leah almost doubted he had ever been there.

CHAPTER TWENTY-SEVEN

Kendra was amazed by how quickly Isaac took care of essentials like the back-country camping permit and a set of maps. At the visitors center they sought out Hank Armstead, who was delighted to show them the best route into Lock Hollow. He helped Isaac pinpoint the locations of the Blackburn and Spurlock farms on Isaac's GPS, as well as the infamous cave.

"You'll see the foundations and maybe more," he said. "Last time I was there, some of the walls were still standing." As a finale, Hank suggested a hut that abutted the Appalachian Trail where they could stay that night.

Once they were in the parking area closest to their starting point, they carefully divvied the gear between Caleb and Isaac.

Kendra's pack, which Caleb would carry, was smaller than Isaac's, so there was no need to explain why the teenager was getting a lighter load. Caleb was new to backpacking and wouldn't understand how a pack that felt comfortable at the trail's beginning could feel like it was loaded with rocks by the end.

Before the carjacking, Kendra had carried her own gear and Isaac hadn't been forced to make many changes in his own hiking habits to accommodate her. Now she felt lucky to be on the trail at all. They would hike three miles today, then two more tomorrow. If all went well, they would return the entire distance on their final day.

"You sure this is enough to eat?" Caleb skeptically eyed the freeze-dried food Isaac had asked him to carry.

Isaac was clearly enjoying himself. "I promise you'll like it. Spaghetti one night, chicken and rice the next. When we get back, I'll treat you to a steak dinner with all the trimmings."

Kendra had a day pack filled with gorp, PowerBars, bottled water and sandwiches they'd bought in Luray. Her old hiking boots felt comfortable, if odd. She and Isaac had talked about buying real boots for Caleb, but new boots were worse than old sneakers. Instead, he wore high-tops with a pair of Isaac's wool socks. Thanks to Isaac's organization, in less than half an hour they were almost set.

He did one last run-through. "Got the map, got the GPS, got the ultraviolet water purifier—"

"How did you camp before you had so many toys?" she asked.

He grinned, then ticked off item after item until he'd finished. Finally he shoved the list in his pocket.

"We'll take our time, K.C. The minute you get tired, we'll stop. The days are long. No matter how slow we go, we'll have sunlight when we set up camp."

She had no desire to be heroic. She knew she had a better chance of making the trip to Lock Hollow if she was careful in every possible way. And she wanted to stand where Leah and Jesse had stood, to add another piece to the puzzle she was assembling of their lives.

"I'll put one foot in front of the other and we'll see how I do," she promised.

She did remarkably well. In a patch of

woodland at the beginning of the trail, Caleb found the perfect walking stick, and she used it to propel herself forward. Her stride had improved markedly in the months since the accident. At the beginning, when she hadn't been sure she would ever walk again, she hadn't envisioned a day when she and Isaac would hike together again.

They took several short breaks but waited until they reached a clearing by a meandering stream before they ate lunch. As they walked, Isaac had explained the concept of "leave no trace" to Caleb. To prove he'd listened, Caleb led them to a clearing on a path that had been used by other hikers, instead of trampling a new one of his own.

They sat on rocks and listened to the stream gently wash over stones and fallen tree limbs.

"Hear that?" Caleb asked.

Kendra was instantly attentive. It was rare that he introduced a subject on his own. A bird fluted and chirped somewhere just beyond them.

Caleb cocked his head to listen again. "That's a hooded warbler."

"Good for you," Isaac said. "I can only recognize a few songs."

"A teacher gave me a CD with birdcalls."

Kendra wondered how long ago that had occurred. "That's one of the reasons you like my woods, isn't it."

"I'm making a list."

"You know, Helen's son-in-law is a birder, and so is their daughter Tessa. Have you met them?" She watched him nod. "They would love to take you with them, Caleb. Do they know you're interested?"

He looked as if explaining an interest to strangers was a foreign concept. Kendra made a note to do it for him. Tessa was on a prolonged maternity leave with her toddler son, Ian, but she was a gifted teacher who genuinely liked teenagers. She would help draw him out of his shell.

As they took the next section of the trail, she thought about the way things were falling into place for Caleb. It wasn't that country people had more time to involve themselves in the lives of their neighbors. People were as busy here as anywhere else, but they had to remain connected to prosper and flourish. Connections made all the difference.

They had made all the difference in her life. She'd come to the Valley to be alone, but no one had let her. The loving attention of neighbors and friends had helped her heal.

"That's what's been missing from our lives," she said out loud.

Isaac was walking beside her, and Caleb was fifty yards ahead, taking photographs. "What's that?"

"Connections." She looked over at the man who was purposely slowing his pace to stay with her. "Neither of us is good at making connections, Isaac. Look at us. No family ties, at least not until this summer. Friends we see only occasionally. Jobs that keep us so busy we don't have time for much else. We throw money at organizations but don't get involved. We even chose a place to live that someone else furnished, so we could ignore that, too."

"Is this one of those 'life in the country is great and life in the city is terrible' conversations?"

"No. I think we could be connected anywhere, if we just wanted to be."

They walked in silence for a long time before he spoke. "ACRE was like a little family when I first got there. I wanted it to be bigger and more professional. I wanted it to be a stepping-stone to something even more impersonal. Maybe I should have thought more carefully about what I wished for."

"What do you mean?"

"ACRE used to be fun. People were always having parties, impromptu get-togethers at bars or restaurants or somebody's apartment. We were a community working toward a common ideal."

"*We* didn't go to many parties."

"I was working too hard. So were you."

She felt a stab of regret. "We've been good at slamming doors."

"And ACRE's not fun anymore. Not since Dennis came on board. Not since we've streamlined and shored up and started instituting rules for every aspect of working life. It's not really safe to say what we think anymore. The others have been more aware of the changes than I have, since I'm higher in management. But it's all coming to a head now."

"That's why you took off this week?"

"You're not the only one who's been forced to reexamine your life."

He didn't say more, but the silence

stretched farther than the next step. She thought it stretched into the next phase of their lives and the way they would live them.

About an hour before dark, they reached the hut where Hank had suggested they camp. He had warned them the site might be crowded, but when they arrived, they were the only ones there. The only other hikers they'd seen had been day-trippers. And apparently no one hiking the Appalachian Trail had yet arrived at this outpost.

They inspected the structure, and when Isaac noted Caleb's obvious disappointment at sleeping "indoors," he announced they were going to pitch their tents in an overflow tent site. Kendra was delighted to see his-and-her privies, and made use of hers while Isaac and Caleb set up camp.

At dinnertime they went to the hut to cook over the fire pit rather than use Isaac's tiny one-burner stove. They snacked on fresh fruit while they filtered and boiled water to reconstitute their meal. Caleb chose the spaghetti, and although it was supposed to serve four, there were no leftovers by the time they finished the chocolate peanut-butter pie that came with it.

As if the pie hadn't been part of the deal, they made peppermint tea and s'mores over the fire. No one had joined them, and the only sounds were the chirping of crickets, the crackling of the dry tinder they'd found in the forest and the barely audible rush of a distant waterfall. Once something crashing through nearby brush stopped their conversation, but whatever had made the noise never appeared.

"We need entertainment," Kendra said, when the s'mores were gone, the last cup of hot tea was finished, and she, at least, had taken a brief sponge bath and brushed her teeth to prepare for a night in a sleeping bag. The stars were entertainment enough for her, but she suspected Caleb needed more.

"We could tell ghost stories," Isaac said. "Only I don't know any."

"Caleb, do you sing?" Kendra asked.

He grinned and shook his head. In the firelight, the grin transformed his face into something wonderful. She glimpsed the man he would be, but even better, she glimpsed a boy finding some pleasure in the world around him and the people in it.

"Well, I have something." Kendra stood

and pulled a sheaf of papers out of the pocket of her windbreaker. "I brought these with me. They're copies of letters from Leah Spurlock to her best friend Puss, who had moved away from the hollow."

She explained how she had gotten them. "I haven't read many of them yet, but I thought I'd read a couple out loud, unless you guys would be bored silly. They're folk remedies."

"What kind of stuff was she trying to fix?" Caleb asked.

Kendra took out the first page and read a little bit. "Well, here's one for something called low blood." She looked up. "Maybe like anemia? From a poor diet, maybe." She scanned a little more. "Oh, that would be it. Here's what she says." She began to read out loud.

" 'I am sorry your brother is looking a little peaked. It is no wonder he feels tired when he works so hard. With spring just beginning, the help he needs is springing to life from God's green earth. Pick him a mess of poke greens and cook them up the way your mama always does. Get only the young ones, and change the water three times. Make him eat all he can. Other greens are good, too, and better if you cook them in an old iron pot with a little vinegar.' "

Kendra looked up again. "Greens are filled with iron, and the iron cookware people used on their stoves actually leached into the food they cooked and provided dietary iron. At least I think it did."

"Leah must have thought so," Isaac said.

"What else does it say?" Caleb sounded interested.

She scanned the letter and smiled. "She says to give him a tonic of sulfur and molasses."

"Yuck."

"Sulfur is sometimes used to kill parasites," Isaac said. "Molasses is another source of iron, and, for that matter, calories."

"A good multivitamin sounds better. And how do you know all that?"

"I took a boatload of chemistry and physiology classes in college. I thought I might want to be a doctor."

"Then you could have worked even *longer* hours."

"Is that possible?" He smiled at her, and she smiled back.

"What else do those letters say?" Caleb asked.

She scanned the next couple. " 'Sassafras root tea if you're feeling puny.' Hasn't sassafras been proved to be carcinogenic?"

Caleb looked interested in the new word. "What does that mean?"

"It means it causes cancer," Isaac said. "And I've heard that, too."

Kendra put the letter behind the others. "I guess we'd better take Leah's advice with a grain of salt. She didn't have lab rats to experiment with."

She read advice from a couple of others until it was clear she was losing her audience. "And that's your bedtime story, boys."

Isaac got up and stretched. "Caleb, let's bear-proof the area."

These were words that would normally strike fear into hearts, but Caleb was fourteen. He nearly leapt to his feet. "Bears? You think some might visit?"

Isaac draped his arm over the boy's shoulder. "Only if we leave stuff where they can get to it. We have to take everything that smells like food and hang it from a tree. Ten feet up, four feet out. Even soap and toothpaste, so we'll wash up first."

Caleb looked as if someone had handed him a bouquet of balloons. They went off to gather up anything remotely edible.

Kendra watched the dying fire send spirals of smoke toward a million visible stars. She started to put the letters away, but noticed that the next one was longer than the others. She scanned it, then read it more closely. The letter was dated June 1934. One sentence stood out.

There are women in this hollow who don't know a thing about what they are saying. If you hear rumors about me, Puss, just remember everything you know in your heart about who I really am. Some people will beleave anything they here, just to make time on this earth a little more intresting.

She felt as if Leah had come back to tell her to dig deeper. Had Leah wanted a relationship with Daniel Flaherty so badly that she had committed murder? Obviously some people had believed it. But Leah hadn't ended up with Daniel. She had ended up alone, giving birth to Jesse's baby in a primitive cabin in Toms Brook. And, more important, the woman Kendra was learning to know was not one who would kill to get what she wanted.

One person would know for certain how intimate that relationship had become. Kendra wondered if Daniel Flaherty was still alive. He would be well into his nineties, so the chances weren't good. But she had the resources to find him if he was.

Or had Daniel been one of the bodies in a cave in Little Lock Mountain?

She was still clutching the letter when Isaac came back to the fire.

"Caleb's gone to bed, but he won't sleep. He's praying for bears. It's going to keep him awake."

She slid the letters into her windbreaker and held out her hand. He helped her up.

"This has been one of the best days we've ever spent together," she said.

He pulled her close and kissed her.

Isaac had spent his working life saving the wild places of the earth. Now, as he stood in the morning sunlight looking over the last traces of the farm where his grandparents had lived, he knew how they must have felt when they realized it would soon be lost to them forever. The irony was extraordinary. Someone in Washington had taken the same position he might have taken had he been working for the government. The earth needed protection. The earth belonged to everyone, and everyone deserved to enjoy this piece of it.

And yet . . .

"Oh, will you look at this?" Kendra came up beside him.

He heard the emotion in her voice. "According to my GPS, that's the Blackburn house."

There wasn't a lot left. Trees and undergrowth had filled in much of what once had been fields and pastureland, of course. But as the ranger had told them, the outline of a foundation was still visible through the summer foliage. The skeleton of one wall had refused to fall. The bottom third of a stone chimney was a monument to another time.

Caleb was already walking toward the ruin, taking photos. Isaac was glad Kendra had bought the teenager a camera. He could not have objectified this moment in a photograph had his life depended on it.

"They woke up every morning, and this is what they saw," Kendra said. "Can you imagine?"

They were standing in paradise, pure and simple. Even through all the trees, they could see mountains on top of mountains in the distance. Gentle hills looking over them. Rocky outcrops like contemporary sculptures. Somewhere the sound of a spring flowing unfettered.

"It looks like there are still remnants of their landscaping," Isaac said, a catch in his voice.

She took his hand. "Let's go down and see."

They walked slowly. For the first time Isaac understood the expression "hallowed ground." For better or worse, he was the last link in the human chain that had been forged in this place. With the exception of Etta, who was only the most distant of cousins, he had never met the people who farmed this land, who lived in this house, who survived sorrows and joys here and then were forced to live elsewhere. But despite that, he was still one of them. He had never stepped foot on this soil, but somehow his roots were here.

"The soil around the house is rocky," Kendra said. "That's why it hasn't grown over. But isn't that a lilac?" She pointed to a flourishing shrub at the near right corner of the foundation.

"I think so."

"I've always wanted lilacs," Kendra said.

"They don't grow on windowsills, do they?"

"No, but something tells me that if there's a viable sprout, I'm going to have one to plant at our cabin when we leave the park tomorrow. And don't tell me I'm not supposed to take so much as a stone with me. I know."

He didn't argue. He understood what she was feeling. In the long run, he would have to agree with the government's desire to save this land from being heavily farmed and to open it for all who wanted to enjoy it. In the short run, he was angry that the family he would never know had been forced off land they had owned for generations. And today, at least one heirloom lilac sprout belonged to him.

When they reached Caleb, he was taking photographs of the ruins. Isaac watched the boy's serious expression as he framed each shot. It would be a worthy collage when he had finished. When Caleb had exhausted the ruins as a subject, the three of them wandered down behind the house and found remnants of what probably had been a barn. The logs were rotting, but the shape of the former building was there to see.

"It wasn't very large," Kendra said.

"I doubt they had more than a cow or two, maybe a mule or a horse, some pigs for fattening."

"It couldn't have been an easy life."

"It might have been a satisfying one, though."

"They sure didn't face traffic jams." Kendra brushed aside a clump of weeds. "Look at this."

Isaac peeked over her shoulder. It was a tool of some sort, cast iron and heavy. He squatted and parted the grass to get a better look. "I think it's some part of a plow. The piece that digs a furrow."

"I wonder how many furrows it dug in its time."

"Let's look around some more."

They spent another hour wandering the immediate area. Kendra dug a lilac sprout and packed it in a plastic bag, watered and sealed it and stuck the bag in her day pack. "I feel guilty. I wouldn't take a native plant. I swear."

"You don't have to convince *me* you're law-abiding and environmentally correct," Isaac said.

"I wonder what Leah brought with her to the Valley. If anything planted at the cabin now came from this place. There are hollyhocks that look old. I've managed to free them from weeds, and I hope they'll flourish."

"If she had anything to do with those bodies, she got out of here fast. I doubt she was engulfed in sentiment."

He looked down at her and saw she was pale and perspiring. "We're going to find you some shade," he said. "And I'm going to locate that spring for some nice cool Blackburn water."

"I don't want to spoil this for you."

"You've been pushing yourself and doing great, but let's not take any chances, okay?"

She nodded, obviously glad to rest.

They spread a sleeping bag under a tree that had been there long enough to observe generations of Blackburns. Caleb had already located the stream and filled the filter bottle. Cold water was their reward. Isaac unpacked gorp and they each took a handful.

"There must be a family cemetery somewhere on the property," Kendra said. "From what I've read, the park didn't move them, but they don't maintain them, either. That's up to the families."

"That doesn't seem right," Caleb said. "Take the land, then tell people they have to come back from wherever they were scattered to care for their dead."

"We'll find it another time. I want to find my way over to the Spurlock place before it gets dark." Isaac put his hand on Kendra's knee. "And I want you to stay right here. No arguments. From what I can tell, the best way to get there is up that ridge and over. It's a tough climb, and you've had enough for the day."

She looked relieved. "I like it here. I'll wait for you and Caleb."

Caleb frowned. "I'll just stay here and wait."

"You don't have to worry about me. I'll be fine. I'm going to close my eyes and take a nap."

"We should have brought Dusty to protect you."

"Dusty the rug would lie right down beside her and take a nap, too," Isaac said.

Caleb looked from one face to the other; then he chuckled. "Well, she'd still have some company."

Kendra took off her cap and used it to fan her face. "Looks like she's got a longer name, too. Dusty Rug. Rug for short, until she gathers some energy. I've got the sun and the sky, and there's a breeze that tells every animal in sniffing distance I'm here, so they'll stay away. Don't worry about me."

The two males filled water bottles after another trip to the spring and took a couple of PowerBars each. Kendra teased them about having enough power between them to walk the length of the park. Then she settled back, cap over her eyes, and left them to their adventures.

Caleb was silent as he and Isaac picked their way up the slope. He kept up without difficulty, a good sign, considering his early health problems. They stopped about a third of the way up, and Isaac took a reading with the GPS.

"Do you want to see the cave where the bodies were found?"

"The whole thing is kind of creepy, isn't it."

"That's a good word for it. It's up to you."

"I don't think I want to go inside."

They cut across the slope and down to a rocky area that backed up to another ridge. Isaac stopped and took another reading; then he looked up. "It should be right over there."

The cave wasn't hard to spot. There was a distinct space among several large boulders. Shielded by another rock, as it had been before the dog squeezed inside, it wouldn't have been noticeable. Isaac imagined children finding this place, playing together inside, neglecting to tell their parents where they had been—parents who had probably played there themselves as children.

"There are probably more caves," Isaac said. "But this is where the ranger told us to look."

"I would like to live out here," Caleb said.

"Me too." Isaac clapped him on the back. "But we can come and visit any time we want."

Caleb took some photos. Then they went back up the slope and continued toward the Spurlock farm.

For a time they walked in silence. Once Isaac asked Caleb to identify a birdcall, and he told Isaac it was probably a wood thrush.

"Do you want to be a naturalist?" Isaac asked.

"Maybe I want to be a doctor."

"Like I said, at your age, so did I."

"A surgeon gave me back my life. I'd like to do that for somebody someday."

"That's a good reason."

"Why did you?"

"We lived all over the world. I saw so many sick and injured people, I wanted to fix them all. Turns out I'm better at fixing the earth. I saw a lot of land that needed help, too."

"I guess there's a lot that needs fixing, no matter how you look at it."

After another twenty-five minutes of hard hiking, they reached the Spurlock farm. Isaac was sure the trip must have been easier when his grandmother and grandfather lived here. Fields had grown up, and paths were used only by the occasional hiker.

Without his GPS, he wouldn't have known they'd arrived.

"Let's see if we can find anything of the house," Isaac said.

They found it at last, a larger footprint than the Blackburn home. There were no walls here, only a foundation and what might once have been a fireplace but was now a rubble pile. He tried to imagine it as it had been. By the standards of today, it had been primitive, at best. By the standards in the Virginia mountains, he thought it might have been a palace. Now what was left of it lay under a tangle of blackberry brambles, wild roses and mountain laurel.

"Wow, see what they looked at every day?" Caleb said after a while. "I'm going over there to take some pictures."

Isaac glanced up and realized that beyond the closest row of trees a mountain rose high in the distance. They were at the farthest reaches of the park. Not far beyond them, park property ended, but of course it ended at a ridge, and there was little below them for a ways—nothing at all until the land leveled off again and could be used for pasture.

But beyond that, wild and still uninhabited, was a mountainside, covered with forest, unbroken by farmsteads or estates or ski lodges. He moved out of the shadow of the Spurlock family homestead and toward the view, until he was standing next to Caleb.

He stared at it for a long time, his heart pounding faster. This was the sight his family had awakened to each morning. The sight that had greeted them as they went about their chores. The last thing they had seen from their windows at night.

"It's a wonder, isn't it," Caleb said, "that it's there like that? Maybe the park's a good thing. I've been wondering. But if it can keep a mountain like that the way God made it, then maybe all the suffering was worth it."

"Unfortunately, that mountain's not in the park," Isaac said. "It's just outside the borders. It's called Pallatine. Pallatine Mountain."

CHAPTER TWENTY-EIGHT

They walked more slowly on the way back to the Blackburn farm. "It must be weird going to a place where your family used to live," Caleb said.

Isaac knew enough about Caleb to understand this was not a casual remark. "Next time we'll hike into Corbin Hollow," he promised. "Kendra tells me that might be the area where your family was from."

"I don't know anything about them. Just what Cissy says."

One part of Isaac wanted silence, so he could consider what he had just seen. The other part wanted to help Caleb put his life in perspective. Apparently that part was stronger.

"I didn't know anything about my family until recently. I was adopted as a baby."

"Nobody wanted to adopt me. I wasn't perfect enough." Caleb said this without bitterness, as if he thought this was understandable.

"It was their loss, but in a funny way it worked out for you, didn't it? You were reunited with your sister, and you're living with people who care about you."

"They don't feel like family. Not Cissy, either." Caleb paused. "Maybe I just don't know what family feels like. Did you learn that from your adoptive parents?"

Isaac wondered why Caleb had chosen *him* to open up to and supposed it was because he was an adopted child. But Isaac didn't discuss his childhood. Even Kendra only knew bits and pieces. On the other hand, he supposed he ought to be glad the boy was opening up to somebody.

"Here's the truth," he said, after moments of silently phrasing and discarding answers that put a positive spin on his life. "My adoptive family was unhealthy, and I grew up thinking I wasn't worth a lot."

"Is that why you're so interested in the family you came from?"

"My birth family?" Isaac started to say that Kendra was the one who was intrigued, but he couldn't. Her quest had become his. "I guess my grandmother reached out from the grave and pulled me into generations of people up here. I felt like I was part of something when I was standing on that hillside with you. Of course, I realize that makes no sense." He was surprised to hear the catch in his voice.

"I wish that would happen to me."

Isaac was touched. "Here's what I think. You learn to love people a little at a time. You don't worry about it. You just stay open to the possibility. You notice how they treat you and listen to what they say. Then one day you realize how much you would miss them if they vanished from your life."

"I used to think I made people vanish, so many did."

"And now?"

"It's just the way things happened. Only maybe they'll keep happening that way."

This time Isaac was surprised he knew how to answer. "There are two kinds of people who'll care about you in your life, Caleb. The ones who are paid to care, then move on, and the ones who care because they can't help themselves. Nobody pays that second kind. They do it out of love. The people who are paid, like doctors or nurses or foster parents or teachers? They know caring about you has to be temporary. That doesn't mean it isn't genuine, but they know it has to end."

"That happened a lot."

"But the second kind? Those people want the caring to last forever. Your sister falls in that category, and I think maybe the Clairbornes do, as well. And later in your life, a woman'll come along and care about you whether you're perfect or not."

They started down the ridge that would lead them to the farm.

"Is that what Kendra did?"

Isaac laughed. "You know, apparently everything you've been through has given you some insight."

"Did living with bad parents do that for *you?*"

Isaac had never thought about his life that way. Had he learned things he could use? Had those early, painful years taught him things that had made him a better person?

In the end, he had to be truthful. "I think I learned more about how not to live. And I think I'm a slow learner, anyway. It's easier for me to shut people out than to bring them into my life. Don't be that way. Start now. Let people get closer. You'll be a lot happier."

"Are there only two categories, do you think? Or maybe there's a third. People who care about you because they just like being with you? Maybe not forever, but while they can."

"I think we call those people friends."

"Then I guess you and Kendra are my friends."

"I wouldn't take 'forever' out of that mix. I hope we'll be friends a long, long time."

Caleb grinned. Isaac punched his arm. On the reticent male-bonding scale, the rating for this conversation was high.

Kendra was standing at the bottom of their trail watching them descend. She waved in welcome.

"A fox came to say hello. A big red one. And there are enough chipmunks around the foundation of the house to make me wonder where all the snakes and hawks are living. Clearly not here."

"Some Indian tribes think a fox has healing powers," Caleb said. "Maybe the fox is your totem."

"What about the chipmunks?"

"They snoop. They're nature's detectives. They want to know everything."

"Like reporters," Kendra said. "Suddenly I believe in totems."

They weren't supposed to make a fire outside an official fire pit, and *this* rule they followed. They ate the freeze-dried chicken and rice, which came with chocolate pudding, and they toasted marshmallows over the tiny flame of Isaac's camp stove for one more round of s'mores.

Since they were supposed to camp fifty yards away from any ruins, they chose a wooded area off the trail. Someone had camped there recently, which made it that much more desirable. Rocks had been cleared so that the larger tent nestled in the space. Between them, Isaac and Caleb cleared another spot a few yards away for Caleb's.

By the time the nightly rituals had been performed, Caleb pleaded exhaustion and went to bed. Between waiting for bears last night, carrying a pack and climbing the ridge, he needed sleep.

Kendra wasn't ready to go to bed. The air was cool, and the moon was nearly full.

Pine and something sweetly floral perfumed the air. She couldn't breathe enough of it to satisfy herself. It was enchanting.

"Let's go for a walk." She held out her hand to Isaac. "Let's see how the ruins look in the moonlight. Bring the lantern."

They told Caleb they would be back, and received a sleepy "uh-huh" in answer. Isaac took her hand, and they started toward what remained of the farmhouse.

"I want to hear what it was like to go to the Spurlock farm," she said, when they were away from the tents. "And I have something I want to show you. We can show Caleb in the morning."

"Do you know what Jesse saw every day of his childhood?" He didn't wait for an answer. "Pallatine Mountain."

She stopped. "You're kidding."

He tugged until she started walking again. "I knew it was close to park property. But when I researched Pallatine on maps at the beginning of our negotiations, I didn't know there was anything special about Little Lock Mountain. It was just one of a lot of smaller mountains in the Blue Ridge."

"You're sure?"

"Oh, no question. It has a distinct shape. And it's pristine. For now."

Kendra could hear the conflict in his voice. "I guess that's a view of it you never thought you'd have."

"I imagine that view was one of the hardest things to leave behind."

She waited, but he didn't say anything else. She knew he was struggling with his part in securing Pallatine for ACRE, and she hoped, when he was ready, he would share the struggle with her.

They wandered past the ruins, which were ghostly in the mist rising from the cooling earth. Shadows moved and reformed as filmy clouds slid across the moon.

"What did you want to show me?" Isaac asked.

The lantern and moon helped, but the darkness was still thick. Kendra had second thoughts. "It's a little farther. Can we see well enough to make it?"

"Just lift your feet as high as you can manage. And you take the lantern."

She led him around the house, but not in the direction of the barn. There was enough of a path that she could see the way to her find. Finally she stopped. A small iron fence was almost hidden by brambles and weeds, and saplings were taking root inside its confines. But this area was not under the guidelines of "leave no trace." Someone had been here in the recent past and had tended to it.

"The Blackburn family graveyard," she said. "I went for a little walk while you were gone, and I found it."

He didn't speak. She moved forward and felt along the top of the fence until she discovered what she was looking for. "Here's the gate."

She opened it and motioned him inside. Isaac seemed reluctant, but he followed.

"I found Leah's mother and father, your great-grandparents. There are just two little stones to mark it. They were buried side by side. Somebody chiseled their first names. Flossie and Dyer." She stopped and handed him the lantern. "Right here. Maybe Leah intended to have real headstones put up but didn't have time or money before she had to leave."

Isaac came to rest beside her. "This feels odd."

"I know."

He was silent for a time, shining the light

on the stones, then away. She waited quietly.

"Are there others?" he asked at last.

"We'd need to clear the brush to get back into the corners. I think there are at least several that aren't well marked. Maybe more. But there's something else you need to see. It's the reason I brought you here without Caleb."

"I'm glad you did."

She hadn't been sure how he would feel. "Can you see that this has been cleared and tended sometime in the past year or two?"

"It looks that way. Hikers?"

"Here's why I don't think so." She led him back the way they'd come in, then skirted the edge of the fence on the inside, stopping directly across from the place they had been. She gestured to the ground at her feet. "Shine the light right there."

He did, and a small gray marble slab glistened. Isaac squatted to get a better look. "I'll be damned," he said.

"I know. I was really taken aback when I found it." She didn't have to look to remember the inscription. *Jesse Isaac Spurlock 1911-1934.* And under that: *Birdie Florence Blackburn 1911-1934.*

Isaac traced the letters, professionally chiseled into the slab, which lay flush to the ground. Finally he got to his feet.

"Somebody knows what happened to them." Isaac's eyes met hers. "Do you think they're buried here?"

"I don't think so. Somebody put this here as a memorial, and fairly recently, at that."

"His middle name was Isaac."

Kendra wanted to touch him, but she knew better. Whatever Isaac was feeling was extraordinarily personal. "I've thought about that all afternoon. I bet your mother made that a condition of your adoption. It was a private adoption through an attorney. She could have asked for almost any conditions she wanted."

"She never even knew him."

"But she imagined him. She told Marion Claiborne that Jesse was a prince. Maybe she wanted to give you some small part of the grandfather you'd never meet."

Kendra knew the simple, intimate act connected Isaac to the mother he'd never wanted to think about. Rachel had given him away, but, like Leah, she had given him what she could.

He didn't speak for a few moments.

Kendra hesitated, then slipped her arm around his waist, and he seemed grateful for the contact.

Finally he asked the obvious question. "Who do you think put it here? I'm sure the park doesn't know. They wouldn't have allowed it."

"Someone who knows Birdie and Jesse didn't run away together, that they died back in 1934."

"Do you have any suspicions?"

"Aubrey Grayling knows more than he told me. If anyone knows who put it here, he's the one. But he won't talk to me."

"Maybe he'll talk to me." Isaac released her and led her out. "Legally, as family, I have the right to tend these graves."

"Are you going to do it?"

"I don't know."

She knew better than to push. But she suspected they would be back in the future, carrying a spade and a saw. She was glad.

As they walked back, the silence was almost oppressive. No owls hooted; even the crickets were subdued. If animals hovered in the forest, they didn't make themselves known.

Kendra shivered and rubbed her bare

arms. She realized she should have worn her windbreaker. As they neared the ruins, she broke the silence.

"You and Caleb are getting along well. You're enough alike, it's like watching brothers together."

He surprised her by taking her hand and sinking to a stone large enough to hold them both. He slung his arm over her shoulders to warm her. "He'd like that."

She was surprised he wanted to talk, and unaccountably wary. The forest seemed to be holding its breath, and now *she* was, as well. "Maybe you would like it, too. You never had one."

He looked down at her. "But I did."

Kendra didn't know what to say. Isaac wasn't forthcoming about his childhood. But at the very least, she thought he'd told her the basics.

"I had a brother for seven months," he said. "I was eight, and he was four. He was an Air Force brat, too. His parents were killed. I don't think anyone ever told me how. But my father and mother volunteered to adopt him. I don't know how these things get worked out, but one day he moved into my bedroom. His name was Davey."

She was almost afraid to ask. "What happened to him?"

"Nothing as bad as you're thinking. My father was a tyrant, but he stopped short of murdering children. Nobody buried Davey in a secret grave."

God help her, she had been thinking that very thing. She had met Isaac's father only once, and it had been one time too many.

"Davey knew what a family was supposed to be like," Isaac said. "Between the trauma of losing his real parents and the trauma of living with mine, he went from a normal little kid to a monster. It makes sense, of course."

"It does." She waited. It took Isaac some time to tell the rest.

"The colonel didn't have a lot of patience. He thought discipline was the answer, of course. But Davey had more spunk than I had, or he'd seen what good parents were like, or some combination. He refused to budge. No punishment my father could devise did the trick, and of course talking to him or showing him compassion was out of the question. So one day my father just gave him back. Said he was the devil's seed and he didn't want him in his house. I came home from school, and every trace of him was gone. My mother wanted to keep him, of course. But she couldn't stand up to the colonel. For months, I heard her crying at night."

She shivered, and not because she was still cold. "That's awful, Isaac. I'm so sorry. Why didn't you tell me this before?"

He didn't answer directly. "I'd been an only child. I wasn't sure I wanted a little brother. I didn't know what to think when I came home and found Davey was gone. I remember feeling relieved, then guilty. Horribly guilty. As if my ambivalence and the tension he'd brought with him had somehow caused his exile."

"Every kid is ambivalent about siblings. And I suspect you knew even at eight that there wasn't enough love in that house to go around. Much less enough for two children."

"For a long time after Davey disappeared, I expected to be next."

"I'm so sorry. I suspect he was the luckier. He probably went somewhere better."

He faced her. "Today I told Caleb I find it easy to shut people out of my life. It doesn't take a psychiatrist to understand why. I've overcome some of it. But there's one thing I can't get past, K.C."

She waited. Somehow she knew the real point of this story was about to unfold.

"I will never be able to adopt a child," he said.

She heard the pain behind his words, but they struck such pain in her own heart that for a moment she couldn't draw a breath. "Never?" she whispered.

He shook his head. His eyes were suspiciously moist. "The scars are too deep. They go all the way to forever. If you've been hoping . . ."

"But we know happy adoptive families. There are so many. Most adoptions are successful."

"Don't you think I know that?"

She understood then that he had given this thought, that perhaps he had been thinking about it since the moment he realized he would never father a child with her.

"You sell yourself short."

He held on to her when she tried to rise. "No. Don't you see? This would always be there. If I was angry at a child, I'd hear the colonel ranting about how I wasn't his real son, that I could never be his real child. If I was strict, I'd worry I was trying to make up for the child's unfortunate genetics. If I wasn't strict enough, I'd wonder if I was just reacting to my own upbringing. Nothing about being an adoptive parent would feel natural to me. Being a parent might have been hard with the role models I had, but I think I could have done it, maybe even well. But being an adoptive parent? There'd be a whole different layer of self-doubt, of memories and feelings I could never work through."

"Why are you bringing this up now?" She was crying. She hadn't realized it until she heard the tears in her voice.

"Because I had to. I've known it for a long time, but I just didn't know how to tell you. I think you still want to have children, and that's the only way we can do it. Then, today, I was talking to Caleb about how he was treated, about how nobody adopted him because he wasn't perfect, and I realized I can never overcome the fury I feel at the whole damn system. And you had to know."

"And is this where I'm supposed to tell you it's okay? That you're wrong, and I don't really want children? That my heart isn't in shreds because I'll never have a baby?"

"Is it?"

"What do you think?"

He framed her face and, as devastated as she was, she registered that his hands were trembling.

"I think that if there was anything I could do, I would do it. If I could give you what you want, I would."

"What *I* want? Don't you care, even a little? Doesn't it eat you up that you'll never be a father?"

"It's a decision people make all the time."

She pushed him away and stood. "Well, I didn't make it, Isaac! It was made for me. And now you're telling me I can adopt kids or I can have you, take my choice. But either way, my infertility is no big deal to you, the way having kids is no big deal. How many times have you pointed out that they'd get in the way? Maybe in the long run you're relieved I can't have them and you can't adopt them!"

He grabbed her before she fled. "You want the truth?"

"I thought I got the truth."

"Yes, I want children! I want my own child,

in my arms, with my eyes and your nose and our genes. Together. I want to turn back the clock so all the things that went wrong for you didn't happen. I want to turn it back so I had adoptive parents who adored me. I want to stand by you in labor and watch our children being born. And what good does it do to tell you any of that? Does it change anything? Because none of it's ever going to happen!"

She stared at him. It changed everything, and Isaac didn't, couldn't, see it. Knowing this altered every breath she would take for the rest of her life.

"*You* can have children," she said. "You can find someone else to have them with."

He pulled her close. "Didn't you hear me? I want *our* children. Together. I have from the first. We put it off. I thought we had time. But I've always, *always* wanted them. I was just waiting until it was right."

"It's never going to be right."

"I know. I know." He held her tighter. "I want to make it right. And I can't."

She began to sob in earnest. And she knew, as his arms tightened around her, that Isaac was crying, too.

CHAPTER TWENTY-NINE

On the first morning after Isaac returned to D.C., Kendra awakened with a sense of loss. She missed him in a way she never had before. Until now, she hadn't been lonely in Toms Brook; the void left by Isaac's absence was new. They had lived together for years, unable to share their deepest feelings, but now that the dam had broken, she knew their marriage had changed forever.

For the next week she kept herself busy to avoid the echoing emptiness of the cabin. And searching for Daniel Flaherty kept her busiest of all.

According to the *Washington Post,* Daniel Flaherty had died in Florida in 1978, definitely not in Lock Hollow. The obituary stated Mr. Flaherty had retired from government service in 1960 and moved to Bradenton. He had been survived by his wife of sixty years and two sons, who asked that in lieu of flowers, donations be made to the American Red Cross. A private Mass had been held in Alexandria, where Mrs. Flaherty and her sons resided.

Clearly Daniel was now unavailable for comment. Which was why, on the Saturday afternoon after the camping trip, Kendra was on her way to Vienna, Virginia, to talk to Daniel's assistant, Charlie Thompkins.

Since the morning when Sandy, Kendra's friend and *Post* colleague, had e-mailed her a copy of Daniel's obituary, Kendra had pondered the implications of those brief sentences. It seemed that the Flahertys' marriage—which would have been well under way when Daniel and Leah were having their evening trysts—had not ended happily. Daniel died in Florida, while his wife was living in Virginia.

There was little hope that the wife was still alive, nor did Kendra have any desire to contact her. She briefly considered, then abandoned, the possibility of finding his sons. Even if Daniel had told them stories about his months in the mountains, it seemed unlikely that he had also recounted the story of his relationship with one Leah Blackburn.

Instead, she did a Google search for the younger Charles Thompkins, throwing in terms like "Shenandoah" and "surveyor" when the first results were, as expected, overwhelming. Gradually she narrowed the search until she came to a recap of an article from the magazine *America's Civil War,* about a Charles Thompkins of Vienna, an amateur historian whose area of interest and expertise was the Civil War as played out in Virginia's Blue Ridge mountains. The recap went on to say that "Charlie" had gotten interested in the subject as a teenager when he helped survey property for the Shenandoah National Park and discovered numerous artifacts.

Kendra had headed straight to the telephone.

Today she had an appointment to meet Thompkins, who lived with his oldest son. Vienna was in northern Virginia, not far from the District, and she had a second reason to make the trip. Last night, on the telephone, she had promised Isaac that she would have dinner with him in a restaurant they had always enjoyed in Arlington. Afterward, if she was still feeling brave enough, she planned to make her first trip into the city to attend an ACRE party and spend the night in their condo. For the occasion, she was wearing the clothes she had worn home from the hospital.

So far, she wasn't enjoying the trip into the city, but neither was she paralyzed with fear. Summer weekends were busy on I-81 and I-66, as vacationers enjoyed the area's historic sites. The traffic required all her attention. By the time she took the second Vienna exit, her hands were numb from gripping the wheel—but not trembling from fear.

Vienna had wide streets, bordered by well-maintained, flourishing lawns. Pink petunias and white impatiens lined flowerbeds, and hostas languished under tall shade trees. Clearly northern Virginia hadn't seen the drought that had plagued the Valley. She found the right house with no difficulty. The redbrick colonial was at the end of a cul-de-sac. The mailbox sported a vinyl decal of a Canada goose in flight.

The man who answered the door had not been sixteen for a very long time. He was nearly bald, and thin enough to worry her.

But his face lit up when she introduced herself.

Charlie ushered her inside. "I'm alone for the afternoon. Would you like to see my collection of artifacts?"

Kendra had a feeling that if she declined, the interview would go downhill quickly. She spent the next fifteen minutes sipping cola and genuinely enjoying the collection. He had firearms and ammunition—some of which he had picked up on his travels across the mountains—belts and belt buckles, framed photographs, medals and fading ribbons. The small study where they were displayed was a mini-museum.

"All from Virginia," he said. "And what's now the park? That was my favorite place. Not everybody up there favored the South, you know. Some of those mountain people were for the Union, and some of the Valley's Germans, too."

"I wanted to talk to you about the park," she said, sensing her opportunity. "Do you have time?"

"You say you're with the *Post?*" He led her to a red velvet wing chair in an oppressively formal living room.

"I am, but this is personal."

He seated himself across from her. "So what can I tell you?"

As briefly as she could, she explained Isaac's story. Charlie had dark, intense eyes, and it was clear he was following every word with interest.

"I remember her," he said when Kendra finished. "Oh, yes, Leah Spurlock. She wasn't much older than me, and I was just a kid. I was supposed to be working with the Civilian Conservation Corps, but I'd done some surveying with my daddy down near Fredericksburg, and when they found that out, they put me to work helping Daniel."

"I guess both you and Leah grew up fast."

"I could hardly say a word around her. She had one of those pure oval faces, like a Renaissance Madonna, and she had a way of carrying herself, like a queen. At least that's how it seemed to me."

"How did it seem to Daniel Flaherty, do you suppose?"

"You sound like you have suspicions."

Kendra kept it simple. "There are rumors."

"Rumors about her and Daniel." It wasn't a question. "You have to understand Daniel, first."

She sat back, content they were on track. "Tell me."

Charlie appeared to choose his words carefully. "First, he was a married man. But he didn't wear a ring, and he sure never let on he was married when he was out in the field. He figured that what he did when he was off at work wouldn't hurt anybody. And I'm not just . . . what's the word . . . extrapolating? He used to lecture me when we were camping out. Like it was a lesson I ought to learn, right along with shaving acres off parcels and calling valuable pastureland a rocky hillside to make himself look good. He taught me that, too."

Kendra had known a number of men like Daniel. She doubted young Leah had known any until she met him. "I found his obituary. I did the math and calculated he was married when he met Leah."

"Daniel was a Catholic. In those days, divorce wasn't in the cards. But I don't think he lived with his wife for much more time than it took to get her pregnant twice. He liked acting free, even if he wasn't."

"You're painting the picture of a sociopath."

He considered. "No, I think he had his

own moral code. Like a lot of folks, he thought the people up in those mountains would be better off somewhere else, so he didn't mind cheating them a little. He figured the government was going to do enough as it was. I guess he also figured as long as he treated women well enough when he was with them, he hadn't hurt anybody. It wasn't like he had dozens, but he had a way of making them think they were special. He made them think he cared. And the darn thing was, I think he did, a little."

He paused. "Particularly about Leah Spurlock. He even found land and a house for her—got it for the back taxes, of course, but it was still prime land."

Kendra tilted her head to encourage him. She hated to interrupt the flow.

"Maybe it turned out okay, though. Because in the end, Leah hurt Daniel more than he hurt her. She wasn't very sophisticated, but she was nobody's fool. When she realized what Daniel really was and what he expected from her, she rejected him. Simple as that. Leah Spurlock was the one who got away, if you don't mind a fishing metaphor. And I just bet Daniel never recovered."

"This is getting interesting," Kendra said. "Do you have time to give me the details?"

He smiled, clearly thrilled to be asked.

Blackburn Farm
Lock Hollow, Virginia
May 15, 1934

Dear Puss,

It is no wonder your insides are upset, what with the news from home these days. I know your daddy is setting his mind toward leaving, though he is not packing. I still hope the lawyer can help, but can one man stop a lightning bolt just by waving his arms at a thundercloud?

I have included some pills made of the root of goldenseal ground up fine. You will find this helps a little. What would help more would be for things to be the way they were. That would help Jesse and me, too.

The friend who wishes you were here
and is also glad you are gone,
Leah Spurlock

After the night at the woodpile, Leah and Jesse stopped speaking to each other. Birdie was their intermediary, carrying messages as if nothing had happened. She seemed oblivious to the tension in the house and went about her chores with smiles for both of them. To escape the silence, most nights Leah found excuses to go outside when she thought Daniel might be waiting for her. Her absences drew no comment from her husband, but even if Jesse had suspicions, they were unfounded. Daniel was never there.

Then, after two weeks, when she was feeling sadder than she had since the deaths of her parents, she found him waiting under the hickory trees with a gift.

Daniel moved out of the shadows into the starlight to greet her. She was so surprised, she clapped her hand over her lips to stifle a cry.

"I was afraid you wouldn't be here," he said in a near whisper. "I've been away, and I thought you probably gave up on me." He held out a parcel wrapped in brown paper. "I brought you something to sweeten your days."

She took the parcel, searching his face. "What is it?"

"Nothing much. Just something I thought you might like."

She untied the string and spread the paper. Inside was a collection of nickel candy. A peanut butter and molasses Mary Jane bar, a Snickers bar, Milk Duds, Bit-O-Honey. She hadn't seen so much candy in one place except at Grayling's Store.

"For me?"

"Your life has had too many sour moments."

She laughed softly. Having someone think of *her* for a change was new and seductive. "Where did it all come from?"

"I had meetings down in Harrisonburg. That's where I've been."

She thought how much Jesse and Birdie would enjoy this treat, but that pleasure was fleeting. How could she share the candy, considering where it had come from? She could hardly tell her husband that she had been meeting a man in secret and he had given her this gift.

Until this moment, she hadn't dwelled on the problems she was creating by meeting Daniel. When guilt nibbled, she told herself she deserved moments with someone who understood what she was going through. There was no harm unless she meant harm. Now, with the moonlight glinting off the colorful wrappers, she realized that harm could be caused unintentionally, as well.

She thrust the package back at him. "You know I can't take anything from you."

He clasped his hands behind his back. "It's yours now. Don't you deserve a little pleasure? You take care of everybody. Who takes care of you?"

Reluctantly, she rewrapped the candy and took her time tying the knot. She had never thought of her life quite that way, but of course, that was what troubled her so. Although Birdie tried valiantly, she still required looking after, and would until the end of her days. And Jesse? Jesse had given up on life and on her. He had resumed most of his chores, but she didn't know how long that would last. She was losing her beloved home, and her husband seemed lost to her already.

She hadn't realized that Daniel had moved closer, but suddenly his fingers rested under her chin, and he tilted her head so she was looking at him.

"You're a lovely young woman. You may not feel it's true right now, but you have a good life ahead of you. And you have choices. Maybe your husband plans to stay here and fight 'til the last, but there's no reason you should be caught up in that. You're very easy to love. A man who doesn't love you is crazy." He brushed a finger gently along her jaw.

One tear trickled down her cheek. "Where would I go?"

"I have a place in mind."

His touch felt so good. Having someone understand her feelings and worry about them felt even better. At the same time, her heart beat a frantic warning. She felt a pull toward Daniel Flaherty that could become as hard to resist as the pull of the earth at her feet. It was possible to feel too good, to lose the power of discernment. And she felt that moment quickly approaching.

"Don't cry," he said softly. Then he moved closer and kissed away her tear.

She wasn't surprised. For a moment she stood there as his lips traveled toward hers. Then, before his mouth reached hers, she stepped back just far enough that he dropped his hand and his head lifted.

"Where?" she asked, forcing the conversation back to what he'd said a moment ago.

He smiled, but not like a man who has been thwarted or even warned. "While I was away, I found some land in the Valley, above the North Fork of the Shenandoah River but high enough it won't flood. With the payment the government will give you for this farm, you can have the land, and some money to start over besides."

"But where would we live?"

"There's a cabin. Not much to look at, but it could be added to. Someday you could build a better house."

"You found it for me?"

"I heard about it and went to see it. I thought of you when I did. My own home's not so far that I couldn't look in on you . . . to be sure you adjust."

"Jesse will have no part of it. I can tell you that without asking."

"Then perhaps you need to consider a future without him."

She couldn't. Thinking of a life without Jesse, even a Jesse who wasn't talking to her anymore, was like thinking of one without stars or sun. When she tried to imagine it, the world went dark.

She gazed down at the ground. "I had a dream last night. I dreamed he was standing on the roof of the barn with a shotgun. Crows were flying at him, flocks of crows like nothing you'd ever want to see. I shouted and shouted, but Jesse, well, he wouldn't get down. And every time he took a shot, nothing came out of that shotgun but . . ." She shook her head, the dream gripping her again.

"What?"

"Blood." She looked up. "Blood came a-running out of those barrels. I told my sister the dream before breakfast. Birdie reckons if you do that, a dream won't come true."

"It's the other way around. If you tell a dream before breakfast, it *will* come true."

She was upset enough, off balance enough, to be worried that Birdie, who lived her life by signs and superstitions, had gotten this wrong. The worry must have shown in her face, because Daniel put his hands on her arms.

"It's just a silly superstition. But here's something that is true. There'll be no future with your husband if he tries to stay here. The government won't tolerate resistance. So far people have left peacefully, but everyone is prepared in case it doesn't always go that way."

"They would shoot us on our own land?"

"It's not yours anymore. It's gone. But this land on the river can be yours forever."

"Two women alone?"

"Perhaps you wouldn't always be alone, Leah."

His meaning was clear. He wanted to be with her. They could live on the river together, and if she divorced Jesse, or he died defending what was his by right if not by law, then one day she and Daniel would marry.

She held out the candy, but he shook his head.

"I brought it all that way for you. It wouldn't be right to take it back."

He pulled her closer. She resisted only a little. Her limbs were heavy; her shoes had soles of lead. He smiled down at her.

"It's hard for me to watch you being treated so badly and to see you worrying so much that you have those awful dreams. You deserve a lot more. When was the last time anyone was good to you? Can you tell me?"

She gave one shake of her head. He sighed, as if he had been afraid of that. His arms tightened around her.

"I want to be good to you."

This time, when his lips sought hers, she didn't deny him.

Behind her, from the direction of the house, the dogs began to bark. Then, as if he was closer than he was, Jesse's voice drifted toward them as he tried to silence the animals.

A door slammed. Leah jumped back, her eyes wide, her lips tingling. "I have to go."

"Tomorrow night, then."

She tucked the parcel under her arm and, without a backward glance, started toward the house. But once Daniel was out of sight, she took a detour to the farmyard and fed the wrapped candy, bar by bar, to the hogs.

CHAPTER THIRTY

To make her trip into the city easier, Isaac had suggested that Kendra park in the driveway of an ACRE colleague who lived near the Metro in Arlington. That way, when she was ready to head back to the cabin, she could take the Metro to her car and never have to brave D.C. traffic.

Of course, Arlington's traffic was nearly as bad. Kendra was glad when she finally found the house on a quiet street in the Lyon Park neighborhood, not far from the restaurant where they planned to have dinner. She parked, then gathered her purse and the overnight bag she had packed. The irony wasn't lost on her. She was packing for a weekend in her own home.

Although she'd gotten to Arlington fifteen minutes early, Isaac was already waiting.

Her undemonstrative husband scooped her into his arms and kissed her before she could walk back to his Prius to stow her bag. She hugged him back.

"It's so good to see you here." He pushed her hair back from her face. "You made the drive okay?"

"I made the drive fine. But have you noticed all the maniacs on the roads?"

"You used to be one of them. You were a take-no-prisoners maniac."

"Well, I'm a recovering maniac now." She smiled at him, glad from the tips of her toes to be with him again. "You look great. Who picked out that shirt?" It was a subtle earth-tone plaid, worn with a nubby linen jacket and a gold tie. The combination made his eyes look even an even darker brown.

"You did."

"I have the best taste."

Reluctantly, he released her; then he took the suitcase, and, arms around each other's waists, they walked to his car. He put her bag in the backseat and hit the lock.

"Since we're early, why don't I show you something before we head for the restaurant."

"Like what?"

"Barry's house."

Barry was ACRE's staff attorney. Kendra hadn't paid much attention to her surroundings except to find the right street and number, but now she turned to look at the house in question. "Oh, nice," she said with real appreciation. "Wow. But what's to see from here?"

"He's out of town, and I promised I'd check on it in exchange for the use of his driveway."

She gladly followed him up a blue flagstone walkway lined with blooming perennials in asymmetrical curving borders. The house was charming, a shingled Craftsman-style bungalow, probably built sometime in the 1920s. It had a deep front porch and a side-gabled second story. It looked perfectly at home on a street of eclectic older houses, all well kept up.

"I wonder how he found this little gem," she said.

"It was a fixer-upper. And he paid a lot of attention to detail in his renovations. I thought you'd enjoy seeing it."

Kendra fell in love the moment she stepped through the door. The house was small, but perfect in every way. Golden oak floors, new wood frame windows, beautifully executed crown molding, a kitchen with granite counter tops and stainless steel appliances. She wandered as Isaac watered a Christmas cactus. There was a small oak-paneled study, a cozy living room lined with bookshelves, a powder room off the kitchen. A family room had been added in the back, sporting a window wall that looked over a stone patio and a tiny yard enclosed with a privacy fence.

"Do you think he'd care if I peeked at the second floor?" she asked.

"Go ahead. I'll be up in a minute."

Upstairs, she wandered, admiring smallish bedrooms and a newly redone bathroom. Then she came to the master suite. It had a loftier version of the family-room view, with windows that framed the attractive neighborhood behind them and a bathroom worthy of hours in the garden tub.

"Barry has excellent taste," Kendra said, when Isaac joined her. "I could move right in here and be supremely contented."

"Well, that's good, because you can, if you want to."

She hadn't suspected. "Barry's selling?"

His smile dipped just a fraction, but she

knew him too well not to note it. "We're experiencing a staff exodus, and unfortunately, he's one who's leaving. He took a job out in Seattle. He's had the house professionally appraised. If we pay his asking price, he won't get a Realtor. It's not cheap, but we'll make a nice profit when we sell the condo. We can swing it."

"But you like living in the city."

"If we're going to keep the Rug and the Rascal, we can't stay there. On the other hand, they'd be perfectly happy in this yard. It means leaving earlier for work in the mornings, but there's a little community center around the corner with all kinds of neighborhood activities, and Clarendon's within walking distance, for restaurants and fun."

Isaac had done his homework and had prepared the sales pitch. Kendra didn't know what to say. There were wonderful neighborhoods right in the city. In fact, Foggy Bottom was one of them. But he knew that a little extra distance from the scene of the crime would serve her well as she continued to recover. She was already in love with the house and the neighborhood.

"You're doing this for me." She put her arm around his waist. "Don't deny it."

"Sure, and for the four-leggeds. And so I'll have a wife again." He leaned his head against hers. "And because I need something in my life besides work and more work. And because this makes the drive to the Valley a little shorter. It's not so much house we can't manage both it and the house there."

"When do we have to let Barry know?"

"He's at a training session. He said we could tell him in two weeks when he gets back. He's not worried. It will sell like that." He snapped his fingers. "But I've indicated a strong interest."

This time, she thought, as perfect as it was, she wouldn't buy the furniture. Not even if Barry was selling it to make moving to the West Coast easier. She would paint the walls her own colors, carefully select bright accent rugs for the beautiful wood floors, choose a mix of antiques and reproductions to highlight the architecture and historical period.

If they bought it.

"We're lucky to have some time." She lifted on tiptoe and kissed him. "No matter what happens, thank you for thinking of this."

Over Vietnamese food in nearby Clarendon, a neighborhood replete with ethnic restaurants and charm, Isaac listened as Kendra told him what she had learned from Charlie. As the restaurant filled to overflowing, he watched her for signs of stress and saw nothing to alarm him. She was doing well. Their lives might get back to normal soon.

He no longer knew what that meant.

She finished her story. "Charlie said that at the end, your grandmother rejected Daniel, but he wasn't able to go into much detail. His son and family came home, and I took off to meet you. At least now we know Daniel Flaherty wasn't one of the bodies in that cave."

"There would have been reports of an official missing in the mountains. You'd have discovered that in your research."

"I know, but this whole thing is so strange, I'm prepared for almost anything." She smiled at him over the remnants of her green papaya salad.

"What's that smile about?"

"I'm just happy being here, being with you, enjoying thoughts of how the night will end."

He especially liked that last part, too. It was almost enough to make him spill the remaining drops of soup. "And going back to the condo?"

"I'm even looking forward to that. Maybe it will be a farewell trip."

He knew better than to follow up too closely. Kendra needed time to think about Barry's house. Theoretically, they should even look at real estate in more neighborhoods to compare. But he had a feeling they weren't going to bother.

"So tell me about the party," she said.

Their entrées came. Chicken with lemongrass and curry for her. Beef with eggplant for him. He figured that even if the house wasn't perfect, living this close to some of the best Vietnamese restaurants in the region would convince her to move here.

He told her who would be at the party and warned her that there might be tension. But when she asked for details, he refused. "I want you to give me your unbiased assessment."

They chatted about everything except the

house and his job. Kendra carried the bulk of the conversation. Caleb was dog-sitting. He had shown her the photos he'd taken on their camping trip, and she thought they were exceptionally good. He had promised to e-mail them to Isaac.

She had caught Ten playing with Dusty, and when she came back through the room ten minutes later, the two were curled up within a foot of each other, sleeping it off.

The tomatoes she had planted in Leah's garden plot were growing so fast she'd already had to put wire cages around them.

He listened to the recital of quiet days and small pleasures, and felt a stab of envy. He wondered if he had always worked hard because he was afraid that if his life lay fallow, even briefly, he wouldn't like what he discovered about himself.

He paid the bill, and they walked to their car. He was surprised at how quickly they got into the city and the historic Foxhall neighborhood near Georgetown, where Dennis had bought an expansive Tudor. Even though Dennis had hired two valets, Isaac found a place on his own and parked on the street. He came around to open Kendra's door.

"He certainly spared no expense," he said.

"You mean the hired help or the house? What on earth does he get paid?"

"The board wanted him badly."

They strolled up the walkway, hand in hand—his idea. A pretty young woman, in black pants and a starched white shirt and bow tie, let them in.

Kendra was swept up in a flurry of welcomes. It was the first time the ACRE staff had seen her since the carjacking, and she was immediately wrapped in good wishes. A caterer in the bow tie uniform of the evening handed Isaac a glass of champagne. Another offered a selection of desserts from a black lacquered tray.

He wandered through the crowd, chatting with colleagues and board members. Although he was congratulated repeatedly for his work on securing Pallatine Mountain, he discovered it was hard to be gracious. Pallatine was like a lump in his throat, and he couldn't clear it away.

Dennis saw Isaac and motioned for him to come to the corner of the formal dining room, where he stood with another man. Light illuminating a side garden filtered in through multipaned leaded-glass windows. The table held an array of finger foods, and a trio of elaborate cheesecakes garnished with candied roses and violets.

"Isaac, do you know Miles Wainwright, deputy secretary of the Department of the Interior?"

Isaac didn't. A nondescript man in his late fifties, Wainwright wore the ubiquitous dark suit, pastel shirt and striped tie of every D.C. bureaucrat. Isaac shook hands and listened as Dennis regaled the deputy secretary with praise for Isaac's contributions. When Wainwright was called away to meet someone else, Dennis turned to Isaac.

"He's a good connection for your future."

Isaac snagged a second flute of champagne. "I hear he knows how to work the administration to get things done."

"Stick with me and you'll make all the contacts you need. I know you won't be with us forever, but when it's time for you to move on, I can make sure you move right into a job you want."

Dennis was not short on ego, but he wasn't exaggerating by much. He had worked his way to the top in both the private sector and government, and his contacts were the major reason ACRE's board paid him so extravagantly.

"I like giving good recommendations," Dennis said. "They're rare enough. I've had to give a few real stinkers in my time. I can't recommend someone who's not a team player."

Isaac knew a warning when he heard one. The introduction to Wainwright, the pep talk, and now the stiletto slipped silently between the ribs. He was tempted to ask Dennis just to spit out what he wanted. But he *was* too much of a team player to be rude.

"I've always given any team I'm in sync with my all," Isaac said carefully.

"You gave your all with Pallatine. We all know that. It was a coup for you and your assistant. What's her name? Holly? No, Heather."

"Heather Griswold."

"It's too bad she's leaving. And under a cloud."

For a moment Isaac thought he'd heard Dennis wrong. "Heather's leaving?"

Dennis raised an eyebrow. "I'm surprised you don't know."

"So am I. What do you mean, under a cloud?"

"She wrote to the board about the construction on Pallatine. Of course they'd approved it themselves, so there was no real point to her letter. But it created a flurry when we needed calm. If she hadn't resigned, I probably would have fired her."

Isaac wondered when Heather had done this. A bigger question was why she hadn't come to him first, and that answer wasn't hard to find. Heather believed that once Isaac's mind was made up, he moved forward. There was no room for doubt. She had told him as much.

"Heather's an idealist," Isaac said. "We need idealists and hard workers. I'm sorry she's leaving."

Dennis clapped him on the back as if they were golf buddies. "We'll find somebody who's able to keep the big picture in front of them. Pallatine is a good thing. Better us than someone else, right?"

Isaac wondered. Would other environmental organizations capable of this kind of purchase have taken the easy way out? Or would they have shopped more carefully for a better solution? Dennis had decided to sell portions of Pallatine to ACRE's largest contributors so that everyone could be happy.

Everyone except Gary Forsythe, the man who was selling them the land so that it would be protected and preserved for all time.

Everyone except Isaac Taylor, whose family had, for generations, looked over Pallatine Mountain, and whose days had been shaped by that pristine view.

"Do you happen to know where Heather's going?" Isaac wished she had consulted with him before she made the move. Heather was too talented to waste her skills.

"Some grassroots group. From what I can tell, she'll be living on beans and singing old Pete Seeger songs." Dennis dismissed more talk of Heather with a wave of his hand. "Pallatine is set to go. We'll be signing the papers next week. Would you like to be there?"

"Does Mr. Forsythe know your plans for financing?"

"There's nothing in the paperwork that requires us to reveal our plans. We'll be meeting the standards that were set and then some. How we're paying for the land purchase isn't relevant to him."

The last sentence was an out-and-out lie. How ACRE was paying was more than relevant. Isaac knew it could change the entire face of the transaction.

"You don't plan to tell him what we're doing?" Isaac said.

"Actually, I think he needs to know. I don't want him finding out later and going to the press. We need to explain it carefully after all the documents are signed." Dennis paused a heartbeat. "*You* need to explain it."

"Me?"

"You're the one he trusts. If you explain it carefully and objectively, get him to understand it was the only way to really protect the mountain, then we'll short-circuit future trouble."

Despite a powerful urge to follow in Heather's footsteps, Isaac draped a hand over a nearby chair to keep himself tethered to the conversation. "I would rather not. I'm ambivalent about this, Dennis. And it'll show."

"Well, we all have ambivalence. I'd like to buy up every piece of wilderness in the whole wide world and keep it exactly the way it is. But that's not the way things work.

You know that better than anyone else on our staff."

Isaac ignored the left-handed flattery. "My ambivalence is twofold. One, that we're going to allow construction where there shouldn't be any. And two, that we're not being up front with Mr. Forsythe."

Dennis smiled sadly. "If we don't do it the way we're planning, it won't get done. Developers will move in."

"I'd like to look for alternatives."

"We have. They don't exist. End of story."

Isaac doubted this. He suspected that in the rush to please significant donors, better options had been overlooked.

"You'll talk to Forsythe?" Dennis prompted.

Isaac gave a curt nod.

Dennis left to mingle with his guests.

Kendra lay beside her husband in the bed they had shared for so many years. Their lovemaking had been tender and fulfilling. But despite Isaac's effort to stay in the moment, she had sensed a certain preoccupation.

Now she propped her head on her elbow and gazed down at him.

"It's the party, isn't it."

"What?"

"Whatever's on your mind."

He tried a smile that wasn't quite convincing. "Are you complaining?"

"Not on your life. But let me in. What's going on in that head of yours?"

He pulled her into the crook of his arm. "What were your impressions tonight?"

"Of your performance a few minutes ago?"

He ruffled her curls in answer.

She grew serious. "People didn't want to be there. They were just putting in time. That's not a champagne and truffles crowd—at least, not the staff. The whole thing was an example of how disconnected Dennis is from the people he works with."

"I think Dennis wants to see a lot of the staff move on. Apparently Heather got the hint."

"Your Heather?"

"What a way to put it. But yes, my assistant Heather."

"Did you hear that tonight?"

"From the man himself."

Kendra listened as he told her what Dennis had said. She felt herself growing infuriated, until she exploded.

"What can you possibly say to Mr. Forsythe to make him think it's fine to build estates on property he sold you specifically so you would protect it!"

"I don't know, but I'll have to think of something."

She propped herself up again. "Or not."

"Do you know any Pete Seeger songs?"

"Did I miss something?"

"Dennis said Heather will be eating beans and singing Pete Seeger at her new job. In other words, she's taken a giant step backward."

"Maybe she's taking a giant step toward a feeling of self-worth."

"Good for her. But if she wants to make a difference, then she's made a bad decision."

"So you're saying that to make a difference you have to compromise your ideals, no matter how bad you feel about it? That logic trumps the heart?"

He turned to face her. "Maybe I don't have a lot of Jesse Spurlock in me. I'm not willing to stand in front of the bulldozers when they tear into Pallatine. I understand the words 'lost cause.' I've done what I can to save most of it. Now I have to move on."

She lay back and stared at the ceiling.

"What?" he said at last. "I can hear you thinking. I just can't make out the words."

"What have the past months been about, Isaac?"

"Retreat." He said it so quickly it was clearly something he'd considered.

"For me or for you?"

"Mostly for you."

"And what does that mean? Did I retreat to lick my wounds?"

"I feel like I'm taking a quiz I have no chance to pass."

"I'll tell you. I didn't escape. I've never been as connected to my life as I am now."

"Wait until you start back to work. Maybe you've forgotten what it's like in a corporate environment, how you have to make decisions every minute and hope they're right, because you have to move on to the next one whether they are or not."

"I'm cutting my hours. I'll have time to consider what I do. I'm not going to work full-time."

He didn't answer. She could feel the tension. "I've already broached it with my boss. I want some free time to write a book about the historical use of eminent domain and the effect it has on the lives of everyone involved. Because I can't live for my work and still remember who I am. There are people who can, but I'm not one of them. And I don't want to make decisions the way you claim you have to."

She rolled over to face him. "I don't want to be you, Isaac. Never again."

She knew by his expression that she'd hurt him.

"You don't want *me* to be me, either," he said.

She heard the anger, but she couldn't back off. "No, I want you to follow your heart. Look at what's happening at ACRE. People are leaving. People are being asked to do things they know are wrong. All in the name of saving the earth? Well, the end doesn't justify the means. I think you were given a gift when you went to the Spurlock farm and saw Pallatine in the distance. A gift, a vision. I think, if you want it badly enough, you can find a way to save it and save yourself while you're at it."

"And lose my job, and all hope of ever being in a position of authority where I really can make a difference."

"Someday you're going to be forced to

look back on the *way* you made a difference. Will it be worth it?"

The anger in his voice was replaced by ice. "You know, this is beginning to sound like a lecture, or an ultimatum."

"Not an ultimatum, a crossroads."

He sat up and swung his legs over the side. "What does that mean?"

"It means I've changed. Maybe you and I will never have children, but we can surround ourselves with people we love. And maybe we'll never get to the top of our career ladders, but whatever rung we stand on, we can know we got there without stepping on anybody to do it. Those are the things that are important to me. Not where I'm heading, but how I make the journey. I learned that from your grandmother."

"Oh, some role model she was."

"I think Leah wanted you to know her story and learn from her mistakes. She and Jesse let the removal rule their lives. They let it separate them. Being forced to leave the mountains was the first great sorrow of their young lives, and it destroyed them. They could have made peace with their future if they had just realized that it wasn't staying on the farm that mattered most.

They could have started over. *We* can start over."

He made to stand, but she rested her fingertips on his arm to stop him. "Don't you have to figure out what's really important, too?"

"My job *is* important."

"Not if it separates you from the man inside you."

"I'm going for a walk."

This time she didn't try to stop him. Instead, after he dressed and the front door closed, she lay awake and thought of a night so much like this one when, in a fit of anger, she, and not Isaac, had traded the security of the condo for dark city streets.

And all the changes that simple act had wrought.

CHAPTER THIRTY-ONE

On Monday and Tuesday, Isaac was the perfect team player. He went through all the motions, meeting with his staff to gauge their rising stress levels, listening carefully, offering advice and pep talks that seemed to be the words of a heretofore unknown alter ego. He worked until the city was dark, editing grant proposals, answering mail and phone calls, making arrangements to speak at professional conferences. By Tuesday evening, he thought he was beginning to gain some control over his feelings of unease, some sense that he could fix what was wrong at ACRE with patience and creativity.

Then Heather walked into his office.

He was more than surprised to see her. He had expected her to return next week to clean out her desk and say goodbye, and he had decided not to discuss her reasons for moving on. Heather was an adult, an extremely competent one, and her reasons for this decision were bound to be good. The right to question her was no longer his.

"Exactly what's going on?" he asked, as his carefully planned speech flew out the window behind him, which was open to catch the evening breeze. "You resigned without even talking to me? You went to the board without discussing that, either?"

"I'm here now. I hoped I'd catch you alone to say goodbye."

He got to his feet and motioned to a chair; then he took the one beside her, so he would feel less like a teacher calling a student on the carpet. "I don't know how I'm going to fill the hole you're leaving."

"Me, either." She smiled, but she looked wary.

"The worst part's that you did all this without my knowledge."

"Isaac, I considered coming to you. In the end, I knew it wouldn't make a difference. Your eye's on the big picture. My complaints would have been a flicker."

There was nothing to argue about. He

saw that clearly. She was leaving because there was no longer room here for personal idealism. No room for the small but important actions that ACRE had been known for. No place to be heard and taken seriously. She didn't want to work for a bureaucracy. In Heather's mind, the big picture was made up of thousands of frames flashing by, and those mercurial images were what concerned her. The little triumphs, the sense that she had made a difference.

"Where are you going?" he asked instead.

She named a small organization that was nothing more than a blip on his radar screen. Dennis hadn't been far off in his description.

He got to his feet, because there was really nothing else he could say. "They'll be lucky to have you." He stuck out his hand.

She didn't take it. "You may not want to do that."

He raised a brow in question.

"If you don't go to Gary Forsythe and explain what's happening here and what ACRE intends to do on Pallatine, I will."

"Dennis already asked me to do it."

"When?"

That, of course, was the sticking point. Honesty after the fact. A caboose carrying what was left of their integrity.

"You need to think this over," she said, when the answer was clear from his silence. "But I'm willing to do the dirty work as a parting gesture of my affection. I think you want Mr. Forsythe to know, but you don't want to jeopardize your position here."

"And if he pulls the deal and developers move in? How will you feel?"

"I'll feel that ACRE didn't do enough. And I won't blame him or the developers."

Isaac didn't ask her to reconsider. He knew he ought to report Heather's intended conversation with Forsythe to Dennis, but he wasn't going to. He was partially relieved that the decision and the repercussions were no longer his. And some larger part wondered what kind of man thought that way.

He walked her to his office door. "The closing's next week."

"I have all the information." She faced him. "You know, you're a good man. But you're heading somewhere you don't want to go." She rose on tiptoe to kiss his cheek; then she disappeared into the corridor.

* * *

Jesse Spurlock had headed somewhere he didn't want to go. In his quest to keep his home, Jesse had refused to look at anything else that was happening. Isaac wondered if tunnel vision was an inheritable trait. He supposed he might find out. Aubrey Grayling had agreed to see him.

On Wednesday morning, Isaac had awakened to the realization that he was, as Kendra had said, at a crossroads. Barely taking the time to call and cancel the day's appointments, he began the trip to Gainesville, where Aubrey lived with his son and granddaughter Jennifer. When he had called to ask if he could visit, Jennifer hadn't sounded surprised.

Almost as if she had been expecting his call.

The drive took a little less than an hour. Gainesville was just close enough to the city to be a bedroom community. Isaac hadn't been in the vicinity in more than a year, but he was stunned at how quickly it had grown from sleepy country town to suburb.

He found the Graylings' house without difficulty and was glad to discover it was still surrounded by farmland. He hoped Aubrey would not have to watch his world change for the worse yet again.

Jennifer Grayling, a perky blonde, ushered him inside. The house was tidy and probably prefabricated. Someone had built a front porch and added a sunroom, and the views of cornfields and cows were somehow reassuring.

"Paw-paw's getting ready," she said. "I have fresh tea."

He followed her to the kitchen, with its yellow walls and white speckled counters adorned with ceramic vegetable canisters. One charged second passed, and he was a boy standing in one of the many kitchens of his childhood, one that had looked much like this one. He recalled, for the first time in too many years, the way his mother had always made sure there were homemade cookies waiting in a candy-apple red canister beside the kitchen door. No matter where they lived, no matter the size or state of the kitchen. Cookies had been one of the safe ways she could show her affection. And there had been others.

"You must like these silly curtains," Jennifer said. "You're smiling."

He focused on the window over the sink.

The curtains were fading patchwork, blocks of vegetable prints with human faces. He cleared his throat. "They're definitely not like any I've seen."

"My mother made them. She's gone now. I can't bear to take them down."

Stored somewhere in a Foggy Bottom closet was a collection of china plates *his* mother had bought in their journeys around the world. She had cherished them. He resolved to find and display them wherever he and Kendra decided to live.

A noise sounded behind him, and he turned to see an old man with snow-white hair and pale blue eyes that probably saw both little and everything. Isaac took the initiative. "I'm Isaac Taylor," he said, thrusting out his hand. "You must be Mr. Grayling."

A trembling hand gripped his. "Aubrey. Saves time."

Jennifer finished pouring the tea and handed Isaac both glasses. "Why don't you use the sunporch? No one can disturb you out there."

She took her grandfather's arm and helped him through the kitchen and small family room, and down two steps to the sunroom. Plants filled the corners and spilled from hanging baskets. A light oak table and chairs sat along one end, a wicker sofa and chairs along the other.

Jennifer helped Aubrey settle on the sofa, bringing him a pillow to put behind his back and a coaster for his glass. "I'll leave you two alone," she said once both men were comfortable. "Paw-paw, you just call if you need me."

"I wondered if you'd find your way," Aubrey said when Jennifer had gone.

"Jennifer gave good directions."

"That's not what I meant."

"You mean you wondered if I would come talk to you?"

"By now somebody's told you how much you look like Jesse."

Isaac set down his tea. More carefully than it warranted. "Etta Norton," he said.

"I have photographs. More than a few. And some of your grandmother, too. I had Jenny put them in an album. They're all ready to take when you leave today."

"Mr.—Aubrey, if you wanted to talk to me all along, why didn't you just call and say so?"

"I bet if you think about it, you'll find that

answer on your own. You might even have it now."

"Because you wanted to be sure I really needed to hear what you're going to say."

"I never did meet a dumb Spurlock. Stubborn, yes. Funny? You better believe it's true. But they also could chew every word that ever came their way and spit it back in your face when the right moment came along. Jesse was like that. When a dark mood come over him, he couldn't see his hand in front of his face. And he sure couldn't see anybody else's."

"Like Leah's."

He grew solemn. "See, the thing was, Jesse thought he ought to be giving Leah the moon and stars. And all she really wanted was him. He was as blind as I'm going to be in a year or two. The thing is, she was, too. They couldn't find their way to each other until it was too late. And neither of them saw the danger. . . ."

Isaac didn't interrupt, but he knew that even if he did, nothing would stop Aubrey now. He had been waiting a large part of his life to tell this story. Isaac sat back and waited for the rest of his grandparents' saga to unfold.

CHAPTER THIRTY-TWO

Blackburn Farm
Lock Hollow, Virginia
May 30, 1934

Dear Puss,

I cannot heal myself. There is no cure for a broken heart.

I will be gone when you come home. There is too much to explane in this letter. I hope someday we will meet agin, and I can tell you all there is to tell. Just remember who I am when things are said aginst me. I did not change, but the world surely did.

Always your friend no matter where we live,
Leah Spurlock

The distance between Lock Hollow houses was considerable, the terrain formidable. But still, news snaked from one part of the hollow to the other, traveling up ridges, along stream banks, over roads so rough that wagons couldn't travel them. On the day Leah began to suspect she at last might be pregnant, the news she'd tried to hide reached Jesse through his stepfather, Luther Collins: Leah had been meeting secretly with Daniel Flaherty, and Flaherty was so taken with her that he had offered her prime land near the Shenandoah River.

The sun was disappearing behind the trees when Leah looked up to see Jesse bearing down on her. She had been trying to repair a hole in the chicken wire surrounding their henhouse, although she wasn't sure she hadn't made the situation worse. A fox had made off with their best layer during the night, and she was afraid that Jesse, who had worked in their orchard all day with his stepfather, wouldn't have a chance to fix the enclosure before the fox made a second raid.

Jesse had spoken to her so seldom in the past weeks that at first she felt a thrill of anticipation. He had come to find her. Maybe at last they would talk about the future. Maybe, if all went well, she could tell him she might be having his baby. Would that give him the reason he needed to abandon his plan to remain on their land even if it meant war with the authorities?

"You Jezebel!"

Alarm filled her. Now that he was closer, she could see the fury written on his features. She knew, without another word, that he had discovered her meetings with Daniel. Guilt and shame told her so.

She didn't cower. She straightened and stood tall, and she didn't flinch when he raised his hand. "No Spurlock hits a woman. And no Blackburn lets him."

His hand hovered in the air, descended, then fell to his side. "You are a faithless Jezebel."

She didn't pretend not to know what he meant. "I've been faithful to you, although why I should be is a puzzlement. You abandoned me months ago."

"Tell me you didn't take land from that man. Tell me you didn't lie with him!"

"I didn't lie with him. And he has offered *us* land, but I reckon it's been hard to tell you so, since you won't speak to me."

"No man gives a gift without getting something in return!"

She wilted a little, because she knew he was right. Daniel clearly had expectations. She was sure he was in love with her, and the things he'd done, he had done because of it.

"I've never led him to expect anything." She thought of the one kiss, and she was sure her cheeks reflected the memory, as well. She pleaded with her eyes. "But I have been so lonely, Jesse, I have spoken to him just to hear the sound of my voice."

He stared at her. His eyes were dark coals. Her handsome, charming husband was suddenly a man who was angry enough to kill. She felt a shiver of fear. The silence stretched; she found it difficult to breathe.

Finally, as if he had made a decision, he turned away.

"You go with him." His voice was tight, as if it were coming from some terrible, smothering place inside him. "You go with that Daniel Flaherty, Leah. And you leave the rest of us here to tend what still belongs to us. You go, and don't come back. Take whatever you will. I want nothing that ever belonged to you."

She felt as if he had hit her after all. "This farm belongs to me."

"Trade it to the devil, then. The Spurlock place is mine by rights. That's where I'll be when they come to burn down this house."

She risked everything by grabbing his arm. "Jesse, it's you I love. That hasn't changed. But you been keeping apart from me. And I don't know what to do about it. We had to plan, and you wouldn't. I . . ." She swallowed. "I think maybe I'm having a baby, Jesse. And a baby needs a place to live, a place where we can be happy."

He shook off her arm and whirled. "And whose baby would it be?"

Her eyes widened. "You can ask me that?"

"I don't remember a time when we were together of late, do you?"

"That night by the woodpile! *I* remember you could hardly do it fast enough."

For a moment something flickered in his eyes—a doubt, perhaps, a realization that he might, after all, be a father. Then his expression hardened.

"We went more'n a year without making a

baby, and you say it happened just like that?"

"That's the way of it."

"Not so I ever heard."

"I reckon you don't know all the secrets of a woman's body!"

"Maybe someday I'll stop by that grand house of yours on the river and look to see if this child you're carrying appears to be anything like me. But you go on now, 'cause I don't think there's much to worry about. You go on, you and that baby's father!"

That he could be this cruel nearly destroyed her. Tears sprang to her eyes. She let out a wail, fell to a stump beside the fence and covered her face.

When her weeping had ebbed, she saw he was gone. The tears had washed away the edge of her sorrow but none of her anger. She had bared her soul, and he had rejected her, her and the child she might be carrying. She saw no hope for them now, no glimpse of a future together. She understood that Jesse felt betrayed. Now she was sorry that she had ever spoken to Daniel, and sorrier still that she had let him comfort and kiss her. And yet Daniel, unlike anyone else in her life, had offered solace and a way to face the unknown.

And Daniel was offering a life after Lock Hollow.

"Leah?"

She whirled to find Birdie limping toward her. She put her hand over her heart.

"Why are you crying?"

Leah shuddered. Birdie had witnessed the way Jesse had treated her over the past months. She'd told Leah it was shameful and Leah deserved better. Although she had been unfailingly kind to Jesse, in the sisters' private moments, Birdie had voiced her qualms. Clearly, she was an ally.

Leah stumbled through an explanation of everything that had transpired. Birdie bit her lip. Her lovely face shone with pity.

"Yesterday a robin came a-flying into the house when I opened the door to shake the rug. I knew then—"

"Birdie!"

Birdie fell silent.

Leah stifled a sob. "Jesse told me to leave."

"Surely he don't mean to say that." Birdie didn't sound convinced.

"How can we stay?"

"Mama said things shouted in anger fester by the first light of dawn. You could tell him you're sorry."

"It's not so simple!"

"Then maybe you should do as he says." Birdie rested her hands on Leah's shoulders. "Hear me. I know marriage binds you forever. But surely there are times, like this one, when vows are only words best forgotten. I been watching, and I seen the way Jesse treats you, and it's shameful. You only want what's best. And you been meeting with that Mr. Flaherty to get what's best for us. I seen it, and I know what I seen. And if you want, I will go and tell Jesse Spurlock myself."

"No!"

"Then what's there to be done? Your husband don't want you. Another man, a better man, does. And he has a place for you. What does Jesse have?"

Jesse had her heart, but Leah was certain now that her heart meant nothing to him. Jesse might be the father of a child they had created together, yet even that news had not caused him to relent.

"Will Mr. Flaherty know what to do?" Birdie asked.

Leah felt numb. If Jesse knew about her friendship with Daniel, everyone in the hollow probably knew the story, too. And whether the story was right or wrong, she would still be shunned. The farm was no longer hers by law. And now the hollow was no longer hers by rumor and innuendo.

"Do you care after this Mr. Flaherty?" Birdie asked, when Leah didn't answer.

"He's kinder than Jesse will ever be."

"Then go to him this night. Tell him what all you told me."

"And what will you do?" For the first time that evening, Leah remembered that Birdie depended on her to make things right. Their mother had left Birdie and this farm in Leah's care. This terrible moment was not just about her failed marriage or about losing the land, it was about her sister's health and safety. She had no choice but to find another home for Birdie and herself, and one was waiting. All she had to do was say yes.

The home first, then perhaps, later, when her heart had mended, she would consider the man who had made it possible.

"I'll wait here." Birdie tossed her head. "I'll

wait until you settle in. Etta will come if I ask. She'll help until you come back for me."

"You could go with me tonight."

Birdie held up her hand. "I cain't be ready tonight. But while you're a-planning what to do, I'll get things prepared. All our things, yours and mine. And when you come back, I'll be ready then."

"I . . ." Leah could think of no other solution.

Birdie nodded. "It's best this way. You know it's so."

Leah didn't know anything except that she had never felt so miserable. Once some neighbor men had gathered to dig a well for a family a ridge away. She and her mother had gone to help with the meal that always accompanied such an event. When the food was nearly done, Leah had gone to watch the excavation, when, suddenly, without warning, the well, which had not been properly reinforced, collapsed on the two men deep in the hole. Her life was like that well. The men had been rescued just in time, but there would be no rescue for her.

"I will go and talk to Daniel," she said with a heavy heart. "I'll go and see the land on the river, so I can decide if it's the right place to go."

"We'll pack just what you can carry."

Leah realized she was crying. Birdie's eyes were wet, as well. "I never thought being married would be like this," Leah said.

"Maybe it's good you never had a little 'un. Maybe that's something to be glad about now."

Leah hadn't told Birdie she might be carrying Jesse's child. And now she didn't want to make the truth about her husband sound even harsher. Jesse and Birdie had always been friends. Birdie deserved to remember him with some degree of fondness.

Jesse was absent when they got to the house. With little conversation, they chose the things Leah would need to take with her. They wrapped the small bundle in a worn sheet and tied it tight. Leah washed quickly and changed her clothes, donned her everyday shoes, plaited her hair. Her hands trembled as she did. She felt as if she were living a dream.

She had no appetite for the supper Birdie had prepared, but Birdie forced her to take a wedge of cornpone and a piece of chicken.

She left her sister at the front door after a fierce, prolonged hug. Both women were sobbing. "I'll be back for you," Leah promised. "You be ready."

"That's what I'll be doing while you're gone."

"You send word to Etta through Jesse, so you won't be alone."

The skies were darkening quickly. Leah started down the road to the farm where she knew Daniel and his assistant were living. She had never been there to meet him, but she suspected the two men were using the abandoned house for shelter. It wasn't much, but it was better than a tent.

She hadn't expected to meet Daniel on the road, but when she was out of sight of her own house, she saw him coming toward her. Unlike Birdie, she didn't believe in signs. But this seemed right and just to her. She didn't have to seek out Daniel. He had come for her.

He seemed surprised to see her, but of course, he didn't know any of what had passed tonight.

"Leah?" He sprang forward and took her hands. "What's this?"

"I'm leaving Jesse. I was coming to look for you."

His face was impossible to read in the moonlight, but he chafed her hands. The air was turning cooler, and he warmed them in his. She knew she should appreciate his touch, but his hands felt soft. They weren't Jesse's hands, hardened by work, hands with long, sensitive fingers. Daniel's fingers were short, and his hands were damp.

"What happened?" he asked.

She told him what she could. "I cain't stay with him," she finished. "He told me to come to you, and here I am."

"You did the right thing. He's treated you badly. You certainly deserve better."

She wished he would drop her hands. And she wished he were standing farther away. She felt the weight of his presence as if his body were flush against hers. For the first time, she noticed the way he smelled. Not like a man coming in from a day outside in the fresh air, but overpoweringly sweet, like the blossoms of valerian, which she grew as a soothing tea.

She took a step back, and he dropped her hands. "You're upset. I understand. Why don't you come back with me? Have you had supper?"

He was being kind. She heard concern in his voice. She wished Jesse had sounded half as concerned, that her husband had gripped her hands in his and tried to warm them. Daniel had done all the right things.

Yet it was Jesse she still yearned for. And always would.

In that moment, she understood that she would never love this man. Not in months, not in years. This wasn't a temporary reluctance, born of the chaos and sorrow of the past hour. For the first time, she saw clearly that even though her marriage was in shambles, she couldn't abandon it. She couldn't abandon her husband. She had taken a vow to love Jesse until death parted them. She had failed, and so had he, but they could try again. She wouldn't use his anger as an excuse to find a better life. She wouldn't use it as a convenient reason for choosing someone else.

"No, I cain't go with you," she said. "I cain't ever marry you. I'm sorry. I was wrong."

"Marry?" He looked puzzled.

"Marry you and live with you by the river.

I don't love you. I love my husband. I'm going to find him and make him take me back."

He looked stunned. "Leah, dear, you don't have to worry about marrying me. But you can still live there. I have the deed right here. It'll be easy to put it in your name. Your husband doesn't want you. Don't forget what you just told me. And when you're settled, I can come and visit you. I—"

She realized the truth. Like lightning over the mountain. "You're already married."

"Not in the ways that matter."

"You're already married!" She was furious, but only at herself. "And you're right, it don't matter. 'Cause I wouldn't have you, Daniel Flaherty, if you had the preacher standing right there beside you and I was a free woman. You're like the fox that preys on my chickens. You're bigger and faster, and you've got the power of our futures in your hands. You think that gives you the right to take anything you want!"

"Think carefully. Where are you planning to go, if not with me?"

"First thing? I'm going to find whoever bosses you. And I'm going to tell him what you tried to do and why. And next I'm going to find one of those news reporters that's been snooping around up at Skyland writing about our misery. And I'm going to tell him a real story he can print. You set out to make me think you wanted to help us, but all you ever wanted was me in your bed. And in the end, you brought a brand-new hell crashing down on all of us!"

Even as she said the words, she knew that all of them shared the blame. Jesse, Daniel and her. Daniel had preyed on her weakness, but Jesse had fed it with his silence. And she? She had done little to help Jesse. She had taken his rejection as a sign that he didn't love her, instead of a plea for help. She had abandoned him when he needed her most, just as he had abandoned her tonight.

"Don't do that," Daniel said.

For a moment, she didn't know what he meant. Then she remembered that she had just threatened him. Threatened him only moments ago, although it felt as if years of understanding had passed.

"Look, I have the deed," he said. "It can still be yours. And there will be money to go with it. I'll make certain of it. Enough to help you get a start."

"I don't want your money!"

"It's yours by right for the land, not a gift."

"You let someone else bring me the deed and the money. It's our money, and I'll take it, glad enough. But I want no part of anything else from your hands."

"You were married. I didn't see the harm in this. I thought I could help you. I thought—"

"You thought you could have me anytime it pleased you! Well, I'll tell you what I think. I think if I ever see your sorry face again, I'll go running for a gun."

She was halfway back to the house before she realized the full impact of what she had done. She was truly alone now.

Until a man stepped out of the shadows.

Jesse stood in the moonlight, his face unreadable. If he had been there all along, he had heard her conversation with Daniel.

"What are you doing there?" she demanded.

"I was coming after you."

Five words. Simple words. And yet they were the sweetest she had ever heard. "Why?" Her voice dropped to a whisper. "If you thought I hadn't been true to you?"

"I guess because you being true wasn't as important as you being here."

She flew into his arms. He held her tight, kissing her forehead, her cheeks, her lips. She slipped her arms around his neck, her bundle falling to the ground.

"I love you, Jesse," she whispered. "Nobody else."

"I thought I'd lost you for good. Then I heard everything you said to him."

He was holding her so tight, she could hardly breathe. She didn't care. She would gladly have died in his arms.

He put his hand below her waist, his fingers splayed against her skirt. "Ours," he said.

"We cain't raise him here, not fighting the government. When the time comes, we have to think of him or her."

"We'll do what's right for all of us." He kissed her. "I been talking to Aubrey. He's coming to see us tonight or tomorrow. Maybe we'll go in on that lawsuit. Maybe we'll move. But we'll decide together."

They were losing so much, but they hadn't lost each other. They would start over. The three of them and Birdie.

"Birdie." She pulled away. "We have to tell Birdie. She thinks I'm gone."

"I have something to do." His eyes flicked down the road where Daniel had waited for her.

She grabbed his arm. "No, Jesse. You forget it. Come with me. Daniel Flaherty's not worth a fight."

"I'll be home soon enough."

She heard the determination in his voice. "I don't want to be the cause of more misery."

"I have a few words to say to him. I'll be home soon enough."

She knew better than to argue. Jesse might have forgiven her, but he would never forgive Daniel Flaherty, and tonight, Daniel would understand what that meant.

"I'm going in, then. You be careful."

He swung her off her feet, around and around; then he set her down and kissed her. "Baby needed a ride."

For a moment she felt young, in a way she hadn't in months. "You hurry, now. I'll be waiting."

She picked up the bundle and started back toward the house as he headed up the road. She wondered how she would find the right words to express to her sister what had occurred. At first Birdie would be skeptical that everything had been made right between them. Then, when she was satisfied that all was well, she would smile and kiss Leah's cheek. And that night she would start a new quilt top to celebrate.

The dogs didn't bark when she approached. She left them behind on the porch as she opened the door. At first she couldn't find her sister; then she realized why. For some reason the lanterns had not been lit. Only the table was illuminated by several of the special beeswax candles scented with rosemary and lavender that Leah made each year to burn at Christmas. Birdie was standing behind it.

"Oh, Jesse, I do know how much you like my chicken. I fixed it just the way you like it best."

For a moment Leah thought Birdie was talking to her and had just mixed up the names; then she realized that her sister, who had put away her glasses, didn't even know she was there. As she watched, Birdie, who had taken down her hair and donned her best dress, held a corner of her skirt away from her legs and did an awkward little dance step.

"I made a peach pie, too," she said, nearly singing the words. "Just for you, Jesse. Everything I do is for you. I knew *she* would leave us alone soon enough. I was the one you were supposed to marry. You see that at last, I know. Well, we can always be together, now that she's gone. We'll go away, and nobody will know that you aren't married to me. We'll start over—"

She stumbled through a turn, then stopped dancing and peered into the shadows. "Who's there?" Birdie fished in her pocket for her glasses, slipped them over her nose and peered at her sister.

Leah felt a jolt of alarm. "Birdie, what are you doing? Who were you talking to?"

Birdie moved closer. "You?"

Leah was growing frightened. Something was clearly wrong. "It's Leah. I came back. Jesse and I worked things out." Leah watched her sister's face, and Birdie's expression worried her more. "He's sorry," she said, speaking faster, as if speed could counter the way Birdie grew still and rigid.

"I don't love Daniel. I love Jesse. He believes me now. And he knows the baby—"

Too late she realized that this was something she hadn't yet shared.

"Baby?"

"I'm having Jesse's baby. Least, I think I'm having a baby. You'll be an aunt. Someone new to love, Birdie. We'll move away together, if it comes to that. We'll find a way to be happy somewhere else. You might even find a man who loves you, the way Jesse loves—"

"Stop it!" Birdie backed away—away from the kitchen and over to the fireplace, where the wood stove warmed their house in winter. "I don't believe you."

"Aren't you glad?" Leah couldn't stop talking. If she kept talking, maybe she wouldn't have to think about what she had seen when she came in. Maybe she wouldn't have to think about what she had heard.

Suddenly Birdie seemed to melt. She began to laugh. "You're fooling."

"Birdie. Stop. You're worrying me. I—"

"Jesse loves me. He don't love you. Don't you know he just married you 'cause he thought I didn't want him? And now that you're gone, he can have—"

"I'm not gone. I'm standing right here."

"He can have me," Birdie went on, as if Leah hadn't spoken. "And I will cook for him and sew his clothes. I'll be the one he turns to at night when—"

"Stop it! Birdie, stop this! All this excitement, this worrying's, been too much for you. You need to rest. Tonight's been too much for all of us—"

"Oh, you think everything is too much for me! You with your perfect legs and strong back and good eyes! You think I don't know? You think I don't see what you are?"

"I'm the sister who loves you."

"Our mama was a witch. First she doomed me by walking through that house and not sitting down. Not even once. Then she traded my health for yours. She made a bargain with the devil. Don't you know why I was the one got the polio? Mama fixed it that way. What else could have done it? And you got everything else, even Jesse. Even though she was already gone by then. I made sure she was gone, and you still got Jesse!"

Leah was dizzy with horror over what Birdie was saying. "You made sure she was gone?" she whispered.

Birdie's laugh was high and wild. "It was

time for her to die! God wanted her dead, but the devil was holding her here. The fever broke after you went to bed, and she fell asleep. I saw she was better. I put that pillow over her head, and she was too weak to fight me. She couldn't fight me and God!"

Bile rose in Leah's throat. She fell to a chair and put her head in her hands. "You're touched." She couldn't believe she hadn't seen it. Yet no one had suspected. Birdie was different, yes. But none of them had understood in exactly what way. No one had understood how deeply the polio and its aftermath had affected her, the constant pain, the resentment of a sister who hadn't been struck down with her.

"No, I got a way of seeing things you cain't see. And I know what's what."

"We'll get you help." Leah rose and started toward the fireplace, where Birdie warily watched her. "Somebody can help. I reckon you don't mean the things you're saying now."

With a speed Leah couldn't have imagined, Birdie reached up and took down the German Luger that Jesse's father had gotten in the war. She aimed it at her sister, clutching the pistol against her chest to steady it. “I know what will help me most. I didn’t want to hurt you. I thought you would just go. That I wouldn’t have to do what I did to Mama. Why didn’t you, Leah?” The last was a wail.

Leah froze. The gun was always loaded. “We’re sisters. We love each other.”

“I have tried not to. You are the devil’s spawn, a sorry bargain Mama made, and I aim to keep myself pure.”

“Birdie, I’m so sorry you were the one who got sick. But maybe I didn’t get sick just so I could be healthy and take care of you. Maybe that’s what God intended. That’s what I’ve tried to do. Haven’t I?”

“You took Jesse!”

“You never told me you loved him. You never showed a sign of it.” But even as she said the words, Leah knew the signs had been there all along. The way Birdie had always opened up to Jesse, the way she had fussed over him, even the way she had paused for such a long time in front of him on Leah’s wedding day, as if Birdie herself were the bride.

“You got between me and him,” Birdie said. “It was me he loved, but you took him, the way you took my health. You are a scourge on my soul."

Her arm shot out, and she held the gun directly in front of Leah. She was shaking, but her aim was straight enough.

The door opened, then closed. Both women turned at the sound. Jesse stood just inside, his eyes wide with astonishment in the candlelight.

"Birdie?" He moved toward them, gracefully, slowly. "What's wrong, Birdie girl?"

"She's trying to take you from me!"

Unlike Leah, Jesse seemed to understand the situation immediately. He kept his voice low and calm, but he moved closer.

"It's been such a terrible day. You've been through so much. But you're our strong, wonderful Birdie girl, and I reckon you aren't going to do anything as foolish as shooting your sister."

"She came back! She was supposed to leave us alone."

"You just let me talk to her. I aim to straighten this out. You trust me, don't you? You know I'll do whatever is best."

"No, she's got the devil inside her. Don't you see it? She made you marry her, when I know you wanted me. You cain't control what she does. Nobody can." She lifted her arm higher.

Jesse darted a frantic glance at Leah. He moved a little closer to Birdie.

"Birdie girl, this ain't no way to start our time together. Not with something like this hanging over our heads. You can see that, cain't you? You want to be with me, then you got to give me your trust. I promise I'll make things right here."

The gun wavered. "We can go somewheres, just you and me, Jesse. But she cain't come."

He glanced at Leah. "Leah, you heard that, right? Now that you understand the way things are, you can go with that Flaherty fellow after all. You just tell Birdie so."

"Yes." Leah nodded emphatically. "Birdie, I didn't know. I guess I just never saw what was in front of my eyes."

Birdie's arm was trembling violently now. She began to lower the gun, and Leah felt a surge of hope. Then, with a cry, Birdie lifted the gun again, this time holding it steadier with both hands.

"No! She's fooling us, Jesse. She's got your baby inside her. That's why Daniel Flaherty don't want her. I see it now. She'll never leave us alone."

"We been married nearly two years, Birdie girl. And do you see a baby? There ain't no baby inside her, either. She just said so to make me sorrier."

Leah nodded. She was crying now. "Just put the gun down and I'll leave. Then you and Jesse can have your supper. Please, Birdie."

"No, you leave first." Birdie motioned with the pistol. "You go on out that door, and don't you come back. Not ever."

"I understand it all now," Leah said. Frantically, she caught Jesse's eyes. He gave the slightest of nods. She knew that once she left, he hoped Birdie would relinquish the gun and he could subdue her. Then Leah could return and they could decide what to do.

"You walk slow. Don't get ideas, Leah."

Leah knew that she had to look as if she really meant what she said. "I'll take my bundle. The one you helped me tie. That's all I'll need. I won't come back here."

"You take it and git."

Leah moved carefully toward the bundle. The moment her back was finally to Birdie, she began to tremble uncontrollably. Seeing her sister with a gun trained on her had been terrible enough. Not seeing her was devastating.

She was almost to the door, almost through it, when she heard a shout.

"No!"

Then a shot.

For a moment she expected to die right there. She waited for the white-hot pain that would come, the cessation of breath and heartbeat. She had seen death enough times to know what would happen.

Time seemed to pause, but she knew it was really only seconds before she whirled. Birdie began to scream. Jesse lay on the floor.

Birdie ran to him and laid the gun beside him. She gathered him in her thin arms. "Why'd you do that, Jesse? I had to kill her. Didn't you see?"

Jesse was still alive, but even in the candlelight, Leah could see the blood pouring from a wound in his chest.

Birdie looked up and saw Leah running toward them. She grabbed the gun again and aimed it at her sister. "You stay away!"

"Let me help him, Birdie!"

"It was you was supposed to die!"

Leah knew Jesse had thrown himself at Birdie before the shot went off. She could see it as clearly as if her back had not been turned. "That don't matter now. Let me help him!"

Birdie looked down at Jesse in horror, then up at her sister. She got to her feet, gun outstretched, as if she intended to follow through on what she had started.

"No . . ." Jesse's voice was barely audible. "No, *you* come with me," he said. "Not her. Leave her here. You . . . Birdie. *You* have to come with me. . . . Together . . ."

His head fell back, and Leah knew he was gone.

"Jesse!" Birdie looked at the gun, then at her sister. "I knew he loved me!"

Before Leah could do more than scream, Birdie turned the gun on herself.

It was over within seconds. Leah stood paralyzed, but the screaming went on and on, and she didn't even know where it came from.

From nowhere, she felt a hand on her shoulder. She whirled and found Aubrey behind her. He gathered her in his arms and held her as the screams turned to sobs.

He was sobbing, too. "I saw it all through the window. As I was coming up. Saw it all. Heard it all. Every bit. I ran, but I couldn't get here fast enough."

"Birdie was touched. We didn't know. She was in love with him. When she realized Jesse and I . . . we were going to get through these hard times—"

"Hush. I know. I heard enough."

"Two times. He saved my life two times. He threw himself in front of that bullet. And he convinced her . . . He . . . Maybe they're not dead. Maybe there's something we can do." Leah fought to turn around, but Aubrey held her firmly.

"There's nothing to be done now." His voice was low and broken. "Except think about what we have to do next."

CHAPTER THIRTY-THREE

Isaac sat in the silence that had fallen after Aubrey finished his story. Finally he shook his head. It was all he could manage.

"I'm sorry, son," Aubrey said. "The rest of my life, I wondered how things would have been that night if I'd just got there sooner. But truth be told, I was reluctant to get to the Blackburn place. Like everyone else, I'd heard the rumors about Leah and that Flaherty fellow. I think Birdie set Etta to telling that story so Leah would feel more inclined to leave with Flaherty and avoid the scorn of her neighbors. With all that, I didn't know what I'd find going on between Jesse and Leah."

"There's a lot I still don't understand."

"I imagine so." Aubrey sat forward as if he

wanted to comfort Isaac. "I can fill in some more, if you're willing to sit."

"I want to know why my grandmother was forced to leave Lock Hollow under a cloud. You could have prevented it by just telling the truth."

"Simpler than you're thinking. See, there were two things at work. The first was about Birdie and the second about the hollow. Let me start with Birdie."

"You'd never seen any sign she was mentally ill?"

"Of course I had. We all had. But none of us knew what we were looking at. She had peculiar notions, yes, and her days were woven around old superstitions. She had a way of looking off when she talked to you, and sometimes the things she said just didn't ring true, like she was answering questions nobody else was hearing. But I just figured it had to do with the way she could never leave the house much, and the pain she suffered. And her vision, well, it was so poor, I just thought that was some part of it. Mrs. Blackburn protected her, you know. She took it on herself to keep Birdie out of harm's way, out of the world's way. In the end, maybe that's what done it."

Isaac was still trying to put the story together. "I don't see what this had to do with Leah leaving Lock Hollow."

"Leah didn't want folks to know what Birdie had done. Leah'd protected Birdie all her life, too. You never saw a more loyal sister. The Blackburns raised her that way. Birdie was Leah's burden. Even after . . . well, everything." Aubrey cleared his throat.

"You mean my grandmother decided to take the fall for her sister?"

"That's about what happened. But that weren't all of it, you see. Part of it was my fault."

"You?"

Aubrey folded his arms. "You learned a lot about the park and what happened since you started looking into this, didn't you."

Isaac gave a short nod.

"You learned the way they looked at us mountain people? You go back, and you look at the stories the papers were printing, the firsthand accounts from people who didn't have a bit of sense about what they were seeing, people who just wanted what they wanted and were happy to get it one way or another. Didn't matter to them who they struck down while they were getting it, either."

"I fail to see how this had anything to do with my grandmother."

Aubrey smiled sadly. "Leah would be glad, I guess, to know someone is defending her at last."

Isaac was surprised at how angry he felt, but everything that had happened had been such a terrible waste. "Just explain it to me."

"I told Leah if the real story got out, it would about do us in. I was trying to use the law to our benefit, to make the world see that we were good, intelligent people who were about to lose everything we had. There was an important court case going on at the time, one that looked promising, and I thought if it ended in favor of the fellow who'd brought it before the judges, then we had a chance of keeping our land."

Aubrey turned up his hands. "Then this awful thing happened. And nobody down below would have seen it for what it was. They wouldn't have seen one young woman, what we now call psychotic, who destroyed a family. No, they'd have seen it as some sort of pathetic lover's triangle, a hillbilly love story. I could almost see the headlines. And it would have doomed the only chance we had to hold on to what was ours." He paused. "Of course, later on that case ended in defeat and we still had to go."

Isaac was trying to imagine this, to move beyond fury to understanding. "And my grandmother went along with that."

"More than anyone, she didn't want Jesse's or Birdie's memories tarnished. She didn't want to hurt her neighbors. To be truthful, she only wanted to get away as fast as she could, too. We couldn't bury them in the family plot. When folks came sniffing around, wondering what happened to Jesse and Birdie, that would have been the first place they checked. We couldn't disturb the dirt and start rumors flying. So I had to think of a solution. Jesse and I played in those caves at the bottom of Little Lock as children. Leah played up there some, as well. We knew them all. I spent the night carrying their bodies up to the one that was the most remote. With the help of gravity and a tree limb, I was able to send a couple of boulders rolling downhill till they covered the mouth of that cave."

"And the quilt?"

"That was Leah and Jesse's marriage quilt. She wrapped them inside it when we got up there. Said she didn't want to look at that quilt ever again."

Isaac considered that. "So the Lover's Knot I have . . . ?"

"It was Birdie's. She'd made two identical tops, you see, but only finished the one. One top for herself and Jesse, because she was fixed on the idea he'd marry her. One for Leah and whoever she chose. When Leah left the Blackburn place for the last time, she packed up everything she could. Maybe it just got mixed in with everything else, maybe she took it on purpose. I'm not sure of that part. But later, when her daughter ran away from home . . ."

Isaac got to his feet and went to a window. "Are you guessing about this part, Aubrey? Because this part happened well after the night my grandfather was murdered in Lock Hollow." He turned and correctly read the expression in Aubrey's eyes. "You were in touch with my grandmother after she left, weren't you."

"After everything, you don't think I would have let her go off without a bit of help? I looked in on her whenever I could, made sure she was doing all right with her little 'un, made sure she could provide for her. I owed her that. I owed Jesse that."

"Just you? No one else ever knew?"

"Not just me. Puss, as well. I told Puss the truth a month later, though Leah didn't want me to. But I figured Leah would need her friendship after everything, and Puss was sworn to silence. They wrote each other at first. In later years, they talked on the phone every week. Maybe they even visited each other again, though I'm not certain of that. But the three of us, we were the only ones from the hollow who ever knew what happened. Years later when she married again I don't think she even told Tom Jackson."

Isaac was putting the pieces together. "Then my mother took off because someone told her what everyone *else* from Lock Hollow believed."

"That's when Leah realized she'd made a terrible mistake by not telling Rachel the truth. And when she found out about you, she started worrying that someday, if you went looking for your birth family, you'd be told she was a murderer, too."

"So that's when she finished that quilt top and made a map out of it."

"She did. She studied on the matter a long time. She wanted to make it possible for you to find out what happened, but only if you were sincerely interested. She didn't want to force anything down your throat. She knew eventually, if you set your mind to looking, you'd find me from my name being on the quilt. She entrusted me with making sure you got the story, but only if you really needed to learn it. That's when I joined up with the folks at The Way We Were. I was watching for you, and hoping."

"You're ninety-two. Did Leah think you were going to live forever? She certainly didn't."

Aubrey grinned. "You met my Jennifer."

Isaac understood at last. "Jennifer knows?"

"Every last bit. I had to tell her some time ago, on account of my being old as a rock, as you pointed out. She's the one had a little headstone made for Jesse and Birdie both and took it up to the park to put in your family cemetery. She said it was the least we Graylings could do, considering."

Isaac sat back, taking it all in.

"And now the truth is this," Aubrey said. "The last little pieces of it. You come from good people, Isaac. Both your grandpa and grandma were special to me. They weren't perfect. You've got that part figured out on your own. But they had integrity, loyalty, strength, and they loved each other as much as I've ever seen anybody love anybody. Maybe Leah was wrong not to let the truth come out. Maybe I shouldn't have asked her to make that sacrifice. But I think she went to her grave believing it was important. Spurlocks and Blackburns, they stand up for what's right. They always did. And they take the consequences when they have to. And that's what you need to know about the people you come from, son. That's all you ever really needed to know."

CHAPTER THIRTY-FOUR

Kendra felt a kinship with Leah Spurlock Jackson. Sometimes she tried to imagine how different Isaac's life would have been if Leah had been alive to guide him. She had finished reading Leah's advice to Puss, and savored the way Leah had taken knowledge learned from her own mother and applied it. Medical science would dispute some of what she had believed, but by the same token, some of it was grounded in reality.

Leah's formal education had been minimal, but she had soaked up every bit of information that had come her way. It was no surprise to Kendra that Isaac was both as smart and inquisitive as he was.

Kendra stopped in the midst of gathering bundles of dried spearmint and lemon balm from the front porch rafters, and gazed into the woods, much as Leah probably had. She hadn't spoken to Isaac since the weekend. She had risen early on Saturday morning, prepared the coffeepot for him, then headed for the Metro. Once she was back at the cabin, she had phoned and left a message at the condo, but he hadn't returned her call. They hadn't talked since.

Back in the spring, she had retreated to Toms Brook to give herself time to think. Now she had retreated to give *him* time. Her leaving was not an ultimatum. She wouldn't abandon Isaac if he made the wrong decision about Pallatine Mountain. She trusted him. He wasn't struggling with black and white, but she hoped they could both live with the shade of gray that was his personal solution.

She was alone at last. The construction crew was beginning serious repairs on the original cabin, and this morning they had torn out the false ceiling in the living room. Even with tarps covering the furniture, the room was a mess. The men had carried out the old beadboard and stacked it in front of the porch to haul away after they ripped the ceiling from the bedroom wing. She had swept and swept again, but a lot more chaos was coming.

Afterward, the lumberyard had delivered assorted materials, and the crew had piled them beside the old boards before heading off for the day. Cash had dropped by to promise that, beginning tomorrow, they would roust her out of bed at dawn and ruin her days straight through until sunset. She didn't need Cash to see what was coming. Before long, she would be forced to abandon the cabin until the worst was over. She wanted to go back to D.C. to spend the bulk of that time with Isaac, but she wasn't sure if she would be welcome.

After all the excitement, the afternoon promised to be too quiet. She had planned to spend it shopping with Elisa, but just before lunch, Elisa had called to say she was catching a cold. The temperature had grown steadily hotter, remaining dry, with a strong breeze that whipped in gusts and brought no relief. Now the woods, where the temperature was always milder, beckoned. For weeks she had planned to wander through with field guides in hand. She liked the idea of brewing her own teas from plants that everyone, including the FDA, considered safe. Today she would settle for picking young blackberry leaves to dry.

And she would think of Leah when she drank the tea.

She had about an hour of sunlight left. Inside, she changed into long pants to thwart ticks. She donned a cap and a long-sleeve shirt, and hooked a bottle of water over her belt.

She remembered that Caleb was coming before dinner to drop off a CD slide show he'd made of the photos from their camping trip, and she scrawled a note to leave on her windshield, telling him where she had gone, in case she wasn't back in time.

"Hey, Dusty. Time for a walk." She stomped on the floor twice to wake the snoozing puppy. Dusty woke long enough to wag her tail, then settled back on the cool wood and closed her eyes. Ten was sleeping not far away. He opened his eyes and watched warily as she approached. Kendra wiggled her fingers not far from his nose. He managed a pathetic hiss; then he batted her finger without bothering to extend his claws and fell back asleep.

Between the two animals, she figured she had the equivalent of about half a pet. But she was a sucker. Despite everything, she had grown outrageously fond of them both.

She was perhaps fifty feet into the woods when she thought she heard a vehicle coming up the driveway. Not long ago she would have had to talk herself into staying calm. Now she was simply curious. But as the engine grew louder, and she heard blasting rock music and men's voices, she finally began to worry. She remembered the last time someone had come and hoped these visitors would leave, too.

She debated what to do, but in the end, she knew she had to go back.

When she arrived, Randy and two other young men were standing by her front porch. One of the young men, a blonde with a Marine haircut and a tattooed eagle on his biceps, had a rifle, barrel down but still menacing.

"Come to shoot that snake of yours," Randy said with a self-conscious swagger. "Like good neighbors."

Fear inched through her. The men had been drinking. A lot. If she'd had any doubts, the beer cans they'd already tossed out of their pickup put them to rest. And Randy wasn't quite steady on his feet.

"You need to leave." She was surprised at the words that emerged easily from her own throat, and even more surprised at how calm they sounded.

Randy looked shocked, as if an idea had just occurred to him. "Hey, you're not s'posed to be here."

She wondered how he knew she had planned to visit Elisa. He hadn't been with the crew this morning, but she remembered that as the men were leaving, she had teased them about never working on the house if she planned to be gone. Another of the Rosslyn and Rosslyn pickups had come in about then to confer or trade materials, she didn't know which. But now she bet that Randy had been in that pickup.

She drew herself up to her full height. "Well, I *am* here. And you're trespassing. With a gun. And you'll notice I've posted my land. Not that it's hunting season."

The man with the rifle hooted, poking the tip of the barrel into the bushes around her front porch. "Hey, we come to help."

The third man, who looked enough like Randy to be a relative, flipped a cigarette butt over his shoulder and pulled out the pack to light another.

"I don't want your help." She spaced the words.

The smoker cupped his hand around the flame, then shook out his match. "I hear you got a snake lives under there as long as a tree trunk." He gestured to the space under the porch as his friend continued to poke the shrubs.

Kendra ignored him and turned back to Randy. "Randy, neither Cash nor his dad is going to be happy about you bringing your friends to a worksite. You'd better get going. I won't say anything. But don't come back like this again."

"I got no job. Quit today!" Randy puffed out his chest, but his eyes looked troubled.

Maybe his inner turmoil was a result of too much beer, or maybe it was genuine regret. She didn't know, but she took a step closer so she could lower her voice.

"Why? Cash told me you're a good worker."

"I do better work than any two men on that crew whether I'm sober or not. He's got no reason to criticize me. I don't have to take that from nobody."

She lowered her voice still further. "Does

this seem like a better way to spend your time?"

He narrowed his eyes. Beer bravado. She'd seen it before. But she also saw it was passing quickly, and the reality of what he'd done was beginning to hit him.

"Go," she said even more softly. "Listen, just get out of here. Go home and sober up, then talk to Manning or Cash. Tell them you'll never drink on the job again. Maybe you can fix this."

"No, we come to kill that snake."

"Randy, I'm sorry I embarrassed you the day you tried to shoot the snake. I really am. But my snake is not what's wrong with your life."

He sniffed. For a moment she was afraid he was going to burst into tears, a scene he would never live down. Then he straightened his shoulders as best he could and beckoned to his friends.

"Lady don't want us, boys. Her loss."

Kendra stepped back and watched the other two men laugh as Randy wove a circuitous path back to the truck. He made it without falling, a feat that seemed to take an inordinate amount of skill.

She stepped in front of the smoker before

he could follow. "I hope one of you had less to drink than Randy."

"Oh, I'll drive." The man gave a forced laugh and flipped another butt to the ground, making a half-hearted attempt to grind it into the earth with the sole of his work boot. "Bet there weren't no snake to start with."

She concentrated on every stone that spun under their tires as they backed toward her Lexus. The pickup had turned and was on its way back down the driveway before the impact of the past few minutes hit her. She was trembling. Her stomach was churning, but she had survived the confrontation. She had stood up for herself. The Kendra Taylor who had covered dangerous stories, who had put herself in harm's way for the sake of a byline, might never emerge again. But she could live with the woman she had become.

The retreat had ended. The rest of her life had begun.

She waited a few minutes to be sure the men didn't return; then, with one deep breath, she started back into the woods.

* * *

Isaac read the note on the Lexus windshield and knew there was no point in going up to the house. Kendra was prowling through the woods, and if he wanted to talk to her, he had to go there to find her.

He was in no particular hurry, and he supposed this was a good time to get used to that. He strolled a short distance in, listening as he went and enjoying the way the temperature dropped. He didn't call her name until he was out of sight of the clearing.

"K.C., are you in here somewhere?"

He heard a noise ahead of him. Then Kendra backed out of a thicket of blackberries about ten yards away. "What are you doing here?"

He covered the ground between them, skirting trees, avoiding spiderwebs and vines. When he reached her, he slipped his arms around her waist. "Didn't anybody ever tell you the story of Little Red Riding Hood?"

She smiled up at him, her eyes sparkling. "The Big Bad Wolf and his friends were just here. You must be the friendly Woodcutter."

"Wolf?"

"Long story. Not to worry."

He kissed her forehead; then he hugged her again, pillowing her face against his shoulder. He realized just how much he had longed for this in the hours since he had met with Aubrey. "I guess you're really not in any danger of getting lost or eaten, are you."

"Not much. Any straightish line will take me back to civilization. And I'm too skinny to tempt any critters." She stepped back so she could examine him. "What's up? You're the last person I expected to see."

"Who was the first?"

"Well, Caleb's supposed to be here pretty soon. You didn't see him, did you?"

"Not yet, but I read the note." He smoothed her hair behind her ears. "I'm glad I found you."

His smile faltered, and she began to look concerned. "Really. What are you doing here? It's Wednesday."

"I was more or less in the neighborhood. Well, a lot less than more."

"Okay, I'm intrigued."

She was waiting, clearly aware that something had changed. He supposed that level of intuition came with the package when a man and woman were intimate.

Now he dug for the right words, words that would explain his feelings easily, until at last he shrugged. "I went to see Gary Forsythe."

He watched the way her smile disappeared in tiny increments. "Should I ask why?"

"I went to tell him exactly what's up with Pallatine."

"Has he signed the papers, then?"

That, of course, was the big question. Had Isaac bought into Dennis's plan? In a way, the question seemed odd to him now. That he had ever considered not telling Forsythe seemed impossible.

"No, the closing's scheduled for next week. Since Heather is leaving, she was going to tell Forsythe herself and take the fall, but in the end, *I* told him, because *I* was the one who needed to."

He could see she understood everything this entailed. She looked worried, but still, despite that, pleased. "I can't imagine how you feel. And now you wait to see what happens?"

"I know what will happen. I gave him the names of two other organizations who will buy Pallatine with the right kind of promises.

All his lawyer has to do is wave the names at Dennis, and Forsythe will get any stipulations he wants. I'm sure ACRE will end up with the land. Dennis will scurry around soothing feelings and finding the money somewhere else. Then he'll brag about what a great deal he made, and how strong his scruples are. Most people will be happy enough, except the ones who were going to build environmentally friendly mini-mansions."

"And you?"

Isaac was surprised to find he was no longer worried. "Me? I'm toast."

"You're certain?"

"Just to be sure nobody's in the dark about who did what or why, I'll write an account of the entire transaction for the board. Then I'll follow it with my resignation, which will be accepted immediately. They'll tell me how sorry they are to lose me. Then I'll be escorted out of the building by a security guard. I'll be lucky if they give me enough time to grab your photo off my desk."

Her gaze softened. She placed her palm against his cheek. "I'm so sorry."

He held her hand in place for a moment; then he kissed it. "There's no reason to be.

I feel better than I've felt in months." He pulled her face against his shoulder again and ruffled her curls. How could he explain that, for the first time in a long time, he felt free? Free to figure out who he was and what he really wanted. Free to follow a path somewhere other than to the top. Free to try new ideas, new approaches, find new solutions.

He tried as best as he could. "I've been walking a tightrope for a long time. Today I just dove off, and there was a safety net below me."

"As long as I've known you, you've been working your way into a job where you felt you could make a real difference. This is going to affect that, isn't it?"

"I hope I can make a difference by doing what I know is right. If I can't, at least I can live with myself."

"I know you, Isaac. You'll find a way."

He yearned to tell her so much, but the words were still hard to find. They always would be, but from now on he would search harder.

"I think wanting to make a difference . . ." He struggled. "It was more than just being concerned for the earth. That's a lot of it.

But some of it was wanting to be a different person."

She hugged him. "You never needed to be. The original is plenty wonderful."

"I have a lot to tell—"

She jumped back, pulling him with her. For a moment he thought she was reacting to what he had said; then the largest snake he had ever seen came streaking through the woods, passing just inches from where they had been standing.

"I—"

An explosion rocked the quiet forest. He clutched Kendra, then immediately realized where the noise had come from.

He began to run. He knew Kendra was somewhere behind him, but he left her to fend for herself. He dodged trees, jumped logs and made it to the clearing just in time to see the western portion of the front porch go up in flames.

Isaac punched 911 on his cell phone, but even as he made the report, a *whoosh* sounded and flames shot through the porch roof.

"Isaac . . . what!" Kendra made it into the clearing, but by then he was already running up the steps to get the animals. Above him, a figure emerged through the smoke.

"Caleb!" Isaac realized the boy was carrying the spitting, clawing cat under one arm and, somehow, Kendra's puppy under the other. He grabbed Ten from the boy, and together they made it down the steps. Caleb deposited Dusty on the ground, but before Isaac could stop him, he ran back up.

"Caleb! Come back here!" Isaac set Ten on the ground, too, and started after him.

This time Caleb ran to the bedroom portion of the house, which was farther from the flames, threw open the door and began to grab what he could and toss it over the railing. Before Isaac made it to the porch, Caleb was trying frantically to save the last of Kendra's mementoes. Isaac saw quilts flying, then framed photos, Kendra's new sewing basket, a jewelry box. He grabbed Caleb's arm and, as the boy protested, he jerked him back down the steps to safety.

Kendra ran closer to grab the things Caleb had managed to save, dragging them to her car and out of harm's way. Then Kendra hugged the teen. "Nothing's worth what you are, Caleb. Don't you dare go back up there!"

"We can beat it out," Caleb shouted. "We can try."

Isaac watched as the flames engulfed the old dry logs. "We can't. The cabin's going to be gone before the fire department gets here. All they can do at this point is keep the fire from moving to the forest and the barn wood."

He put one arm around Kendra and another around the boy, and pulled them farther away from the heat and smoke. Dusty followed to whimper at their feet. Ten had climbed a tree behind them and was yowling angrily.

Kendra gulped; then she began to cry. "A cigarette. That's why Cash won't let his men smoke around the cabin. I should have checked. There were some men here earlier, and one of them was smoking. I didn't pay enough attention where he threw his butt. It's been so dry. It must have smoldered all this time in the old beadboard until something else caught. The crew brought supplies today. Something fed the flames."

A butt, something dry, something volatile. Isaac could see how it had happened.

They were in rural Virginia, but the Toms Brook volunteer fire department was organized and efficient. Over the crackling of the flames, he heard the faintest sound of a siren.

"They're on their way." He didn't want to give false hope. "But not in time."

"At least I got your quilts, Kendra." Caleb sounded as if he was near tears himself. "They were in a stack by your bedroom door. At least you have those."

"I know. I know. Thank you. I . . ." Suddenly she turned to Isaac. "Oh, Isaac, not all of them. Your grandmother's quilt. Leah's Lover's Knot was in the other part of the house. On a chair under a tarp." She started to sob again. "The quilt, the house, everything Leah left you . . ."

Isaac shook his head and pulled her close, keeping one arm around Caleb, too, to be sure the teenager didn't try anything foolish.

"K.C., listen. You, too, Caleb. Let it go. We'll build another house here. The cabin doesn't matter. The quilt doesn't matter. They've both served their purpose. Trust me. All the things Leah really meant for me to have are still right here."

The siren grew louder. Soon the clearing would be filled with firefighters struggling to save what no longer mattered. They stood together, and as the cabin burned, Isaac silently thanked his grandmother for everything she had given him.

EPILOGUE

Kendra slammed the front door and tossed her keys on the aluminum television tray, fairly sure she had beaten her husband home. The clank of her keys on the metal always drove Isaac crazy. The sight of the tray, something Barry had rejected and left in the basement when he moved, drove Isaac crazy, too.

She couldn't blame him. Three months had passed since their move to Arlington, and she still hadn't found the right piece of furniture to put beside the door. She wanted an authentic Limbert side table, and the search was going slowly. The little Craftsman bungalow was still more than half empty. Between resuming her job part-time, researching her book, moving here and starting from scratch on plans for the house on the river, time to meander through antiques stores was at a premium. But she made the time whenever she could, and she refused to be rushed. Making a home was an experience to savor.

Something crashed in the kitchen, and she froze. Then she heard Isaac's voice.

"That's it! I've had it! Out you go."

She heard the door slam and laughed, knowing exactly what had happened. Isaac was home after all, and the animals were not behaving.

She walked through the house, still with the slightest of limps. She was at peace with her body, and she viewed the limp as a reminder to slow down and view the world around her. She did that now, savoring the things she and Isaac had already managed to do.

The walls were painted warm earth tones; the polished floors were dotted with Oriental carpets she and Isaac had fought over, compromised on and now loved dearly. Two Gustav Stickley rockers flanked the fireplace. Harold Doolittle etchings of mountains and evergreens adorned one adjacent wall, and photographs, including copies of some that Aubrey had given Isaac of his grandparents and some Caleb had taken of the Blackburn and Spurlock land, lined the other.

A plush garnet-colored chenille sofa proved the Taylors were eclectic enough in their tastes to be comfortable. The log cabin album quilt she'd been given by Helen and the other quilters embellished the back of it. Upstairs, the other quilts in her collection hung from a rack beside their bed, including the top she was still piecing from the old blocks Helen had given her. She had managed to attend two meetings of the SCC Bee since moving back to northern Virginia. She was enthusiastic, but no one had yet proclaimed she had talent.

She reached the kitchen and leaned against the doorframe, enjoying the twin aromas of lemongrass and garlic as she watched her husband cook. His mother's collection of china plates decorated the tops of the cabinets, providing a homey, feminine accent above his head.

"I almost picked up Peruvian chicken. I'm glad I didn't. Is that your famous pad thai?"

Isaac looked up, and Kendra watched his eyes light.

"Hey, I didn't hear you come in."

"The Rug and the Rascal took care of that."

"Dusty's found her inner puppy. I cleaned up an entire roll of toilet paper, starting in the bathroom and ending upstairs. It was a map of the day's pursuits."

"Ten probably helped."

"No doubt he was the instigator." He switched off the burner and came over for a kiss.

She put her arms around his waist and leaned against him. "How did your day go?"

"Terrific. We had a meeting and decided that everyone had to take pay cuts. I'm now making fifteen percent less than I was last week, which was nothing. Think of it as a bigger donation to charity. And yes, it's pad thai. To win you over to our cause."

She laughed because she could. She knew how lucky she and Isaac were to be so financially stable that he could take this kind of risk. He had added his talents to a roster of a dozen disenchanted ACRE employees and was now the chief operating officer of an organization so new the staff was still arguing missions, job titles and, most of all, a name. Someday soon they had to work their way to funding sources.

But Isaac was in his element, creating the right kind of organization from the ground up. She had never seen him happier. And, with his usual artistic flair, he had already designed their logo, the unmistakable peaks of Pallatine Mountain, with an eagle soaring high above them.

"You don't need to win me over," she said. "They need you. Eventually you'll whip them into shape."

"If I live that long." He squeezed, then let her go. "Jamie called."

"Are they coming for Christmas?"

"You're supposed to call back. But let's just say we can't avoid furnishing the guest rooms much longer." He went back to his pan, flipped on the burner and began to stir. "Tell me about *your* day."

She would, she knew. She would open a bottle of wine and pour each of them a glass. She would lean against the counter while he finished cooking, and they would laugh together over things that had happened in the newsroom. Eventually they would welcome the pets back inside. Maybe they would plan for their upcoming weekend at Gayle Fortman's B and B on the Shenandoah, and talk about where they would go out to eat on Friday night with Elisa and Sam, and how long they could steal Caleb from the Clairbornes on Saturday for a hike in the mountains. They might even look at the newest set of house plans, or discuss the merits of timber frame versus log construction.

It would be an ordinary evening.

She found herself smiling.

"You look happy," Isaac said, looking up from the stove.

"You know, you're a perceptive man."

He smiled, too, and went back to cooking their dinner.